Acclaim for THE LAST CHINESE CHEF

"Crackling with energy and ambition . . .

"Using Chinese culinary history, language, ▪▪▪▪▪▪▪▪ ▪▪▪▪▪▪▪▪▪ of fine cuisine, Mones shows how food can both nourish the body and the soul."
— **Liane Hanson, National Public Radio** *Weekend Edition*

"Maybe you're not hungry. Maybe you've never considered the imperial heights of Chinese cuisine. Nicole Mones can change that with the flip of a page . . . *The Last Chinese Chef* brims with vividly rendered meals and stories about the cooks who have created them for centuries." — *Charlotte Observer*

"Outstanding and beautifully written . . . a great story about the discovery of one's self." — *Willamette Weekly*

"Remarkably, Mones entrances both the serious cook and those of us belonging to the 'How long do I microwave this?' school. In her care, the lovingly prepared meal is both a conscious act of culinary craft, meticulously described, and a metaphor for meaningful spiritual exploration. As a wise uncle of Sam's reflects: 'Almost anything could be recalled or explored through food.'"
— *Seattle Times*

"You may have had Chinese food; you may think you know it well. However, this novel will transport you into the world of a hidden culinary culture rarely experienced outside China . . . Mones's characters are genuine. You will care for them so much you won't want to put the book down until you've learned their fate." — *Northwest Asian Weekly*

"An entertaining and erudite novel cleverly interspersed with mouthwatering details on one of the world's greatest cuisines." — *Northwest Asian Times*

"Mones's latest achievement appeals not just to devotees of fiction but equally to anyone interested in Chinese cooking, its theory, and its craft." — *Booklist*

"Mones has a subtle touch when portraying growing affection between genuinely nice people . . . Warning: Avoid reading while hungry."
— *Kirkus Reviews*

"Sumptuous . . . Early in her visit, Maggie scoffs at the idea that 'food can heal the human heart.' Mones smartly proves her wrong." — *Publishers Weekly*

Books by Nicole Mones

LOST IN TRANSLATION

A CUP OF LIGHT

THE LAST CHINESE CHEF

THE LAST
CHINESE CHEF

Nicole Mones

A MARINER BOOK
HOUGHTON MIFFLIN COMPANY
BOSTON • NEW YORK

First Mariner Books edition 2008
Copyright © 2007 by Nicole Mones
ALL RIGHTS RESERVED

For information about permission to reproduce selections from
this book, write to Permissions, Houghton Mifflin Company,
215 Park Avenue South, New York, New York 10003.

www.houghtonmifflinbooks.com

Library of Congress Cataloging-in-Publication Data
Mones, Nicole.
The last Chinese chef / Nicole Mones.
p. cm.
ISBN 978-0-618-61966-5
ISBN 978-0-547-05373-8 (pbk.)
1. Americans—China—Fiction. 2. Food
writers—Fiction. 3. Cookery—Fiction. I. Title.
PS3563.O5I9L37 2007
813'.54—dc22   2006030469

Printed in the United States of America

Book design by Robert Overholtzer

DOC 10 9 8 7

The lines on page 269 are from the poems "Summons of the Soul" and
"The Great Summons," in *The Songs of the South: An Ancient Chinese Anthology
of Poems by Qu Yuan and Other Poets;* translated and annotated by David
Hawkes (Penguin Books Ltd., 1985). Copyright © David Hawkes, 1985.
Reproduced by permission of Penguin Books Ltd.

THE LAST
CHINESE CHEF

Apprentices have asked me, what is the most exalted peak of cuisine? Is it the freshest ingredients, the most complex flavors? Is it the rustic, or the rare? It is none of these. The peak is neither eating nor cooking, but the giving and sharing of food. Great food should never be taken alone. What pleasure can a man take in fine cuisine unless he invites cherished friends, counts the days until the banquet, and composes an anticipatory poem for his letter of invitation?

— LIANG WEI, *The Last Chinese Chef,* pub. Peking, 1925

Maggie McElroy felt her soul spiral away from her in the year following her husband's death; she felt strange wherever she was. She needed walls to hold her. She could not seem to find an apartment small enough. In the end, she moved to a boat.

First she sold their house. It was understandable. Her friends agreed it was the right thing to do. She scaled down to an apartment, and quickly found it too big; she needed a cell. She found an even smaller place and reduced her possessions further to move into it. Each cycle of obliteration vented a bit of her grief, but underneath she was propelled by the additional belief, springing not from knowledge but from stubborn instinct, that some part of her soul could be called back if she could only clear the way.

At last she found the little boat in its slip in the Marina. As soon as she stepped aboard she knew she wanted to stay there, below, watching the light change, finding peace in the clinking of the lines, ignoring the messages on her cell phone.

There was a purity to the vessel. When she wasn't working she lay on the bunk. She watched the gangs of sneakered feet flutter by on the dock. She listened to the thrum of wind on canvas, the suck of water against the hulls. She slept on the boat, really slept for the first time since Matt died. She recognized that nothing was left. Looking back later, she saw that if she had not come to this point she would never have been ready for the change that was even then on its way. At the time, though, it seemed foregone, a thing she would have to accept: she would never be connected again.

She stayed by herself. Let's have dinner. Join us at the movie. Come to this party. Even when she didn't answer, people forgave her. Strange things were expected from the grieving. Allowances were made. When she did have to give an excuse, she said she was out of town, which was fine, for she often was. She was a food writer. She traveled each month to a different American community for her column. She loved her job, needed it, and had no intention of losing it. Everybody knew this, so she could say sorry, she was gone, goodbye, and then lie back down on her little bunk and continue remembering. People cared for her and she for them — that hadn't changed. She just didn't want to see them right now. Her life was different. She had gone away to a far-off country, one they didn't know about, where all the work was the work of grieving. It was too hard to talk to them. So she stayed alone, her life shrunk to a pinpoint, and slowly, day by day, she found she felt better.

On the September evening that marked the beginning of these events, she was leaving the boat to go out and find a place to eat dinner. It was a few days after her fortieth birthday, which she'd slid past with careful avoidance. She found the parking lot empty, punctuated only by the cries of gulls. As she reached her car she heard her phone ringing.

The sound was muffled. It was deep in her bag. Living on the boat kept her bag overloaded — a small price to pay. She dug, following the green light that shimmered with each ring. She didn't answer her phone that often, but she always checked it. There were some calls, from work, from her best friend, Sunny, from her mother, which she never failed to pick up.

When she looked at the screen she felt her brows draw together. This was not a caller she recognized. It was a long string of numbers. She clicked it. "Hello?"

"Maggie? This is Carey James, from Beijing. Do you remember me?"

"Yes." She went slack with surprise. Matt's law firm kept an office in Beijing, and Carey was one of its full-time attorneys. Matt had flown over there more than a few times, on business. Maggie'd even gone with him once, three years before. She'd met Carey — tall, elegant, faintly dissipated. Matt had said he was a gifted negotiator. "I remember."

"Some year," he said, his manner disintegrating slightly.

"You're telling me." She unlocked the car and climbed in.

"Are you all right?"

"I'm surviving." What was this about? Everything had been over months ago with the firm, even the kindness calls, even the check-ins from Matt's closest friends here in the L.A. office. She hadn't heard from any of them lately.

"I'm calling, actually, because I've come across something. I really should have seen it before. Unfortunately I didn't. It's a legal filing, here in China. It concerns Matt."

"Matt?"

"Yes," Carey said. "It's a claim."

"What do you mean? What kind?"

Carey drew a breath. She could feel him teetering. "I was hoping there was a chance you might know," he said.

"Know *what?* Carey. What kind of claim?"

"Paternity," he said.

She sat for a long moment. A bell seemed to drop around her, cutting out all sound. She stared through her sea-scummed windshield at the line of palms, the bike path, the mottled sand. "So this person is saying —"

"She has his child. So I guess you didn't know anything about this."

She swallowed. "No. I did not. Did you? Did you know about a child?"

"No," he said firmly. "Nothing."

"So what do you think this is?"

"I don't know, honestly. But I do know one thing: you can't ignore it. It's serious. A claim has been filed. Under the new Children's Rights Treaty, it can be decided right here in China, in a way that's binding on you. And it is going to be decided, soon." She heard him turning pages. "In — a little less than three weeks."

"Then what?"

"Then if the person who filed the claim wins, they get a share of his estate. Excluding the house, of course — the principal residence."

To this she said nothing. She had sold the house. "Just tell me, Carey. What should I do?"

"There's only one option. Get a test and prove whether it's true or false. If it's false, we can take care of it. If it turns out the other way, that will be different."

"If it's true, you mean? How can it be true?"

"You can't expect me to answer that," he said.

She was silent.

"The important thing is to get a lab test, now. If I have that in hand before the ruling, I can head it off. Without that, nothing."

"So go ahead. Get one. I'll pay the firm to do it."

"That won't work," said Carey. "This matter is already on the calendar with the Ministry of Families, and we're a law firm. We'd have to do it by bureaucracy — file papers to request permission from the girl's family, for instance. It would never happen by the deadline. It won't work for us to do it. But somebody else could get the family's permission and get the test and let us act on the results. That would be all right."

"You mean me," she said.

"I don't know who else. It's important, Maggie. We'll help you. Give you a translator. You can use the company apartment. You still have Matt's key?"

"I think so."

"Then get a flight. Come in to the office when you arrive." He paused. "I'm sorry, Maggie," he said. "About everything, about Matt. It's terrible."

"I know."

"None of this was supposed to happen."

She took a long breath. *He means Matt, hit by a car on the sidewalk. Killed along with two other people. Random.* "I've wrestled with that one," she said. "So this child —"

"A little girl."

She closed her eyes. "This girl is how old?"

"Five."

That meant something would have to have happened six years ago. Maggie scrolled back frantically. It didn't make sense. They were happy then. "If you'll give me the months involved I'll go back through my diaries and see if he was even in China then. I mean, maybe it isn't even possible. If he wasn't there —"

This time Carey cut her off. "Winter of 2002," he said softly. "I already checked. He was."

The next morning she was waiting in the hallway when Sarah, her editor, stepped from the elevator.

"What are you doing here?" Sarah said. "You look terrible."

"I was up all night."

"Why?"

"Bad news about Matt."

"Matt?" Sarah's eyes widened. Matt was dead. There could be no more bad news.

"Someone filed a claim."

Sarah's mouth fell open, and then she closed it.

"A paternity claim."

Sarah went pale. "Paternity! Let's go inside." She unlocked the door and steered Maggie to the comfortable chair across from her desk. "Now what is this?"

"A woman filed a claim against him in China, saying she has his child."

"Are you *serious?* In China?"

"Yes, and because of the agreements between our two countries, this claim can be ruled on in China and collected from there."

"Collected," repeated Sarah.

"Generously," said Maggie.

"What are you going to do?"

"Go there, right away. I have no choice. I've never asked you, in twelve years, not even when Matt died, but now I'm going to need a month off."

"Please! Doll! We run old columns all the time when someone has an emergency. You're the only one who's never asked for that. Don't even worry about it. And a year ago" — Sarah looked at her, eyes soft with unspent empathy — "I told you to take off. Remember? I practically begged you."

"I know." Maggie reached over and clasped her friend's hand. "The truth is, work kept me going. I needed it. I've always been like that. I'm stronger when I'm working. I don't know how I'd ever have made it through without it." She looked up. "I'm better lately. Just so you know."

"Good. By the way, your last check came back." Sarah showed her the envelope. "Do you have a new address?"

"I got a new P.O. box, one closer to where I'm living."

"Where are you living?"

"In the Marina," she said, and left it at that.

Sarah wrote down the new mailing address. "Thanks. Anyway, of course you can go, take a month off, we'll use an old piece. Don't even think about it. Maybe it'll be good for you, actually. You should make the best of it. Recharge."

Maggie spoke carefully. "Do you feel I need to recharge?"

"No. No, it's not that, it's just . . ." Sarah paused, caught between friendship and responsibility. "Lately you don't seem that excited about food. You must have noticed it too. I don't get the old sense of wonder."

I don't either, Maggie thought sadly. "In which stories did that bother you?"

"Well. The one on the Pennsylvania Dutch. Couldn't you have found anything charming about them?"

"You're talking about people whose principal contribution to cuisine is the pretzel. Who make perfect strangers sit at a table and share fried chicken. Whose idea of a vegetable is a sliced tomato. And don't get me started on their pie!"

Sarah smiled. "See, you're as wonderful as ever. Just go off like that. Let yourself go."

Maggie laughed.

"And don't forget that part, too. You always found the happiness in food."

"I'll try."

But now Sarah's small smile melted, and concern took its place. "Do you think — there's no possibility this is true, is there?"

"You mean Matt? I have no idea. Did he tell me anything or lead me in any way to think anything? No. He went to China on business sometimes, but so did all the lawyers in his office."

"You went there with him."

"I did, once, for a week. Three years ago. Nothing. And you know me. I am watchful. Being attentive is the way I write, and it spills over. I sensed nothing. But this, if it happened, would have been a few years before that. I can't think like this, Sarah, is the truth; I'll go crazy. I have to go and get a lab test, and that's that. Then on from there."

"It's going to be a difficult trip," Sarah said, now as her friend.

Maggie nodded. "And just when I was getting the guy kind of settled in my mind, you know? And in my heart. Plus, to be honest, Sarah, even though it's necessary and all, it's not really a good thing for me not to be working, even for one month. I perform better at everything when I'm working."

"Are you saying you'd rather work?" said Sarah.

"Of course I'd rather work, but I can't. I have to go there and see to this."

Now a new smile, different, the impish smile of an idea, was playing on Sarah's face. "Would you like to work while you're in China?"

Maggie stared. She wrote only about American food. "How?"

"File a column from there. We can run an old one — I already told you, it's no problem, you have some classics I'd love to see again — but we also have an assignment in China. It just came in. I can give it to anyone, in which case I'd have to send someone. Or I can give it to you, since you are going, and it can be one of your columns."

"You don't think I'm an odd fit?" said Maggie. She did do ethnic food, of course. From the Basque country-style platters of the San Joaquin Valley to the German sausages of central Texas, it was impossible not to. American cuisine had so many incoming tributary tastes. She knew them all. What she never did was *foreign* food.

"It's a chef profile. American guy, born and raised here, but half Chinese."

"Hmm. That's a little closer."

"He's not cooking American," Sarah said. "The opposite — back to the old traditions. He's descended from a chef who cooked for the Emperor and in 1925 wrote a book that became a big food classic, *The Last Chinese Chef.* Liang Wei was his name. The grandson's name is Liang too, Sam Liang; he's translating the book into English. He's a cook. Everything he does is orthodox, it's all according to his grandfather, even though Beijing seems to be spinning the opposite way, new, global."

"I like it," Maggie said.

"He's about to open a restaurant. It's going to be a big launch. That's the assignment, the restaurant."

"Look, I won't lie, for me it would be ideal. I would love to write it," said Maggie. "Not to mention that it would keep me sane. It's just — I don't know how you can give it to me. I'm the American queen."

"Sometimes it's good to mix things up. Anyway, you're going. When are you leaving?"

"Tonight."

"Tonight! You must have a ticket."

"I do. And I'll have a rush visa by midday. Tell you what, Sarah, if you just reimburse me for the ticket, I'll take care of all the other expenses. I do have to go there anyway." And she did have the company apartment.

"I can sell that," said Sarah. She shone with satisfaction. She loved to solve a problem. "Are we there yet?" she said. "Is that a yes?"

They knew each other well. Maggie had only to allow the small lift of a smile into her gaze for her friend to read her agreement.

"Good," said Sarah. "So." She handed Maggie the file. "Sam Liang."

In Beijing it was late evening. Yet people were still out, for the autumn night was fine and cool, faintly sharp with the scent of the chrysanthemums along the sidewalk. It was the local life in his adopted city that Sam Liang loved the best, like here, the people shopping and strolling on Gulou, the street that went right up to the dark, silent drum tower for which it was named. Sam barely glanced at the fifteenth-century tower, which rose in the center of the street up ahead. He didn't look into the brightly arranged shop windows, or the faces of the migrant vendors who had set up here and there on the curb. He searched ahead. There was a cooking-supply store on this block. His Third Uncle Xie had told him about it. Xie lived in Hangzhou; when he came north to Beijing he always stopped there.

Sam was hoping to find a chopping block, heavy, round, a straight-through slice of tree trunk, the kind that Chinese chefs had always used. He had two for his restaurant and he needed a third; a busy restaurant really needed three. Every place he'd tried had cutting boards, but they were the plastic ones — the new, modern alternative that had taken hold all over the capital. Plastic was cleaner, people said, safer; it was the future.

Sam didn't agree. He hadn't come all the way to China to switch from the traditional tree slab to plastic. Plastic ruined a fine blade. Besides, it was true what his grandfather had said, that wood was a living thing beneath a man's knife. It had its own spring.

Ah, he spotted the store ahead — its lights were on, it was open. If any place still had the old-style chopping blocks, it would be this one.

More than once Xie had explained how to choose one. "Never buy from a young tree, only an old one. Make sure its rings are tight with age. See that the block's been conditioned properly with oil, that it has a sheen. Don't bring home the wrong one."

"And what kind of wood?"

"When I was young all chefs used soapwood. Now most chefs use ironwood, though some like the wood of the tamarind tree from Vietnam. Listen to Third Uncle. Choose the wood that feels best under your hands. Forget the rest."

Sam opened the door to the shop. In one hopeful sweep he took in the long shelves with their stacked woks and racks and sieves and steamers. He saw the cutting boards, white plastic, in their own section. He saw only plastic; no wood, no tree trunks.

"Ni zhao shenmo?" said a woman's voice, What are you looking for?

It was the proprietress, a white-haired woman Sam recognized from Xie's description. "Elder Sister," Sam said politely, "I seek a chopping block, but the old kind, wood."

"We no longer have them."

"But why?"

"They are not as hygienic as the plastic. Especially now, you know how it is, everything is supposed to be clean."

He knew what she meant — the Games. "But if I may ask, when you stopped selling them, did you have any left?"

"No," she said.

His hope was sliding. *"Zhen kelian."* Pitiable. "My Uncle Xie told me he thought I could find one here. Do you know him? Your old customer? Xie Er?"

Her old eyes widened. "You know Xie Er?"

"He is my uncle."

She looked hard at him. He could feel her weighing the Eurasian mix in his face. Everyone did it. He was used to it. It was the light above his head, the air in which he walked. She wouldn't find anything in his face anyway, for Xie Er was his uncle not by blood but by other ties. "His father and my grandfather were brothers in the palace."

"You're a Liang," she said.

"Yes," he said, surprised.

She slid off her stool, stiff, and opened a back door behind her. Sam moved closer. She touched a switch, lighting a storeroom of crowded shelves and boxes. "In here," she said, and he followed her. "This one." She moved some papers to the side.

As soon as he saw it, he knew. It was about two feet across, seven or eight inches thick, still ringed with bark, everything finished to a dull gleam. A heavy metal ring was embedded in one side, for hanging, as such a block should be stored vertically when not in use. He could imagine it ten years from now, twenty, its cutting surface worn to a gentle suggestion of concavity, changing with him, with his cooking, under his hands. He wanted it.

"I could pay you cash for it," he said. "I'd be so happy to do that."

"Do you cook?" She was eyeing him. "Yes?" she said at his emphatic nod. "Then just give me a moment. I'll think of a price."

"Please take your time," he said softly, but inside he was overflowing. He reached out a practiced hand to feel the chopping surface. "And sister, if you happen to know, this is what sort of wood?"

"That?" she said. "That is the old kind. Soapwood."

Maggie stood in the airport in front of the candy counter. Matt had always given her candy corn. It was their signature candy, something she used to say every relationship should have. For them it was more of a sacrament than a food. The first time he brought it home he'd had in mind a joke on her American food specialty, but that was soon forgotten and it became his parting token. He would present her with a little bag before leaving on a trip. She could still picture how he'd looked one morning in their bedroom, in the slow-seeping dawn light, packed, dressed, ready to go. When? A year and a half ago? They both traveled so often that they rarely rose for each other's early departures. That particular morning she was half-awake, drifting; she could hear the rustle of his pants and the crinkle of plastic as he dug in his pocket for the little bag of corn. She heard him settle it by her bedside lamp and lean down to kiss the frizz of her hair. Just that. Too nice to wake her. Then the click of the door. Remorse bubbled in Maggie now. So many times she had let him go like that.

She walked over to the plexiglass tube filled with orange-and-white kernels and opened a plastic bag underneath. On the day he left for San Francisco, the last day she saw him, he did not give her any candy corn, because he was coming back that night.

In the year since, she had not eaten a kernel. She pulled the lever now and they gushed into her bag, a hundred, a thousand. She got on the plane and ate steadily, sneaking the sugar-soft kernels into her mouth one by one and letting them dissolve until her teeth ached and her head felt as if it would balloon up and float away. Queasy, full, she refused the meals when they came. She started a movie and turned it off. She sat washed by waves of guilt, guilt she'd felt many times this past year as she remembered that she and her husband, in truth, had always loved each other best when they were apart. And now it was for always. She closed her eyes.

She felt her computer bag between her feet. She hadn't even thought yet about the job. What with getting her visa, collecting a sample for Matt from the hospital where he had banked blood, delivering it to the DNA lab, getting the collection kit, packing, speeding to the airport — with all this she had not given the first thought to her interview with the chef. Actually it had been a relief to have to move so fast. Grief, which had become half-comforting to her, almost a companion, had seemed finally to take a step back. She felt like a person again, even if she barely made it to the gate on time with her carry-on.

Then she was strapped in, with her candy corn. She attempted to face the situation. Was it possible? Could the claim be true? She let her mind roll back once again. She lingered over every bump, every moment of discord; she knew where each one was located. They were all inside her, arranged since his death alongside love, rue, and affection. She threaded through them now. Another woman? A child? It just wasn't possible to believe he could have kept it from her. He was such a confessor. It was a *joke* among people who knew him. This was the kind of thing he could never, ever have kept to himself.

Especially since the question of children was one that came up between the two of them. Originally they were both in agreement. They did not want children. Halfway through their decade together, though, Matt changed his mind.

At first, when it started, she reminded him of the ways in which parenthood did not suit them. She traveled every month, and so did he. If they had a child, someone would have to stop. That would have be her, clearly; he earned most of the money. The thing was, she didn't want to stop, not for a while. She loved her column. Let me work another year, she would say. Matt was patient. He was the one, after all, who had changed his mind. But always the subject came back.

He could never have hidden a child. This thought seemed clear to her in the humming silence of the plane. The other passengers were sleeping. After a long time of shifting uncomfortably in her seat she got up and went to the back of the plane, to the hollow where there is always a tiny window. She looked out through the trapped streaks of moisture to the deep darkness, thinking. Finally she crept back to her seat and fell asleep.

When they landed in Beijing she felt a little sick from the sugar, and she dragged her feet past entry agents who stamped her passport and waved her ahead. She stopped at a currency booth to change a few hundred dollars and, thus fortified, stepped out of security into the crowded public area.

Touts swarmed. "Hello?" said one. "You want taxi?"

"No, thank you."

"Taxi. This way."

"No." She rolled her bag toward the glass doors, outside of which

she could see people in line for taxis. On her right she passed a European man. "How much into Beijing?" she heard him say to one of the men.

"Three hundred," the man replied, and the European agreed. She kept walking.

Meanwhile the first man was still following her. "Taxi," he said, and then to her shock actually wrapped his fingers around her arm.

"Get away from me," she said, and shook him off with such force that even she was surprised. He stepped back, the loser, his smile derisive. She strolled to her place in the taxi line and felt herself stand a little taller.

Her turn came and she showed the driver the firm's Beijing business card, which bore the apartment address, then let herself melt in the back seat. She had done it; she was here. A freeway sailed along outside, dotted by lit-up billboards in Chinese and English for software, metals, chemicals, aircraft, coffee, logistics. What was logistics? Not knowing made her feel old.

She still had a few loved ones, at least. She flipped open her phone. It chirped to life. The first number was her mother's. Maggie didn't call her often, but every time she got a new phone she put her number first, at the top of the list, anyway. Her mother had raised her alone and done it well, even if she hadn't been able to make much of a home for Maggie. She deserved to hold the top slot.

Next came Sunny, her best friend and most frequently called number. Then Sarah; her other friends. And Matt's parents. Her heart tightened, as always, at the thought of them. Their suffering had been like hers.

She closed her phone as the car swooped down off the ring road and into the city. Right away she saw this was not the Beijing she remembered from three years ago. The boulevards were widened, the office buildings filled in, the street lighting redone. Maybe it was the coming of the Games. Or maybe it was just the way Beijing was growing. She remembered Matt saying it had been under construction all the time, going back more than a decade. Always building, investing, expanding, earning.

The driver turned down a side street and stopped in front of the building she remembered. She paid the fare — ninety-five *kuai*. She smiled at the thought of the man in the airport agreeing to pay three hundred. It was like being her old self for a minute; she'd always loved to be the better tourist.

Inside and up the elevator, she let herself into apartment 426 and clicked on the overhead lights. It was the same. The couch, the television, the windows that faced the city.

She rolled her suitcase to the wall. Her steps were loud in the silence. There was an envelope on the coffee table. *To Mrs. Mason,* it said. From the law firm. She opened it. *Welcome you to China. Please come to the office in the morning.*

Only someone who didn't know her would call her Mrs. Mason. She had never changed her name. No doubt they didn't know her; Carey was likely to be the only one still in the office who had been there three years before, when she came. She remembered Matt telling her that, aside from Carey, the Beijing office was never able to hold on to foreigners for long. That was one reason the lawyers in the L.A. office, like Matt, had to go there. Then in the last few years they'd hired two Chinese attorneys who had gone to university and law school in the States and then returned, and the pressure eased. Matt didn't go at all the last year and a half before he died. In any case — she checked her phone again — it was too late to call the office now. Calder Hayes would be closed.

It was early enough to call the chef still, but first she had to do some reading. She slid out the file with Sarah's writing on the tab, *Sam Liang,* and made herself into a curl with it on the couch.

The first thing she saw was that he was a chef of national rank, which had to be near the top in the Chinese system, and there was a list of prizes and awards. That was fast, she thought. He'd been here only four years. Then she came to an excerpt from his grandfather's book, *The Last Chinese Chef.*

Chinese food has characteristics that set it apart from all other foods of the world. First, its conceptual balance. Dominance is held by *fan,* grain food, either rice or wheat made into noodles and breads and

15

dumplings. *Song* or *cai* is the flavored food that accompanies it, seasoned vegetables, sometimes meat. Of the latter, pork is first, and then aquatic life in all its variety. The soybean is used in many products, fresh and fermented. *Dian xin* are snacks, which include all that is known under the Cantonese *dim sum*, but also nuts and fruits. Boiling, steaming, or stir-frying are preferred, in that order, stacking food when possible to conserve fuel. Chopsticks are used. Of the world's cuisines, only Japanese and Korean share these characteristics, and everyone knows they have drawn their influence from the Chinese.

She looked up and out the window at Beijing. The urban shapes of progress gleamed back at her, the cranes with their twinkling lights, the tall, half-built skeletons. Clearly a city on the move. And yet this chef seemed to be reaching back into the past.

Fine, she decided. Contradictions were promising. They gave depth. She reached for her cell phone and punched in his number.

It rang twice, then clicked. *"Wei,"* she heard.

"Hello, I'm looking for Sam Liang."

At once he turned American. "That's me."

"I'm Maggie McElroy. *Table* magazine?"

"Oh yes," he said, "the restaurant article. Wait. You're not here already? In Beijing?"

"Yes —"

"I didn't send the e-mail yet, or call. I should have."

"What do you mean?"

He fumbled the phone and then came back. "I hope you didn't fly here just to talk to me."

"What?" Wasn't that the idea? Wasn't she supposed to do that? Sarah had told her he was ready to go. "Only partly," she said to him now on the phone. "I did have some other business."

"I'm glad to hear that," he said. "Because right now, as of this morning, my restaurant's not going to open."

"Why?"

"I'm afraid I have lost my investor."

"But you can get another, surely — can't you?"

"I hope I can. I'm going to try. But until that happens and while it's all up in the air, I'm sorry, I can't do the story."

Maggie didn't think well on her feet. She always came up with the right response later, when it was too late. Writing worked better, allowing her time to sort things out; hence her choice of profession.

But she had to try to come up with something now. "The piece doesn't have to be about the restaurant. A profile of you would be fine."

"A profile of me? Whose restaurant is not opening?"

"Not like that —"

"With what just happened I can't say it seems like a good idea. I hope you understand."

"That could be a mistake." Her mind was whirling, looking for strategies, finding none. "Really."

"Please — Miss McElroy, is it?"

"Maggie."

"Accept my apology. And please tell your editor too, I'm very sorry. I had no idea this was going to happen."

"I know," Maggie said. "Do you want to at least think it over? Because I'm going to be here for a few days."

"I'll think if you like. But I don't see how I can give you an interview about a restaurant that is not going to open. Or how I can do a profile when something like this has just happened."

"I understand," she said. She was disappointed, but she also felt for him. A lot of attention had been trained on this opening.

"Enjoy your trip."

It was an American thing to say, polite, faintly strained, distancing. *He wants to get rid of me.* "Take my number in case."

"Okay," he said. He took it down dutifully, and thanked her when she wished him good luck. Then they said goodbye, smiled into the phone, and hung up.

Three qualities of China made it a place where there grew a great cuisine. First, its land has everything under heaven: mountains, deserts, plains, and fertile crescents; great oceans, mighty rivers. Second, the mass of Chinese are numerous but poor. They have always had to extract every possible bit of goodness and nutrition from every scrap of land and fuel, economizing everywhere except with human labor and ingenuity, of which there is a surfeit. Third, there is China's elite. From this world of discriminating taste the gourmet was born. Food became not only a complex tool for ritual and the attainment of prestige, but an art form, pursued by men of passion.

— LIANG WEI, *The Last Chinese Chef*

Sam Liang turned the phone off and replaced it in his pocket before he turned to face his First and Second Uncles, Jiang Wanli and Tan Jingfu, who stood glaring at him. They were older by thirty-five years, friends of his father and, with Xie Er in Hangzhou, the nearest thing he had in China to clan relatives. They'd also been his guides in the kitchen and his ties to the past. From every conceivable angle, they had unlimited rights to harangue him.

"Was that a female person?" demanded Jiang in the Chinese they always spoke.

Sam sighed. "Yes."

"I trust you invited her to meet you?"

"No, First Uncle."

"The times I've told you to try harder are more than a few! Have we not talked of this? Yet whenever an opportunity crosses your path with a female person, you show your white feather!"

"Uncle. That was a business call. Anything else would have been inappropriate."

"Huh!" Tan raised a finger. "My English is not so poor! She was from the American magazine. A writer. Probably a food specialist!"

"Exactly right," said Sam. "And the restaurant is off for now. There is no story."

"You are not trying very hard," said Jiang. "You should do an article with her. It would bring you attention."

Tan leapt in. "You could have at least suggested the two of you drink tea! You could have discussed the matter as a civilized person."

Sam understood. A civilized person meant a Chinese person. After the first few years of instructing him in the kitchen — the two of them barking directions, shouting at his mistakes, harrumphing their approval when he cooked well — the two old men had turned to teaching him etiquette. They showed him the web of manners and considerations that held together the Chinese world. Unfortunately, he had been raised in America; he was possessed of willful foreign ways. And he was only half Chinese. Luck was with him that the other half was Jewish, as Jews were admired for their intelligence, but still, here in China, it was bad to be only part Chinese. This was always the first thought of Sam's detractors.

Those critics called him an outsider even though he was old-school. They didn't seem to care that he was one of the few still cooking in the traditional way, that all the other top cooks in China were showcasing some modern edge. But he had determined to do what his grandfather had written and his uncles had taught him. He knew cooking well was the best revenge.

"I wish you had invited the female person to meet you," Tan said.

"Yes, Uncle." Sam did not argue. In their minds, being single at his age was almost an affront to nature. It was something they felt a duty to correct. He had long ago understood that the best way to love them was to let them interfere. Let them scold him and insist upon meetings with the female relations of their acquaintances. These meetings were at best a waste of time and at worst painful — and not only for him. What he'd quickly realized was that the women didn't want the introduction any more than he did. They too were there only to appease elder relatives.

Certainly there were beautiful, intelligent Chinese women to be met in the internationalized top layer of Beijing society, but so far Sam had not found the connection he wanted. Part of it was them. For Chinese women who liked foreigners, he was not foreign enough. For those seeking a man who was Chinese, he was too foreign. His status placed him somewhere below all of the above on the instant-desirability scale.

It had not been like that at home in Ohio. There, his dark, high-cheeked face had seemed exotic to women, especially corn-fed girls with athletic strides and sweet smiles. The women here were lovely too, but different, sinuous, cerebral, fine-skinned. They were cultured. He found them fascinating. It was never hard to begin affairs with them. What was hard was to connect.

That, he sensed, was his fault; he wanted a connection that was complete. Here, he could never get over feeling that he was using only half of himself, the Chinese half. Everything from before, from America, now hid unseen. And he wanted to be seen. At home in the West he'd had a similar feeling, only it was the Chinese part of him that lay dormant. He'd had the idea that coming here would change things. No. He was still half.

"You could have talked to the American about the book," Tan said.

Sam shook his head. "Respectfully, Second Uncle, I don't see them doing an article about a book that came out in 1925 — oh, and *in Chinese*."

"You are translating it."

"It's not done."

"You're no further?" said Jiang.

"I ought to be more hardworking," Sam said, which was the evasive and Chinese thing to say. Actually it was his father who held up the translation. Now retired from the post office, Liang Yeh spent most of his time in a dark room with books and the things he remembered. Sam couldn't get him to do his part, which was rendering his own father's formal, premodern Mandarin into a rough English-and-Chinese mix Sam could understand.

He had not told Tan and Jiang this, preferring to let them admire the old man. To them, Liang Yeh had triumphed. He had made his way to America. He had established a family. They didn't know that Sam had been largely raised by his mother, the no-nonsense and tireless Judy Liang, née Blumenfeld, while his father was mentally remote. Exile was in the heart, and Liang Yeh carried it with him everywhere. He seemed determined to never let it go. In time exile became his most important aspect, his shadow, closer to him in a way even than his family.

Therefore, when complaints were raised about the slow translation, Sam took the blame. It eased a needy and chronically sad part of him to hear his father praised, and he did whatever he could to leave his uncles' good opinion intact.

"You will finish it when you can," said Second Uncle, for though they were hard on him they always forgave him. Tan was walking out of the kitchen now, where he had been fussing with the tea things.

"Uncle, you shouldn't," Sam said. "I'll make tea."

"No!" Jiang raised a hand. "You sit. We have a special matter."

"You want to introduce me to another of your relatives," said Sam.

"Very good!" said Jiang. "My grandniece is coming from Jilin. But that is next month. Younger Born! You tell him."

"Very well," Tan said. He set the tray down with ceremony. *His* grandfather had been the great chef Tan Zhuanqing, who had been one of the top cooks in the palace, and whose apprentice had been the young Liang Wei — Sam's grandfather. Great was the Tan name even now. Tan leaned over his cup and paddled the steam toward him with swollen hands. "Very secret!" he said importantly.

"Only a few know! The Chinese Committee for the 2008 Games is going to run its own Games here, an Olympics of culture. They are going to have competitions in Beijing and Kunqu opera, in dance, which is to include martial arts, and in cuisine! Competitions on TV! All China will watch!"

"You see?" said Jiang. "The Liang name will fly to the four directions!"

"You're getting ahead, Uncle."

"You are on the audition list!" Tan cried. "We can confirm it!"

Sam felt a twist in his stomach. A great opportunity, but the timing was terrible. His restaurant wasn't even opening. "Why me?"

"Fool!" Tan raised a hand as if to cuff him. "If we've told you one time it's a hundred! You are in a direct line from Tan Zhuanqing. Your grandfather was trained by him. People eat your dishes and they talk about them all across the city. You have not even opened a restaurant yet, and you are known."

Sam swallowed. "How many will audition?"

"Ten, for two spots. Two spots for northern cooks on the national team. The rest of the team will be Cantonese, Sichuan, Hunanese, and Shanghainese."

"What's the audition?" He felt as if he were clinging to a rope high above the rapids.

"Each candidate will prepare a banquet for the committee. Nephew! You must make a celestial meal for them!"

"Sure," said Sam. With a lurch he saw the complexity of it. This was not the four or five dishes chefs prepared on those TV contests — this was a banquet. It was the complete symphony, the holy grail of Chinese food art. It required not only great dishes but also concept, shape, subtlety, and narrative force. "Who are the others?"

"Wang Zijian," said Tan. "Pan Jun. Also Lu Fudong."

"Right," said Sam. He knew them. Good chefs.

"Zhan Ming," said Jiang.

"Yes," said Sam. "He's good too."

"And Yao Weiguo," said Tan.

"Ah." Here was his real rival. Yao was exceptionally good. And he did the very thing Sam did not: he came up with something new each time. He improvised. Yao's way of working was like that of a European or an American. He riffed, cooking in the style of jazz, while Sam remained the old-fashioned formalist. "I'm worried," he said. "Yao can cook."

"So can you," said Jiang, touching his arm. "It does not have to be complicated. The perfect meal is balanced, not ornate. Remember the words of Yuan Mei. 'Don't eat with your eyes. Don't cover the table with dishes, or multiply the courses too much. Bean curd is actually better than bird's nest.'"

"Those are nice, naturalistic sentiments, Uncle, but don't you think the people on this panel are going to eat with their eyes?"

"Yes! You are right! And you must impress them. But that is secondary. The true perfection of food is a surprisingly modest thing. It is what is right. There you will find what you seek."

Sam sighed. *"Zhen bang."* Great.

The next morning Maggie awoke to a tugging fear about whether the clipping she had brought was still in her computer case. She padded out of bed and to the small living room, where she unzipped the case's side pocket. There it was. A square of newspaper, with a picture of her husband, knocked down, probably dead already, at the scene of the accident. It had been snapped moments after a car driven by an elderly man plowed up onto a sidewalk in San Francisco and killed Matt and two others. There he was. People around him, bending over him. A woman kneeling.

She couldn't bear to look at it. She just had to make sure that she still had it. She did, so she zipped it away and turned to the day, just beginning. The morning outside was gray-shrouded. The buildings were spires of lead.

She took a taxi to the New World Building, where she rode to the seventeenth floor.

Then she pushed open the door to Calder Hayes and felt herself stepping back into America. Magazines on the reception room table — it looked like an office at home. It had been the same way when she'd come here before with Matt.

"May I help you?" said the receptionist, young, Chinese, smart-looking.

"I'm Maggie McElroy," she said, and when this drew a blank, she added, "Mrs. Mason."

"Oh! Hello. Welcome you."

"Thank you. Is Carey here?"

"Mr. James is in Bangkok today. Please wait a minute." She pressed a number code into her handset and spoke in a brief, rapid flow of Chinese. She looked up to see Maggie still in front of her and smiled brightly, pointing to the chairs. "Please."

Maggie sat, pacing her breathing, gathering calm. Soon a small, sturdy woman came pumping out, pushing black glasses up her nose. "Pleased to meet you," she said. "I am Miss Chu." Her accent was clipped, precise, faintly British.

"Maggie McElroy. The same. Your English is perfect."

"So-so," the woman qualified. "I'm very sorry about your husband." With a frank, sympathetic squeeze she took Maggie's arm to walk her back down the hall.

In the conference room, Miss Chu handed her a file folder that opened to reveal the claim. Maggie scanned the lines of English and Chinese, which repeated the information Carey had given her. "I think," Maggie said, "that first we should go see the mother. Immediately. I need her permission to take a sample from the child."

"You see, though," said Miss Chu, "right now we do not know where the mother is."

Maggie felt her eyebrows squeeze together. "Isn't her address in here?" She pointed to the file.

"That is the grandparents. They are the ones who filed the claim. The child lives with them."

"Not the mother?"

"No."

Maggie sat back. "And the mother . . ."

"It is just that right now we do not know where she is," said Miss Chu.

"Okay." Back up, Maggie thought. "The main thing is the child, the permission, the sample." *Though I want to see this woman. I need to see this woman.* "So if the grandparents are the guardians, let's go to them."

"But this address is not in Beijing. It is in a town called Shaoxing. It's in the south."

Maggie closed her eyes. "Then let's go there."

"It's far."

"How far?"

"Near Shanghai. The problem is tickets," said Miss Chu. Her British accent was softened by Mandarin consonants. "One of our biggest holidays is coming, National Day. Everyone will be off work. Everything was sold out long ago."

"Like Christmas?" said Maggie.

"Yes," Miss Chu said. "Like that."

"What about a train?"

"Same problem."

"Can we drive?"

"Possible. We can hire a car. But it will take too many days."

"So what do you suggest?"

"I think it is faster to wait. Let me try to get the tickets." Miss Chu saw that the American had large, thickly lashed eyes and would have been pretty if not for the freckles spattered across her nose and cheekbones, and the excessive, almost masculine point of her chin. She did have unusual hair, though, even for a *laowai,* a dark mass of coiling curls that bounced around her face and softened her angles. Hair and eyes like these were assets, but this foreigner seemed not to care. She wore plain clothes, no jewelry, little makeup. Her hands were knotty. She looked anxious, too. She had reason, thought Miss Chu. "Try to wait a bit," she said. "I have a lunch later today that might help."

Lunch? Maggie thought. "All right. I'll wait." She didn't want to wait, she wanted to move. Her *Table* assignment had already bombed. She couldn't let the DNA test go down the drain too.

"Let us talk after the lunch. Oh — call me Zinnia. That's my English name."

"Zinnia," Maggie repeated. "And your real name is?"

"Chu Zuomin."

"That's nice," said Maggie, "but I'd mangle it. Okay. Zinnia."
She rose. "Here." She passed across her business card with her cell
number circled. "That phone's on all the time. I'll be waiting." She
paused on a breath. "By the way, besides Carey, is there anyone else
still here, now, who knew my husband?"

"I think no," said Miss Chu. "Only Carey. He will be back late
tomorrow."

"Tell him I came in," said Maggie.

On the street she saw herself in a glass window, face shadowed,
her steps moving through the Chinese crowd. She heard a beeping
from her phone. She took it out. When she got back to the U.S. she
would turn it off for a week at least. Zinnia, already? No, a text
message from *Table*. She opened it.

How's everything going? Thinking of you, sending hugs. Sarah.

Guilt tightened around Maggie's neck. She should answer. She
should tell Sarah that the Sam Liang story was off, that his restaurant was not opening and he had canceled. She would send an
e-mail or a text message. She stared at her phone screen. She really
shouldn't wait any longer.

First, though, she had to eat. It had been a long time since she
left L.A., time in which she'd eaten very little besides the candy
corn.

She had brought the apartment's guidebook. In it she scanned
her sector of city restaurants until she found a courtyard house,
close by, that served nineteen kinds of dumplings. This sounded
good to her, and healthy. She needed to eat. She waved her hand for
a taxi.

At the restaurant she was given a table in a lantern-strung court
and a menu in English, with pictures. Many of the small creations
looked like the Chinese dumplings she'd had at home, though with
exotic fillings. Others were fantastical, sculpted creations made to
look like miniature durian fruits and white-tipped peonies and
plump, fantailed fish with red dots for eyes. Each was a marvel. But
she was too hungry for the exotic ones and so she chose a plain

dumpling, something substantial, filled with eggplant, cilantro, and dill.

The shape was familiar, yet the dumpling sounded different from anything she'd ever had before, and it sounded *good*. The truth was, she had never really liked Chinese food. Of course, she'd had Chinese food only in America, which was clearly part of the story. She'd always heard people say it was different in China. Yet even three years before, when she had visited with Matt, they had eaten at more Italian and Thai places than Chinese.

The trouble with Chinese food in America, to her, was that it seemed all the same. Even when a restaurant had a hundred and fifty items on the menu, she could order them all and still get only the same few flavors over and over again. There was the tangy brown sauce, the salted black bean; the ginger–garlic green onion, the syrupy lemon. Then there was the pale opal sauce that was usually called lobster whether or not lobster had ever been anywhere near it.

The menu in her hands held a square of text, framed by an ornate border in the style of scroll-carved wood. At the top it said A BRIEF INTRODUCTION TO CHINESE FOOD. For tourists, she thought, and started to read.

No matter which way you look at history, the Chinese people have been more preoccupied with food than any other group in the world. Compare our ancient texts to the classical works of the West: ours are the ones dwelling endlessly on the utensils and methods and rituals of food, especially the rituals. Food was always surrounded by coded behaviors that themselves carried great meaning. Consider, too, the economics of dining. Take any dynasty; the Chinese were spending more of what they had on food than any of their contemporaries around the world. China has always revered good cooks, and paid them well. Even the most archaic descriptions of early towns tell of restaurants and wine houses jammed along the earthen streets or riverfronts, doors open to the smells of food and sounds of laughter, banners flapping to announce the delights within. Wu Ching-Tzu, in his eighteenth-century novel *The Scholars,* described these places as "hung with fat mutton, while the plates on the counters were heaped with steaming trotters, sea slugs, duck preserved in wine, and freshwater fish. Meat dumplings boiled in the cauldrons and enormous rolls of bread filled the steamers." Still today, few things to us are more important.

It was signed by a Professor Jiang Wanli, Beijing University. What he was describing certainly didn't sound like the food she knew from home. Moreover, the air around her was undeniably bright with good smells and the sounds of chattering pleasure. Each table was filled. Waiters strode past, steamer baskets held high. Bubbles of laughter floated up. Slowly she took in the shrubs, the tasseled lanterns, the cranked-open latticework windows that revealed other dining rooms filled, like this courtyard, with loud, happy, mostly young Chinese.

Could the food in China be truly exceptional? It was possible, she thought now. Well then, she would eat; she would keep an open mind. Of course, writing the article about the chef would have been the perfect way to find out more. Again she felt the stab of regret that he had canceled, so sharply this time that her hand crept into her pocket and lingered on her cell phone. Should she really let it go? No. She should call him again. One more time.

She scrolled through the recently called numbers to his, took a breath, and hit SEND.

It rang, and she heard fumbling. *"Wei,"* he said when he got the phone to his mouth.

"Mr. Liang? It's Maggie McElroy again."

"Hi." Pause. He was surprised. "How are you?" he said.

"Fine. Thanks."

She could hear a scramble of voices behind him. He half covered the phone, hissing, and then came back. "Sorry. My uncles are here."

"I'm interrupting."

"No. They want me to talk to you."

"Why?"

"They've figured out you're a female person."

"Ah." Funny, she thought. She had somehow forgotten how to even look at it in that way. "Actually I'm calling one last time about the article. I don't want to overstep, but — I had to ask you again, since I'm here. Won't you give it some thought?"

"Look —"

"I don't have to write about the restaurant. There are so many things. The book. Aren't you doing a book?"

"Translating, with my father. We're doing it together. It's a book my grandfather wrote."

"The Last Chinese Chef," she supplied.

"You know," he said.

Naturally. You're my assignment. "We could write about that."

"I'm sorry, but it's the wrong time. I should do that when the book comes out."

"True," she admitted.

"Also," he said, "I'm swamped."

She was getting the signals, but she never heard *No.* Not the first time, anyway. "Swamped by what?"

"By an audition to get on the Chinese national cooking team. The 2008 Games in Beijing are going to have their own Olympic competition of culture — things like opera, martial arts. It's an adjunct to the opening ceremonies. Food is one of the categories."

"An audition for the national team?" She digested this. "What do you have to do?"

"Cook a banquet for the committee. There are ten chefs competing for the two northern-style spots on the team. The rest of the team has six spots — two for southern style like Cantonese; two for western, which includes Hunan and Sichuan; and the eastern school, which is Shanghai, Jiangsu, and Zhejiang, basically the Yangtze delta."

"So ten of you are competing for two northern spots."

"Right. Each night for the next ten nights, one of us puts on a banquet for the committee. They'll choose two. Seems I drew the last slot — mine is a week from Saturday. The tenth night."

"The last one. The best. So two win out of ten. What sets you apart from the others?"

"I'm the only one rooted in imperial — it's very rarefied. The emperors had dishes brought in from all provinces, so in some ways I have more flexibility, but also a more rigid artistic standard."

"And you have ten days to prepare."

"Yes. Well, nine. The first banquet is tonight."

"But as a story for the magazine, this is wonderful! Forget the restaurant. Really, Mr. Liang. *This* would be great."

"Sam."

"Sam. I could follow you through the process. I would not get in your way. You could tell me things — just a little, just what's comfortable. I'd do a good piece. Contests are one of my specialties." Why was she having to work so hard to sell this? Most chefs paid PR companies to get them features in places like *Table*.

But he said, "I don't know. I might not even have a chance. I'm kind of an outsider — the only one doing true traditional, on top of everything else."

"Whether you win or not, it's a great story. I can almost guarantee you'd be happy with it," she said. In fact, with just this one glimpse she could see it take shape. Beijing was a gleaming new city, all that steel and glass forming only a partial façade over its celebrated past. The old and the new were locked in a dance. The winner would be the last one standing. Would it be the old or the new? Some jazzy avant-garde local or this guy, who came back to take up where his grandfather had left off? Whatever happened, it was alive. She hadn't had this kind of feeling about an article in a while. *Please,* she begged him silently.

"Let me think."

"I'll come to where you're working — only when you say." She stopped. This was as far as she could go.

Again she heard the little bubble of whispered Chinese behind him. "Shh!" he said, and came back. "Okay. They'll kill me if I say no. And you're right. It would be good for me."

She waited on the edge.

"But you have to forgive me. I can't dress nicely and meet you in restaurants and hold forth. Not now."

"Why would I want to do that? I'll just come and watch you work. You talk when you can. I'll listen."

"All right. Let me think — I'm basically going to be slaving every minute in order to get this together. Tomorrow? You want to come tomorrow?"

"Okay." A smile rose around the corners of her mouth. Again the same strange feeling, of something good.

"Afternoon? Two?"

"Fine," she said.

"Call me when you're getting the cab. I'll tell the driver where to go."

"Okay," she said, and just before he disconnected she heard him talking to his uncles, switching back to Chinese with them in mid-thought, without a breath, the melodic pitch, the soft rolling sounds of the words, and then *click,* he was gone. She grinned at her phone for a second, giddy with relief, and then tapped in a text message to Sarah: *Thanks for your message. I'm getting by. Meeting the chef tomorrow. Love, M.*

She looked up. A waiter was moving toward her through the pools of electric light and the clanging dishes and the voices — was his steam basket for her? Yes. She leaned toward it — delicate, translucent wrappers and a savory mince of vegetables within. The aroma encircled her. She felt she could eat everything in the room. She tried the dipping sauce with a finger: soy, vinegar, little circles of scallion. "Thank you," she said in English, looking up. But he was already gone in the crowd.

Yuan Mei, one of China's great gourmets, once asked his cook why, since he was so gifted and could produce great delicacies from even the most common ingredients, he chose to stay in their relatively modest household. The cook said, "To find an employer who appreciates one is not easy. But to find one who understands anything about cookery is harder still. So much imagination and hard thinking go into the making of every dish that one may well say I serve up along with it my whole mind and heart."

— LIANG WEI, *The Last Chinese Chef*

The chef lived in a low, ancient-looking building facing a narrow, tree-lined finger of lake called Houhai. The street that ran along the lake was lined with gray, age-polished buildings. Some were houses, with laundry spilling from their windows and women out front, on stools. Others had been converted to cafés and bars, the latter marked by the buckets of empty beer bottles that had been set out from the night before. The chef's place faced the street with nothing but a stone wall and a massive red wooden gate, unmarked except for a small house number on the side. Maggie knocked.

From the other side of the wall she heard steps on gravel, and then a man almost precisely her size, with sharp cheekbones and black hair pulled back to a smooth ponytail, swung the gate open.

He could have been foreign — South American, Mediterranean — yet in his way of standing, of relaxing against his joints, she saw instantly that he was American.

"Sam," he said, and put out his hand.

"Maggie."

"I'm in the kitchen." He waited while she stepped over the raised lintel, then re-latched the gate.

In front of them was a green-and-yellow ceramic spirit screen. She paused, unable to stop herself from touching its raised-porcelain design of rolling dragons. "Doesn't this have something to do with evil spirits?"

"Yes. Supposedly they can travel only in straight lines. This has been here a long time. When I remodeled for the restaurant I left it, thinking I needed all the help I could get with spirits. Bad ones out, good ones in."

"I don't know if it works," she said, "but it's beautiful." On the other side of the screen lay an open courtyard with potted trees and mosaic-paved paths. Four rooms with ornate covered verandahs faced inward.

"This is the old layout of a Beijing-style house. There aren't many left. Up here," he said, and took her three steps up to the covered porch of the room facing the gate.

"Did you rent it, or buy it? Can you buy property here now?"

"Yes, though you don't have the same long-term security as in the West — things can change. But this house has been in my family since 1925. It was much bigger then — eight courts, not one. By the time we got it back, a few years ago, it had been whittled down to this."

"I didn't know people got property back."

"Some did — if the government had no use for it. And I know there's a chance I might not have it forever, either. But for now it's mine, so I'm going to use it."

"Great room," she said, following him through a dark, high-ceilinged dining room, empty but for one table and a gleaming expanse of black tile floor.

"You see the floor? They soak the tiles in oil for a year. They did that in the Forbidden City. Yesterday I took the tables out. I put them in storage. Couldn't stand to look at them after my investor backed out. Here's the kitchen."

He held open the metal swing door for her to walk in ahead of him. She caught her breath. She had been in a lot of kitchens, but this one was stunningly organized. Every inch of wall was lined with shelves that held bowls and containers and bottles and jars filled with pastes, sauces, and spices. Down one side ran two Western-style restaurant stoves and a formidable line of wok rings. Behind were the large refrigerators and prep sinks. An island formed a raised counter down the center, with three cutting boards that were polished, circular slabs of tree trunk. "You have really thought things out."

"I had great teachers."

"Who were?"

"My uncles. Two here, one in Hangzhou."

"It's a beautiful kitchen." She eased toward a stool that was tucked under one end of the island. "And I meant what I said, I don't want to hold you up. Go to work. Shall I just sit over here?"

"You can sit there. That's fine. How long have you been in Beijing?"

"This is my second day."

"What do you think of the food?"

She looked up, face brightening. "Amazing! I've had only a few meals so far, mind you, but it hasn't been like any Chinese food I ever tasted. Not that I'm an expert."

"You don't write about Asian food?"

"No." Maggie dug her little book out of her bag along with her pen. "I do American food, and not the haute stuff, either — everyday food, regional food, the human story — you know, cook-offs, fairs. Festivals."

"What a lot of people really eat," he said.

"Exactly."

"To the Chinese way of thinking that can be very profound. We have a long tradition of valuing the rustic. Of all food we find it the closest to nature, the most human. How long have you been doing it?"

"Twelve years."

He studied her. "So why'd they choose you for this?"

"Because I had to come anyway."

"Right. You said something about other business."

"I did," she said, and moved on. The less he knew about that, the better. With him she had a job to do. Besides, nothing made her appear old and pitiful faster than saying she was a widow; she had seen this fact clearly since Matt's death. "To your question, though. To me the Chinese food here is completely different. I may not be a specialist, but, I mean — I work for a *food* magazine, for God's sake. I have eaten in my share of Chinese restaurants. And what I've had all my life does *not* taste like what I've had here. Not even remotely."

"But anybody who knows the food here could have told you that."

"Really?" She folded back the book to a clean page.

"Chinese-American is a different cuisine. It's really nothing like Chinese-Chinese. It has its charms, no question. But it's not the same."

"How?"

"Chinese-American evolved for a different reason — to get Americans to accept a fundamentally different way of cooking and eating. They did this by aiming at familiarity, which was kind of weirdly brilliant. From the time the first chop suey houses opened, that's what they were selling, the thing that seems exotic but is actually familiar. Reliable. Not fast food, but reliable in the same way as fast food. Here it's different. It's the opposite. Every dish has to be unique, different from every other. Yet all follow rigid principles, and all aim to accomplish things Western cuisine doesn't even shoot for, much less attain."

She was scribbling as fast as she could.

"I'd better get to work," he said. He lifted an apron from a hook on the wall, looped it over his head, and tied it. He turned his back to her and stood still for a second, head bent, silent.

She stared at his ponytailed black hair for a second, and went on writing. *Casts his eyes down while he ties his apron. Looking for something, like an anchor falling, seeking the depths.* She watched, saying nothing.

First he piled plump shrimp in a colander and tumbled them under cold water, then worked a towel through them until they were dry. In went egg white, salt, and something squeaky-powdery that looked like cornstarch. She watched his brown knuckles, lean and knobby, flash in the mixture. He slid it into the refrigerator and washed his hands. "Now," he said.

She liked that he had turned his back to her to work. It was good that he was comfortable with her here. That made her feel at ease too. He seemed to be finished with the shrimp, at least for the moment, so she ventured another question. "You said Chinese cuisine in China tries to accomplish certain things."

"Yes."

"Things that set it apart from the cuisines of the West?"

"Yes." He thought. "For one thing, we have formal ideals of flavor and texture. Those are the rigid principles I mentioned. Each one is like a goal that every chef tries to reach — either purely, by itself, or in combination with the others. Then there's artifice. Western food doesn't try to do much with artifice at all."

"Artifice." She wanted to make sure she heard him right.

"Artifice. Illusion. Food should be more than food; it should tease and provoke the mind. We have a lot of dishes that come to the table looking like one thing and turn out to be something else. The most obvious example would be a duck or fish that is actually vegetarian, created entirely from soy and gluten, but there are many other types of illusion dishes. We strive to fool the diner for a moment. It adds a layer of intellectual play to the meal. When it works, the gourmet is delighted."

"Okay," she said, "artifice."

"Call it theater. Chinese society's all about theater. Not just in food. Then there's healing. We use food to promote health. I'm not talking about balanced nutrition — every cuisine does that, to some degree. I'm talking about each food having a specific medicinal purpose. We see every ingredient as having certain properties — hot, cold, dry, wet, sour, spicy, bitter, sweet, and so on. And we think many imbalances are caused by these properties being out of whack. So a cook who is adept can create dishes that will heal the diner."

"You mean cure illness?"

"Yes, but it's more than that. People have mental and emotional layers to their problems, too. The right foods can ease the mind and heart. It's all one system."

"You cook like that?" she said. "You yourself?"

"Not really. It's a specialty."

"Okay," she said, writing it down. "Healing." *As if food can heal the human heart.* "Is that it?"

"One more. The most important one of all. It's community. Every meal eaten in China, whether the grandest banquet or the poorest lunch eaten by workers in an alley — all eating is shared by the group."

"That's true all over the world," she protested.

"No." He looked at her, and for the first time she saw a coolness in his face. He didn't like her disagreeing. "We don't plate. Almost all other cuisines do. Universally in the West, they plate. Think about it."

"Well . . ." That was true. Every Chinese restaurant she'd ever been to had put food in the middle of the table. "I concede," she said. She was going to write *Does not like to be crossed* but instead wrote *All food is shared,* because it was true. He was right.

Now he had taken a rack of pork ribs out of a plastic bag of marinade and was cleaving them off one after another. His tree trunk barely shuddered. She watched him swing his arm and his shoulder. He was wiry but strong. "Your grandfather was a chef," she said.

"Right."

"And your father too?"

She saw him hesitate just a moment before resuming. *So — some problem there.* "Yes."

"Then he was the one who taught you to cook?"

"No. My father stopped cooking when he went to America. I learned here."

"How?"

"Well, first of all, I had always cooked. I learned the basics from my mother — brisket, chicken soup, challah. But four years ago I decided to change my life, and really learn to cook. I came here. I told you, my uncles. They're incredible chefs, they're older, retired — they taught me. Full-time. I spent the first few years basically cowering beneath them. They were rough. What you might call old-school."

"Are those the guys I heard on the phone?"

"Two of them. That was Jiang and Tan, whom I call First and Second Uncle. Jiang Wanli and Tan Jingfu. There's a third one, Uncle Xie, who lives in Hangzhou. Xie Er."

"Are they your father's brothers?"

"No. Xie is the son of a man who worked with my grandfather in the Forbidden City. Tan is the grandson of my grandfather's teacher, Tan Zhuanqing, who was a very famous chef. Jiang grew up in Hangzhou with Xie; they were best friends. So we aren't blood relations, but our ties go back for generations. Those kinds of connections are very strong here. Stronger than in the West."

"And all three were chefs?"

"Tan and Xie were chefs. Jiang is a food scholar, a retired professor."

"I knew I saw that name somewhere. I read a little introduction by him on a restaurant menu."

"That's him. He cooks, too; he says he doesn't, but he does."

"And they were hard on you?"

"Terrible! They called me names. They'd hound me, shout at me, slam utensils to the floor when I didn't move fast enough — and then if I made something that wasn't perfect, they dumped it in the garbage."

"Ah!" She was writing, enjoying his words and the scratch of her pen on the paper. "And then your father. You say he just stopped cooking? Why?" She looked up.

Again he hesitated, his hand in midair with the cleaver. Then back to chopping. "It was too hard for him in America."

"Still, I wonder why he didn't teach you."

For Sam Liang, answering this question was always hard. Everyone in China remembered his grandfather as a chef, fewer his father; still, everyone assumed his father would have been the one to teach him. In truth, Sam would have given anything for his father to have taught him, to have cared — even if he'd yelled at him, insulted him, and cuffed him the way his uncles did. But his father refused. He said no Liang was ever to cook again, certainly not his son. Chinese cuisine was finished. It was dead. Great food needed more than chefs; it needed gourmet diners. These people were as important as the cooks. But the Communists had made it illegal to appreciate fine food or even remember that it had once existed. They had the masses eating slop and gristle and thinking it perfectly fine. In America and Europe, too, Chinese gourmets were all but nonexistent. There were some left in Hong Kong or Taiwan, but that was it. So said Liang Yeh.

When Sam had tried to suggest to his father that things had changed, that a world of art and discernment and taste was being reborn in China and that going back might be worthwhile, the old man erupted. "Never return to China! Never set foot there! It is a dangerous place, run by thugs!"

In fact, even though Liang Yeh was pleased that Sam had graduated from Northwestern and become a schoolteacher, he really had asked only two things of Sam in life. One, never go back to China. Two, marry and have a son. On neither front had Sam delivered. He brought the cleaver back down again between the ribs.

The American woman seemed to read his silence. "So okay, your father didn't teach you, your uncles did. But am I correct in saying you're still cooking in the style of your grandfather?"

"Definitely."

"And like him, do you feel you're the last Chinese chef?"

"Not the last," he said. "Maybe one of the last. I think I'm more optimistic than my grandfather. He thought it was all over. He was convinced imperial style would die with his generation. My father's generation thought the same. Yet there always seemed to be a few who kept it alive."

"Why?"

"Because it was the highest thing. Not only did it incorporate all China's regions, all its schools of cooking, it was a chef's dream like no other. In the Forbidden City's kitchens you could create anything. They had the finest ingredients from all over the world. Hundreds of people cooked for one family."

"So who became a cook?"

"Ah," he said. "Not what you think. Not only certain people. *Any* person could do it. It was one of the weird democratic aspects of feudal China. Some chefs were rich and educated, some poor. Cooking was one of those jobs that relied purely on talent. Any man who excelled at it could get to the top. People respected great cooks. In fact, one chef in the eighteenth century B.C. was made a prime minister, his food was so good. His name, Yi Yin, is still spoken with awe thousands of years later. To this day, when people talk about negotiating matters of state, they say 'adjusting the tripods,' in honor of him and the bronze vessels of his time. You'll see for yourself, the longer you stay here: we are ultra-serious about food."

He talks of the Chinese and says "we," she wrote. *He has a dark face, indeterminate. If I had not known he was Jewish-Chinese I would never have guessed. He could be Greek, Afghan, Egyptian. He could be from anywhere.* "So what kind of person was your grandfather before he became a chef?"

"A slave."

"There was slavery that late?"

"China was feudal until 1911."

"So he was owned by someone." She wrote, *Descendant of slaves.*

"But he wasn't born that way. He sold himself. It was either that or starve with his family."

"Where was he from?"

"Here. Beijing. The back alleys. You should read the story." He pointed his knife at the far end of the counter. "I set it out. It's the prologue to the book. It was the first thing I put in English. You can take it with you if you like. Or read it here."

"Really?"

He turned back to his ribs. "Either way. Right now I have to cook."

"Should I go in the next room?" she said, even though she hadn't seen any place to sit in there. Just the one table. No chairs.

"As you like." He was gathering minced green onions in a mound.

Maggie watched him for a second. She liked the rhythms of the sounds he made, and the raw, unblended smells. Everything he thought and felt and said was condensed into the food under his hands. And it was comfortable here — which was odd to her, because she felt in most people's kitchens the way she felt about homes in general: wanting to leave as soon as possible. Do her interview, get her notes down, and leave. "I guess I'll stay," she said.

He was focused now on cooking and gave only a distracted nod. So she leaned on her elbows and turned past the title page, *The Last Chinese Chef,* and started to read.

❦ ❦ ❦ My name is Liang Wei. I was born in the nineteenth year of the reign of Guangxu, the year they in the West call 1894, into the lowest rung of society. My family were alley dwellers. Five of us lived in one room, but we had city pride. We were folk of the capital. At least we knew we were better than millions of others.

My father was a vendor who went every day to the great open squares inside the Fucheng Gate, to sell glasses of tea to the men who streamed in alongside lines of camels and mule-driven carts. In the heat of the summer and the numbing ice of winter, he went. The caravans bought, or they did not. Too often not. As the years went on, his face became set with the etchings of his fate.

By my seventh year we were starving. The decision was made to sell one of the children. Usually a family would sell a girl, but the girl in our family was the youngest. Too young to sell. I said I would go. It was time for me to be a man.

At least with this move I knew I would eat. There was a reason why families as poor as mine sold their children into the restaurant trade. It was slavery, but it came with hot meals, three times a day. And if the young one proved gifted, there was nothing really to stop him from reaching the top. With food a man could advance on merit alone, without money, lineage, or education.

And thus it was for me. Being sold was my life's beginning. A broker resold me into the employ of the palace. Never before was there such a place; never will there be again. In those years, the last of Ci Xi's reign, there were five divisions: meat, vegetarian, cereals — which meant rice, buns, and noodles — snacks, and pastries. An incredible variety of food was brought to the palace, not only game and birds and seafood of all description but also the fruits and vegetables specially chosen at the dedicated farms, each piece plucked from the bottom of the plant, the place closest to the root and thus to life. Tribute came from local officials all over the empire. From the northwest came redolent Hami melons and sweet grapes; from the south, oranges, tangerines, longan, crystal sugar, and litchis. The governor of Shandong sent lotus seeds, dates, dried persimmons, and peanuts. From Liaoning and Manchuria came hawthorn berries and pears. The repertoire of the palace kitchen covered four thousand dishes. The most important creations — those most favored by the imperial family — sometimes became the lifelong concentration of one celebrated cook.

I lived with two other kitchen boys, Peng Changhai and Xie Huangshi, in a small rented room in the Tartar City, a half-hour's walk from the palace. In this walled enclave that encased the Forbidden City like a larger square lived the Manchus. Relatives of the Emperor and the lords of the Eight Banners, they in turn supported a whole second world of servants, craftspeople, laborers. We, kitchen assistants in our little brick room with its few small windows, were on the bottom of this generally privileged sector of the city.

But at least we were slaves and not eunuchs. Eunuchs could live in the palace. They held unimaginable power. But any man who still had his three precious, his private parts, had to be out by sunset. And so we came here, to the Tartar City, to our small room.

Xie Huangshi was the much younger brother of Eunuch Xie, who directed the Empress Dowager's exclusive kitchen, which was called the Western Kitchen. Their family had also been poor — once. Then the eldest Xie brother had sat for the knife, and passed into the brilliant, painted world of the Forbidden City. He took control of the kitchens and quickly rose in power. Finally he brought in his baby brother, Xie Huangshi — but as a slave, not a gelding. Eunuch Xie remained outwardly aloof, but everyone knew he favored the boy. He put him under one of the greatest cooks of the palace, Zhang Yongxiang. Zhang knew no limits. His most famous dish involved hollowing out fat mung bean sprouts with wire, then stuffing them with minced seasoned pork and steaming them to delicate perfection. Xie Huangshi trailed him like a shadow, never so much as lifting his arm without trying to do it like the master.

Peng and I went under Tan Zhuanqing. There has been no accident in my life luckier than this. It was not only that Lord Tan was the greatest chef of his generation, as he was; it was that he was a man of great accomplishment. All Manchus were pensioned at birth — Lord Tan used to say that this had been the downfall of the tribe — but even among them Tan Zhuanqing came from an especially wealthy and powerful family. From a young age he was famous for his intellectual attainments. By twenty-six he was a member of the Hanlin Academy. It was said he had written the best eight-legged essay in memory. He knew everything about antiquities and was a sought-after expert on cultural relics. He was an aristocrat. He had money, position. He could have spent his life doing whatever pleased him. And what pleased him was to cook in the palace.

"Why?" I would say. "The Old Buddha takes only a few bites."

"It is not her. Ten thousand years to her, of course, but she cares only for little cakes that comfort her and carry her back to other times. It's the princes! Gong, Chun, and Qing — General Director Li Lianying. It is they for whom I cook."

No more than a small remark, but it was one that made me see how all things fit together. There was a shadow audience for the palace kitchens, a discriminating and highly appreciative one. What happened to the food every day, after every meal, was no accident.

Each time the Empress Dowager entered the hall and ate, she left many dozens of elaborate dishes untouched. We packed these into large lacquer boxes, divided into sections, each box containing a meal for a family of eight, and tied them with hemp. These were carried by eunuchs to the homes of princes and high officials. There they got tips and gifts beyond imagining.

When I went out into the city it was with Tan Zhuanqing. He liked to select his own provisions. Everyone knew him. He was famous. I heard people ask him: Why not leave the palace? Open your own restaurant. And he would always say there could be no higher calling than cooking for the Emperor. He was correct. But behind that truth was another one, which was that he also cooked for the cognoscenti. The gourmet was as important as the chef. *Liang tiao tui zou:* the art walks on two legs. To have one, you must have the other.

I learned from him. Sometimes I saw him come up to a stockpot when he believed no one was looking, and add a secret pinch of something from his pocket. We all saw, we all begged him to say what it was, but I was the only one he would tell. Then of course I told Peng and Xie. We were brothers.

Lord Tan arranged our education. He saw that Peng and Xie and I had gifts, and that meant we had to learn to read. "You must read the food classics," he said. "No Chinese can call himself a chef without doing so." We would have thrown ourselves off cliffs for him, done anything, so we worked hard for his tutor. We burned candles until daybreak, and in this way the door of words opened. Lord Tan gave us passage to a higher world. There everything had been recorded, the accumulated truth of all things past. I felt myself leaving my old world, in a way, when I learned to read — certainly leaving the limited world of the immediate, which until then was the only world I had ever known. I found that everything I needed had been somewhere known, and somewhere written. Now that in this paradise of food the hunger of my early years had been satisfied, my appetite was for words. I wanted to know all that men had known before.

Yet what I read was not recipes; they were almost never written down. The way of cooking a dish was always secret, and exclusive, and the only way to learn it was by watching. So in my years of study, what I did was watch Lord Tan.

There was the day we prepared a midday meal for the Empress. He was creating his glazed duck. His secret for this dish was full concentration on the primary essence of the food itself. Thus he used duck fat, rendered from another duck, and duck broth, distilled from yet several others. Duck should taste entirely of duck; duck should be used in every way. This is what he taught me. It did not matter if four or five ducks were used to make one. This was the pursuit of perfection. And this was his secret: by doubling and tripling the essence of the duck he was able to reach *nong,* the rich, heady, concentrated flavor and one of the seven peaks of flavor and texture.

He was wiser than any alchemist. His dishes brought him all the glory under heaven. And he did it just as easily from coarse simple food as from rare delicacies. He often said that the best food was simple and homey; it reminded us of when we were young, or felt loved, or were lit up with believing in something. This was why the Empress Dowager always ordered *xiao wo tou,* crude little broom-corn cakes made with chestnut flour, osmanthus, and dates. They reminded her of when the imperial family had fled to the northwest during the Boxer Rebellion. Not that those who fled were heroic, he whispered to us, his young charges — they abandoned their capital. But it was over now, it was past, and she could remember what it had been like to be on the road, in the open air, eating rough corn cakes.

On that day Lord Tan paid close attention to the duck. *Nong* was a quality that could go too far. Timing was all.

But Tan was a master who effortlessly synthesized knowledge. He always knew to remove the duck at its most sublime. When it was time for the meal to be served I went outside and stood in a row with the other apprentices, all of us in our flapping blue robes with white oversleeves. The Empress ate in the Hall of Happiness and Longevity. I could barely see it down the long brick walk. They were setting tables up in there now.

Then came the call. Each of us took a lacquer box on our shoulders and set off in a foot-whispering line. In the hall we laid out the dishes in places chosen by the geomancers and protocol officials of the Western Kitchen. Everything was according to pattern, order, harmony. There were hot and cold dishes, roast fowl, soups, fish fried and steamed and braised, and all manner of sweet and salty northern-style pastries. From the far south came crabs preserved in wine and fresh cold litchi jelly. There was shark's fin sent by the king of the Philippines, and bird's nest from the Strait of Malacca.

We set down the plates and withdrew as always. That day we did not return to the Western Kitchen but waited in another hall nearby, empty, wood-dusty, ringing with our footsteps and our chortling jokes. Then we trotted back and packed the food into the dragon-embossed lacquer boxes as usual. We tied them with green and red strings and fixed them to poles.

Yet Old Li, the eunuch who always took my pole, walked up to me and stood there. "Boy," he said, "you know the Houhai District?"

"Of course, sir," I said, for I had grown up there.

"Then take this to the Gong family palace. Do you know the road?"

"Like my hand. But honored sir, it is not my place to go there. It is yours."

"Don't you think I know that? Curse fate! But it's urgent. I am being called back. You'll take it?"

"Yes, honored sir." Before I had even finished speaking he swung his robes and walked away. His pole was still in my hands.

I shrugged it on. It settled easily into the notch on my shoulder. Prince Gong's mansion lay near the lake. I knew the spot. I walked toward the back of the palace, for it would be best to leave by the Shen Wu Gate.

Then it was out into the teeming city, my blue and white robes fluttering with importance, the imperial lacquerware bouncing with my steps. People moved out of my way. Crowds parted. I wore the colors of the palace.

At the front gate of the Gong mansion the pole and boxes were recognized at once, though I was not. "Honored lord," I said to the gatekeeper, "Master Li could not carry these boxes today. I am an unworthy apprentice."

The gatekeeper called to someone. A gate to the inner gardens opened and a beautiful girl came out with a servant. "Ah! Where's Uncle Li?"

"He was detained."

"You came instead?"

"Yes, miss." I made a reverence.

46

She put on an amused look and reached into her purse for coins. "What's inside?" she said.

"Lord Tan made his glazed duck."

"Ah! Wonderful." She handed me the coins.

"Pleasure belongs all to me, miss. Thank you." I closed my fist around them. I bowed low and long, until she and the servant with the food had withdrawn.

Quickly I slipped out to the street. I walked down along the lake with its waving fronds until I was under a pool of yellow light, beneath the buzz and hiss of a gas lamp. Only then did I unfold my hand to look.

Five coins. They looked like —

I bit one. Gold. I had never seen it before, but I knew. I closed my hand tightly again and kept walking, south, away now from the lake.

When I reached Huang Cheng, to return to the palace, I should have turned east. Instead I turned west — toward my family. I would run like light itself. I would be no more than a moment late. Lord Tan would never know.

When I came to my old neighborhood and turned panting around the corner to my own lane, the first thing I saw was my mother sitting outside the doorway on a stool, scrubbing a cabbage. "Zhao Sun," she said slowly, half stumbling with surprise and wonder. She used my milk name, the name they called me as a baby, which I had not heard for a long, long time. I made an obeisance, but it was stiff. "Liang Wei has returned," I said, and then she leapt to throw her arms around me.

"Ma," I said, the single syllable strangling out of my mouth. She was so small! I was tall and strong; I had not realized how much I had grown. My skin was scrubbed, my queue plaited. I stood holding her in what had for a long time seemed to be only my apprentice clothes, but which now shone in this dark alley as brilliant robes of imperial silk.

"Come," she said, and pulled me quickly in through the low, stooping doorway. As my eyes adjusted to the dimness of the clay-walled room, my little brother and sister appeared from the shadows, eyes large, barely believing. It was as familiar as a dream: the cracked basin, the faded flowers on the bedding. My mother's dented pans.

I was glad my father was not there. I had another father now — Tan Zhuanqing. My life was his.

"I can't stay." I gave Erhui and Ermo a squeeze. They were thin and not much taller than I remembered them — not flush with good food as I was. "Go outside," I told them. "Let me talk to Ma."

When they had slipped out into the sunlight and dropped the quilted cold-weather robe back down behind them, I took her elbow, opened her hand, and dropped in one of the coins. "Do you know what this is?"

"By the Gods," she said, "yes." She looked up at me. "Where did you get it?"

"I earned it." I was as tall as the sky then, a man. I bent over it with her. "Is it enough for the winter?"

"Yes. More than."

"Then I will return with this much every year."

Her eyes filled and spilled over with gratitude as she slipped it into a secret pocket she always kept within her clothes. Then she let out a small cry and dropped to grasp me by my knees.

"Ma, stop," I said. I pulled her up, but my heart swelled with gladness. "I must go," I said. "Take care of the young ones."

I ran back through knotted lanes and beaten-dirt intersections where as a child I had played and hidden and stolen crisp autumn pears and seed-studded wheat buns from the carts of vendors. It was the world to me then — neither good nor bad, rich nor poor. Old men lounged on marble steps as they always had, bulky wadding inside their socks for warmth. Small children wore clothes handed down, much mended. Old ladies walked in gray cotton with their hands behind their backs. And here I passed in bright silks, leather on my feet, gold coins gripped tight in my fist.

At the Forbidden City I was well known by the guards and passed quickly through the gate. Avoiding the grottoes and gardens around which were arranged the private halls and apartments of the royal family, I took one of the outer passages back to the kitchen complex. These minor avenues connected an outer web of halls and courtyards, where lived relations and forgotten concubines. They did not matter in the palace, yet they could never leave.

Finally I came to the kitchen. I passed the snack section, the pastry section, the meat section. Usually it was in this section that Master Tan worked. Today, though, my instructions were to meet him in another part of the kitchen. He was to give me a different lesson in *nong*, by making fermented mung bean curd. It was a difficult dish. Reach the rich, heady top point, and it was a dish so delicious one could not stop eating it. Ferment it too far — even a little — and it was repulsive. This was *chao ma doufu*, and we were going to make it in the vegetarian section, a place where they generally specialized in brightly nuanced, mock meat and fish dishes of bean curd and gluten.

I was late, but not by much. If Lord Tan said anything I would throw myself on the ground. "Master," I would say, "I know. I beg you. Forgive this miserable child who is unworthy —"

I stopped short in the door to the vegetarian section. No one was there. The counters were cleared and the ranges still cooling. Where was my master? He never came late.

I walked back the way I had come. I passed the rice, bun, and noodle section, where many boys were at work. Some were making thick hand-cut noodles and others a fragrant porridge of lotus root and lotus seed. "Have you seen Lord Tan?" I called, for they were apprentices like me, and between us there were no formalities. No, they had not, and where had I been? "Nowhere," I said, and silently touched my finger to the four coins in my pocket. I would tell no one until I saw Peng and Xie.

I returned to the meat section. It too was quiet. The great black ranges stood in a row, the glow in their fireboxes snuffed down to red embers. The woks were clean and back on their rack. "Master?" I said, and my voice sounded small and childish in the air.

No one. But I felt something. I felt him. I continued walking toward the back room where the meats were hung and where long banks of prep counters were lined with endless bowls in blue and white filled with all manner of sauces and condiments and accent vegetables, all fresh minced to perfect uniformity.

Then I noticed something.

There were shards scattered on the floor, blue and white; someone had broken a bowl. I froze.

There were his feet. He lay curled around himself as if still in agony, both hands pressed to his chest. I didn't need to touch him. I didn't need to feel for his pulse. I knew he was dead; I could tell. The light of knowledge had gone out of him. All he knew had escaped into the air. I glanced around frantically, as if somehow I could find it and gather it back. *It's in books,* he would say to me if he were here, *go find it.* But he was gone. He was empty and inert.

I dropped and kowtowed to him three times. After the third time of pressing my forehead to the cold tile floor, I rose and began a long and agonized wail for help, not stopping until I heard the jumbled footsteps, the eunuchs and the kitchen workers, the scuffing and clattering. Their faces, their eyes when they stumbled in and saw him, were pale and sick and horror-struck. It was as if civilization itself had died. It was the beginning of the end. All of us knew it somehow, and all together we lowered ourselves to the floor before him. Men and eunuchs crowded into the doorway, ten deep, twenty, and when they saw, they too fell to the ground.

The call was going out. I heard a bell clanging. Suddenly I knew, from deep inside me, that he was going to have one of the greatest funerals the capital had seen in decades, with a banquet lasting three days for his family, his friends and admirers, the princes and the great scholars and the high officials. And I would prepare his glazed duck.

 ⚘ ⚘ ⚘

When Maggie finished she sat for a moment in silence. This man in front of her was part of a pattern that went back in time, across generations; he was connected. Not merely to a single person, such as a spouse — she knew how quickly that could be torn away — but to a whole line. No, she thought, a civilization. She watched him move around the kitchen as if from a distance, from a boat offshore, from a life that would never be like his. Not that she felt envy. She had made it one of Maggie's Laws this past year not to covet the lives of others. She had learned to guard against such feelings in order to continue to have friends, to have a life; almost everyone she knew still possessed what she had lost, which was normalcy and love. She didn't know yet about this man's private life, but now that she'd read the prologue, she did see he had something else, something that clung to him like a light. It was a connection over time, insoluble.

As a state of mind, a multigenerational sense was new to Maggie, or at least foreign; she was from L.A., where many people, including her own responsible but solitary single mother, had come from someplace else. People made their own lives; that was what Matt had always said. He'd done it. He placed himself in the world. He spent lots of time on jets and married a woman who did the same. And in his mid-thirties, after years of loving her *because* she was the peripatetic observer and writer he had come to know, he began vexingly to still love her but to wish that she were different. Then the moment he felt it, he had to tell her; that was the way he was. He started waking her early in the morning with his hand on her abdomen, on the warm spot in her center. *Think about it,* he would say in her ear.

What? she'd ask, sleepy, but then she'd open her eyes and see his gaze and know. She loved this about him. Even when they didn't agree — as happened, halfway through their marriage, with children — he was a natural river of honesty. She had learned with him to be honest in return, and so she told him the truth, which at first was some version of "I don't know." *Let me work a little more,* she would say. *Let me think about it.* They both knew it was not what they'd agreed. Still, she'd consider it. *Give me a year.* In this way they bumped along.

She watched the chef drop the shrimp into a sizzling wok and swoop them around with his arms. She took up her pen and wrote, *He has a shape like a marmot.* It felt good to write, not to think about Matt. Now he was adding something to the wok — what? — which made the shrimp fragrance climb. She didn't want to break the spell by asking. He turned the shrimp onto a plate and cranked off the hissing ring of flame.

Only then did he turn and see that she'd finished. "Hi," he said.

"I love this." She touched the pages. "Can you tell me what happened to them?"

He wiped his hands on his apron. "First the dynasty fell. That was 1911. They had to leave the palace. They all opened restaurants, Peng and my grandfather Liang Wei here in the capital and Xie in Hangzhou. They did well. My grandfather wrote *The Last Chinese Chef* and it was a sensation. Everyone prospered, for a while."

"Until?"

"Communism. The new government closed the restaurants down. They kept a few places open for state purposes. My grandfather's was one of those liquidated. That turned out to be lucky, because a few years later they were jailing people who ran imperial-style restaurants.

"That was what happened to Xie. His place in Hangzhou was one of the ones they left open. But later, having his restaurant was what got him sent to prison. He died there. But he'd had a son in the thirties, who grew to be a great chef too. This is my Uncle Xie in Hangzhou — the one I call Third Uncle."

She looked at her notebook, checking the names. "What happened to Peng?" she asked.

"Peng's fortune was not shabby." He pronounced the name back to her the proper way, *pung*. "He was admired by the Communist leadership, especially Zhou Enlai. No matter that he cooked imperial — he was that good. They wanted to keep him. They gave him a restaurant in the Beijing Hotel, Peng Jia Cai. He became *their* imperial cook. In the 1950s that place was the be-all and end-all. He was amazing. Even my father said that of the three of them, he was the best."

He put down a plate of pink shrimp under a clear glaze. No additions or ingredients could be seen, though she had watched him add many things. The aroma seemed to be sweet shrimp, nothing more.

He took one and held it in his mouth, dark eyes flying through calculations.

Her turn. She put one in her mouth and bit; it burst with a big, popping crunch. Inside there was the soft, yielding essence of shrimp. "How do you make it pop like that?"

"Soak it in cold salt water first. That's what I was doing when you first came in."

"It's great," she said.

"Good," he corrected. "Not great. I can still detect the presence of sugar."

"I can't."

He smiled. "Remember I told you we strove for formal ideals of flavor and texture? This dish is a perfect example. One of the most important peaks of flavor is *xian*. *Xian* means the sweet, natural flavor — like butter, fresh fish, luscious clear chicken broth. Then we have *xiang,* the fragrant flavor — think frying onions, roasted meat. *Nong* is the concentrated flavor, the deep, complex taste you get from meat stews or dark sauces or fermented things. Then there is the rich flavor, the flavor of fat. This is called *you er bu ni,* which means to taste of fat without being oily. We love this one. Fat is very important to us. Fat is not something undesirable to be removed and thrown away, not in China. We have a lot of dishes that actually focus on fat and make it delectable. Bring pork belly to the table, when it's done right, and Chinese diners will groan with happiness."

"*That's* different," she said, scribbling. "What else?"

"That's just flavor. We have texture. There are ideals of texture, too — three main ones. *Cui* is dry and crispy, *nen* is when you take something fibrous like shark's fin and make it smooth and yielding, and *ruan* is perfect softness — velveted chicken, a soft-boiled egg. I think it's fair to say we control texture more than any other cuisine does. In fact some dishes we cook have nothing at all to do with flavor. Only texture; that is all they attempt. Think of bêche-de-mer. Or wood ear."

Maggie considered this. As a concept, texture was not new to her. Many of the greatest dishes she had experienced on the road delivered their pleasure through texture: fried oysters, with their dazzling contrast of inside and out; the silk of corn chowder; the crunch of the perfect beach fry. But all of these relied on flavor too. "You must do something to give them a taste, surely?"

"Yes — we dress them with sauces. But plain sauces, way in the background. Anything more would distract. The gourmet is eating for texture.

"Once you understand the ideal flavors and textures, the idea is to mix and match them. That's an art in itself, called *tiaowei*. Then we match the dishes in their cycles. Then there is the meal as a whole — the menu — which is a sort of narrative of rhythms and meanings and moods."

"My God," she said, writing rapidly.

"Everything plays in. The room. The plates. The poetry." He plucked up another shrimp with his chopsticks and chewed it thoughtfully. "The problem is, this shrimp falls short of true *xian*. *Xian* is the natural flavor. If it doesn't taste natural, the chef has failed to create it."

"So you're saying, it's the natural flavor, but it's concocted."

"And there's the paradox," he said.

She smiled and wrote it down. "You concoct it how?"

"By adding supporting flavors, mostly. Every flavor has a specific effect on every other flavor. But all this must be invisible. Believe me, a Chinese panel will know this. And this shrimp — right now — is not quite there."

"So are you going to use it in the banquet?"

"Not unless I get it perfect."

She ate another. "I think it's pretty great." There was a silence while they both ate and her eyes wandered to the prologue. "Could I borrow this?" she said, touching it. "I'd like to read it again."

"Take it. I printed it out for you."

"Thank you."

"I'll give you more of the book later, if you want."

"I do. But right now I'm going to clear out and let you work." She packed everything up into her bag.

"I hope you'll come again," he said. "Come on. I'll walk you out."

They pushed through the door and crossed the large, darkened dining room, him moving a few steps ahead to hold open the wood-and-etched-glass door out to the courtyard. "You know?" he said. "We've been talking about food all this time. I didn't ask you — what's the other thing you're doing here, in Beijing?"

She turned, halfway down the steps. The raw sadness of the last year came back over her, the sudden slam that could never be undone, the frantic constriction, the struggle to get control. Sometimes even the ministrations of her friends couldn't get through to her. It was in her job that she'd found a small tunnel of light, especially during the weeks of each month she spent away, writing about other people's lives. There'd been the kindness of the Malcolms, the retired Maryland couple on the Eastern Shore who worked six commercial crab pots and consumed their entire catch, eating crab at every meal through the season. There was Mr. Loeb, the stout pastrami man in Nebraska, delicate and graceful with a knife, the last counterman in the Midwest to slice the fragrant rosy slab by hand. Being with those people helped her. In their normalcy they relieved her. They didn't ask questions. She didn't have to tell them about the mess that was her life.

Now Sam Liang was waiting.

"I'm a widow," she said. "A year ago my husband died."

She waited while he took this in, while compassion, and some of his own fears, crossed his face. She had seen it in people's faces so many times by now. "I'm sorry," he said.

"Thank you. It's been difficult, but I'm better. It's been a year." That, she thought, was enough to say. He didn't need to know how raw it still felt. And he certainly didn't need to know about the widening sea that separated her more and more from other people, about the long days this summer she had spent lying on the bunk on her boat, ignoring the messages on her cell phone. She made her voice brisk. "My husband did some work here, and some matters in China came up related to his estate, so I had to come."

"I see." A lift of his eyebrow acknowledged the potential for a challenge. "I hope it goes well. Good luck. Are you very busy with that? Do you have the time to come back again?"

"Oh, yes," she said. "I'll be going out of town in the next day or so, but until then I'm okay."

"Do you want to come tomorrow, late morning?"

"That will work," she said, and stepped past him over the sill.

"Maggie," he said, as she turned for the street. "What you told me. I'm really sorry."

"Thanks." *Not that you know anything about it.*

"See you," he said.

She raised a hand and walked all the way to the turn in the road along the lake before she looked back. In that blink she saw him withdrawing, his blue jeans, the old-ivory skin of his hands, and then, *click,* the gate closed.

4

Let us return for a moment to the popular view that poverty, specifically scarce food and fuel, stimulated China's culinary greatness. Certainly it is true in the case of cooking methods, and when it comes to the unsurpassed ingenuity of Chinese cooks in making delicious dishes out of everything under heaven, all the plants of the earth and sea, all the creatures, all their parts. These are the legacies of scarcity. Yet truly great cuisine, food as high art, did not arise here; it arose from wealth. It was the province and the passion of the elite. Throughout history, gourmets and chefs tended to reach their heights in conditions of plenty, not need.

— LIANG WEI, *The Last Chinese Chef*

The following morning Sam Liang came back home from delivering some birds to his poultry farm outside the city. It was not his farm, exactly; he leased space there for his fowl before slaughtering them. He followed Liang Wei's dictum, which was that a bird one wished to eat must spend at least the last few weeks of its life running and exercising in the fresh air. This made for better meat, according to *The Last Chinese Chef*. It was a brutal way of looking at it, a Chinese way: care for the creature, love it, pamper it, then eat it. Of course anywhere one went one found eating to be a cruel business. Here, though, there was no pretense. You knew a healthy animal tasted best, and so you raised it or at least fostered it. You knew fresh meat and fish were the most delectable, and so you did the slaughtering yourself. There were even dishes with live ingredients. In drunken prawns in the Shanghai style, for example, the prawns were not quite dead when eaten but so inebriated from being soaked in wine that they lay perfectly still for your chopsticks. No Chinese diner would flinch at the faint flutter of movement in the mouth. On the contrary. To the *meishijia,* the gourmet, this was the summit of freshness.

At first, Sam had been a bit disturbed by this. It seemed to echo the faint streak of sadism he saw in China's past. Every country had its dark history, but in China there were certain convulsions, like the famine and the Cultural Revolution, that seemed needlessly cruel. And the privatized Chinese business world, right now, in the twenty-first century, was cruel too. Things ran on opportunity, not principle. No one thought in terms of win-win dealings but only about who would win and who would lose. Every man watched his back at all times. In the America of Sam's youth, he had heard people say they lived in a "dog-eat-dog" society. Here in China, they said "man-eat-man." *That* was the economic boom.

With each passing year in China, though, he saw that the true situation was more subtle. It was not so much that China was crueler than the West, only more honest. The frankness of life, even of death, was always in front of him here — certainly when it came to food. It was more honest to take home an animal and slaughter it than to buy its meat in a square, shrink-wrapped package, more honest to keep a fish alive and swimming until the moment you wished to devour it. His appetite stirred at the thought. He so loved the *xian* of fresh fish.

As for the business world, it had its treacheries but also a massive and marvelous saving grace: *guanxi. Guanxi* was connection, relationship, mutual indebtedness. It was the safety net of obligation and mutuality that held up society. The best opportunities and connections were kept for the family, the clan, the friends, in an outwardly rippling circle. You gave one thing to the world; you gave something higher to your own group. As an American, Sam had been put off at first by this, for all he could see in it was cronyism. Later, when he came to know it as a way of life, he saw its mercies as well.

He saw too that it was food — people eating together, whether at banquets or daily meals — that kept the engine of *guanxi* going. Perhaps this was why chefs in China had always been so important.

As he walked the last stretch from the subway stop and came to the early-morning edge of the lake, he was also thinking about texture. On his way back he had stopped by a dealer who sold all kinds of dried mushrooms and fungi and water weeds and flowers, just as the man was opening up. Sam had bought several varieties of *mu-er,* wood ear, so called because of the way it grew on trees. One bag was the delicate white ruffles called cloud ear; the others were the more common crisp brown flaps. When reconstituted they had a robust vegetarian crunch, one that no amount of cooking could soften. No taste beyond the faintest metallic sense, easily corrected by other ingredients. All texture. Whether added in slivers or pieces, they could transform many dishes.

He saw his own gray stone wall ahead, set back slightly from the sidewalk. It was noisy here on the street, busy, but inside his place it was quiet. Perfect for a restaurant. And out front was the long, thin tendril of lake. It was classic feng shui, and not in any obscure sense either, for no one could arrive or leave without taking pleasure in the sight of the lake.

This district had changed even just in the last few years. Once characterized by graceful, crumbling residences, moody water, and a few far-off shapes of pagodas and skyscrapers above the willows on the opposite shore, it had become a theatrical sightseeing spot. Young men pedaled tourists in rickshaws. For blocks at a time the sidewalks were crowded with cafés and bars, their doors flung open, Chinese pop blaring.

Nowhere else on this strip was there a restaurant like the one he was going to open, but that didn't matter. Fate had put his family in this neighborhood. And he loved it. He loved the summer, with its repeating cicadas and hot, hazy air; the winter, when the sky was bright and cold and itinerant vendors sold hot meat skewers and char-fragrant roasted sweet potatoes. In fall the light turned golden and men sang their way along the lake's edge, under the trees, offering fanned sticks of candied crab apple.

He unlocked his gate and brought the big brass joins together again behind him, carried his bags to the kitchen. He needed to put the food away and leave. It was time to go meet Jiang and Tan.

That morning Zinnia called and asked Maggie to meet her at a Shanghainese restaurant near the Calder Hayes office, even though it was too early for lunch. Maggie hurried there, hoping Zinnia would have the tickets. It had been almost two days. After leaving the chef's house on the lake the day before, she hadn't done much except sit in the apartment thinking about Matt. She had been in the same apartment with him three years before, in the same rooms; he came easily to mind. Yes, they had liked being apart. And yes, they were happiest of all when they were first reunited again, in the golden space before questions and qualifiers started, once again, to resurface.

So they specialized in reunions, and in separations; that was all right. They came and went, living on takeout containers, his and hers, one side of the refrigerator and the other, experiencing their joy in cycles. Even on the downslope, when they'd started contracting back into their own agendas and dropping seeds of irritation, they were honest. She always felt she knew what was in his heart, good or bad.

And that was the problem that had kept her up late the night before, looking out at the still, shimmering city. Now there was this claim. So maybe she had no idea what was in his heart. *Did you do it?*

No.

Do you know this woman?

No.

Then how did this happen?

She sat on the couch throwing silent questions, imagining answers. She visualized his kind, big-jawed face and felt sure he was saying no: no, it was not true. She decided she believed him, as she always had; then she changed her mind and threw him out of her heart and ceased to accept his denial; then some hours later she took him back again. By the time the deep night had come and the street below had gone silent she was exhausted. She slept as if unconscious, without dreams, and when she awakened she felt tired, as if she'd barely slept at all.

She pushed open the door to the Shanghainese restaurant. Inside, the world changed. She felt pushed back in time. Around her were dark-wood walls and brass lamps, waitresses in old-fashioned side-slit gowns. Only the diners were modern, with their crisp clothes and multiple, faintly chiming electronic devices. Among them she saw Zinnia, who waved her over.

"Sit!" she commanded when Maggie reached the table. "How are you? Are you well?"

"Well enough. Did you hear anything about the tickets?"

Zinnia's earnest smile evaporated for a second.

Maggie saw she had been abrupt. "I'm sorry — I guess I thought maybe that was why you asked me here."

Zinnia nodded. "I don't have the tickets yet. Unfortunately I did not receive your file until I was assigned to help you, and that was the morning you arrived. So I have just started. But I will do my best. You should not worry."

"You are determined," Maggie said admiringly. "I believe you'll do it."

"I will. *Ni fang xin hao.* That means you should put your heart at ease. The day we met I had a lunch. The person couldn't help me. But then last night I had dinner with a friend from China Northern. It is one of the biggest domestic airlines. We had ten courses and wine. Very good. Long talk. Now I am waiting for his call."

"Good," said Maggie.

Their business clarified, Zinnia looked back at what she'd been studying when Maggie walked in, which was the menu. "I want to have the jellyfish. It reminds me of my childhood. My son likes it too. Have you had it?"

"Yes," said Maggie. "You have a son?"

"Yes. Two years old. He's a good boy," she said proudly, still looking at the menu. "When you had jellyfish, did you like it?"

"It didn't have much taste."

"You are right! Actually jellyfish is not taste food. It is texture food."

"Fine." Sam Liang had told her all about texture. "Let's have some."

"*Hao-de.* Then some other dishes."

"What exactly did you ask him?" said Maggie. "The guy from China Northern."

"I didn't ask him. I only mentioned the facts in passing."

"I thought you meant you had dinner to ask him for tickets."

"Yes. But that was the request, the dinner. The only thing left was to mention the matter in passing. I did. Now I must wait."

"I see." The jellyfish arrived, handed off by a waitress on her way to another table. "So do you think it's possible we could leave today?"

"Maybe tonight, more likely tomorrow." Zinnia reached out and snagged Maggie a pale, translucent heap of gelatinous curls. "Try," she said.

Maggie took a curl up on her chopsticks and ate it. The flavor was mild, barely discernible, but Zinnia was right about the texture: it was the mouth-feel of the food that snapped her to attention, crunchy and spongy at the same time. "Hey," she said. "Not bad."

The younger woman grinned. "That's what we say! *Bu cuo.* Not bad. It means so-so in English, doesn't it? But it's a sincere compliment in Chinese. Did you know that? It means you like it. Good." Zinnia took some on her own plate. "Are you free after we eat?" she asked.

"I have a meeting." She looked at her watch. She was going to see Sam Liang again.

"Can you stop at the office first? Carey James is back from Bangkok. He asked to see you."

"Yes," Maggie said immediately. For this she would call the chef and see if she could be a little late. Carey had memories of Matt, memories she hadn't tapped. He'd have images or nuances still new to her — events, jokes, snippets of remembered conversations. She may have had this new blade of uncertainty about her husband buried in her side, but she still knew that she would take anything. Anything about Matt. Even just the chance to talk about him a little bit with someone who remembered him. "Of course," she said.

"Good," said Zinnia. "Now come." She pointed with her chopsticks at the food. "Every person needs to eat."

"You have to decide what manner of menu you want," Second Uncle Tan told Sam. They were in a restaurant having midmorning snacks, restaurants being far and away the best places to meet in China at any time of day. Homes were small, while the world outside was filled with public places where people could eat or even just sip tea.

"There are three kinds of menus," Tan said, "the extravagant, the rustic, and the elegant."

"And within the elegant there is the recherché," Jiang said, breaking his Chinese only for the French word. "This is another possibility: nostalgia. There are certain great classics still remembered by the people."

"Jiu shi," Tan agreed, It's so.

"You could make crisp spiced duck," said Jiang. "Carp in lamb broth. And old-fashioned hors d'oeuvres — dipped snails, fried sparrows."

Tan looked over with a snort. "Too intellectual. Such dishes are only for true aficionados."

"Afraid I'm with Second Uncle," said Sam. "That's not for this panel. And a rustic menu wouldn't work for them either. You and I know, to cook plain food brilliantly is one of the hardest things of all. But they won't see it."

"Just two hundred years ago Yuan Mei himself said that the most sophisticated thing of all was to use the cheapest bowls and plates," Jiang said.

"But today?" Sam said. "Now that everything is about money? Suicide. Impossible. However," he added, "we could go with the elegant. For instance — what about tofu in the shape of a lute, stuffed with minced pork, flash-fried? And a chicken's skin removed whole, intact, then stuffed with minced ham and vegetables and slivered chicken meat and roasted at high heat until fragrant —"

"Impressive," said Jiang.

"— and the skin is snapping-crisp, *cui* —"

"Texture!" said Tan. "Yes. You should make this point clearly. What other cuisine controls texture as ours does?"

"He is right," Jiang said.

Sam understood the implication. Be Chinese. Let the other, native-born cooks take chances and improvise. He would be what his grandfather had been, what his father would have been, a cook of tradition. Beijing might be wide open, aggressive — profane, even — in its run for the future, but people still longed for the past.

That was one reason he and his uncles liked this restaurant; it was old-fashioned and therefore restful. While they talked they picked at a few dishes. One plate was heaped with braised soybeans mixed with the musky chopped leaves of the Chinese toon tree; another held rosy-thin slices of watermelon radish in a delicate vinaigrette. Uncle Tan had proposed ordering wine, but had been overruled with a sharp reproof from Jiang. Sam agreed. It was not even lunchtime. Too early.

"For texture you could consider silver fungus, or your stir-fried prawns," said Jiang. "Ah, yes! Those prawns. First crunchy, then inside, soft as mist."

"I made those prawns just yesterday," said Sam. He thought of the American writer in his kitchen, her ease as she watched him cook, her careful eyes, her perception that never lagged no matter how much he told her. The inflection of her speech, which was sunny and American and sounded like home to him. Even though what she told him just before she left, about her husband's death, fell like a heavy weight. "I made them for the woman writing the article."

"Ah, the woman!" They leaned forward.

"Forget it," Sam said. "She's in a bad situation. Her husband died —"

"A widow," clucked Tan.

"— and there is some matter here in China over his estate." He stopped at the sound of an American voice behind him.

"What are you guys talking about? That's some fast Chinese."

"Hi," said Sam, turning. It was David Renfrew, one of the shifting crowd of foreigners he had met here. He had thought he would find friends among them, as they, like him, were outsiders, but so far he had not. "We were actually talking about prawns," he said. "Have you eaten?" It was a traditional Chinese greeting, but said in English, from one American to another, it had an agreeable irony.

"Just did," David said. "I heard you were on TV last night. You're up for the cooking games."

"Auditioning for the team," Sam said.

"Good luck."

"Thanks. Meet my uncles." Sam circled a hand around the table. "We were just going over what I should cook. David Renfrew, Jiang Wanli, Tan Jingfu. Jiang is a retired food scholar, Tan a retired chef. David is a banker."

"Pleased to meet you," said David.

"Pleased," they both murmured back in English.

"So." David turned back to Sam. He still spoke little Chinese after all his time here, and didn't really try. That was typical. David had been here a bit longer than most, the average expatriate stay being only about two years, but he still lived the *laowai* life. With occasional excursions for variation, this generally meant shuttling between the office and the circuit of clubs and hotels and gyms and restaurants that were aimed at foreigners.

"When was the last time I saw you?" David said. "Hold it, I know. That party at the Loft. Right?"

"I think so." That had been one of those nights when Sam had gone out even though he hadn't really wanted to.

"You know who else was at that party?" said David. *"Her."* He trained his eyes on someone across the room. "I saw her that night. She was a friend of someone I used to know. Damn, what's her name?"

Sam leaned to the side in his chair to follow David's gaze.

"Where?" he said to David, and then, "Oh, I know her." He recognized her short, tentative posture, her straight fall of hair. She worked in the Sun Building. He'd met her through a Dutchman who knew her there, a guy who managed a shipping company. Piet. What had happened to Piet? Gone back to Europe. Then he had seen this girl occasionally at parties. She seemed young, maybe a little naïve, but nothing about her had really caught his attention. "That's Xiao Yu," he said.

"Xiao Yu! That's it. Thanks."

"Do you know her?"

"No. Well, I met her. At my friend's place. That was a while ago. Forgot her name." A possibility ticked across his precisely edged Teutonic features. "I'm not stepping on toes, am I?"

"You mean her and me?" said Sam. "No."

"Just asking."

"We're barely acquainted." Sam sent a glance to Xiao Yu. "I mean, feel free," he said to David.

"Thanks," the American said. "I will. Hey. It's been a long time, hasn't it? We should catch up."

"We should," Sam said.

"Call me. We'll have coffee. I'm at work all the time." David turned his smile on the uncles. "Nice to meet you," he said. Then he left.

"Your friend?" inquired Uncle Jiang, and Sam nodded.

"Did he want you to make an introduction to that girl?"

"No," said Sam, watching David move away through the tables. "He met her before. He just forgot her name."

Jiang raised one white eyebrow.

But Sam had his gaze beyond his uncles, still on David. Now he was coming up behind her. She didn't see him. He reached a hand out to her shoulder. She started, and turned, and all the way across the room Sam could see the gladness in her eyes. She was so open to him. It made Sam sad. Why? She was no child. It was none of his business. He looked away. Maybe the feeling arose in him because of the American woman. He felt sorry for her too.

"Let's go back to texture," Jiang prodded.

"Good." Sam turned.

"So far we have been talking about things that are *cui,* crunchy. Consider the spongy quality of intestines. Take the Nine Twists, the way they make the intestines into soup in Sichuan. And in Amoy they stuff them with glutinous rice and cook them and slice them cold with soy sauce."

"Don't forget Hangzhou!" Tan put in. "There they stuff the intestine not only with rice but also with smaller and smaller intestines, so it slices into concentric rings. So clever."

"Flavor rich, texture delicate," Jiang said with a sigh.

Sam rolled his eyes. "Intestines are out."

"You should consider," said Tan. "At least you should learn to make them. Hangzhou style. No cuisine has more richness behind it. Or more literary history. Of all the times you have visited Little Xie there, did he not show you?"

"Not that dish," said Sam. He was in some ways closest of all to Uncle Xie, his Third Uncle — so called because he was the youngest of them. The best part of Sam's apprenticeship had been sweated through in Hangzhou, under the old man's displeasure and his tantrums and his praise. Xie had taught him many dishes, but not the intestines.

"Xie could really make that dish," said Tan. "But your father did it best. Even better than Xie. Don't tell me he didn't show you."

"He didn't," said Sam. Jiang and Tan still didn't grasp the fact that his father had taught him nothing. When Sam was small, Liang Yeh had gone to work and come home every day and then sat alone in his little study. He would read and let himself wander, staring at the wall while unspooling scenes from paintings and operas, movies, and the classics of art and philosophy. In his mind men fought with swords, leapt and floated in the air. He was often far away when the young Sam would walk into the room looking for him. His mouth would be loose and his hand a light flutter on his book. "Hey," Sam would say, and his father's eyes would bounce to him, surprised.

To Sam as a child, this seemed merely like his father. But by the time he reached high school he understood that Liang Yeh was different. At games and other obligatory events, his mother, who had enough vitality for three people, managed to anchor all the interactions. Liang Yeh would stand apart, remote, attentive, his hands jammed for warmth into his layers of jackets and shirts. "How is it you Americans do not feel the cold?" he would say to the other parents — and that was if he spoke to them at all.

But Sam was in China now. Heaven had given him the gift of his uncles. "I have been thinking," he said. "I am allowed to have three assistants at the banquet. What about the two of you and — you don't think Xie will be well enough to come, do you? I worry that he's not over his illness." For *illness* Sam used the word *maobing*, which literally meant "hair of an illness," showing his optimism that any indisposition would soon be over. "In which case I will just have two," he finished, "the two of you."

They exchanged looks. "Nephew," said Jiang, "Xie is far beyond helping you cook. He is worse; to speak truly, he is gravely ill. *Bing ru gao huang.*" The disease has attacked his vitals.

"What?" Sam said. Sometimes the little four-character sayings went right past him. Chinese was a living web of references and allusions, a language that was at its best with short verse and metaphorical sayings. So much of the web of civilization was out of his reach that plain conversation often eluded him.

Tan shook his head with a gravity that made the meaning clear.

"That bad?" said Sam.

"*Yu shi chang ci,*" Jiang said after a moment, He's going to go away from this world for a long time.

"I thought he was better," said Sam.

"A little," Tan answered. "For a while."

"Then I have to go to Hangzhou," he said.

Jiang nodded. His face was pale.

"I was going to go after the audition."

The interval of silence sent unwelcome recognition around the table. "Maybe that will be too late," said Jiang.

"Then I'll go now."

"Nephew," said Tan, "it is filial of you. But there is the contest. You must prepare. Xie would want you to do that."

"True," said Jiang. "And even if you try to go, you may not get a ticket. It is almost National Day."

None of that changed anything.

"Stay and prepare," Jiang repeated.

"Xie will understand," added Tan.

Sam knew this was demurral and not truth. Jiang and Tan *wanted* him to go see Third Uncle. They expected it. But they had to counsel him not to, then later reluctantly agree when he insisted. "I'm going," Sam said.

"Well," said Jiang, as if resigning. "Then ask him to give you a dish for the banquet. One of his specialties."

"The pork ribs," said Tan. "Oh! *Ruanyiruan,*" So soft. "The meat falls away in your mouth. He marinates them, then rolls them in five-spice rice crumbles. They are wrapped in lotus leaves and steamed for hours."

"Soft as a pillow," said Jiang.

"I could eat that right now," said Sam. "Okay. I'll start working on the ticket right away." His eyes wandered back to David and Xiao Yu. Where they had been talking was only a blank patch of wall. They were gone. Had they sat down? He scanned the tables, the waiters moving sideways through the aisles. No. They had left. He felt the twinge again inside him, the odd feeling he'd had before, the pleasantness of the hour with Maggie McElroy. Where had David and Xiao Yu gone? He kept thinking that the next time he glanced over he might find them standing there again, restored. But he did not.

On his way to the office Carey had tried to settle on what he would tell Maggie. Too little would disrespect her, while too much would hurt her unnecessarily. He fiddled with what to do. Tell her the truth, of course, but only when she asked and only that part of the truth which pertained.

He remembered, when he'd met her here in Beijing three years ago, being aware right away that she did not know. *She has no idea,* he remembered thinking. *Matt never told her.*

Carey was not surprised. He would not have told either. So Matt had gone a little wild; so what? He'd pulled his reins in quickly enough, and by himself, too. Let it be, was Carey's feeling. He was a nice man, Maggie seemed like a nice woman, no need for them to suffer. Let them be as happy as they could. That's what he had thought. Now of course he half wished Matt had told her himself, so he wouldn't have to.

Not that it was what Matt would have intended. Matt was a steady man, a man of rules; this Carey had seen about him from the first moment. He could still see Matt at the airport, with his hyper-organized luggage, his smooth, clean face smelling of the shave-soap provided on the plane. The man had force. His legal work was like that too, meticulous, powerful, unbending. He stayed with the rules. He was, Carey knew, exactly the type who sometimes had to break out.

It was a pattern he had seen before. He guessed one in twenty were like Matt, good, hardworking guys who bolted their traces when they came to this place where everything was on offer, where a wild, clubby economy turned cartwheels around the power center of government, where any desire could be satisfied.

"Let's go out," Matt had said at the end of his first day in the Beijing office, on his first visit, seven years before. That was the beginning. He had left even Carey in the dust, and Carey was known far and wide as a king of the night. They roamed from one pulsing spot to another on Sanlitun. After the crowded bars and the costume raves Matt would walk away and negotiate with the women who worked the clubs. Carey tried to tell him there were finer women to be had elsewhere, only marginally more expensive, women with something close to beauty, even class. A phone call away, come, let's go — No. Matt would go for the bargirl. And he would walk up to the African drug dealers too, relaxed, companionable. He'd ask them what was up, like they were in New York. Not a blink. They'd always tell him what they had, hashish, ecstasy, LSD. He bought hashish and rolled it with tobacco. That was where he drew the line. His restraint when it came to drugs fit with the other Matt, the married man, the one Carey had met at the airport. And that was the Matt who showed up at the office after their nights on the town — always on time, frayed but ready — and put in a full day's work. This impressed Carey. The man was a rock.

But Matt started to feel guilty. On his second visit, later that same year, he came into Carey's office one afternoon and said he'd decided he should just go ahead and call Maggie now and tell her everything.

"Have you lost your mind?" Carey remembered saying. "Why would you tell her?"

"Because I tell her everything."

"Things like this?"

"I never did things like this before."

"You tell her *this* and you'll change everything. Ask yourself — are you going to do it again? Is this going to be your new lifestyle?"

"No! I feel bad already."

"Then don't do it anymore. And don't tell your wife. She doesn't need to suffer." His hand strayed to the file he had been working on. The clock had been running on the client and he didn't like to stop. "It's okay, man," he added gently. "Everybody slips a few times."

Matt had thanked him, and agreed that yes, this was the thing to do. "You'll have to find a new late-night companion," he joked, and Carey told him *that* would be no problem. At the same time, he was not surprised Matt had climbed back into himself, red-faced, so quickly. This too he had seen before.

But two evenings after that, Matt buzzed him again, on his cell. It was late. The office was almost empty. Carey was ready to leave anyway. And there was Matt again, that same excited edge in his voice, saying, "I know what I said, but can't help it. Let's go out."

"Okay," Carey said, feeling his own smile form. At moments like these Matt was as willful and open as a child. He acted on his needs. There was something almost like purity about him, an up-rush from inside. Maybe it was because of this that Carey indulged Matt in those first few years, went out with him, shepherded him. They were two friends who knew each other only at this single crossing in their lives. The two men rarely spoke when Matt wasn't in China. The last year before Matt died they had not talked at all.

And then he was gone. Carey was well aware of the fact that he had other friends he knew better. Still, it was hard to think of Matt now, this past year, without a bolt of sorrow.

From outside his door he heard the tones of his secretary and beside her another voice — Maggie. The door opened and in came the widow, her walk slow, hyperconscious. She had changed in the three years. Her face, always too sharply arranged to be called pretty, had started its turn toward the elegant concavity of age. Her body looked ropier than he remembered, under loose, neutral clothes. Care and grief had her in a cage, leaving only her large eyes, which now burned with extra intensity, as if compensating for the rest of her. "How are you?" he said, uselessly, and rose to give her a hug.

"Had better years," she said into his shoulder.

They sat a few minutes talking. Their words made circles around Matt, remembering him, trying to laugh about him, talking about the shock of his death — "Christ, that's one phone call you never want to get," said Carey. After they talked about Matt he inquired elaborately into the comfort of her flight, and the apartment. She told him about her assignment. And then she noticed the file, which he'd laid out on the table between them. "You've seen this already," he said, "right?"

"Zinnia showed it to me." She opened it. "Talk about being blindsided."

"Me too," he said.

She looked up abruptly. "You mean what you said before? You knew nothing about a child?"

"No," he said, and repeated: "Nothing about a child."

The way he said it hinted at more. "Then what about the woman who's named here as the mother? Gao Lan?"

He exhaled. "Yes," he said. "Her I knew about." He watched her eyes widen and almost instantly glaze over, as shock was followed by humiliation. *Tell her the truth.*

"What exactly do you know?" she said.

"Just that it did happen between them."

"Her and Matt."

"Yes."

"Was it at the right time?"

"Yes. It was brief, though. I don't want you to think it was a relationship."

"Why?" she said, her voice sharpening. "Does it count for less if it wasn't?"

"No," he said.

"Especially when there's a child."

He raised his hands; she had him. But it did count for less. It would have been worse if Matt had actually loved this woman. He hadn't, and that mattered. Right now, though, Maggie couldn't see it. Understandably.

"Tell me what happened," she said, and he did. He started with the night Matt met Gao Lan.

Nice girl, Carey remembered thinking when he first saw her under dancing, roving lights. Pretty. But there were endless girls who were pretty. He knew that. Matt, still somewhat green in China, did not. He saw Gao Lan across the room and begged and pestered Carey until the two of them went over to Gao Lan and her friend and bought them a drink. To Carey it was boring. They were such ordinary girls. There were better girls elsewhere. But he could not get Matt to leave that night and go somewhere else.

The way Carey told it to Maggie, he took his leave early and could only infer what had happened later. It was easier for him to convey it this way, even though it was not the truth. Actually Matt and Gao Lan had been the first to leave; they left together, and Carey saw them go. He could still see Gao Lan turning her perfect oval rice-grain face up to Matt as they walked to the door. She'd had a porcelain femininity that made her quite the opposite of Maggie, across from him now, angular, sad, intelligent.

"Was it just that one night?" she asked. "Or did it happen more times?"

"Only the one night." Carey couldn't be sure of that, of course, but it was what Matt had told him.

That winter Matt had come to China twice. On the second visit Gao Lan called him, and what Matt told Carey afterward was that he had broken it off with her then and there. He didn't share any of the details, just said he didn't want to see her. Didn't want to talk to her.

At the time Carey had thought it unfeeling. Carey's sympathies, if they lay anywhere, were snug in the lap of male prerogative — but there was no reason to hurt a woman, either. Matt had sheared Gao Lan away with one swipe. She didn't like it. Carey had seen her only once since then, at a reception. She'd given him an icy stare and turned away.

"I felt sorry for her at first," he admitted to Maggie now. "Bad about what happened. Not anymore. Not after I saw this." He tapped the claim form. "I know he could be the father, I admit it, but at the same time I still don't believe it. If she had his child, why would she keep quiet all this time? And — I know this sounds strange, but it's hard to imagine a child coming from a liaison that meant so little to him." Carey felt no need to tell Maggie that this had actually seemed to be a little more, emotionally, than the one-night stand it probably was. "A liaison that he regretted."

"Nature doesn't care about your feelings for someone," she shot back. "And how do you know he regretted it? What makes you say that?"

"He told me," Carey said, and closed his eyes. He could hear the clang of the metal door and see the bright fluorescent lights and see Matt, in the office men's room, his head over the sink, guilty from the night before. "I shouldn't have done it," he said to Carey, raising his face, and Carey, who did not inhabit Matt's universe of commitments and barely understood its layout, nevertheless read the wild mix of remorse and terror on his face. It was then he sensed that hearts had perhaps been open, along with the sex. "Do you think I could have screwed up my life?" Matt had asked from his well of misery over the sink.

"He loved you," Carey told Maggie now. "He felt terrible after it happened because he was afraid he might lose you. He was abject. That's why he cut it off with her. And it never happened again. One night only. I don't know if it makes you feel any better, but he was in agony afterward."

"How nice," she said, voice going slightly flat. "But from what you're telling me, the child could definitely be Matt's."

"I'd say there's a good chance," Carey said, "yes. But chances mean nothing. You need the absolute truth."

"I need the test," she said.

The classics tell us that the mysterious powers of fall create dryness in heaven and metal on the earth. Of the flavors they create the pungent. Among the emotions they create grief. Grief can neither be walled away nor be held close too long. Either will lead to obsession. For someone grieving, cook with chives, ginger, coriander, and rosemary. Theirs is the pungent flavor, which draws grief up and out of the body and releases it into the air.

— LIANG WEI, *The Last Chinese Chef*

Maggie had called Sam Liang to say she would be late, but even so she had only a half-hour from the time she stumbled out of Carey's office to the time she was due to present herself smiling at the chef's front gate. She got in a taxi and lashed herself into a humiliated state. She'd been made a fool of. Matt had been with this woman, Gao Lan, and he'd been with her at the right time. And she never had a clue. She loved him unflaggingly, until the very last day of his life. Loved him still. Or did she?

This is boxed away, she was telling herself when she came to the chef's front gate, for now she had to work. *This will be sealed until later.* His gate was ajar. So she stepped in, called out a greeting, and followed the pot-clanging sounds to the kitchen.

His back made a curve into the refrigerator. When he stood up and turned around he was holding a whole poached chicken on a plate, its skin a buttery yellow. "How are you?" he said.

That, you don't want to know. I am the last stop on the bottom of creation. "Fine." She dropped her bag on the same stretch of counter she had claimed the day before. "How about you?"

"Stressed. I need a better source of live and fresh fish, for one thing, and I need it fast. And I'm cooking until all hours."

"Trying dishes for the banquet?"

"Trying to conceive the meal." He leaned against the counter in a brief exhaustion.

"When did you go to sleep last night?"

"Two." He amended. "Three."

"We don't have to do this today." One hand still rested on her bag. She could turn and leave. She had her own problems, from which, she knew, this would barely distract her anyway. "It's no problem for me."

"Not at all," he said. "Stay. Sit down. I made this for you."

She glanced at the whole chicken, plump, tender-looking. "You shouldn't be making anything for me, with all you have to do."

"I did, though."

She inhaled. "It smells good."

"It's not finished."

She leaned closer. "But it's not whole. I thought it was. It's cut up." *And so precisely reassembled.*

"Yes," he said. "It's in *kuai*, bite-sized pieces."

"How'd you cook it?"

"It's in *The Last Chinese Chef.* You put the chicken in boiling water —"

"How much water?"

"That's in proportion to the chicken. After you do it once or twice you know. Bring it back to a boil and turn it off. Cover it. Let the chicken sit until it cools. Perfect every time."

"Just water?"

"Oh, no. Salt. And different things. Today ginger and chives. They are always good for chicken — they correct the metallic undertone in its flavor." He paused. "They do many things."

"So flavors correct other flavors."

"All foods affect each other in some way. We have a specific system."

"For example?"

"There are techniques. Breaking marrow bones before cooking to enrich flavor. Cooking fish heads at a rapid boil to extract the rich taste. Whole set of techniques for texture, too, ways of cutting and brining and soaking.

"Then, at the next level, you use things to modify each other. There is a long list of flavors that modify other flavors — things like sugar and vinegar. Then there are just as many flavors used for their controlling or suppressing qualities, like ginger and wine. Then we have a bunch of things we use to affect texture. That's where our starches and root powders come in."

While he talked he set a wok on one of the rings and whuffed up the flame. "I'm going to finish the chicken," he told her. He let the wok sit for a minute, heating, and then added the oil.

"First you heat the pan?"

"Hot pan, warm oil." He dropped in ginger to hiss and rumble, then added chives. The fragrance flowered instantly. He shut down the flame and poured this boiling, crackling oil over the chicken. Then he sprinkled cilantro leaves on top. "Now it's ready."

She took the chopsticks. The smell of chicken had bloomed to a warm profundity. It smelled like home to her. Her childhood may have been narrow, just her and her mother, but wherever they lived, the aroma of chicken was there with them. And this smelled as good as anything she could remember. Better.

"Try it," he said. "It's cut bone-in. Chinese style. Can't get the flavor without the marrow. Just spit the bones out. You okay with that?"

"I am."

He laughed. "You're so serious."

If you only knew what I was trying to hold down. She plucked a morsel from the side of the bird, low on the breast where the moistness of the thigh came in, and tasted it. It was as soft as velvet, chicken times three, shot through with ginger and the note of onion. Small sticks of bone, their essence exhausted, crumbled in her mouth. She passed them into her hand and dropped them on the plate. "But it's perfect," she said. "All chicken should be cooked that way, all the time. I may never have tasted anything so good."

"Thank you."

"I mean it." She bit into another piece, succulent, soft, perfected. It made her melt with comfort. It put a roof over her head and a patterned warmth around her so that even though all her anguish was still with her it became, for a moment, something she could bear. She closed her eyes in the bliss of relief. She finished and passed out the bones. "Are you going to make this for the banquet?"

"No," he said. "This I made for you."

She looked up quickly.

"These are flavors for you, right now," he explained, "to benefit you. Ginger and cilantro and chives; they're very powerful. Very healing."

"Healing of what?" she said, and put her chopsticks down. She felt his human force suddenly, as if he were standing quite close to her instead of sitting across the counter, and she sat up in apprehension.

"Grief," he said.

"*Grief?*" The unpleasant nest of everything she felt pressed up against the surface, sadness, shame, anger at Matt. Anger at Sam for presuming, for intruding; gratitude to Sam for those same things. Her voice, when it came out, sounded bewildered. "You're treating me for grief?"

"No," he insisted. "I'm cooking for you. There's a difference."

She tried to master the upheavals inside her. She would *not* cry in front of him. "Maybe you should have asked me first."

"Really?"

"It's a bit difficult for me."

"Well, for that I'm sorry. Forgive me. You're American and I should have thought of that. Here, this is how we're trained — to know the diner, perceive the diner, and cook accordingly. Feed the body, but that's only the beginning. Also feed the mind and the soul."

Maggie thought about this. "A chef in a restaurant can't do that," she protested. "They don't know the diners."

"Right. That would happen only with their friends or frequent customers — who were many, by the way. But restaurants through history were only one part of things. There were also the chefs who cooked for the wealthy families and knew their diners intimately. There were the famous gourmets who left behind their influential writings; they too had long relationships with their cooks. The cooking relationship is a bond like family. Supporting the soul is naturally a part of it." He scanned her face. "Look. I didn't mean to offend you. This is how I was trained by my uncles. It's also how my mother raised me, to do things for people. She called it a *mitzvah*. I'm sorry if it felt too close for comfort."

"It's not your fault," she said. She still felt invaded, a little; now she also felt guilty for it.

"It's only food," he said more gently.

"I know." She put a hand up to shield her eyes. *No. Not in front of him.* "I probably shouldn't have come today. I should have canceled." A tear rolled out. She couldn't stop it. Quickly she wiped it away.

"It's all right," he said.

That led to another. And another.

"It is," he said. "Really."

He was looking at her as if he really didn't mind, as if he wanted her to cry. *But I don't want to.* "Sam, I can't," she said.

But she did anyway. It came out faster, until she was gulping. She covered her cheeks, her eyes, but was unable to shield it. He sat across from her, watching her, rapt. He didn't move. He accepted her raw outpouring like a man at the pump on a hot day, as if he'd once known something like this, and he missed it. Why? she wondered, even as he passed her a towel and she accepted it. Most of the men she knew did not like to see a woman cry.

"You okay?" he said after a time.

She nodded, and handed it back.

"Why did you say you should have canceled today? Is everything all right?"

"It's just — I got disturbing news. Remember I told you I was here because of something related to my husband's estate?" She sighed. *I never wanted to tell you. I wanted to interview you and do this article without your ever finding out.* "Here's the truth about that something: it's a paternity claim. There's a woman here who says she has my husband's child, and her family has filed a claim."

She saw the instinctive flutter of distance cross his face — no one liked to stand too close to something like this — before compassion took over. "I'm sorry to hear that."

"Right. Well, I have a very tight window in which to get a lab test, and I'm on it, of course, but all this time, until today, to tell you the truth, I didn't believe it."

"And this was your news," he guessed.

She closed her eyes. She needed to do anything that might calm her. "Today I found out that he did have an affair with the woman who had the child, and at exactly the right time, too."

He stared at her for a second and then said, "Here." He plucked tender pieces from the rich underside of the bird to arrange upon her plate. "You need these."

She made a half-smile and brought one to her mouth. It tasted so good, so *necessary* to her, that she quickly ate all the pieces on her plate, while he sat across from her, also eating chicken, watching her.

"How did your husband die?" he asked, putting more on her plate. "Was he ill?"

"No. He was standing on a street corner in San Francisco, that was all. Waiting for a light. A car veered into him and two other people."

"Oh," he said slowly, and put down his chopsticks. "That's bad."

"It was," she agreed. She ate another piece. The chicken was soft, sublime; it cushioned her against these things that were hard to say.

"So have you met the other woman?"

"Not yet. Actually the child lives with the grandparents. They are her guardians, the ones who will have to give their permission. Unfortunately they don't live here. They live in the south. We are trying to get tickets. That's the holdup."

"It's impossible to get tickets now," he said. "It's almost National Day. Everybody has a week off and they go places. I'm trying to get a ticket too. I've been trying all afternoon, in fact."

She sat up. "Ticket to where?"

"Hangzhou. I have this uncle there. Remember the uncles who taught me to cook — two here, and one in Hangzhou? Uncle Xie, the one in Hangzhou — he is dying. I don't think he can make it even until my banquet. So that's what I'm trying to do. Get down there to see him, just for a day, before the end. But I can't get a ticket."

"I'm sorry, Sam," she said simply. "That's very sad. We haven't been able to get tickets yet either."

"And where are you trying to go?" he said.

"Shaoxing."

He jumped.

"That's where they live," she added.

"But that's incredible. Shaoxing is right next to Hangzhou. Literally. A half-hour drive."

"Really?" she said, and then shrugged, because it didn't matter. "Anyway. Good luck to both of us on the tickets."

"Good luck," he echoed. "I hope you feel better. And I hope what I did was okay. The chicken, I mean."

"The chicken was great. I wish I could eat it every day." She lifted her bag onto her shoulder. She knew her eyes were probably puffy and her skin streaked. The strange thing was that she was starting to feel better. "It's just that now is not the best time for us to sit and talk. I hope you understand."

"I do," he said. His kindness was cut by a drift in his attention. It was subtle, but she could feel it. He had to get back to work.

"Thanks."

Instead of answering he rose and turned, snaked his hand to the back of a shelf, and came back with a simple, lightweight box of lacquer. He wiped it with a clean towel and started to pack the chicken in it. She thought he couldn't possibly be giving her this box. It was too nice a container. She'd have to clean it and bring it back. But maybe that was what he wanted her to do — come back.

"Here," she heard him say, atop another soft slice of sound as he slid the box across the counter. "Don't forget to take the chicken."

The minute she was gone Sam left the kitchen and went back to his east-facing room, where he lived, where his computer glowed on the desk and his books were turning into uneven pillars against the wall. He sank onto his unmade bed with the cell phone pressed to his ear, listening to the far-off ring that sounded in Uncle Xie's house, a thousand kilometers to the south. He had tried calling before Maggie arrived, and no one had answered.

At last he heard a click, and then, *"Wei."*

Relief washed him when he heard the whispery voice of Wang Ling, Uncle Xie's wife. "Auntie. It's me. How is he?"

"Not well, my son. He is asking for Liang. He means your father."

"Can I talk to him?" said Sam.

"Right now he is sleeping."

"Oh, let him sleep."

"Yes." Then she said, "Are you coming?"

"Aunt, I am determined. *Zhi feng mu yu,*" he said. Whether combed by the wind or washed by the rain. "But I cannot get a ticket! Not yet anyway. It's the holiday."

"You must try, my son."

"I will," he swore. He could tell that Uncle didn't have long, maybe only a matter of days. Sam's father should come to China. He could do it, easily. It would mean so much. But he wouldn't, and Sam already knew it was probably useless to try to convince him. All the more reason why he himself had to find a way to go.

As soon as they hung up Sam went back on the computer with one hand and used the other to press his cell to his ear and call every person he could think of who had any possible connection to travel. He didn't get a ticket, but he kept trying. As he did he watched the clock advance. Soon he'd have to leave; Uncle Jiang was taking him to meet the man who was, without dispute, the city's greatest fish purveyor. If this man were to take him on, what an advantage he would have, what exquisite quality! The trouble was, he never took new clients. It had been years since he had done so. In fact, it was whispered that the only time he would take a new one was when one of the old ones died. But Jiang knew him, and had arranged the meeting.

No ticket. Nothing. *Third Uncle, stay alive for me.* He closed the computer program, locked the gate, and took the subway one stop to An Ding Men.

Just as he came up aboveground his cell phone rang. It was her.

"*Wei,*" he said, joking. "How are you?"

"Much better," she said.

"Did you eat your chicken?"

"I ate all my chicken," she admitted. "I ate it right away. I couldn't even wait for the next meal. And then I got my tickets."

"No wonder you feel better." He felt a covetous pang. "When are you leaving?"

"Tonight. I won't see you for a few days."

"Hopefully when you get back I'll be gone. I'm still trying to get a ticket to Hangzhou. It's just National Day, you know, and Chinese New Year. The rest of the year it's normal, go anywhere, whenever you want. It's just these few weeks that are impossible."

"I'm sorry, Sam." Her voice seemed full of feeling. "I hope you get your ticket."

"I will," he said. And then, into the pool of silence, he took a risky plunge. "Who's going with you?"

"Zinnia. She works in the local office of my husband's law firm. She set up the meeting with the grandparents — called them and got them to agree to meet with us." She paused and he could almost hear her mind ticking. "Sam," she said, "you're not asking me if you can take her place, are you?"

"Of course not," he said. He was sincere, even if he protested too much. "I want to make sure you have what you need."

"Thanks. I'll muddle through."

"Try me when you get back. Maggie? I'm in the lobby of a building now, about to get on an elevator. I'll have to go."

"Okay," she said.

"Have a good trip."

"Thanks."

He clicked off and the doors whooshed shut behind him. The car rose twenty stories at the kind of showoff speed that always left a barometric drop in his midsection. Well, he was high up in a building now, at least, close to heaven, so he sent off a small prayer to any deities who might happen to be nearby. *Help Third Uncle live until I can get there. Let me see him one more time before he goes.*

Sam stepped into a plush waiting room lined with refrigerated cabinets and one wall of bubbling crystal aquariums. After he sat he refocused his thinking and sent out a new set of prayers, these concerning fresh fish. First Uncle would be here soon. And they had to make the most of this meeting.

While Sam was rising in the elevator and stretching out to half close his eyes in the quiet of the waiting room, Jiang walked up An Ding Men Boulevard toward the Century Center. At first he had liked all the new modern buildings. They were a relief to him after the square stone mantle Beijing had worn for so long. But they had quickly grown too numerous. A good many were not aging well, either, and already showed signs of disrepair.

Yet life for the food lover was fine. Restaurants were booming. Cuisine was back. With good food everywhere and top cooks in agreeable competition, the art form was riding another curve. And the gourmet, the *meishijia*, was back in the equation, for once again there was an army of diners. As in the past, they were passionate. They had money to spend and discernment to spare.

Yes, they were in a high cycle now, a flowering — surely one the food historians would remember. Perhaps he could develop a future lecture out of this idea.

Though retired, he still came back to the university annually to speak on restaurant and food culture. This past year his topic had been a single phrase: *xia guanzi*, to eat out, to go down to a restaurant. In an elegant sixty-minute loop he conjured all of *xia guanzi*'s meanings over the last eighty years. At first it meant something positive and exciting — pleasure and company, good food. There was the embroidered charm of teahouses and pavilions, the urgency of urban bistros where men met to plan China's future, and the magnificent clamor of great restaurants. Then came the mid-1950s. *Xia guanzi* became a forbidden phrase. It was counterrevolutionary, bourgeois, a hated reminder of decadence. There followed a long, gray era of enforced indifference and even, during some stretches, communal kitchens. Finally there came a loosening, and then privatization, which hit restaurants almost before it came to any other industry. Eateries sprang open. People swarmed to them. To eat out was glorious! To go down to a restaurant was once again a wonderful thing. It was not just food — it was friends and family and togetherness. It was life coming full circle, a society learning to breathe again. When he was done the audience rose and applauded. Ah, he was a lucky man in his retirement, especially as he had lived to see this day when once again there was real cuisine, everywhere.

He crossed the lobby and rode the elevator up. He was here to introduce Nephew to a seafood purveyor named Wang Shi, whom they all delighted in calling the Master of the Nets, after Wangshi Yuan, the Garden of the Master of the Nets, which was a famous place in Suzhou. Homophonous humor — Wang Shi being close in sound to Wangshi, though the characters were different — was one of Mandarin's little pleasures. Wang had heard the nickname and approved. Association with such a sublime and enduring work of art as this garden was a compliment, and he knew it.

Jiang was here to ask Wang to take Nephew as a customer. For success, the boy needed a peerless purveyor of fresh fish. Yuan Mei himself said that the credit for a great dinner went forty percent to the steward and only sixty percent to the cook. *A mackerel is a mackerel, but in point of excellence two mackerel will differ as much as ice and live coals.* So the great man had written, two hundred and twelve years before. Yes, Jiang knew how vital it was to help the boy get the right source for fish.

Nephew already had a source who did preserved seafood, top-grade dried shrimp and squid and cuttlefish from all over China. This man sold the best miniature smoke-dried fish from Hunan and the subtlest, most musky freshwater river moss from the Yangtze delta, so beloved for mincing with dried tofu in a cold plate, and adding a complex marine taste to the batter for fried fish . . . Perhaps, Jiang thought with a dart of excitement, this could be next year's lecture. Preserved seafood and aquatic vegetables.

Seafood became prized very early in China's history. Everyone demanded it, even the vast population in the interior. Preserved seafood — dried, salted, or smoked — was soon sought after and expensive, for it yielded powerful flavors all its own. It often cost more than fresh. Perhaps, thought Jiang, Nephew should prepare for this contest a tangle of tiny silver fish — crispy, slightly smoky, lightly salty, almost dry, with a touch of sauce and wafer-thin rings of bright-colored hot pepper . . .

But to fresh and live fish. This was what Nephew now needed. Unfortunately the Master of the Nets was much too exclusive to take new customers. Still, he was an old friend. Jiang had to try.

"Uncle," the boy had said, "he doesn't take *anyone*."

"Speak reasonably," Jiang had reproved him. "I've known him a long time."

And so the boy had come, and waited here in Wang's reception area, with its tanks and its refrigerators. It was smart to have the office this way. Fish was visceral. It had to be seen, smelled, observed. Ah! Jiang thought. It would be good to see his old friend again.

"Liang Cheng," he said to Nephew with affection. "Have you eaten?"

"Yes, Uncle." Sam rose. "You?"

"Yes. What about your travel? Did you get a ticket to see Third Uncle?"

"No. I've tried everything. I can't get a seat anywhere. Not for a week."

"I fear he will not last that long."

"I know."

The click of the door, and they stood as a solid man with a bull's neck and white hair bobbled out. Wang Shi. He had a jovial mouth and small eyes that lifted happily when he saw Jiang.

Right behind Wang came another man, young, floppy-haired — it was Pan Jun. Sam knew him. He was one of the ten competitors, a young lion of Shandong cuisine. *He* was a customer of the Master? How was that possible? He was not so very famed for his skills. Indeed, he was one of the lesser-ranked chefs among the ten contestants. Sam was surprised he'd even been chosen.

"Good to see you!" Sam said, jumping to his feet. "How's it going? Are you day and night working? I know I am."

"Oh, yes." Pan rolled his eyes. "I never sleep."

Sam grinned in his frank Midwestern way, which worked to dissolve the whiff of rivalry. "I wish you luck," said Sam.

"Same to you," Pan said with a smile.

"But you will both prevail!" Mr. Wang cried. "There are two northern slots on the team — is it not so?"

Yes, yes, they all smiled at each other. But there were others, eight of them, and they were very good. Especially Yao. Pan Jun said his goodbyes and moved toward the door.

Finally all the warm wishes were finished and the door closed, and at that moment Wang changed abruptly. He burst with apologies. "Old Jiang! Esteemed friend! And your nephew, of whom so much has been heard — how miserable I am to have kept the two of you waiting! It could not be helped! When Pan stopped by, I was as a fish swimming in a cooking pot. I had to drop everything. And not because of his cuisine, for all say that you outshine him — you and Yao Weiguo both. That's the real battle, isn't it? You and Yao! But oh, there is no question, when Pan arrives I must jump."

"Why is that?" Jiang asked.

"You do not know? He is the son of Pan Hongjia."

This brought a gasp from First Uncle.

"Who's Pan Hongjia?" Sam said.

First Uncle whispered to him in English, invoking a moment's shield of privacy. "He is the vice minister of culture."

Sam's heart dropped. All the hidden parts of the pattern came suddenly into view. "I see."

"And the Ministry of Culture is the *danwei* over this event."

"Right." Sam knew what that meant. It was more than just rank. He was cooked. Cronyism, for better or worse, was how China worked. The key was to always know it, to always be aware, be Chinese. Face the truth.

If Pan Jun was a vice minister's son he would certainly be given one of the two northern spots on the team.

That meant one spot left. That one would be between himself and Yao.

"Fu shui nan shou," First Uncle said softly now, in his ear, Spilled water is hard to gather. "You must go ahead."

Sam nodded.

The old man turned to the Master of the Nets. "Old friend," he said. "Dear friend. This will be a battle to the finish line; you can see that. You and I have known each other a long time. Young Liang needs the finest, the freshest fish."

Wang Shi nodded. *"Wo tongyi,"* I agree. He hooked a puffy, inclusive hand around each. "Come inside."

Sam felt a glad rush of surprise. *"Zhen bang,"* he said, Great. He walked with them into the rear office, the wide double entry open. This is the back door, the *hou men,* he thought, glancing up at the frame as it passed over his head. Right now I am walking through it. He watched First Uncle and Wang Shi exchange smiles. "My old friend," he heard Wang Shi say. "How good it is to see you."

Maggie's cell phone rang. It was a long number, a phone in China. Not Sam's, though. That one she already knew. "Hello?"

"Maggie, it's me." It was Carey, his familiar voice sounding aged right now, even though he was only a few years past her.

"Are you okay?" she said.

"Yes. Look, I'm standing outside. I need to talk to you."

"Outside here? Did something happen?"

"Can I come in?" he said.

"Of course."

"You have to buzz me."

"Oh." This was the first time she'd had a visitor. She had to look around the living room wall for a second or two until she found the button. He came up the elevator, and by the time his tall steps whispered down the hall she had the door open. "Sorry," she said when he walked in. "I didn't know how to do it."

He waved this away. "How are you, Maggie?"

"Energized," she admitted. "We leave in a few hours."

"I know. That's what I came to talk to you about."

She felt the black bolt of an all-too-familiar fear, that things would come apart. "Tell me," she said.

He walked over and looked out the window, as if it was easier without facing her. "I feel bad about this. It happened suddenly. We have a big presentation tomorrow. The client I went to see in Bangkok? He's coming. Bad timing — I'll be working all weekend. We have to do the whole show."

"Is it that you need our tickets?" she said, not understanding.

"Tickets?" He stared. "No. I need Zinnia."

"Oh."

"I know I promised her to you. And she's great, isn't she? Whatever it is, she does it. But that's why the firm needs her tomorrow. I'm sorry. It's not easy for her either. Most people have the whole week off for National Day."

"I understand," Maggie said, but still, now what? Carey was right about Zinnia — she had the steady power of a rolling train.

"Now look, you'll still leave, same schedule. I'll get you another translator. I'll have someone within the hour — not Zinnia, no one can be her, I can't promise that. But someone good."

"Someone from your office?"

"No. From a service. But they're excellent. We use them all the time."

"Carey?" She waited until he turned from the window. She wanted his clear attention. "I can't say I'm happy about this — I was counting on Zinnia — but I understand. I really do. And I do appreciate your coming over here to tell me in person."

"I had to come in person," he said. "I feel awful about it."

"I know. But this is out of your hands."

"Yes," he said, looking grateful.

"Look, you have a lot to do. I don't want to keep you. But there's one thing I'm going to ask."

"Anything," said Carey.

"Hold off on getting this person. Twenty minutes. Maybe half an hour, tops. Just until I call you."

"Why?" he said.

"Because I might have my own person."

His eyes bored into her. "Your own person?"

"Just give me a few minutes to check something."

And he raised his hands, acquiescing, gracious. It was the least he could do.

She waited until she'd heard the elevator doors close behind him before she picked up the phone. Calling Sam Liang was not something she wanted to do in front of Carey.

And once she picked up the phone she found herself dialing Zinnia first, quickly, just to make sure she knew everything she'd need to know.

"*Duibuqi,*" Zinnia said as soon as she picked up the phone, "I'm sorry. Carey called me. Now I have to be in the office tomorrow."

"I know. But do you have anything else about the situation that might help me?"

"Let me think," said Zinnia.

"What were they like when you called to make the appointment?"

"For one thing, they did not sound like country people or uneducated, no, the opposite. Right away they agreed to your visit. They said you can see the little girl. They seemed sure she is your husband's daughter."

"Hm," said Maggie.

"So I suggest, when you go, see yourself as their relation. That is not something you say but the feeling you will carry underneath. Do you understand?"

"I think so," Maggie said, though she wasn't sure she did at all.

"Also hope." Zinnia gave her short, no-frills laugh. "Pray. I think that is the best thing, yes. Pray."

"Okay," said Maggie, "I can do that." Even though she had no idea which way she would even direct a prayer, were she to try to make one, having been raised in a world of people who prayed only if they were something exotic, like Buddhist or Muslim. "I'll pray."

From the other end Maggie heard the persistent high pitch of a child. "Is that your little boy?"

"It is. Naughty boy! His *ayi* says he knows I am going. Now I am not, but he doesn't understand that yet." She hushed him with a quiet stream of Chinese and then returned to the phone. "As for while you are gone, I will return to looking for Gao Lan as soon as the presentation is done. She is in Beijing. We will find her."

"I believe you're right," said Maggie.

"Now, this person . . ."

"How could you know so fast?"

"I told you, Carey called me."

"He can do a great job."

"He's Chinese?"

"Half."

"He can talk?"

"Definitely."

"A friend of yours?"

"Not really. A business acquaintance, through my regular job. Someone I am interviewing for a story." She backed off from it and formalized it, naturally, since she was talking to Zinnia, but she knew there was a little more, and this was why she wanted him, she knew, and not some translator from a service. She and Sam seemed to be in the first stages of alliance people pass through while deciding whether or not to become friends. Already they seemed to be looking out for each other, at least a little. She would do better with him, she felt. He would try. "But actually, Zinnia, I think we're getting ahead here. I haven't asked him yet. I need to call him, in fact, right now."

"Oh. You haven't asked him. Why do you think he would want to go?"

"He has his own reason. A family matter. His uncle is dying in Hangzhou and he needs very much to get there."

"Oh! A family matter. That is different. Quick, let us hang up. Call him," said Zinnia. "Right now."

*   *   *

Sam had come back to his place, ecstatic with the quality of the fish he was going to get. The first sampling would not arrive for a few days, though, so for the moment he had turned his attention to the tender transformations that were possible with beef shank and tendon. Right now he was steaming a dozen beef shanks in two stacked baths of complementary broths.

As soon as the beef was on the boil he turned to his laptop, which he had carried to the kitchen, and checked for tickets again. The first one he could get was seven days away; that was the night of the banquet. He had to go and come back much sooner. He put his name on several more notification lists for cancellations. Right now this was all he could do.

Now it was up to the Gods. He didn't keep an altar in his kitchen — that would have been going too far into the Chinese past for his hybrid self — but he had slowly come to sense that his Gods were there. There were times, like now, when he asked them to intercede, but he knew they were capricious and had minds of their own. Sometimes they granted what he wanted and sometimes they did not.

His cell rang. He looked; it was Maggie. "Hi," he said, leaning close in and smelling the steam from the beef. "Aren't you leaving?"

"I am. First I need to ask you something. My law firm had a rush come up. The woman I've been working with, the one I mentioned who was going with me — now they need her to stay here. It's not a huge problem for me, they're going to get someone else from a service, but I just thought — I mean, Sam, you did sort of give me the feeling you might consider it. So I'm throwing it out there. If you're willing to do what she was going to do, go to this meeting and translate and help me and all, then you're welcome to the other ticket. You have to tell me now, though. They need to get someone in the next half-hour."

Sam was holding the phone to his ear in awe. "Are you serious? Are you even asking? Of course I will."

"Just one problem. You're in a huge hurry to get to Hangzhou. I understand. But I'm in a hurry too, that's the thing —"

"Of course," he cut in. "Your thing first. We'll go to your meeting. Then — what were you going to do with the sample?"

"I was going to come back here and express it."

"No," he said. "Express it from Hangzhou. It's a hub. Save half a day."

"Good," she said, surprised.

"And then I'll go to my uncle's. Only then. How's that?"

"It's great."

"How long are the tickets for?"

"Two nights. She booked one night in Shanghai, second night I thought in Shaoxing, but I guess now it will be Hangzhou. Then back here the next morning."

Perfect, he thought. "Is this okay with your husband's company, that I go?"

"I don't know why they would care. Actually the woman I was going to go with, when I was just talking to her, she asked why an acquaintance of mine would be willing to do this. I explained about your uncle. She said since it was a family matter I should call you right away and make the arrangements. As if that trumped everything."

China, he thought, loving the place. "Well, you know my answer already, don't you? Yes. I will do it. Thank you."

"No problem," she said, and he heard the touch of relief in her voice, too.

"When are you leaving?"

"Flight takes off at seven-thirty. Can you pick me up at five?"

"I'll pick you up at four. I'll pick you up at three."

"It's past three now," she told him.

"Is it?" He looked again at the double-steaming shanks.

"It's three-thirty. You'd better get ready. Can you make it?"

"In my sleep," he said, counting the pounds of meat in front of him and judging cooking times as he tried to remember where his suitcase was. "Don't worry. I'll be there."

6

Yi Yin was the greatest of all Chinese chefs. Three and a half thousand years later, his writings are still read and discussed. He personifies the sanctity and power of cuisine through China's history. He was born a slave. Yet he could cook so brilliantly that the Emperor appointed him Prime Minister. A man who could fine-tune the mysteries of the bronze tripods, the Emperor knew, could run the state and manage its alliances. This dynasty lasted six hundred and forty-four years.

— LIANG WEI, *The Last Chinese Chef*

When he heard Sam's voice on the phone saying he was on his way to Hangzhou, Xie Er had himself carried down to the kitchen to wait. He told his son and daughters he would not move until Nephew arrived.

The Xie family lived in a two-story, four-bedroom, white-tiled house up in the hills beyond the botanical garden. It was quiet there, everything a soft shade of green, one of the last places on a two-lane road that petered out under stands of bamboo. The fronds were dry now, in the breezy sun of late September, and rustled all around the house. The bamboo had never flowered in Xie Er's lifetime. This was not surprising. Bamboo did its spreading underground and sometimes did not flower for a century or more. Still, he had lived a long time. He had thought he might see it. He listened to the soft, clicking fronds as he lay on the rattan recliner where they'd settled him to wait for Nephew.

He would not see it bloom. He knew what was coming even though they did not tell him. Huh, old Dr. Shen, he was a fool if he thought Xie could not grasp his euphemisms and decode his grave glances to Wang Ling. Actually, it wasn't so bad. The pain he had felt in his limbs for so long was gone, replaced by numbness. His body was failing, spiraling away from him, his hands quivering when he could raise them at all. Yet he was clear. Steel cables sang in his mind. He remembered everything about his life. And while he could feel the next world, feel its sounds and urges and movements beyond the veil, at the same time he knew he had never been sharper or more astute about this one. He saw everyone and everything, not the surface but what was true inside. Most of what he saw made him content.

He watched the square of window with its pattern of bamboo and blue sky, listening for the calls of water birds and the faraway promise of Nephew's car roaring up the road. The boy was more like Xie's child than any of his own — except for Songling, who smelled food and tasted it and understood it in all its multiplying facets the way he did, and Nephew did. She would have been his equal had she been a man. But it was not her fate to be a man. She became a restaurant manager. It was a good life for her. Women could not become chefs. There had been a time, in the Song Dynasty more than a thousand years ago, when there was a trend of female chefs in the great houses of Hangzhou, but it was a brief movement, one that died with the dynasty. There were women who were great home cooks and teachers, but not true chefs. They lacked the upper-body strength. They might hold up half the sky, as the saying went, but they couldn't flip the heavy woks in a restaurant kitchen. No, a female person like his adored Songling had too steep a hill to climb to become a chef, but she could be a *laoban,* a boss, a restaurant manager, which was far better: less work, more money. It was the right choice for her. Everything now was money: houses, cars, phones, clothes, jewels, vacations. Money was life.

Now the world had changed and changed again. His father had died in prison. Money and gourmet food and discriminating consumption — that was evil in the 1950s and '60s. To have ever participated in it became a crime. His old father confessed to everything they asked of him, made all his self-criticisms, groveled, yet they let him bleed to death in his cell from his stomach ulcer anyway, shitting blood, vomiting it, crying out for a doctor. Fornicators, he thought.

But he, Xie Er, had survived, and with Wang Ling had gone on to produce a son and three daughters.

He also managed to bring back the restaurant after decades of closure, an homage to his father, who surely could not have imagined such a thing during those last days in his cell. When Xie Er reopened in 1993 under the original name, Xie Jia Cai, Hangzhou people flocked back to it as if it had been closed for only a few weeks — old people, who remembered the original, and young people, who had heard the stories. The timing was perfect. Privatization was just beginning. The economy was picking up speed. People needed venues in which they could entertain each other, sit, converse, negotiate, extract information, and ask for help. This was how things got done in the Chinese world. It had always been so. A favor would be bestowed, in the form of a great meal, and a favor asked in return. Then there was the social side of life: families and groups of friends needed a place to gather, lovers a place to meet. All of them came back.

Xie Er ran the place for twelve years and then sold it, his debt to his father repaid, the family secure, his bank accounts safe in Hong Kong and Vancouver. He disliked banks and he disliked foreign countries. He had lived long, however, and had seen China change too many times to take chances.

Outside his window he noticed a change in the bamboo fronds — a deepening of color, a brittle scratch to their movements. He had never seen the plants look this way before. But now everything looked different. The world looked different. He was dying. His boat was pulling away from the shore.

Xie let his eyes wander to his worn copy of *The Last Chinese Chef* on its shelf above his head. How much pleasure the book had given him. How right and correct for Nephew and his father to put it in English. Perhaps now, he thought, the world would finally grasp the greatness of his nation's cuisine, not to mention its long history. People sometimes said the cuisine's long history was the very thing that made it special, but it was not the longevity of the art itself that counted — no. Rather, it was the cuisine's constant position as observer and interpreter. Throughout history chefs created dishes to evoke not only the natural world but also events, people, philosophical thought, and famous works of art such as operas, paintings, poems, and novels. A repertoire was developed that kept civilization alive, for diners to enjoy, to eat, to remember. Almost anything could be recalled or explored through food. Indeed, a great dinner always managed to acknowledge civilization on levels beyond the obvious.

The Western people did not understand this, was what Liang Yeh had told him by phone from far away in Ohio. A meal for them was nothing but food. When it came to the food of China they had their own version, a limited number of dishes that always had to be made the same way with the sauces they would recognize from other restaurants. Sameness was what they wanted. They went out for Chinese food, they ordered their dishes, and they did not like them to change. Liang Yeh said he had met other chefs who'd tried to offer real Chinese dishes on their menus too, but each said the foreigners wouldn't order them, and each, in time, gave up. Liang Yeh had heard there were enclaves in New York and Los Angeles and other cities where discriminating diners demanded real food, but these diners were always Chinese, never American. There was money in the West but no gourmet, was what Liang had concluded. Xie still remembered the sadness in his voice.

Liang Yeh's son could change that. This was Xie's hope. Nephew would be the bridge. So the question was not whether he would succeed in the contest, for he must. The question was how.

As soon as Xie had heard about the Chinese culinary team, he knew the competition was a door that had been opened by fate. The boy had to serve a banquet greater than any Beijing could remember. It had to be such that it would immediately pass into leg-end and become magic, join the pantheon of stories that swirled around China's Gods and great adventures. It had to be so fantastic that people in the future would argue about whether it had ever existed at all.

Xie felt a smile touch his own pouchy and soft-hanging face. He thought of raising a hand toward the window, toward the bamboo, but his fingers only fluttered in response. He looked down at them sadly. These hands had been as precise as any surgeon's. He'd been able to flash-cut vegetables almost thin enough to float up and away like butterflies on a breeze. He had been strong enough to fling an iron pan across the room in a second's displeasure.

Now all he had was his voice. Never mind; he could still use it. And he would, too. Nephew was coming. He lay still with his eyes on the door.

"Let's talk about our strategy," Maggie said to Sam the next morning on the bus to Shaoxing.

He turned, still looking only half-awake despite their quick inhalation of tea and small *baozi*, plain steamed white buns, before they left the hotel at six-thirty. That was after landing in Shanghai at ten the night before and then going out again, because of course they had to eat.

Shanghai was a gleamingly futuristic place that looked as though it had been built overnight, out of a dream. Tall, jaunty buildings were topped with finials in the shapes of stars or balls or pyramids. The Pearl TV tower, brilliantly lit against the night, looked like a spaceship about to lift off as they looped past it on an elevated expressway. Exuberant capitalism seemed to have been crossed with a 1960s sci-fi TV show. In fact, she thought, the principal design influence on the city really appeared to be *The Jetsons*. The kitsch of her childhood had become the city of tomorrow: *Meet George Jetson. Jane, his wife.*

Shanghai ran around the clock, even more so than Beijing — Sam had explained that to her on the flight down. Beijing had the profundity of government and history, but Shanghai had the aura

99

of culture and excitement. And don't forget money, he told her. When they came near to their hotel and drove down Huaihai Lu, with its brilliant glass-fronted department stores, the sidewalks were as crowded as they might be at high noon. And after they checked in at the hotel he walked her through the French Concession neighborhood to the restaurant, the plane trees rustling overhead, past the blocks of old stone buildings with their tall windows and wrought-iron Juliet balconies.

She saw people look at him. He didn't seem to see, though maybe he did and was just used to it. With his angled bones and precisely bumped nose he looked enough like them and enough unlike them to make people stare. And then there was his hair, always bound at his neck by a coated elastic band. Few Chinese men wore long hair. Judging from what she'd seen on the streets in the four days she'd been here, those who did were the young and bohemian, not men Sam's age. So this too set him apart. It was a choice. It made certain things clear about him at a glance.

By the time they finished dinner it was late. They walked back to their hotel and said good night in the corridor quickly, exchanging only brief wishes for a restful night before retreating to their rooms. She felt grateful for the respite. They had been together for many hours, and even though she was surprised at the ease they had felt, talking throughout the plane ride and the drive into the city and the meal, she was hungry for privacy. Thoughts of Matt and what he had done with this woman were constantly in her, and she had to face them and feel them by herself. She had cried in front of Sam once. That was enough, even though he had seemed not to mind, had actually seemed to like it. She would not do it again.

She latched the door, lay on the bed, and looked down at herself. She saw her pants, unattractively wrinkled in fanned sitting lines. Her shirt had hiked up to show a soft white stripe of stomach. She laid a hand on herself. Middle-aged widow in a Shanghai hotel room. She thought back to walking on the streets outside, the lights, the late-night crowds. Everyone she saw on the street seemed to have been tied to someone else, in pairs, in groups, connected, while she walked beside Sam Liang, acquainted but apart. They were here for other reasons, for business. They were here by arrangement. They talked, they joked, they were companionable, but she was sure they both knew why they were here. In the stretches during which both fell silent, she could feel this awareness bumping against them.

This would be her life now, outside her small circle of close friends. This would be the kind of time she'd have with people, people she interviewed, people she met. She had her friends. She had her family — her mother, anyway — and the people she knew from work. If there was nothing else after that, just business acquaintances like Sam Liang, she could accept it. That would be all right. One thing she would *not* allow herself to do was become an aggrieved woman. That had been another one of Maggie's Laws for living through this past year. Now it was even worse, for he had cheated. But she was sticking to the rule she'd set.

At midnight Shanghai time, Maggie dialed Sunny. It was morning in Southern California; her best friend would be up. "Hey," Sunny said warmly, picking up, knowing it was Maggie. "How are you doing today?"

"Things are moving, at least. This has been an amazingly long day. I'm in Shanghai, seeing the grandparents tomorrow, but I'm not with the original translator — *he's* with me."

Sunny was surprised. "The chef?"

"Yes. He's down the hall." Maggie told Sunny what had happened in the twenty-four hours since they last talked, and felt immense relief just at telling her, sharing it, and thus by some subtle magic of friendship dividing her burden of news and surprises in half. This was what people did for each other when they were in alliance. It was the blessing of connectedness. She hung up feeling not just alive again but more peaceful, as if she'd been transported back to a gentler time, before. As soon as she turned out the light she slept.

In the morning she woke up tired, with rings under her eyes. He didn't look much better when he met her in the hall and went downstairs with her to breakfast. She wondered if he had stayed up too.

Now it was time to plan. He was spread out on his bus seat, thinking. Shanghai was long gone. They streaked along a flat, eight-lane highway, past delta farmland cut into green-ruffled squares.

Finally he said, "The meeting is just with the grandparents?"

"I think the child will be there too."

"Any of them speak English?"

"Not that I know of."

"Will they bring a translator?"

"I don't know. I didn't think of that, since I needed to bring one anyway, just to get here."

"That's not really true," he said.

"Consider my state of mind," she answered.

"Okay," he said. "Well. Say they do bring a translator. If that happens, then having me translate is not only redundant, it wastes whatever advantage I could offer you. So if it happens — just *if* — say I don't speak Chinese. Say I'm your associate, or your lawyer."

Maggie eyed his ponytail. "I don't think you could pass for a lawyer."

"I'm American. I can pass for anything."

"To me you look Chinese."

"Here I look foreign."

They rode in silence. "Actually that's good," she said after a minute. "Though most likely you'll be translating, so it'll be moot."

"And the most important thing will still be your strategy," said Sam. "What kind of face you will put on, what you will project."

"What do you suggest?"

"That depends. Let me give you an example." He softened his voice. "What if you walk in and you meet this child and you see a girl who looks just like your husband? Are you prepared for that?"

"You can't always tell by looking at a child."

"No. But there are times when you can. Say it happens. Stop now to think: what will you show? Be ready. When people deal with each other here, no matter what it is, business, personal, big issues, small, a lot rides on the show. The theater. People put great energy into making things *seem* a certain way. It's how things work. It's why you can rent an office here for a month or a year but also for an hour — so you can pull off that important meeting by pretending the office is yours, right down to the secretary, the coffee, the co-workers who are possibly just your friends, dressed up for the day. Everybody does it — individuals, companies, the government. Everybody. Westerners get upset because they're not used to it; they say it's dishonest. Here though, everybody knows it's happening and knows to always watch behind them, so there's no deception. Put aside your old self. Think this way. They will."

"Put on a show," she said. "But what kind?"

"That depends on what you want. You want a sample, isn't that right? Consent and a sample. Fast."

"I've had the kit right here in my purse since I left L.A. The grandparents are the guardians; they're the ones who have to agree."

He nodded, thinking. Finally he said, "I think this is a job for *guanxi*."

"What's that?"

"Connectedness, relationship. If she is his daughter you will be connected to them. You will be like family. Have you thought about how that would feel?"

Yes, she had thought. It would be beyond belief that she could see something of Matt again, something living, going on. When she imagined it she could almost see another life for a second, as if through a break in clouds. It was like an opening into a sweet valley.

He was watching her. "Well," he said, "feel that, think that. Project your welcome for them, and for her. Believe that you want what they want."

"So they'll want to have the test."

"Exactly."

"But how do I do that?" she said.

"The Chinese way of answering that would be to tell a story." He waited until she smiled with her eyes to go on.

"It's the story of the Sword-Grinding Rain," he said. "There was this famous general, Guan Gong. Now he's the God of War, but like a lot of Chinese Gods he was once a real person. He lived in the Three Kingdoms period, around the beginning of the third century.

"So Guan Gong had this famous, incredible sword called Green Dragon on the Moon. He was a great fighter. And one day he was invited to a banquet by the evil Duke, archenemy of his lord. Don't go! his friends all cried — it's a trap! No, he said, I must go. And he went, alone. He took no one. At the door of the Duke's mansion men surrounded him, as he had known they would, and ordered him to surrender his sword, Green Dragon on the Moon, which he did.

"From there, into the banquet chamber. All the lords of the enemy kingdom were seated. No guards or men with weapons were visible, but he saw the ornately paneled walls ringing the room and he knew what those panels meant. Each concealed an assassin, armored, quick, ready to impale him. He was unarmed. He had only one weapon, himself. Just his courage and his intelligence.

"So he bowed low to his hosts, paid them compliments, and offered wishes of health and longevity for their families. Then as the meal was served he started to talk. No one knows what he said, so many times has the story been retold in eighteen centuries, but supposedly he held their attention for hours while he made the case that they should be friends instead of enemies. At the end not only did all at the table stand and applaud, but the very assassins who had been ordered to leap forth and kill him stepped out, cast down their weapons, and embraced him. It was the *guanxi* of genius."

She stared at him.

"This is what you need to do with the family."

"Like *that's* going to be easy to do?"

"No one said it would be easy," he said. "It's delicate, subtle, difficult, but not impossible. It's basically an attitude; when you walk in, are you with them or against them? Anyway, when Guan Gong left the banquet that night a servant knelt and offered him back his sword. No sooner had Guan Gong taken Green Dragon on the Moon from him than it was lifted right out of his hands and whirled up to heaven by the Gods. It has been there ever since.

Around the banquet's anniversary every June, in Beijing, it rains a special rain. That's when the Gods take out Green Dragon on the Moon and polish it. Everybody calls it the Sword-Grinding Rain."

She thought. "It's September now," she said finally, "but maybe it will fall." And indeed, when she raised her eyes and looked down the aisle past the driver, through the big curved windshield, she saw that the road ahead led straight toward a lowering sky.

7

There is always a tension between imagination and reality, between what we wish for and what it is the Gods have granted us. Civilized man finds appeasement through the system of gestures and symbols used to mediate between the two — the careful grooming of appearances, the maintenance of face, the funeral feasts and wedding banquets we put on even as we know they will ruin us. Rich or poor, people feel the same. During my childhood in the alleys of Peking, we were always hungry. If we ate at all it was *cu cha dan fan,* crude tea and bland rice. Yet on this we never failed to congratulate ourselves, as if this were our choice, our philosophy. We would proclaim simple but nutritious fare the best, and our lives, for a moment, would satisfy us.

— LIANG WEI, *The Last Chinese Chef*

In 1966, the year Nainai died, I was seventeen. I was born in the same year as our nation, a fact that gave me pride and also my name, Guolin, the country's Welcome Rain. This was my generation. Later we were termed the Lost Ones because we had lost our educations, but I always bristled at that. Being lost was a state of mind. On the contrary, we showed we had the fierceness for anything. When we were sent to the countryside in 1970 we endured privations such as even our mothers and fathers never did. I went two years without oil and salt. That is something most people today cannot imagine. Yet those ten years of chaos did not break us. The one thing that did break us had already happened, might in fact have made the Cultural Revolution possible, and that was the famine. Looking back, I have thought that only people who were starved as children could do the things we young people did.

We were town people. We did not suffer like those in the countryside, but still, of 1961 I remember mainly hunger. We hoarded every grain, every stalk of wilted vegetable. An egg was a miracle.

We sold everything possible to get more food. Nainai, my grandmother, wanted to sell her coffin. At this my father put his foot down. "Impossible," he said. "You have had it for years. Leave it." And indeed the coffin was one thing they never sold off, and she was to use it to be put in the earth as she planned, five years later.

But what I remember, back further, is the day in May 1956 that Nainai went to buy the coffin. She journeyed to a dark little shop in a small village outside the city, on a day deemed auspicious by her almanac.

At seven, I was too young to accompany her, but I did go with her in the years that followed. We would travel to the village together to visit the shop, where she would look at her coffin and reassure herself that no one had made off with it and that it was indeed as fine as she remembered.

It was. The renowned local wood was oiled to a dull gleam, and there was a strong iron latch to seal it tightly within the earth. To see it comforted her. She knew that safe within, she would never have to wander in some murky, in-between world. She would remind me of this as the old man hunted through the stacks of coffins in his little warehouse to find the one that belonged to her.

When he located it in the pile he would light a little bean-oil lamp for us in the darkened storeroom, so we could sit there for a while. "A good coffin is important," she would say. "How else are the Gods to know I led a supremely good life and am to be treated well in the next world?"

"They will know," I used to tell her. She was to be buried in her ancestral village, after all, which lay in the hills a little farther to the south and from which one saw a long way, across a green valley.

The beauty of the place alone would bring her to the Gods' attention, I felt — if there even were Gods. At that time we were taught that there were not. In fact at certain times it was dangerous to even say such things aloud, but we were in a warehouse at that moment, out in the countryside. No one was near. So I let her talk.

After the famine passed her health declined. She had grown very thin, like all of us, but when we rebounded, she did not. It was another five years or so until she went away. In those last years she was small, sharp-edged, but still clear. Mother dressed her bound feet every day, and her long linen dressings hung in looped rows at the end of her bed, their peculiar fragrance dusting the air around them even when they'd just been washed. She did not so much walk as plant one foot in front of the other, and when she went outdoors she usually had one of us at each elbow. In her walk there was a delicate pathos, graceful even in her advanced age. I can say that now. Back then, when I was young and saw her as a feudal old lady with little more left in her than a whiff of dry breath, she infuriated me. She was the past. She was everything we hated. I thanked the heavens I was born in my own time, so I could serve my country in free, natural health.

Up to the end, though, once or twice a week, she cooked. She made the dishes she loved from her childhood, fried tomatoes and tofu, hot and sour cabbage, soup noodles with pickles. Once she made a rich soup of tilapia with matchsticks of daikon. To buy a live tilapia at that time was sufficiently extravagant to attract attention. Once was all right; it could be explained as a family celebration. But she could not cook it again.

My mother sat down with Nainai and explained why. "The idea now is that everybody eats simply. You know, *cu cha dan fan.*" Crude tea and bland rice. "We should eat only the most basic foods. To cook anything else is not wise, even if we had the money, which we do not." She was gentle and clear. Nainai may have nodded submissively, but she was already deciding not to listen. She may not have called for tilapia again, but within her constraints she cooked what she wanted.

In August of that year the railways and hostels were thrown open to youth, free of charge. We could ride anywhere we wanted in China, mix with *laobaixing,* or old hundred names — the masses. Our job was to talk with people and in this way advance revolution.

I had to go. I was compelled by my age, by the times, by the depth of my beliefs. People don't like to say it now, but those times, though they were bad, also had some good. We were living for something. Between people there was a kind of *ren qing,* human kindness, which I don't feel anymore.

It was a flame I was, at that age, unable to resist. My little bag was packed in minutes. My mother begged me not to leave. She said it was dangerous. She wrapped her arms around me as if she could keep me. I lifted her hands off. "Do you think this is something for me and my friends? We are supposed to exchange revolutionary ideas. Besides, I am seventeen. I'm a grown woman."

I could see how this drained both my mother's and my father's faces. They were children of the modern era; they had gone against their own parents, insisting, for example, on choosing their own marriage partners and careers. Of this they'd always been proud. That it was my turn made them less happy. They were silent.

Nainai did not say anything either. Most likely she did not hear anything. She was cooking with her back to us. A friend of hers had visited her earlier with some foodstuffs from the south, and with this she was preparing a meal. I shouldered my little pack and went to say goodbye to her. Despite how old she was I never thought this was the last time I'd see her.

"Deng yixia," she said when she saw I was leaving, Wait a moment. "Let Nainai prepare you a box to take." Before I could even answer she had taken a tin box and begun to arrange food in it.

"I don't need dinner," I told her. We needed food to sustain our lives, of course, but according to new thinking, it was a necessary inconvenience. "I don't want it."

She was calm. "Who's going to feed you where you are going?"

I had no answer for this, and the truth was I did want dinner, badly, and so after I had gone one more time to trade stiff, anguished goodbyes with my father and share an embrace with my mother I returned to Nainai, and embraced her too, and took her box.

When I reached the station I was grateful they had not come with me, for the huge hall was an ocean of parents, terrified, tearful. I don't know if I could have endured their being part of it. As I made my way through the crowd I felt the strangeness of being alone. Which train would I take? To what place? Beijing. That was the heart of the country, and I was the Welcome Rain. I hurried toward the track with hundreds of others like me, part of a moving current. When we got close I saw a stocky comrade up ahead raise his hands and roar, *"Beijing che lai!"* Beijing train's here! We surged together, one undulating form, toward the great staircase that led upward. There was chattering and laughing around me. I was pushed and buffeted. I shoved and shouldered back.

When I reached the upper concourse I could see, through the windows that gave out onto the tracks, that the train was already full and then some. Young people were climbing on through windows, pushing one another into doors, even staking out spots on the roof.

I stopped. People behind me jostled past and kept trying to get on. I saw it was useless. Older men, tired-looking men in work-stained clothes, got off the engine in front and shouted at people to get off. Youths only stuck their heads and arms out of windows and shouted back at them. Finally some *Hong Weibing,* Red Guards, jumped off from the front of the train and went up and down the track pulling people off. "The people's train has to run," I heard one of them admonish a boy as he pulled him off and dumped him on the platform. The workmen climbed back on and the great chuffs swelled to life and the *Hong Weibing* leapt aboard, one by one, as it started to roll. Finally with a scream it pulled out.

"You might as well try to fish the moon out of the ocean," someone said at my elbow. I turned, and there was a girl my age watching the scene beside me. She had long hair in braids and a white blouse, as I did, but otherwise we looked nothing like each other. She was small, with a face the shape of a teardrop, while I had a more angular face and a longer build. "You have to be waiting up here when they arrive," she said, "and be the first one on."

"What we really need is a southbound train that ends here, so it will empty out. I'm Zhang Guolin." I touched a finger to my nose.

"Huang Meiying," she answered, of herself. It is a strange thing, because this was a girl I knew for only fifteen or twenty hours of my life, more than forty years ago, and yet I remember her name with utmost clarity. I remember what I thought when she told me, too: Meiying, pretty and brave. It was a common name. A bit old-fashioned, maybe, but because of the "brave" part, most girls felt no need to change it.

We worked together. One held the place in front while the other scouted for rumors of arrivals. Finally there was a southbound train that ended here and would turn around for Beijing, and we were in front. We held our prearranged stations at the platform's edge. No one would move us. The shout went up and people poured up the staircase, onto the concourse, to the cement expanse where we stood, unyielding.

"*Tongzhimen!*" came the howl from the front, Comrades! The engineer, distinguished by his age and the filth on his clothes, leaned from his car. "You will board the cars in an orderly manner!"

People laughed at this as the passengers streamed from the train, a river of blue cloth and young black heads which had to part and flow around us because of the way we stood our ground. The instant the cars were empty we pushed and shoved our way on, and found ourselves running, laughing, down the empty aisle of a hard-bed car, rows of plain wooden berths, six in each open cubicle, with one common aisle. It was littered, and it still smelled of close-packed youth, but what was that to us? It was our car. It would take us to Beijing.

Not that we were to lie down; there would be far too many people for that. But we had a place to sit, pressed side by side on a lower berth, she by the window and I next. That was more than most had. Many stood in the aisle, or leaned nodding in half-sleep between the cars through the journey. The luckier ones managed to find space to slump to the floor. But we were comfortable. And because we had each other we could get hot water while it lasted, or relieve ourselves after it was gone. One could get up while the other defended our place.

In our little bay, designed for six passengers, at least twenty had pressed in. Everyone was hungry.

After some hours and the exchange of many revolutionary ideas, it was agreed that anyone who had any food would bring it out for all in our knot to share.

As I dug in my bag I glimpsed the kinds of foods others were drawing forth: peanuts in a twist of newspaper, dried fruit, small packages of crackers. And then I put out my tin box.

All eyes flew to it. It had the weight and size of real food; when I cracked the lid, the aroma rushed out, unstoppable. "What is it?"

"I don't know," I answered, for I had taken the box from Nainai without looking inside.

Now I lifted off the lid, and drew in my breath. It was *Guangzhou wenchang ji,* a Cantonese dish Nainai loved. Velvet-braised chicken breast, thin-sliced Yunnan salt-cured ham, and tiny tender bok choy were layered in an alternating pattern. All three were meant to be taken together, in one bite. The arrangement glistened under a clear sauce. As soon as I saw it my mouth longed for it. That must have been what Nainai's friend brought her from the south, Yunnan ham. So special. It had been meant for me, and now everyone was staring at it. With a plunging heart I realized how opulent and bourgeois it appeared.

"What's that?" someone said.

"She said she didn't know," said another.

"How could you not know?" said a third, this time to me.

I held the tin box, terrified.

Then Huang Meiying, next to me, spoke up with a boldness I had not expected. "She doesn't know because an old lady handed it to her on the way into the station. I saw it. I was right behind her."

"What old lady?"

"I never saw her before," said Huang.

"Did she say anything?"

Silence. It was my turn. Little Huang was looking at me. I cleared my throat. "She said, Long live Chairman Mao."

"Maybe it's poisoned," someone said.

"It's not poisoned," scoffed another. "I'll show you. I'll eat some." He tasted it, lifting one set of the three slices in the incandescently simple sauce and dropping it in his mouth. I wanted to scream at him. I was about to collapse from hunger. And this was ham, from Yunnan, made for me by my Nainai. I wanted it.

I still remember the feeling of tears burning behind my eyes when he swallowed and his face registered such pleasure that everyone else had to have it too, and I saw it handed around. Quickly it was gone. Everyone had something to say. It was rich, it was ostentatious, it was not the plain food we were supposed to eat, yet they ate it in a blink. Huang Meiying saw my tears. She pressed my arm. Then someone in the cubicle said he wished he could find the old lady and teach her a thing or two, and after that both of us sat quiet for a long time, afraid to say anything at all.

Hunger kept me from falling asleep that night. It was not the first time or the last. How many young people today could do what I did? Could my own daughter do it, Gao Lan? No. Yet that was when my character was forged, especially when I was sent to the northeast in 1970. And it began four years earlier, that night when I fell asleep hungry, wedged up with my back straight on the train to my adulthood. In my memory hunger is mixed up with those times the train stopped and sat on the tracks, far from anywhere, the window open, the night air cool, the countryside black and formless. I made a promise to myself that night. No matter how much work it took, I would not be hungry, and neither would my children.

It was for this reason I told Gao Lan we must file the claim against Shuying's father, so the two of them would never, ever be hungry.

As for Gao Lan's secrets, I decided to let them rest. I had told her long ago that Old Gao, her father, did not have to know the whole truth. We would file the claim. That would be all. It was a necessity. She and the child needed support.

To this she agreed, for it was the undeniable truth that no matter how much Old Gao and I loved the little girl, we were growing old. "All life's uncertain," I said to Gao Lan. "Should we just wait for our death with folded arms? Or provide for her?"

"I don't think you will go to see Marx anytime soon," she had answered, invoking the old joke that had been popular under communism when referring to death, *jian Makesi qu.* Going to see Marx.

I understood that my daughter would only speak lightly about these things. Yet it was important to be pragmatic. In time she understood, and we filed, and my old husband and I agreed to receive the American widow and her escort.

And then it was the day of their visit. They were coming to meet Shuying. I awoke filled with anticipation. I believed I would know at a glance whether or not the American saw her husband in our little girl.

Teacher Sheng arrived first. His black hair was brushed back with an unexpected pomade, and his narrow shoulders twitched beneath a dark suit. He proclaimed himself delighted to be here and assured me that he, the middle school English teacher, would take care of everything. We talked together about the weather. A storm was coming.

Then they were at the door. Sheng and I went together to open it. The woman was not what I'd imagined, though when I saw her I also found that what I had imagined was something I could no longer quite remember. She was small for a foreigner, only an inch or two taller than I, and dark, though her halo of curly hair immediately made her different. The man with her, Teacher Sheng explained, was her lawyer.

"Lawyer?" I said. "He's no lawyer. Look at that hair." To me he appeared more like a mathematician, or an artist.

"He's a lawyer," said Teacher Sheng.

I went into the kitchen to prepare tea. While I was there Shuying poked her head in at the door. "Naughty little treasure!" I hissed, seeing the small curly head, loving her. "I told you to stay in your room until we call."

"I want to see them."

"Not until I call you." I was firm. She ran back to her room. We had spoken in the local version of the Wu dialect, which was the language of Shaoxing and the only tongue we used with Shuying. When my old man and I didn't want her to understand us, we spoke Mandarin. Our privacy in that language would be finished the following year, when she went to school and learned it.

I carried the tray out front and set a teapot in the center of the low table, surrounded by cups. I did not serve. It was not ready. In deference to foreign ways I also set out cold cans of Coca-Cola, one for each person. No one opened them or touched them or even looked at them. This was proper, of course, though I was surprised, for they were Americans.

Teacher Sheng leaned toward me. "She says her hope was to meet Shuying."

Of course it was her hope, I thought, why else had she come here? And yet even I had not expected her to care so much about seeing the child. Gao Lan had told me a little bit about this woman's husband. He had loved her, his wife, but he was not happy. He wanted a child. She was not ready. These things he had confided in Gao Lan, and she in me, and I held them carefully in my mind now as I looked at the woman. "A step at a time," I told Sheng. "I'll call Shuying out in a minute. Here. Drink tea." Now it had steeped, so I poured. My husband came out, Gao Fei, and introductions were exchanged between him, the widow, and her lawyer. I poured another cup.

Finally the widow spoke. Teacher Sheng translated. "She says if this child really is her husband's daughter, she wants to take care of her. No question. But she says to do that, to make everything work with his estate, she needs a lab test. She hopes you agree."

Gao Fei and I looked at each other.

"The outcome will be positive, right?" my husband said in Mandarin, just in case Shuying was listening. "It cannot be otherwise. So we should do it."

"No test," I said. I heard the stubbornness in my voice.

He looked at me. His gray brows rose toward his hair.

"No need to do more," I said. "We filed the claim already."

"But you heard what the widow said. And it's clear, isn't it? Anyone can see Shuying's father was a foreigner. It is not as if we are trying to pass off fish eyes as pearls."

I felt my heart trembling. "Teacher Sheng," I said, "will you let us speak between ourselves?"

"Certainly! Yes!" He all but fell over himself trying to get out of the room to leave Old Gao and me alone. Of course the widow and her lawyer were there, but they were foreigners. They did not understand.

"The truth," Gao Fei demanded. "What's this about?"

"It's something our daughter didn't want to tell you." I was trying to soften him by invoking her, but I knew I was equally culpable. I had agreed with her to keep this hidden.

"Well?" He was growing heated.

"She had another man at the same time. Another foreigner."

He stared, his understanding slow in building.

"Another boyfriend," I said.

He caved back from me slightly, ashamed, almost as if someone had punched him. "Does she know which is the father?"

"No," I said sadly. "She has never known." For Gao Lan had never been able to say clearly, not when Shuying was a baby, not when she became the precious child she was now. Just then I saw the American man watching us. He felt my gaze and looked away.

"Why her husband, then?" Gao Fei's gaze traveled briefly to the wife, the widow, who sat across from us watching. She looked naïve. She looked kind.

"Because Gao Lan won't go to the other one," I said.

"Why?" His eyebrows looked stuck together.

"She's afraid of him."

"Afraid!"

"That's what she says."

He trembled, drew a pack of cigarettes from his pocket, shook one out, and lit it. He smoked silently, his eyes fixed on me. Blue smoke formed a cloud of displeasure around him. "You didn't tell me this."

"The Gods will strike me now that I have told!"

"The Gods striking you?" he said sourly. "That would be the dragon and the tiger matched in battle indeed! I have no doubt who would win. I see done is done. These things we cannot change now. Call Sheng back. Let's hear what else they have to say."

"Teacher Sheng!" I cried. The translator in his stiff suit hurried back from the kitchen.

When we were all seated again the widow's lawyer took his turn to speak. Sheng listened and turned to us. "He says that for all the purposes of acting on the claim, speaking of the law firm that executes the man's estate and also the bank that has his holdings, all of them will need to see proof of paternity."

Gao Fei and I looked at each other. "You see why I don't want to do it," I said softly.

"Yes."

"They both stress that she wants to take care of the child," Sheng said. "As a matter of principle. She just has to know for sure that the girl is his."

Those were good, upright words, but I was scared. Best just to let her see Shuying first, I decided. Start with that.

I sent the signal to Gao Fei. The lines on his walnut face creased deep into a smile. If anyone indulged her more than I, it was he. "Shuying!" he called out. "Come here!"

Tiny footsteps spattered down the hall and our little treasure with her sparrow's body eased around the door frame. She darted over and wedged herself between my legs.

"Gao Shuying," announced Teacher Sheng.

The widow's eyes fastened on the child as I had known they would. Her gaze took in everything from her head to her little feet.

Did she see her husband in her?

Protectively I pulled the girl close. My little meat dumpling. Nothing would ever take her away from me. We were joined, like form and shadow, by blood, by affection.

"Does she say the child resembles her husband?" I put this to Teacher Sheng, and he asked her in English.

When he turned back to me he said, "She is not sure. She wants to believe. Her heart is unreliable. She says, if you will please give permission for the test, she will live by whatever it says. It's a touch to the inside of the mouth, that is all. She has the kit and the forms in her bag."

I listened. My heart was still pulled in two directions.

"Gao Lan's working as hard as she can at the logistics start-up," Gao Fei said, in Mandarin so Shuying wouldn't understand. "I don't think she can work any harder. This is her rice bowl. It's important."

"I know," I said, and I did. I had promised myself I would never forget. Even now. "Tell her yes," I said, turning to Sheng. "Tell her we give our permission."

Sheng conveyed this, and the American woman drew a small box out of her shoulder bag.

"Little Dumpling," my husband said to her in the local Shaoxing tongue, "I want you to let Auntie touch a stick inside your mouth."

The widow got up, took a few steps, and knelt in front of the child. Her face was serious. Now it could not be stopped.

She unscrewed a vial and took out a swab.

I was unable to look. I busied myself by pouring a cup of tea for the long-haired man, who still sat in a watchful silence across the table. Something about him needled me. Who was he, really? I filled the cup, set down the pot, and then reached forward with my two hands, offering it. This was an old-fashioned gesture. Any civilized person knew that the cup must be taken with two hands as well. Outsiders rarely knew. I think I wanted to see him falter, show his ignorance. Maybe I even wanted to feel the brief comfort of derision, at the very moment I felt frightened that I might have lost something. I extended the cup.

Without seeming even to think, he lifted two hands to take it. As was civilized. Proper. My eyes narrowed. Was it an accident? No. I felt something in the air of the room change. He was not an outsider.

Yet the thought barely had time to form in my mind. "Open your mouth for Auntie," I heard my husband say.

Maggie and Sam stepped out the front gate of the complex, walked to the corner, and veered left onto busy Jiefang Lu before they turned to each other, ready to burst with all they had to say. "We did it," she breathed first. She had the signed forms and the sample in her bag.

"You were wonderful," he told her.

"*You* were."

"We both were. And you haven't heard anything yet." He raised his hand for a taxi.

"Where are we going?"

"Hangzhou, are you kidding? As fast as possible, to mail your sample. Then get me to my uncle's." A car pulled over and they climbed in. "Next bus is on the half-hour." They settled in the back. "Now. Are you ready for this? There were two men in Gao Lan's life. Two foreigners — at the same time. The right time. Either one could be the father. They don't know which."

She stared. "Then why Matt?"

"For some reason Gao Lan's afraid of the other guy. Wouldn't approach him. Wouldn't file against him. That's why this came to you."

Maggie swallowed down this new and slightly darker understanding. The taxi jolted to a stop outside the bus station. They paid, jumped out, and ran into a concrete palace of a depot far too large and full of useless echoes for its light trickle of passengers. After buying their tickets they went to stand in line at the gate. "You know what doesn't quite make sense?" said Maggie. "That she doesn't know who the father is. Shuying is not a baby. She's a girl. She must look more like one than the other."

"Well, you saw her too," said Sam. "What do you say? Is she Matt's?"

Maggie thought a long time. "I suppose I can't be sure. Maybe. She could be."

"If you had to guess?"

She hesitated. "I'd guess no."

"Before you went in, did you want her to be his?"

"Not at first. Definitely not. Later — I have to say, I thought about it. He's gone, is the thing. It would be like part of him came back. It would be like something happened that he wanted, too, wanted at least by the end of his life, and that was to have a kid."

"He wanted a kid?"

"Not at first. By the end."

"You never had one."

"No. Neither did you," she added, as if compelled.

"I was never married."

"Well, I was, I had a family. Matt and I were a family, a family of two." She paused. "Then he wanted three. I couldn't go up to that number. At least not so fast."

The bus pulled away and quickly climbed onto an open highway with little traffic, only a few whizzing cars and trucks. On both sides of the road were factories, extending for miles. "You okay?" said Sam.

"Yes. Fine." She wiped at her eyes.

"You should be happy. You did great today. You got what you wanted."

"It was luck," she said.

"Maybe. But I told you the story and you applied it. And the heavens, in case you haven't noticed, are about to salute you." He aimed a triumphant look through the bus window to the world outside. They had left the line of factories behind and now were crossing the flat river country — low, green, featureless, brimming with insects and birds and unseen creatures. In front of the bus, the straight ribbon road narrowed to a point. Black clouds grumbled above it. "You know what that is?"

"A storm?"

He gave the wry smile that said no. The bus barreled into the dark bulkhead of sky. The pressure dropped. Daylight ebbed away as electricity rose. They could feel the dark charge in the air around them. Grass rippled across the marshes.

Lightning flashed up ahead; then thunder rumbled. She saw that he was smiling next to her. The first drops came down and the big wipers at the front of the bus started up. She watched, mesmerized. Big drops tapped on the roof and the windows, a few at first, and then more quickly until the rain poured on them, a furious volley, a fusillade of gunshots slamming the roof and spraying all over the windows. It was like going through a car wash.

"Do you know what it is yet?" Sam said.

She shook her head. Water was sheeting across the road. The wheels sent up fans of spray. The wetlands were cloaked with darkness.

He leaned close so she could hear him, and said, "It's the Sword-Grinding Rain."

8

The major cuisines of China were brought into being for different purposes, and for different kinds of diners. Beijing food was the cuisine of officials and rulers, up to the Emperor. Shanghai food was created for the wealthy traders and merchants. From Sichuan came the food of the common people, for, as we all know, some of the best-known Sichuan dishes originated in street stalls. Then there is Hangzhou, whence came the cuisine of the literati. This is food that takes poetry as its principal inspiration. From commemorating great poems of the past to dining on candlelit barges afloat upon West Lake where wine is drunk and new poems are created, Hangzhou cuisine strives always to delight men of letters. The aesthetic symmetry between food and literature is a pattern without end.

— LIANG WEI, *The Last Chinese Chef*

Sam had told her Hangzhou centered on a magnificent man-made lake, and that if she wanted to spend the night downtown while he stayed at his uncle's, he could book her at a hotel with a room facing the water. It sounded nice, but so far nothing Maggie had seen of the crowded gray city into which their bus disgorged them even hinted at such a fairyland. The streets, crawling with cars, were narrow canyons of glass-and-steel buildings. Sam waved over a taxi, explaining that the DHL office was outside town. She climbed in beside him, grateful. The rain had stopped, and everything was wet and washed clean.

They soared on a half-empty freeway along a river, past farm fields and intermittent housing developments, to an enormous and newly built business park. In this labyrinth the driver somehow found his way to the DHL office with its fleet of red-and-yellow trucks, and with Sam translating she signed forms and paid and dispatched the package. Done. She walked out feeling oddly numb. Her steps seemed heavy, the building and the parking lot unreal. It was finished. It was sent. She climbed back into the car, not quite believing it.

She stole a glance and saw him giving her a hopeful look. "Are you hungry?" he asked. "Because I have to eat immediately."

"Starved." She had already decided she would eat as soon as he dropped her off, but it would be so much better to eat with him; he knew where to go, what to have, and how to tell her about it. Every meal here had been a breakthrough into the unexpected, but the food she had eaten in his company had been something more. With him, this world of cuisine seemed not only intricate but coherently beautiful. It did what art did, refracted civilization. "I'd love to have lunch with you," she said. "But I absolutely don't want to keep you. You need to get to your uncle's."

"It's past one o'clock, I have to eat. I'm Chinese that way. Or I've gotten that way."

"Meaning?"

"Nobody delays meals here. Everybody eats by the clock. Meetings in offices stop at twelve sharp even if they're only ten minutes from concluding. By now, too, lunch will be over at my uncle's house, and I don't want to arrive hungry. It's part of my job as a family member to think ahead and avoid inconveniencing the people I care about."

"Kind of like Southerners in America."

"Yes," he said, brows lifting in surprise at her, "you're right. As opposed to say, New Yorkers, who just throw out their requests and expect you to be the one to say no, sorry, it's an inconvenience."

"Exactly."

"So you do want to eat," he said.

"I do."

"Good." He laid a hand over his midsection, as if to reassure himself food was coming. He had a long waist anyway, the Chinese part of his body. Her eye followed his hand to that part of him.

He gave instructions to the driver. "Where are you taking me?" she said.

"Lou Wai Lou. Might as well go to the quintessential Hangzhou restaurant. It's been around forever, and they're still bragging about the Qianlong Emperor coming down to eat in Hangzhou in the eighteenth century. Through its history it's had a close connection with the Seal Engraving Society, which was a gathering place for the scholar crowd. Classic Hangzhou cuisine. If a person like you eats in only one place, it should be this."

"I was just thinking about this world of food you've been showing me," she said, "and why I never knew about it before. Why do you think haute Chinese hasn't made it in the West? Haute Japanese has. Haute Italian has."

"You're right. Every year the lists of the world's fifty greatest restaurants come out, and not one of them mentions a single Chinese place. I think it's because people don't know it. Chinese-American food is so different."

"But that was true once of Italian," she protested. "Spaghetti, pizza? We got past that. Why not Chinese?"

He considered. "Could it be the money?" he said. "People value what's expensive. It's instinctive. They see Chinese as a low-cost food, so they think it can't be high-end. It can be totally high-end, and it can also be expensive, which they're not used to. Of course, no more expensive than any other high-end cuisine, but still. It's Chinese. The funny thing is, actually, that what drives up the price of high-end Chinese cuisine is often the rarity of the ingredients. If you order high-end but forgo those dishes, it's not always that pricey."

"So what are the ingredients that are so expensive?"

"Exotic parts of exotic creatures. Chinese love them. It is a constant push against the envelope to wring delicious taste and texture out of the unexpected. These are the dishes, along with ones that are ridiculously labor-intensive, that make the high-end cuisine stand out. But let's say you go to one of the world's greatest Chinese restaurants —"

"One of the ones the list makers never heard of."

"Right, and you refrain from ordering the exotica. You will still have unbelievable food, and yet some of it at least will not be priced in the stratosphere."

"I don't know," she demurred. "Those animal parts might be hard to pass up."

"I could put you to the test on that," he said.

She smiled. She knew that if he cooked it, and if he said it was good — bear paws, camel humps, dried sea slug, whatever — she would eat it.

Traffic slowed as they reentered the city, and soon they were in the urban knot again, crawling through dense fumes of exhaust between buildings that towered on each side. Once again she wondered when she was going to see this lake.

Then their street ended at a T intersection, beyond which stretched a dreamy blue mirror of water dotted by islands and double-reflected pagodas. Hills covered with timeless green forest ringed the opposite shore. Small, one-man passenger boats sculled the surface, their black canopies making them seem from a distance to be random, slow-moving water bugs. As far as she could see around the lake, between the boulevard and the shore, there stretched a shady park filled with promenading people. The noises of the city swallowed themselves somehow into silence behind her. She felt a sense of calm spreading inside, blue, like the water. She glanced at him. He was smiling with the same kind of pleasure. "What's on those islands?" she asked.

"Pavilions. Zigzag bridges. Paths."

"You know what? Maybe you should just stop and let me out. I'll stay right here. Get old here. Never leave."

"And you will stay here tonight — lucky you. If you want me to get you a room on the lake. Don't you? Yes. That's what I would do in your position. But first, lunch."

Lou Wai Lou was a stately old building on a broad, crescent-shaped peninsula hugging the shore of the lake. They got off at the main road and walked down the causeway to the restaurant. The water's edge was clotted with luxuriant patches of floating, round-leafed lotus. Sheltering trees rustled in the wind.

The restaurant was a stone building with huge windows and grand dining rooms. Sam showed her the building for the Seal Engraving Society next door. "The society members, the calligraphers who created the chops and seals used by educated men, were Lou Wai Lou's original *meishijia,* their gourmets. Some say that's how it got started that Hangzhou cuisine was about literature."

"Literature?" she repeated, not sure she was hearing right.

"This is the literary cuisine."

They sat down. "You mean what, writers eating together?"

"No, the opposite — eaters writing together. Poetry would be written in groups. People would get together and dine and play drinking games and write poetry — like a slam. So here, food and poetry developed side by side. Always modifying each other."

"You mean this is the food of the literati."

"Yes. Even today, dishes quote from the poets. You'll see! We'll order *dongpo rou.*" And he called for a waiter. "It was named for Su Dongpo. Famous poet who wrote some of his gems here. Oh," he said to the waiter, "and another dish," and he asked for sliced sautéed lotus root with sharp-scented yellow celery, garlic shoots, and Chinese sausage. Finally he ordered beggar's chicken, because it was a famous local dish and he said she must have it at the source.

Sam Liang sat back after that, and stopped himself. Three dishes were enough. Uncle Xie would have him cooking the moment he arrived at the house, driving him, insisting he do better, teaching him something he needed for the banquet, which was now in five days. He would work hard, prepare a huge meal for everyone tonight. Better to eat lightly. *Qi fen bao.* Seven parts of ten. He knew that. And nice to have one more hour in this woman's company.

Admit it, he thought, you like being with her. Hour after hour it was the same, and this was the second day — unusual for him. He usually didn't do well when he took trips with women. Of course, that was usually because they were lovers and not friends, and it had always been hard for him to be with his lovers around the clock. This woman was not his lover; maybe that was why he got along with her so well. An acquaintance. Maybe a friend. Sometimes — the evening before, for instance, when they had said good night in the hallway — he thought he saw a sexual woman in there, waiting for someone to come in and find her. Other times he wasn't sure. *That's a question for some other man to answer. Not you.*

Yet he had been impressed with her today. She had handled herself perfectly in the meeting, waiting to speak until all the pleasantries had been exchanged, then offering herself as exactly what they might hope for, the widow wanting nothing but to support her husband's child — if she was her husband's child. That was her only sine qua non and she held fast to it, at the same time making it seem utterly reasonable. He himself had spoken in support of her, in English, only once, and it had been enough. She had taken a message that was essentially metaphor, the Sword-Grinding Rain story, internalized it, and played it back as strategy. He hadn't expected that.

"I really don't know much about you," he said now. "I know about your husband and this claim and the things that brought you here. But not about your life."

She thought. "One of the things about writing a column for twelve years is that you have to build a sort of persona. I've done that. I have a public self. That person would answer, I have no home. My home is the road, the passageway between the tents at the state fair, the alley where the oyster place is, you get the idea. And I do live like that, about ten days a month."

"And the rest?"

"I spend the rest of the time at home. Writing, mostly."

"And you live in L.A."

"In Marina del Rey. Actually on a boat. I live on a boat."

"Seriously?" His awareness went up.

"It sounds cool and minimalistic, but it's not. It's kind of screwed up, to tell you the truth."

"You moved there after your husband died?"

She nodded.

"You can't cook on a boat," he said.

"Sure you can. But I don't. I never cook."

"Never? And you're a food writer?"

"Not if I can help it. On this, I can tell you, my husband and I were in perfect accord. Neither of us knew how to cook. My mother was a wonderful woman but terrible in the kitchen; his mother could cook but refused to show anybody how. So we kept a refrigerator that looked like a forest of takeout containers, his and hers. Matt loved to eat, but he had no interest in cooking."

"Opposite man from me," said Sam.

"What about you? I know you studied with your uncles, but where'd you learn before that?"

"My mom. Not Chinese, of course. Jewish food. The basics. Comfort food. Here." He flipped up his phone and touched the buttons and flipped it around to show her the corded grin of a pleasant-looking gray-haired woman. "Judy Liang," he said, his love evident. "My childhood home cook."

"She looks nice," Maggie said, which was the truth.

"She is." He put the phone away. The food came. *Dongpo rou* was a geometrically precise square of fat-topped pork braised for hours in a dark sauce. Maggie lifted the fat layer delicately away with her chopsticks and plucked the lean, tender meat from underneath.

"Ah, you're so American," he said. "The Chinese diner is in it for the fat."

"Let me see *you* eat it."

He scooped up a piece and popped it in his mouth. Then he said, "Truth is, I don't like the fat much either."

She laughed. She couldn't stop eating the pork, which was succulent and delicious. "Would you say this is high food or low food?"

"Both. That's like so many things here. It's low in that it's one of the most common dishes in this city. They cook it everywhere. It's high in the sense that to make it right — with tender, succulent meat and fat like light, fragrant custard — is a rare feat."

"Will you put it in your banquet?"

"I will," he said, surprising her. "But I think in a different form."

"Good," she said, "because I love it." She turned to the second platter, which held lotus root and crisp, strong-tasting yellow celery and sausage. Also delicious. Then the beggar's chicken. It looked at first like a foil-wrapped whole bird, but he undid it, folded back layers of crinkly baking bags, and broke the seal on a tight molded wrap of lotus leaves. A magnificently herbed chicken aroma rushed into the air.

Maggie couldn't wait. She picked up a mouthful of chicken that fell away from the carcass and into her chopsticks at a touch. It was moist and dense with profound flavor, the good nourishment of chicken, first marinated, then spiked with the bits of aromatic vegetable and salt-cured ham which had been stuffed in the cavity and were now all over the bird. Shot through everything was the pungent musk of the lotus leaf.

At once she knew she should write about this place. She should give the recipe for this dish, catch the glorious bustle of this restaurant, describe these tall windows looking over the majesty of the lake and the virgin green hills beyond. Her one column was inadequate — inadequate even to tell the story of Sam Liang, which was so much richer than anything she could contain in a brief piece. And in addition to him she had so many moments, like this one, this lunch at Lou Wai Lou.

After they ate they walked outside and stood on the steps to look out at the lake. "The thing I can't believe is that behind me" — she waved back over her left shoulder — "is that gray, honking city. While over there" — she pointed across the water — "I see nothing but trees and hills. No development. In this day and age that's amazing! What's over there?"

"Monasteries and stuff," he said. "Temples." Then she looked around and saw that his attention was focused away from her and the lake, trained on the bottom of the steps, where an older man used a bucket of water and a brush as long as a mop, which he dipped in the water and swirled on the wide smooth pavement.

"What's he writing?" she whispered.

"A poem. Unless it's a short one, the beginning will be gone by the time he gets to the end. It will evaporate away. That's the idea. It's like a recitation."

"But who is he?"

"Just a guy out enjoying the day."

"Can you read the poem?"

"Me? No! Impossible." He looked at Maggie. If she stayed here, in time she would understand more. Only half the beauty of what the man was doing was the poem, beyond doubt some beloved classic. The other half was his calligraphy, which rendered each character into something like an abstract painting, beautiful, but all the more indecipherable to Sam. "Elder Born," he said in polite Mandarin, "may I trouble you as to the author of this poem?"

"Su Dongpo!" the man cried up the steps, delighted.

"It's the guy the pork dish was named after," Sam said to her.

He knew how strange the connection between food and poetry seemed at first; he remembered his Uncle Xie explaining it to him. "The number-one relationship is between the chef and the gourmet, my son. The chef must give the *meishijia* what he wants. Here in Hangzhou, for a thousand years, the *meishijia* have been the literati, so we give them dishes named for poets. We create carvings and presentations to evoke famous poetry and calligraphy parties throughout history. We strive for dishes of artifice which inspire poetic musings. The highest reward for any Hangzhou chef is to hear poetry being created and applauded by his diners out in the dining room — oh! Nothing else in my life has given me such a good feeling, except my wife and my son and my daughters — and you, my son, of course. This is what you must understand if you are to be a true Chinese chef. Eating is only the beginning of cuisine! Only the start! Listen. Flavor and texture and aroma and all the pleasure — this is no more than the portal. Really great cooking goes beyond this to engage the mind and the spirit — to reflect on art, on nature, on philosophy. To sustain the mind and elevate the spirit of the *meishijia*. Never cook food just to be eaten, Nephew!"

Sam had tried, but here he truly was held back by being a foreigner. He had been born, raised, and educated in America. He lacked the dizzying welter of references and touchpoints that would have been his if he had grown up here. He had only his uncles. They had done their best to fill him in on five thousand years of culture, starting the moment he arrived. For this he not only accepted their abuse, he was grateful for it.

In another taxi they sailed back up the road toward the lake and the hotels. It was time now. He needed to get on to his uncle's.

He had called. He was told Xie had been carried down to the kitchen and was waiting for him. His wife, Wang Ling, was there beside him, and since yesterday all four children had been home — three daughters and a son. Only one of the daughters, Songling, still lived in Hangzhou; she managed another venerable restaurant called Shan Wai Shan. She was the only one of the Xie children who had followed her father into the world of cuisine. The other two daughters, Songan and Songzhe, and the son, Songzhao, all had professional careers and families in Shanghai. They were Sam's generation, and he thought of them as one thinks of far-off cousins, rarely seen but always spoken of with fondness. When they were born, their father had insisted upon using the traditional generation name, so that their given names all shared the same first syllable. By then, in the 1950s, this was hardly ever done — but that was Third Uncle, a stubborn reprobate, still using the generation name even after his own father had died in prison for being an imperial cook.

The old man had used the same iron will on Sam. No one was harder on Sam than Xie. None had used harsher names. Xie had called him a worthless lump of mud and a motherless turtle. He told him he didn't deserve to be a Liang. More times than Sam could bear to remember he had taken away what Sam was in the middle of cooking and dumped it out. *"Zai kaishi yixia,"* Uncle would order, slamming the clean wok back down in front of him, Start again. And Sam would swallow back the humiliation and know that Uncle would not be teaching him if he didn't believe he could learn it, could do it. Each time Sam would resolve to keep trying.

And now Uncle was slipping away from the earth, and all Sam wanted was to get to him, quickly, and be with him once again, while he lived.

She turned to him in the back seat. "If you can just tell me a good place to eat tonight. Near my hotel."

"By yourself?"

"Of course by myself."

"You can't eat alone," he said, and even as he spoke he asked himself what he was doing. Why not just say goodbye? It was time for him to go to Uncle's. "I told you, that's one of the important things about Chinese food. Maybe *the* most important thing. It's about community."

"I'm okay eating by myself. I always eat alone on the road, and always *always* since Matt died."

"That's bad luck. I might have to try and change you."

"You can't change me," she informed him.

"But to eat alone is anti-Chinese."

"I'm not Chinese. Look, Sam, you're being so nice and you really don't have to be. It's just, I'm here. I don't want to waste a meal. Tonight I want to go someplace good. Just tell me. That's all."

"I could easily give you a place. But the thing you should really do is come with me. Eat with the Xie family. Then I will bring you back here."

"I don't want to get in between you and your family."

"You won't. You'll be watching a lot. I'll be the only person you can talk to, and I might be occupied. You okay with that?"

"Yes," she said. "I'm a writer. I love to observe. But this is your family. It's a sensitive time."

"But I would like you to come."

"Okay," she said after a minute.

He felt himself smile. He was relaxed with her, which he hadn't felt in so long. She was a friend. Nothing wrong with it.

They had reached her hotel parking lot. She slid out the door and pulled her bag behind her. "Will you wait for me a moment? Just let me put this stuff in the room. I'll be right back."

"Okay," he said.

Maggie closed the door and trotted away from him to the entrance. She was aware that he was watching her from behind. When she was younger she would have worried about whether her shape was pleasing or not, but not now. She was old, forty, and besides, he was not interested. Still, she was glad she was going along. She felt a pull to him. Maybe they'd be friends after all.

She ran upstairs and put her things in the room and then came back down. Another thing: it would be a blessing to have company tonight, not to be alone. She had done it, got the sample, sent it off, and there was always that sense of letdown when a difficult task was finished. There was also the sadness, the finality; if Shuying wasn't Matt's, then she, Maggie, would never see his face in any living form, ever again. In time she might even forget his face. She would remember it only the way it had been captured in pictures. She was going to see herself get old in the mirror, and never remember him any other way but young.

"You okay?" said Sam when she got in the car.

"I am," she said, and she closed the door behind her.

Xie must have fallen asleep because he awoke to the sound of the car door. Then a second door. Voices. A woman. His shaggy brows lifted. Finally, after all this time, the boy had brought a woman here! An instant web of thoughts bloomed and branched out in his mind as he heard their steps coming up to the door.

"Men kai-de!" he called. Door's open!

The door pushed open and in came Nephew, smiling, wet-eyed, and behind him an outside woman with large, dark eyes and unruly hair.

Nephew dropped beside him and held him in the Western way as he murmured to him in Chinese. Then he said, "Uncle, this is Maggie McElroy," and raised a hand to the girl. Xie did his best to give her a smile. She was pleasing in spite of her face, which was too sharp. Of course she could have looked like a dog and he would

133

have been happy, considering that she was a woman and Nephew was bringing her. *"Huanying, huanying,"* Xie said.

"He says welcome."

"My pleasure to meet you," said Maggie.

"Ta hen gaoxing renshi ni," said Sam.

Xie had been watching her eyes. He could always tell when someone understood. "She can't talk?" he said abruptly in Chinese.

"No, Uncle, not a word."

"Too bad."

"No! No, Uncle, it's not like that. She's not my girlfriend. She's a writer, she's doing an article about the competition. It's no more than that."

"Did *I* say something?" Xie demanded. "Did this worthless old lump say anything to her but welcome?"

"No. Sorry. Anyway, I'll run her back to her hotel after dinner."

"She is your good friend, she is welcome."

"She's not — oh, never mind." Besides, she was his friend, in a way.

Uncle Xie was looking sternly at him. "Enough." The old voice was imperious. "Show me your wrists!"

Sam unbuttoned his cuffs and rolled them back. He knew he wasn't going to have enough new scars to please Uncle. Serious Chinese cooks always had a signature pattern of mottle-burns. These burns could extend past the wrists all the way up the forearms. Just reaching across the stove, a chef could be burned by spattering oil, and the burns left their own special marks. Even American immigration officers checking incoming Chinese chefs with work visas knew to check the wrists and forearms for the spatter-pattern of scars.

Xie craned his neck. "Closer!" he rasped, and then when he got a look he let out a weak snort. "What do you do all day, lie about? Do you ignore your prayers to your calling? When are you going to rush to clasp the Buddha's foot — the day of the banquet? Don't you know by then it will be too late?"

"Uncle, I have been thinking, and trying dishes —"

"Flush your thinking! It is the American in you that thinks somehow everything you need will arise by magic inside you! Wrong! You have to learn! To learn you have to work!"

"But Uncle —"

"If you were working you would be burned!"

Behind them Maggie stared. Though she didn't understand their Chinese, it was obvious that, as sick and weak as the old man was, he was hitting hard. Yet Sam didn't seem to mind. He could feel her watching and turned around. "Don't worry. It's his way of saying I matter to him."

"It's fine," she said.

Then Uncle Xie cut back in with his rasping Mandarin. "I'm waiting! And since you did not bring this foreign female here to tell me you had a special feeling for her, why are you talking to her? Lump! Dogmeat! Do you think I have so much time left? Wash your hands! Tie back your hair! You should cut it. It looks terrible. Prepare!"

"We're going to be cooking now," Sam told Maggie. "You'll have to forgive me."

"Nothing to forgive. I'll watch. That's why I'm here." She crept to the side and sat down. "You're fun to watch."

"See, that's why I wanted you here. You're nice to me. I get nothing but tough love from my relatives. Ah, here's Wang Ling, Uncle Xie's wife." And he bent to hug a small, white-haired bird of a woman.

He spoke in Chinese to the old lady, introducing Maggie, after which she took Maggie's elbow with a surprisingly strong little hand. She sat beside Xie and soothed him while Maggie settled on her small worn stool against the wall.

First there was soaking of lotus leaves, which Maggie gradually saw were meant to wrap short ribs. She watched as Sam followed instructions from Uncle Xie and mixed a marinade of soy sauce, scallions, ginger, sugar, peanut oil, and sesame oil, plus a spoonful of something. "Bean paste," he shot back at her over his shoulder. Her notebook crept out of her purse practically of its own accord, and she started writing things down.

The ribs and the marinade went back in the refrigerator. "They have to steep," said Sam. Then he lifted the lotus leaves out, wet and limp like elephant ears. He stared at them for a second. "I see my mistake," he said to Maggie in English. "I should have cut them with scissors when they were dry."

"Worthless," sniffed Xie.

"Completely," Sam agreed, and started sawing on them with a serrated knife.

After half an hour his uncle said, "All right. Take the ribs out. First, take all the pieces out of the marinade, the scallions and ginger — throw them away. Leave some of the marinade on the meat. You're going to put two bite-sized ribs in each lotus leaf. First roll them in the five-spice rice powder — get a lot, now, make a paste. Get some larger rice crumbles. Large enough for the mouth to feel. That's it, now roll them. You have the plate ready? Line them up. No! Turtle! Smooth side down! You're going to turn them over to serve, remember? Just witness your stupidity!"

"He doesn't seem happy," said Maggie.

"It's not as bad as it sounds," Sam said.

Now Wang Ling was bending over the old man, telling him it was time to go up and nap. "Yes, Auntie," Sam agreed. "You are right. Uncle, I'll carry you up. We'll awaken you in two hours when the ribs are finished steaming. Would you like that?"

"Like it!" said Xie. "I'll swat your worthless head if you don't!" Then he broke apart, coughing.

"Come, Uncle," Sam said, and he lifted the thin old figure in his arms like a child and bore him gently toward the stairs. Wang Ling bent to take the empty rattan chair.

"Oh, no," Maggie said quickly, "let me." And she scooped up the chair, which was light, and followed Sam into a central hallway and then up a straight single flight of stairs between whitewashed walls. At the top they turned into the second bedroom.

It was warm with the sweet vinegar of old people, the books, the glasses, the cups of tea, the medicines. Sam laid Xie on the flowered bed. Curtains lifted in the breeze. "Thank you, my son," Xie said to him, voice flickering, exhausted.

Now, Maggie thought, he did look sick. His skin was yellow

parchment, his hands weak and palsied. His chest rose and fell with effort. He was trying to talk to Sam.

"Guolai," he whispered, Come here.

Sam bent close.

"I don't suppose you have any miserable idea for a menu, do you?"

"Not yet, Uncle."

"I have written one out for you, my son. Songling helped me. Songzhe, Songan, and Songzhao are bringing back all the food you will need for it. You are to prepare it for tonight. When you are done, even if you do not use any of the dishes from it, you will understand the classical progression."

"Yes, Uncle. I'll start when they get here."

"Awaken me the moment the ribs are ready." He lifted his head off the pillow, the only thing left he could move. "Don't make me come after you!"

"No, Uncle," Nephew said, tenderly tucking the cover. Xie watched as he and the curly-headed foreign woman slipped out. He himself could feel the soft bath of sleep coming on. Sleep was his comfort now, sleep and memories, along with the kind gaze and gentle hands of his old wife. And his children. And Nephew, now that he was here.

The injections his wife gave him took away the pain, even as they made his mind as clear as glass. Everything around him was like a dream. What had been far away was near. The days of his youth, particularly, seemed as pure and immediate as if they had just occurred.

Hangzhou was a food lover's dream then, and had been for a thousand years. Even the most ancient texts recorded its "abundance of rice and fish." By the time of the Southern Song in the twelfth century, restaurants and teahouses were two-thirds of the city's establishments. In order to outdo one another, Hangzhou chefs turned to the lavish use of ingredients, even rare ones, not even to eat, but simply to flavor the others — prawns used as a seasoning, crab roe as fat. And then there was decorative cooking. He must remember to bring this up with Nephew. At certain points in Hangzhou's history, presentation had reached virtuosic, garish heights, with elaborate mosaics of brightly hued hors d'oeuvres and the cutting of main-dish ingredients into floral and animal shapes. Oh, and there were the local delicacies: the Zhenjiang black vinegar and the Shaoxing wine.

It was right that Nephew should have his final lesson here in Hangzhou. Nowhere else in China were the people so occupied with gastronomy. Oh, he thought, shivering with delight, for so many centuries cultivated men had thought nothing of spending long hours over wine and poetry, debating which was better: the fresh pink shrimp flavored with imperial-grade green tea leaves, or the skinned shad wrapped in caul fat and steamed with wine.

Diners such as these deserved flattery, and so in Hangzhou a new element of Chinese cuisine was born — the pleasure of the compliment, made by the chef, delivered to the diner. This in turn gave rise to a whole sub-school of dishes characterized by surpassing subtlety, dishes that would be apprehended only by those with genuine taste.

Into this food fairyland had been born the young Xie, with his best friend and sworn brother, Jiang Wanli. The two families lived in adjacent compounds, and the little boys seemed joined to each other in all things.

They waited on private banquets together at the restaurant, not serving, just watching from the side in their gray silk gowns and black overtunics, ready to refill wine cups or change plates. Here they learned the esoteric lessons of cuisine. Food was not just to eat. It was a language. It was a regulator. It set the ladder of power. Each time the boys served, they observed this. Each meal was art, was a delight, but also a revelation of hierarchy.

Before a banquet they would wait for their guests at the entry, its pond and arched bridge and feathery trees laid out in the style of ornate containment which had long been the region's signature. As they led the arrivals back to their private dining room, ready-set with cold dishes, they were already trading calculations silently, through no more than glances. Who would sit in the *shangzuo*, the seat of honor facing the door? Who would sit in the lowest seat, with his back to the door? What dishes were selected? Who served food to whom? What toasts were proposed, in what order? Which prestige foods would be served? These were the parts of the banquet language which had meaning. The conversation, the words that were said at table, meant next to nothing. It was through etiquette that the verdict was passed. The boys saw subordinates demoted, successors selected, the revelation of a traitor in the group. Sometimes they saw the bland manners that meant the banquet with its formal mix of supplication and magnanimity was just a show, the successful candidate having already been secretly agreed upon via the age-old back door.

Ah, Xie thought in an agony of hope, the boy's meal had to be brilliant — in every way, on every level. All the right messages had to be sent out through the dishes, all the right resonances struck. He watched the long-pointed fronds of the bamboo outside the window and wondered once again what it was that made their movement so odd now, so brittle in the breeze. This was the last thought he had before he slept.

Down in the kitchen Maggie and Sam found the four Xie children, all in their forties, all with the crosscut Xie cheekbones of the patriarch. None of them looked like the delicate, narrow-faced mother, not even the son. Sam introduced them: Songling, the oldest, Songan and Songzhe, the other two girls, and Songzhao, the son.

Sam had told her they spoke a bit of English, but she didn't hear any. All were talking in Chinese at once. Cornucopia-stuffed string bags of food spilled onto the counters. Gourds and herbs and cabbages and all manner of flowering chives were spread out, tubs of rosy-fresh roe, a great live fish slapping in a plastic bucket, and two live chickens, caged.

"These you're going to kill?" said Maggie.

"Not in here," he said. "There's a place outside the kitchen door for that. Don't worry. It won't be when you're around."

"Give me some warning. I'll take a walk."

"Come to think of it, maybe you should watch." The thought made him smile. "You're in China. Actually, Maggie, the sisters have a plan for you, if you like. They're all going to get a massage. They want you to go with them."

"A massage?" she said.

"They always do this together when they come home." He was making separate piles of the vegetables, the sliced-in-place pads of fresh pasta, the eggs.

"*Women shunbian qu,*" one of the sisters offered.

"They're going anyway," he translated.

"To a *massage* parlor?" she said.

He laughed. "It's not that kind. Oh, there are those here too, believe me — just not this place."

"I wondered," she said. "I saw girls in Beijing."

"Wonder no longer," Sam told her. "It's everywhere." Indeed, prostitution had sprung back to life alongside the restaurant business in the 1990s. It took all forms and went through every kind of channel, one of them being massage establishments whose true purpose was immediately made obvious by low lights, bed-furnished cubicles, and so-called masseuses clad in skintight gowns slit to their pale hipbones.

In the dim lights, the girls who worked there were usually pretty. By Western standards they were inexpensive, too. Added to that was the fact that prostitution here was not hidden away in secret, seedy places the way it was in the West. It was forthright, visible. Sexual services in token guises were openly offered in the best hotels and business centers. Outcall services supplied whatever was desired in more private settings. At the highest caste level were all the women who were kept in apartments and on retainers for their sexual services: contract mistresses. If what you wanted was paid sex — and Sam didn't, personally, not because he was ashamed but because for him paying seemed to knock the whole point out of it — then China was a great place to be. Plenty of Chinese men were into it. Some *laowai* men too, though they mostly stuck to the bargirls and masseuses.

"I won't lie to you," he said to Maggie now. "Massage parlors of that kind are everywhere. Very big here, with Chinese and with foreigners too. But so is the other kind, the legitimate kind, where the workers are trained and it's totally therapeutic and they just do massage, on men and women alike. It feels great. You should go. The sisters want you to."

They spoke up now, chorusing in Chinese, obviously saying yes, yes, she should go.

"We can't really talk to each other," said Maggie.

"That doesn't matter. You're getting a massage."

"I think I could use that," Maggie admitted. Except for hugs and handshakes, she hadn't really been touched by anyone this past year. Everyone was kind to her, but their kindness was in the heart. She had not felt anyone's hands on her. No one held her. So often she had lain on the boat and wrapped her arms around herself, even in the daytime, the curtains tight against the bright light and the faint slap of the lines in the wind.

Sam said something in Chinese, and Songling linked her arm through Maggie's. "Come," she said, and led her outside.

"Bye," Maggie called back to Sam, and he just looked at her with a smile, one that seemed to penetrate through her shell to the inside of her, one that said, *You're about to feel good.*

Songzhe sat beside her in the back of the car, and Songan rode up in front with Songling. They curved down through a green pelt of trees rich with bamboo. When they passed an entrance gate with a sign in English and Chinese she saw they had been driving through the Hangzhou Botanical Garden. The sisters batted back and forth like birds, happy to see each other, and Songzhe kept leaning over to squeeze Maggie's arm. Everyone was so physical here, Maggie thought. That was one reason she liked it. That and the fact that people went around in groups. Sam, for example; even though she had mostly been with Sam alone, he seemed to have a herd of family members supporting him in the background. They were quarrelsome, but they were there. It was a form of sustenance. It was not Maggie's life, never had been, but she liked it.

When they drove up in front of the massage place, she saw that it did indeed look like a clinic. Chinese women in white coats and flat shoes checked them in and led them to a room with eight leather recliners separated by side tables for drinks and reading matter. A wall-mounted TV was blaring a Chinese travelogue. The Xie sisters chattered and laughed. They soaked their feet in plastic-lined wooden tubs of hot water with herbs. She could feel how happy they were to be together, even if it was for their father's final illness, even if their eyes were brimming at the same time they talked and laughed. Each had gossip and revelations and new digital photos on their cell phones, which they made Maggie look at and admire. Maggie knew how they felt. She understood happiness, and she understood grief. Many times during the last year she had been pulled between the two, the way they were now.

"He shenmo?" said one of the white-coated women, standing next to her, and Songzhe translated, "Something to drink?"

"Water," said Maggie. "Please. And could we turn that off?" She indicated the TV, now showing footage of mountain peaks set to tinny music.

At once all three sisters waved dismissively at it, chattering; they didn't like it, they hadn't been watching it, they didn't care. Maggie received a water bottle, took a drink from it, lay back, and submitted to the hands of the girl who took her feet out, dried them, balanced them on the stool, and began to massage them. The woman was confident and strong-fingered. Maggie felt her anchor lift, her beleaguered self finally rise and float and start to spin downstream. The world fell away. In time she saw only disconnected images and scattered, luminous thoughts.

Likewise the conversation between the sisters gave way to the silence of pleasure as the masseuses released the legs and feet and then moved around to each woman's head, neck, shoulders, and arms. Maggie drifted. In a half-dream she saw Matt's face. *How far did you go with her? What did you do? Were there others?* But he didn't answer. A glass wall seemed to separate them. She could see the humorous light in his eyes and the stubble on his chin. See his Welsh face, sheepish and brave.

Is she your daughter or not?

She floated with the woman's strong fingers kneading up her shoulders and her neck to her scalp, then dropping to her upper spine and starting again. Maggie's muscles were hard and tense. As their outer layers relaxed and released, images of Matt rose like bubbles, burst, and vanished. Maggie felt the Chinese woman's hands now on her neck. She remembered Matt two years ago, taking her to a birthday party for his friend Kenny's little son. She remembered complaining on the way over that people shouldn't invite grown-up friends to a party for a three-year-old, but Matt broke through her crust, as he usually did. He was the gracious one. He was the reason their relationship had manners. "You know what?" he said. "Kenny's more proud of this little guy than of anything else he's ever done. So it's fine."

At the party she knew hardly anyone, except Kenny's wife, so she stood with her in the kitchen to help. They chatted and cut melons and pineapples, bananas and grapes, for fruit salad. On the other side of the pass-through, guests buzzed at the food table and formed a laughing circle around Kenny and Matt as they played with little William on the floor. Both men lay on their backs on the floor with their knees up, whooping and hollering, riding the boy on their knees and passing him aloft from one to the other while he shrieked with joy.

"Look at Matt," said Valerie, Kenny's wife. "He loves it."

It was true. Matt's face was alight. His eyes were dizzy with pleasure. So tender, the way he held the boy. *He wants one. Look at him. Look.* It was so undeniable that Maggie thought her heart would crack. "You're right," she said softly. "He does."

Valerie put the last fruit on the platter and wiped it once around the edges. "So when are you two going to have one?"

Now, years later, on her back with a Chinese woman's fingers working their way down her arm, spreading her hand, massaging it, Maggie remembered the way she had fished for an answer, how Valerie had seen her discomfort and kindly retreated. She remembered the silent thud inside her that told her Matt would never rest, never be content, until he had one of his own. She knew this wish would now define their life together. As it did, in the short time left to them.

It's no use thinking about him. He's never coming back. She felt the old sadness. One of the sisters murmured softly in Chinese; the sister next to her released a little laugh. Maggie made an involuntary half-smile in response. She didn't understand. It didn't matter. They were happy here together, and they made her part of it. It was *guanxi,* the deep kind, family. She thought she was beginning to understand it. *Make this the start, then. Go on from here.* The thought was soft and clear in her mind. The room grew still, just the sound of their breathing, soft, like falling snow. She let go of the world and slept.

Sam counted down the last minutes until the ribs came out of
the steamer. He had already gone upstairs and whispered to
Songzhao, who would rouse Uncle from his nap. While the ribs
were steaming he had started work on the menu, killing and cleaning the chickens, preparing the cold dishes, mixing pastes and
sauces. Still so much to grasp. He should have started younger. But
life had been good in Ohio, and easy. He had let it go on too long.

Teaching school had been moderate in its demands, with lots of time off. And a man who taught school was a woman magnet. That was a huge plus. Women loved a man who worked with kids. Double that for a man who could cook, and who cooked for fun. He almost always had someone, and life was sweet even if that someone kept on changing. It wasn't until he was past thirty, with most of his friends paired off, that he started to grow tired of traipsing from one abbreviated version of connubial life to another, his scuffed-up suitcase of self in hand.

At the same time he started thinking about China. He decided to put aside Western food, ignore his father's warnings, and start to learn Chinese. The rest of that year he drove often to Cincinnati for long beans and pea sprouts, bottles, pastes and sauces. He took a lot of time to think. China was half of him too. He was the grandson of the Last Chinese Chef. He could either avoid it or commit to it.

He made his father sit down with him, dictionaries at their elbows, and start putting *The Last Chinese Chef* into English. Sam's own two years of college Chinese had woefully underprepared him to do it alone. But once he knew what the characters were and could look them up, he could take his time with it. He loved the Chinese language, its allusive elegance. He loved the whole sense of history that came with it. And after months of reading and cooking he loved the food, too, even though he knew he'd barely scratched the surface.

"I want to go, Ba," he said. "I'm going back."

"Where?" His father was reading the Chinese newspaper from Chicago and only half listening.

"China."

"Speak reasonably," said his father.

"I mean it. The uncles are getting on. I want to go while they can still teach me. I'm going to cook, Ba. I'm going to learn. I'm thirty-seven. If I don't start now, I never will."

"So learn!" Liang Yeh barked. "You want to throw your life away, urinate on everything, including your education which your mother and I worked so hard for, who am I to stop you?"

"Don't, Baba."

"I suppose my opinion is worthless —"

"Of course not."

"— but even you know you are not a Chinese chef! You are good with food, I admit. Everything you cook is excellent. But to become a Chinese chef you must start young. You must be trained like steel."

"I can learn," Sam said, stubborn.

"Zi wo chui xu," his father shot back, You talk big. "You think you can do it? Learn to cook, then! Just don't go back to China."

"But I must go back to China. It's the only place I can learn."

Liang Yeh was trembling. "Force words. Twist logic. You can go to Chicago."

"Ba," said Sam, "you yourself are the one who said a Chinese chef cannot cook in America! Remember? No cuisine here. No audience."

"That's true! But you can't go back."

"Look, I understand what you went through. It was bad."

"You don't understand! I should write it down so you truly do."

"Yes! You should! Do that! But why can't you see — whatever it was that happened — the world has changed? It's never going to turn back to the way it was. Other things might happen, but not that."

"You know nothing!" his father bellowed. "What if they arrest you? They can do anything!"

"You're crazy! Why would they arrest me? I'm an American."

"I am your father! I escaped!"

"Ba, they don't care. That's history."

"You will throw away everything!"

"First of all, you're wrong. Nothing's going to happen to me. Second, as for your opinion about my life, you're wrong there too. I really believe that. I actually feel for the first time that I'm doing something right. I *want* to go. I'm going."

"What one thing have I always asked you?"

"Never to return to China. But it doesn't make sense anymore. I'm sorry." In that moment his tone changed, no longer arguing, now consoling. He knew what he was going to do.

Liang Yeh felt it. "So you will do this no matter what?"

Sam nodded. "Come," he said to his father, as he took his arm. "Sit for a while. Let's have something to eat."

Now the ribs were ready and Uncle Xie was up. Sam and Songzhao bore him downstairs. Sam saw that Xie's color was worse. He was the mottled pearl of a turtle's belly. They positioned him in the middle of the kitchen, nothing but thin, frail bones under the blanket. *"Shi ji cheng shu,"* he directed, The time of opportunity is ripe. "Quickly!" And Sam cranked off the flame, lifted the lid from the steamer, and released a fragrant cloud.

"Take them out," Xie quavered. "No, don't touch them yet. They ought to rest. Ten minutes. Come and sit by me."

Sam pulled up a stool and sat close beside him. After a time he heard the little car whine up the hill. The three sisters and Maggie came in. The blissful look on Maggie's face was nice to see. "You seem to have enjoyed it," he said.

"I loved it," she corrected him. "They were so nice to me." And she gave Songan and Songzhe each a squeeze on the arm.

"You're in time for the ribs." He used heavy gloves to flip the steamed plate over onto another one. Now the lotus packages, each of which held two succulent pieces of pork rib, were seam side down. "Lotuses are special to Hangzhou," he said to Maggie.

"I saw them in the lake. Great clumps of them."

"You should come sometime when they bloom, in midsummer. When you get close to one and smell it, it's the most surprising thing. The blossom doesn't smell like a flower at all, it smells camphorated. Like a Chinese medicine shop. But the leaf has its own flavor, which comes out in the cooking." And he transferred one lotus wrap to a small plate for everyone in the room.

Inside the leaves, the rib meat came away under their chopsticks, rich and lean and long-cooked with a soft crust of scented rice powder. Underneath, the darker, more complicated flavor of the meat, the marrow, and the aromatics. Maggie thought it was wonderful. She ate everything except the rib bones, which she nibbled clean and folded back up, polished, inside the leaf. She wished she could lick the leaf, it was so good — and she wasn't even hungry. She sent an assessing glance around the room. Songan and Songzhe and Songzhao were eating happily. Songling was slowly, patiently, giving bits of the meat to her father. And then all movement in the room stopped.

Xie's face was falling in disappointment. "Throw them out," he said sadly.

Sam swallowed. What was there to throw out? Everyone else had eaten them.

Xie turned his gaze to Songling. She removed his portion and carried it back to the kitchen.

"What's wrong with it?" asked Sam in Chinese. Everyone sat, uncomfortably silent.

"I will concede that scallions and ginger uplift pork," said Xie. "They carry its flavor, which is a dark flavor, up and out into the light. This is their function. But this is a dish of refinement! Sophistication and subtlety are what is most important, not the peaks of flavor. Everything must be intelligently stated. Every flavor must be a play on texture, while every texture suggests a flavor. This cannot be accomplished with extremes. Ever. The spicy, the flagrant, the hot — these things will never work."

"So their flavors were too strong."

Xie made a small nod. "You can be rustic, but never coarse. *Always* believe in the intelligence of the diner. *Always* reward them with subtlety." His words dissolved into a sharp, spiking cough. Songan patted his shoulder, Songling stroked his hand.

"Baba," said Songling, "you will tire yourself."

"Yes, yes." He bobbled his chin at Sam. "Well? What are you waiting for? Start again!"

Sam exchanged discreet glances with the four siblings; none wanted the old man to be exhausted. They carried him to a quiet corner of the kitchen, leaving the two Americans alone.

Maggie watched Sam turn and draw another package of ribs out of the refrigerator. It was clear to her that the old man didn't like the ribs. Why? She had vacuumed up her own portion shamelessly after the first bite bloomed in her mouth: lovely, mahogany-deep pork with bright accents of onion and ginger.

"What was wrong?" she said.

"He thought the flavors were too strong."

"Onion and ginger?"

He sighed over the new row of lean, rosy-fresh ribs. "You noticed."

"That doesn't mean I thought it was a problem."

"He's right. A meal like this has to be subtle." He cut with irritated clacks of his cleaver. "I ought to have known that."

"Well," she said. She sat listening to the rhythm of his cutting. This was a sound she liked. In time she noticed that the kitchen was a litter of sauces, chopped piles, covered dishes, and used bowls, and she walked to where he was standing. "I think you should move over, Sam. If you could. Make room at the sink. I can't cook in the slightest. I would never think of trying to help you. But I can wash. I happen to be very good at washing, and there's a lot of it here. Let me clean up behind you."

"You can't do that. You should sit down. You're a guest."

"You want me to be relaxed, right? Comfortable?" She waited for his confirming glance. "Then let me help. You're American. You know visitors like to help."

"But you could go upstairs — to the room where I'm going to stay tonight. You'll see my things. It's quiet. We'll call you for dinner."

"Sam. I want to help."

"Okay."

His tone was resigned, but she could tell he was glad. She cleared a space on a counter and covered it with towels, then started scrubbing used dishes and bowls and upending them in a pyramid on the towel. When she finished building it, she dried and then started again.

"You're precise," he observed, of her stacking.

"So are you," she said, of his cutting. "You were taught well." She watched him. "Why'd you start so late?" she said. "I've been wondering."

"Underneath, I think I wanted it too much."

She upended a clean, dripping enamel basin on the outer flank of her pyramid. "Meaning?"

"Did you ever want something so deeply you were scared to let yourself have it?"

"Like love," she said suddenly, and then wished she hadn't. She swallowed. "Like being in love."

"Yes," he said slowly. "Like that." He swept the ribs into a new bowl, washed his hands, and retied his hank of hair behind his neck. "Like a desire so great you know you will never forgive yourself if you fail. So you hang back." He washed scallions and cut them into green circlets. "And then you wake up one day and you realize if you don't do it now, it will move out of reach forever." He looked sideways at her. "You know?"

"I do," she said. "I know."

He nodded. "So I came here."

"I think you belong here."

"And in some ways I don't."

"No doubt. But I love seeing you with your family. They are so good. Even your uncle, even when he's on the warpath." She looked behind her at the frail man beneath the blanket, dozing now, each breath scratching. "He is hard on you."

Sam smiled down at his uncle's chopping block, which she saw was like the ones he had in his restaurant kitchen in Beijing, a massive, well-worn slice of tree trunk. "There was a famous Chinese food writer and gourmet in the eighteenth century named Yuan Mei. His advice was, if you want truly good food, be hard on the cook. He said the Master should always send down a stern warning, *before* the food is served, that tomorrow the food will have to be better. Or else."

Maggie laughed.

"It's not just him, in other words."

"So it's cultural," said Maggie. "But it's personal, too. He loves you."

"He does," Sam agreed.

"So go ahead," she said, and swept her eyes over the counters filled with food. "Pull one out for him tonight." He smiled. She took a fresh towel and started from the top of her new, perfect structure, dismantling it in order, drying.

Dinner was a kaleidoscope of twelve courses and two soups which Maggie, on a purely visceral level, ranked among the best meals in memory. It was oddly comforting to be the outsider at a family table where everything was said in Chinese. She understood nothing, but she understood everything too. They were giddy with the food, with one another, happy to be together despite the anticipatory grief that already surfaced in rogue tears and trembling looks. They took turns encircling the mother and sitting close to the father. They said things to make the others laugh. They cried out with elated admiration each time Sam brought a dish to the table. And no one expected her to do a thing.

It was a perfect position from which to observe the rhythm of the table, and to begin to see how their manners worked. It was quickly clear to her that the object was to serve others while avoiding being served in turn. She could see this was what they were doing with one another, so she played along.

It suited her, to resist being served too much — especially tonight, when she was eating the way she ate when she was working. She consumed a small amount of each thing, but with heightened attention. Over the years she had found that she couldn't eat a lot if she was eating critically. To be truthful, her limit for genuinely attentive eating was four mouthfuls; after that she wasn't tasting, only eating. So when she was working, though she spent a lot of time researching and scheming and ferreting out food, she actually ate but little.

Her friends used to ask her how she could do her job and not grow fat; she would answer that it was the opposite, that it was working with food that kept her thin. To do the job, she couldn't just close her eyes and eat. She had to go slow, think, pay attention, and stop after rather little. It was a good thing, too. Food writers weren't supposed to be fat.

On this night she focused on the perfection of the food. First the appetizers, served at room temperature: an herb-scented puree Sam told her was hyacinth bean, then toothsome puffs of gluten in a sweet-savory sauce, pan-roasted peppers, and some kind of minced salad of dry tofu and macerated wild herbs. She loved the crisp spiced duck with buns, the *dongpo* pork, the one they'd had in the restaurant — pork lean beneath the fat that peeled off to leave the meat in a rich, mellow sauce. But best of all was the second soup. It brought gasps around the table, even from Uncle Xie. The live fish had been transformed into pale, fluffy fish balls, light and airy and ultra-fresh. These floated in the perfectly intense fish broth with shrimp, clouds of soft tofu, and tangy shreds of mustard green. She felt when she was eating it that it nourished every part of her; it was a soup she sensed she would remember all her life.

At the end he served a sweet mold of rice and dried fruits, and then finally he sat down. He said this was called *ba bao fan,* eight-treasure rice. She was so pleasantly full that she couldn't believe he was bringing out one more course, much less something sweet, but as soon as she took the first bite of her portion she knew she would eat every morsel of it.

"That soup was genius," she said to him afterward.

"That's a recipe from Songling's restaurant, Shan Wai Shan. The soup is one of their specialties." He turned and spoke to them in Chinese, listened to Songling's answer. "She says they sell eight hundred orders a month. People come from all over the world for that soup. True believers can even buy one of the blue-and-white tureens to take home. They're made exclusively for this soup in Jingdezhen. It's a whole industry, this recipe."

"A great meal," she said. "Great. Your uncle loved it. Everyone loved it." A clamor of agreement rose around the table, and Sam was toasted and applauded.

Then he turned his attention to Third Uncle. This was the opinion he really wanted.

"The drunken prawns were very good, and the fish in crispy tofu skins. This is the use of meaning in a meal. Well done," Uncle Xie pronounced, and sent him a look of pride.

Sam understood. As soon as he had seen drunken prawns on the menu, he knew that Uncle was paying him a compliment. The dish was included as an homage to Yuan Mei. Sam recognized the dish from Yuan's writings. "Every chef since the eighteenth century owes part of his learning to Yuan Mei," Uncle had told him. "Read him, my son. Only then will you deserve to call yourself a Chinese chef." By including this dish, Uncle was betting that Sam had done what he was told and would recognize the reference. Sam did. And he returned the compliment, this time flattering Uncle. He did this by adding a fish and crispy tofu-skin dish first described in the seventeenth-century literature of Li Yu, another of history's famous gourmets. Uncle was pleased. Sam loved these layers of learning, these meta-levels that made a meal an act of poetry. "Thank you," he said to his uncle.

After that the three sisters banished them from the kitchen while they cleaned, and Sam and Maggie sat in the front room with Uncle Xie, Wang Ling, and Songzhao. A few questions were put through Sam about Maggie's work, the kinds of articles she wrote, and then they asked the inevitable *Are you married?* — to which she replied, fast and flat, that she was a widow. This was her default reply. She no longer had to give an explanation or tell the story. She just said it.

Sam looked at the clock and twisted his torso suddenly up from the chair; the new batch of ribs was done. She heard the talking and the laughter from the kitchen, the click and clatter of dishes, the thump of the hot bamboo basket. In a minute he came back with a steaming row of lotus packages and small plates and chopsticks. They waited ten minutes; then each of them had to open one and taste it.

They all unwrapped. It smelled even better than the last batch. It smelled wondrous. Maggie couldn't wait to taste it, full as she was from dinner. *You'd better not eat like this,* she thought, and then immediately took up a piece of rice-crumbled, tender pork anyway. It was heaven in her mouth, rendered and lean, but rich from its soaking in fat and marrow.

Sam sat next to his uncle and lifted a bit of meat to the old man's lips. Xie chewed the meat and closed his eyes. At first Maggie thought he was happy. But then she saw he swallowed with effort, and refused more. Maggie lowered her chopsticks. She thought these ribs were wonderful. The first batch had been good and this batch was even better. But Sam's uncle was delivering some reasoned, labored criticism. *Oh, please,* she thought. Yet Sam listened intently.

She followed him into the kitchen. "Now what?"

"The flavors are less obvious, but not seamless."

"Isn't there a possibility he's missing the point? There's a symphony of flavor in this dish. It's that matching of flavors you were talking about, what did you call it —"

"*Tiaowei,*" he said.

"Right," she said, as if she remembered, which she did not. "Plus there is the texture. The rice coating is just the right consistency to mellow the feel of the pork. It also rounds out its taste. What is that flavor in the rice powder, anyway? Anise?"

"It's called five-spice. It's a spice blend. Very common here."

"Ah. And then there's the flavor of the lotus leaf. *I* say the ribs are brilliant."

"Thank you." He smiled wearily. "I appreciate that, but I have to make them again. I told him I would. Can you give me just a few minutes? I'm sure you want to go back now. Just let me get this next batch in the steamer and I'll take you. Songling will watch the flame while I'm gone."

"Of course. Take your time. But I'm going to go upstairs, if it's okay, to the room you mentioned before. Can you come get me when you're done?"

"Sure," he said.

"It's a long time since we left Shanghai."

"Was that this morning?" He closed his eyes. "It seems like a month ago."

She nodded.

"Go," he said, and pointed her up the stairs. "When the ribs go in the steamer I'll call you."

At the top, in the second room, she saw Sam's things in a small pile on the bench at the end of the bed. He was neat, but she already knew that.

There was a low light burning. She closed the door and sat on the bed. She kept seeing the elfin face of Shuying, the eyes, the curls. *If you are his, then I'll see his face again.*

It would be days until she found out. Right now she had done all she could. Now was the time to wait, and to be tired. After a few minutes she got up and turned out the light and returned to the bed. She lay down. Instantly quiet and ease settled over her. She thought she had never been anyplace so peaceful as this little Chinese room. She'd just rest there for a second, she decided, but then she closed her eyes and she slept.

Sometime later in the dark she awoke to feel a hand touching her, and she lifted her head, slow and faraway. "Shh," Maggie heard. She opened her eyes.

The door was half-open. Light was coming in from the hallway. Songling was bending over her. Maggie saw her triangular cheeks and chin. *She looks like Uncle Xie,* Maggie thought as she closed her eyes again. She felt Songling pulling her shoes off. *Dear Songling. Thank you.* Then she felt the Chinese woman covering her with a blanket. Warmth settled softly on her. Songling's small steps went out and the door closed, and everything was darkness.

Maggie awoke on the bed. It was late night; dark. Where was she? Yes. She had fallen asleep. It was late now. The whole Xie house was completely still.

She slid off the bed and crept to the window. There were no lights outside, only trees and bamboo, but the moon was full and the pale mercury of it just enough for her to make out the time on her watch.

Three-thirty. Damn. Deep night. Everyone was sleeping. So where was Sam?

She crept to the door and eased it open. The light was still shining in the hall. It hit her harshly and she squeezed her eyes shut a long second before she opened them again. And then she saw him. He was rolled in a blanket at her feet, sleeping.

"Hey," she said. He didn't move. She bent and wrapped a hand around the knob of his shoulder. "Hey, get up."

He lifted himself to his elbows and looked at her. "It's all right," he said. "I'm okay." And he twisted to lie back down.

"No. Come on." She pulled him by the arm until she had him lurching to his feet. She drew him into the room and shut the door. Again the darkness. Good. She steered him to the other side of the bed and he fell, gratefully, going quiet and still again almost instantly. She lay down on the other side and drew the blankets up over them both. They had on all their clothes. He was like a narrow mountain range behind her, one dark-ivory hand curled on the white pillow. She turned her back to him and went to sleep.

When Maggie opened her eyes the sun was pouring in and she heard low, far-off sounds, the clink of dishes, the rise and fall of laughter and Chinese. She drifted her hand out and felt the other side of the bed. It was empty. Now she could hear his clear voice down below, spiking up above the others.

She stepped out of the bed into the warm light. At the sound of her feet on the floor, a flurry of footsteps came down the hall and hands knocked on the door. Immediately the door opened.

It was the three sisters. *"Ni qilai-le,"* said Songling, with the happy air of someone who had grown tired of waiting for Maggie to show some signs of life. They set a towel and washcloth on the bed and then crowded around her, touching her fluffy hair with frank interest. Now that she had spent the night in their house — or maybe it was now that she appeared to have spent the night with the man they knew as their cousin, she wasn't sure — their link had tightened. Songan brought a hairbrush from the drawer. Maggie had to stop her. "No. Never." She took a pick from her tote bag and showed them, and then they all wanted to do it. Songzhe combed out her hair first, then each of the others took a turn. It felt good to Maggie, the hands on her shoulders, the musical sound of their talk, the rhythmic soft pulling against her head. Almost, she could go back to sleep sitting up.

Then she heard Sam's footfall on the stairs. Strange that she knew his step already. He reached the door and knocked and pushed it open, then froze at the sight of the three women around her.

"I'm getting a 'do," Maggie said.

"Ah. I see. Do you want to take a shower? And then we'll have breakfast."

Of course, she thought, another meal. "Does someone else need to use the bathroom?"

"Not now. They're Chinese. They bathe at night. You slept through it."

The sisters got up and trickled out, sly, smiling, as if now was the time for Maggie and Sam to be alone.

"They like you," he said. "They told me so."

"They think we're together."

"No," he said. "I told them we're just friends."

"Well, I'm sorry. I took your room."

"Not in the end," he said.

She stared, suddenly aware that this was a moment that needed to be broken. "Okay," she said, "let me wash. I'll be quick. I'll come right down." And he turned quickly and left.

Breakfast was congee, rice porridge with shreds of a briny, pleasingly marine-flavored waterweed and crunchy, salty peanuts. Hardboiled eggs, pickles, and fluffy steamed buns flecked with scallion surrounded the pot. Two kinds of tea were poured, Dragon Well green, which was Hangzhou's local specialty, and a light, flower-scented oolong that Sam said was from Fujian. The women sat around her, smiling and laughing. They gave her occasional little pats and presses of affection. *He's a good man,* their looks seemed to say. *Take care of him.* They misunderstood, of course. They still thought she was his woman. Even the patriarch sent her an indulgent, welcoming smile. She caught Sam's eye. He shrugged, as if to say he sensed it, but what could he do? Actually she didn't mind;

she liked it. She liked the feeling she had when she was among them.

But soon Sam had to say goodbye. They needed to catch a train in time to make their flight. He embraced everyone for a long time and longest of all his uncle. Maggie embraced them too, pressing her cheek to each of theirs in turn.

They rode down in Songling's car, with Songzhao in the front passenger seat and Maggie and Sam behind, comfortable, leaning back side by side, easy in the green curves of bamboo light. They came to the lake, with its boats and its tree-shaded serenity, and they curled around it for a while until they reached the hotel. The car idled in the big, looping driveway while she ran up and retrieved her bag, rode the elevator down to the lobby, and checked out. She had never used her room.

They turned away from the lake now and into the crowded streets. Traffic crawled between the tall commercial buildings. Songling and Songzhao were talking softly up front in Chinese. Sam was content, tired. His hair was pulled tightly back in his ponytail, but here in the bright daylight of the car she could see the silver strands weaving back from his temples. "What?" he said, looking at her.

"Nothing."

"My gray hair." He reached up and brushed a hand above his ears.

"How did you know I was looking at that?"

"How could I not know? I'm sitting right next to you."

She nodded, but inside she was thinking no, that does not explain it. Because she had been sitting next to people all her life and most of them never had any idea what she was thinking. Even people she knew fairly well. He seemed to know, though, at least sometimes.

"Maggie," he said, a bit tentative. "I wanted to say sorry about last night."

"Sorry why?" she said. "I'm the one who fell asleep in your room."

"I feel bad, though. I wanted to say something to you. I really did mean to spend the night in the hall."

Songling and Songzhao were still talking in the front. Songling let out a little laugh and they went right on in Chinese.

"I like you," Sam said. "I would never want to disrespect you. I went to sleep in the hall *because* I would never do that."

Got to respect the widow, she thought with a flash of hurt. "I wasn't offended," she said.

"Because I would never do that kind of thing lightly," he said. "Never did and never have. Well" — he made a small confessional cringe — "I can't say never. But even though I'm clueless on almost everything, I have managed at least to figure this much out, by this age — that there is nothing casual about people being together that way."

"It wasn't like that," said Maggie. "I made you come in because you were sleeping on the floor. Besides," she added, as they stared out the window side by side, "I would never do that lightly either."

"Okay," he said. The subject was closed. There was a Chinese comic monologue on the radio, punctuated by laughter from a studio audience overlaid by chuckles from the front seat and even, once, a small chortle from Sam. Maggie was getting used to this world she could see around her, the Chinese world, one she could float across like a cloud. It was strange to sense it, to begin to recognize it, but she felt free here. She felt good.

Then they were at the station, and they piled out and hiked the straps of their bags up on their shoulders. Emotional goodbyes went back and forth, and Sam and Maggie exchanged quick embraces with Songling and Songzhao. When she hugged Songling the woman delivered a musical stream of Chinese in her ear, and Maggie gave her an extra squeeze of assent in reply. Whatever Songling said, she agreed with it. Sisterly support. Part of her wanted never to leave, wanted to stay here forever in this place where she couldn't even understand anyone. The car was running. Sam was behind her. She turned away, reluctantly, and followed him up the steps and through the doors that led into the station.

10

Chinese cooking accumulates greatness in the pursuit of artifice. Although we say our goal is *xian,* the untouched natural flavor of a thing, in fact we often concoct that flavor by adding many things which then must become invisible. Thus flavor is part quality of ingredients and part sleight of hand. The latter can go to extremes. The gourmet loves nothing more than to see a glazed duck come to the table, heady and strong with what must be the aromatic *nong* of meat juices, only to find the "duck" composed entirely of vegetables. The superior cook strives to please the mind as well as the appetite.

— L I A N G W E I , *The Last Chinese Chef*

They landed and shared a cab into town and pulled up in front of her building. "Well," he said. A bubble of silence rose between them. They shifted in their seats. Neither had thought of what to say at this moment.

"Okay," she said. She pulled her bag into her lap, ready to get out.

"Look, I'm going to be working like mad now, but if you have any questions —"

"Please," she said, "go ahead, good luck. Don't worry about me."

"Thanks."

"I'm going to start writing."

"You have enough?"

She laughed. "I'll say." She knew perfectly well she didn't need to interview him or even see him again; all she needed was to know the outcome of the contest. She had enough now for three articles. One of her little books was filled almost to capacity with her notes on what she had seen and observed and heard him say; another book held the obsessively careful printed list she always made of everything she had eaten. Never in fact had she accumulated a list so heavily annotated with descriptors, explanations, anecdotes, as this one was. She had enough. Too much. The hardest thing was going to be sorting through it and choosing where to place the spine of her piece. She turned to him. "Do call me, please, after it's over, and let me know how it went. To say I'll be waiting to hear would be a monumental understatement. Five days, right? Saturday night? I'll be burning candles."

"Do some voodoo for me."

"I will, the best voodoo of all. I'll write your story."

He laughed, the open, unexpected laugh that she knew somehow, every time she heard it, was the laugh he had brought with him from home. This was the boy part of him. She liked it. She had liked a lot of things about him these last two days. "Good luck," she said. She took his hands and pressed them between hers, then climbed out of the cab.

Inside the apartment nothing had changed. There was her computer, her suitcase, which she had left behind these last days in favor of a tote. Down the hall was the bedroom where she'd slept with Matt three years before and which she had — admit it — avoided on this trip, staying at night in the living room until she could barely stand, then feeling her way down the hall in the dark and toppling into bed. In the bathroom hung her one towel. Already she had worn her little groove here.

She stood for a while, staring through the darkness at the glittering columns of buildings outside, noticing that she felt different for the first time in many months and interested in the change. It was China maybe, the brash thrill in the air, the unmoored freedom of being far away from her life. Yet it was also the pleasure of the days with Sam in Hangzhou. She still had her grief, but it no longer felt lodged in all her cells and fibers. She had assumed she would grow old with grief, that it would become like her face or her walk or her habits of speech. Now she saw that grief too was a thing that could change.

She turned away from the window and the city. It was time to start work on her piece, even though Sarah had generously told her she did not have to hurry. "Forget your usual deadline," she had said when she called from Los Angeles a few days before. Maggie had explained to her that the competition wouldn't culminate until Sam's banquet on Saturday night, and the article couldn't be filed before it did. "Fine," said Sarah. "Take extra days if you need to. Stay longer. Just get home in time to do your holiday column."

"Are you kidding? Like I'd miss that one." Maggie was famous for her holiday columns, which were petulant triumphs of grinch humor. She hated the holidays. Holidays were about home, which, as a societal concept, she had never really understood. Each year she took her column in exactly the opposite direction, writing about having Christmas dinners at lunch counters, or waking up in cheap hotels in winter beach towns, or cruising convenience stores to see who else, like her, slipped out that day to buy a six-pack and some chips. "Don't worry," she said to Sarah. "I'll be back for the holiday piece."

Now it was time to start on Sam Liang. She moved to the couch with a blank pad, a pen, and her notebooks. She had always worked this way. Before she moved to the computer she began by hand, making a web of all her best thoughts and images and ideas and memories. She read through her notebooks and picked out everything that she loved. That was her first cut; she had to love it. If she didn't love it, why would anybody else?

Then she traced through her jottings to find lines of meaning and pick out moments. When these were repatterned on a fresh page she could usually begin to sense her centerline. Then she would start to write.

Thoughts tumbled easily through her now, and she quickly filled the page with memories of the Xie family. The truth was she had been happy with them, happy for long stretches, hours. She had managed to forget the darkness and feel like she used to feel — like a friend to her life, engaged. It was Sam, yes, and China, but she had to admit that it was the family, too. They had such a net of connectedness between them. Even though it was not hers, rightly, she felt blessed to have been near it and been bathed in it for a while.

She took a fresh sheet of paper, wrote *Guanxi* in the center, and drew a circle around it.

That was it. *Guanxi*.

Then right away she questioned it. Could a column on food really be about the Chinese concept of relationships? But the more she looked at it the more she knew this was the way to write it. Because this was the heart of the cuisine, at least the part Sam had managed to show her. From the family on out, food was at the heart of China's human relationships. It was the basic fulcrum of interaction. All meals were shared. Nothing was ever plated for the individual. She realized this was exactly the opposite from the direction in which Eurocentric cuisine seemed to be moving — toward the small, the stacked, the precious, above all the individual presentation. The very concept of individual presentation was alien here. And that made everything about eating different.

Food was the code of etiquette and the definer of hierarchy too. Sam had made her see that a meal was food but also a presentation of symbols, suggestions, and references, connecting people not only to one another but to their culture, art, and history.

She paused. She wasn't sure — did *guanxi* apply only to the connections between people or to ideas as well? She took a separate sheet of paper and wrote this, her first question for Sam, at the top. Then she set this page aside. They had said goodbye for now; she wasn't going to call him. She wanted to. She found it difficult to get used to being without him. But he needed to work. She would wait.

The next morning when he woke up Sam thought briefly about how much money he had spent on his cell phone this month, then decided that it didn't matter, because this was Uncle Xie. He punched in his father's number. "Please," he said when Liang Yeh answered. "Won't you come? He's asking for you. You still have time."

"Do you think I do not want to?" Liang Yeh lashed back. "It is not easy, this thing you say."

"It's not. I know. It's hard for you."

"You say you know, but you do not."

"Well, if you want me to know, write it down. You've always said you would."

"I already have," said his father.

"What?"

"You heard me. You will see! I will send it to you by e-mail."

"When?" said Sam, thinking, *He may have started, but this could take months.*

"Right now," said Liang Yeh. "My computer is on. Is yours?"

"You already wrote it? You finished it?"

"Yes," said the old man, and a minute later it appeared in Sam's in-box. He could hardly believe it. He had pushed his father for years to write down what had happened. Sam noticed the size of the file. A long document.

He saved it and backed it up, and then put it aside to read later. He had to focus on his menu right now.

It was not just the perfect dishes — and getting those right alone would take all of the next few days — it was the play of the menu itself, its rhythm and its meaning and its layers of reference. On the surface it was a banquet of at least twelve courses, to be staged for the panel on a specific night. It sounded simple, for those were the rules in their entirety. Sam knew, though, that the meal would be judged on so many other levels.

He needed help. He needed sustenance. So he opened *The Last Chinese Chef,* to the section on menu.

⅗ ⅗ ⅗ The menu provides the structure and carries the theme and atmosphere of the dinner. The theme can be witty or nostalgic, literary or rustic. It is developed in the meal like a line of music.

Before beginning, give consideration to opulence. Too much of it is perverse. Yuan Mei said, don't eat with your eyes. But extravagance of some kind or another, whether in ingredients, effort, or talent, belongs in any great meal.

There is no one structure to a feast. Many forms can be used. Yet there is a classical structure, and this can serve as the chef's foundation: four hors d'oeuvres, and four main courses plus soups; or for larger and more extravagant circumstances, eight and eight.

The hors d'oeuvres should amuse while they set the theme of the meal and fix its style. Then the main courses. Start with something fried, light, gossamer thin; something to dazzle. Then a soup, rich and thick with seafood. After that an unexpected poultry. Then a light, healthful vegetable, to clarify, then a second soup, different from the first.

After this you reach the place where the menu goes beyond food to become a dance of the mind. This is where you play with the diner. Here we have dishes of artifice, dishes that come to the table as one thing and turn out to be something else. We might have dishes that flatter the diner's knowledge of painting, poetry, or opera. Or dishes that prompt the creation of poetry at the table. Many things can provoke the intellect, but only if they are fully imagined and boldly carried out.

To begin the final stage the chef serves a roast duck. Then a third soup, again different. The last course is usually a whole fish. The fish must be so good that even though the diners are sated they fall upon it with delight. And then, almost with an air of modest apology because the dishes have been so many, a dessert course is served, something contrived of fruits or beans or pureed chestnuts or even rice, which would only now be making its first appearance at the table as a pudding or a mold, or as a thickener in a sweet bean soup. If the chef's skill is great, no matter how grand the meal has been, this too will quickly be eaten. ❦ ❦ ❦

Sam put down the book. Clearly, he was going to need an underlayer. There had to be a unifying principle. The more he thought, the more he wanted it to be something literary.

What better place to start than with Su Dongpo, the poet? That was what Third Uncle would recommend. He could almost hear the old voice saying it. The pork dish that still carried his name was probably the dish Sam found himself most frequently served when in Hangzhou. When it was right it was perfect in its way, the pork flavor deep and mellow, the fat sweet and soufflé-soft. Simple. The recipe left behind by the poet himself could not have been plainer: a clean pan, the pork, a little water, a low fire, and the willingness to wait. Patience above all. Chefs over the centuries had added the enhancements of soy sauce, wine, spring onions, and ginger in the initial two hours of simmering, then removed the aromatics and bathed the pork in only its juices for four hours of steaming. Correctly prepared, the dish was a triumph of *you er bu ni,* to taste of fat without being oily, paired with *nong,* the dense, meaty, concentrated flavor.

Sam had been thinking of a variation. Why not make the dish in eight-treasure style, steaming it in a mold the same way one made the sweet rice pudding *ba bao fan*? He could pack the pork in with rice, lily buds, ginkgo nuts, dates, cloud ear, dried tofu . . . He could put the braised pork on the bottom, upside down. Keep the fat there. Steam it for four hours. So rich, though, as the rice soaked up the fat; too rich. Maybe he should dislodge the mold slightly, tip it an angle to drain the rendered fat before flipping it over onto a plate.

This notion came from Sam's American half; no Chinese chef would get rid of the fat. But couldn't he achieve *you er bu ni* with a lower proportion of fat? He would have to try it, test it, taste it. That meant making the dish at least five or six times before Saturday. He reached for the paper that held his list and added this new task: figure out how to reduce the fat.

Life in Beijing had changed, after all. Fat had once been a critical part of the local diet, and for good reason. Never in Ohio had he felt anything so bone-cracking cold as the frigid Beijing winter. In earlier times the open-air style of the capital's traditional courtyard homes provided little protection. Heating systems had been localized — the *kang,* or family bed, built over fire-fed flues, the braziers that defended only parts of rooms against the icy wind from the north. Many people back then had simply worn heavily padded clothing during all their waking hours, inside and out. They loved and needed the fat in their food. Then there were the poor people, who ate mostly *cu cha dan fan,* crude tea and bland rice. Meat was too expensive to serve as a major source of calories, so they ate fat to fill out their diet. As these shadows of the past had come clear to Sam through his years in the city, he understood more and more why heart-clobberingly fatty dishes like *mi fen rou,* a lusciously savory steamed mold of rice, lard, and minced pork, had been longtime favorites. But people had central heat now. Even the lowest laborers ate animal protein. It was high time, Sam decided, to drain some of the fat.

Learning about the food of Beijing had been one of the side pleasures of his four years here. Historically, the capital seemed to have drawn its main culinary influence from the Shandong style. With an emphasis on light, clear flavor and subtle accents such as scallion, this cuisine gave birth to at least one somewhat distant descendant that became well known in the West, wonton soup. When done right, this soup was typical of Shandong style in its clarity and its fresh, natural flavor.

Yet the cuisine of Beijing was also the cuisine of the imperial court. From the Mongols to the Manchus, successive dynasties brought the flavors of their homelands. Certain rulers, such as the Qianlong Emperor in the eighteenth century, expended considerable energy seeking out great dishes from all corners of the nation, going so far as to travel incognito in order to sample these dishes at their original restaurants and street stalls. Qianlong was even said to have boarded a lake boat poled by a simple woman, and to have paid her to cook for him. Any dish that interested the Emperor was immediately tackled by a team of chefs. In this way the food of every province became part of the palace kitchen. These things Sam had learned from reading *The Last Chinese Chef.*

What had happened to food in the decades since his grandfather's book was published also interested him. As Beijing had grown and molted, especially during the building frenzy that began in the early 1990s, the city was awash in migrant labor. Construction could not proceed without it; in this respect China was much like America. But in China the migrants didn't come from other countries; they came from rural areas and remote provinces. As workers from Sichuan flooded in, restaurants, cafés, and stalls opened, and soon Beijingers developed a taste for *hua jiao,* prickly ash, Sichuan peppercorn. It became a hot condiment; everyone had it in their kitchens. Workers from Henan brought their *hong men yang rou,* stewed lamb; those who came from Gansu brought *Lanzhou la mian,* Lanzhou-style beef noodles; and from Shaanxi came *yang rou pao mo,* a soup of lamb and unleavened bread. From the northeast came *zhu rou dun fen tiao,* stewed pork with pea or potato starch noodles, and *suan cai fen si,* sour cabbage with vermicelli.

Then there was the food of the far northwest, which was Islamic. In the 1980s, along with the first inroads of privatization, illegal money-changing bloomed. Waves of Uighur migrants from Xinjiang were drawn to Beijing, where they helped revive street-food culture with their signature kebabs and dominated the black market in currency. They also left a lasting stamp on the food of the capital, with their great round wheels of sesame flatbread, their grilled and stir-fried lamb, and their incredibly fragrant Hami melons.

Sam brought his attention back to the steamed *dongpo* pork and rice dish he had in mind; yes, he would drain the fat. He knew enough about food now. He had the confidence. When he steamed it and turned it over he'd have a rich, deep brown dome of treasure-studded rice with the pork now on top, cut into the exact squares so important to the dish, the precision of the shape setting off the softness of the flavor.

Of course he would have to leave at least a thin layer of fat. For the Chinese gourmet, it was everything. It should be light and fragrant, with a *xian* taste like fresh butter. It should melt on the tongue like a cloud, smooth, *ruan,* completely tender. Sam knew he would have to make the fat perfect. Before beginning the simmer he would salt-rub the meat to draw out the flavors that were too heavy, and then he'd blanch it several times for clarity.

He put a stack of CDs on shuffle-play and set to work. He felt happy for the first time since he left Uncle Xie, since he held the papery body to him and felt the stale breath of the dying on his cheek. His uncle was going to go soon, but he would want Sam to cook, to make a great dish like this one. They had said the last goodbye. He put the square of pork on the board and rubbed it with coarse salt.

Carey was in his office worrying when Maggie called. His mother was in the hospital again back in Connecticut, and she was failing. He had to weigh whether to fly back. It was not the first time. He had flown back several times before. Each time, they had said goodbye, and he had told himself that the next time, even if it looked like the end, he would not return. Still.

In so many ways Beijing was starting to feel too far away from his old life, from the person he used to be. It was not just his mother, now dying, and his sister and her sons, now in elementary school — it was his friends, too. He was gregarious. People were an asset he had always known how to accumulate. He had made enemies as well — a few — but these were not so much kept as discarded along the way. He had little trouble blocking them from his mind and heart. Carey went out of his way to maintain a positive picture of himself, and accordingly it was not his practice to look at his dark spots. He covered them with many, many friends. Quite a few lived in America. As he grew older and lived farther away, he should have missed them less, but the opposite happened. He thought of them more. Perhaps it was because his links with his old friends still felt untarnished. He had been a younger man when he knew them, more generous, more true.

He should move back. This thought came to him often lately, but he never did much. What he had here was far too pleasing. At first Carey had seen only the obvious freedoms, the ones that had made Matt so wild so quickly. In time Carey understood that China would allow a man to re-create himself, from the inside out, as someone new. A foreigner could make of this world what he wanted. For some it was the unimaginable wealth one had in the local economy, for others the success with women. He'd even seen some who came to China as modern ascetics; those were the respectful ones who donned the shabby clothes of the scholar and disappeared into rented rooms in the *hutongs,* the back lanes, to learn Chinese. Whatever one's dream picture, China, incessantly indulging Westerners even as it did not fundamentally welcome them, provided the frame.

The trouble was, eventually the dream was over. One woke up. Morosely he fiddled with his phone.

The receptionist called through to him to say Maggie was here. "Send her back," he said.

As soon as she walked in, he saw that she looked different. Her eyes had been circled by care and sadness. Now she looked almost glad. "Congratulations," he said. She had every reason to feel good.

"Thank you. Here are the permissions, signed." She passed the pages across the desk. "I've kept copies. In six more days I'll hear from the lab."

"That's quick!"

"I paid for rush service. And I shipped it from Hangzhou instead of bringing it back here."

"Smart," he said. "So." He folded his hands. "Did you see her?"

"Yes."

"Did she look like Matt?"

"That was a strange thing," she said. "No. At least at first I didn't think so. She's a big-eyed, pretty little thing. She looks like an elf. None of the gravity Matt's face had. But then — I couldn't understand anything she said, of course — there'd be a certain light in her eyes, a way of turning her head and looking, and I'd be stabbed by this feeling, Carey, I mean stabbed. Really. Like it was him."

He felt a bolt of sadness, listening to her. She could so easily have been imagining things. "Lucky you're getting the results so fast."

"Yes," she said. "But talking about that — seeing Shuying did make me wonder. What did she look like, Gao Lan? Do you remember?"

"I think so," he said. She may have sounded casual, but he was not fooled. Any wife would bide her time, pretend not to care, and then pounce when the moment was right to ask. "She had an old-fashioned kind of Chinese look, an oval face, like a woman in a painting."

"What did she do?"

"If I remember correctly, she was a midlevel office worker. There are so many young women with modest English skills like her in Beijing. I didn't know much about her."

"How old?" said Maggie.

"Let me think. By now I suppose thirty, or thirty-two."

He watched Maggie absorb this. Surely she must have guessed that Gao Lan was not as old as she.

"So," said Maggie, "explain this to me. Why, all this time, has Shuying been raised by the grandparents?"

"Oh. That's very common here. A lot of people do this. Historically all the generations lived together, in one compound — not now, now they live apart, but many grandparents still take care of the children. They say, if you need an *ayi*, why give away money to a stranger? Give to your own parents."

"But Gao Lan works so far away."

"Perhaps she can't make a living in Shaoxing."

"Her living — that's another thing we learned. She's working at a logistics company. We didn't get the name. Just, logistics."

He made a note. "That's pretty broad. Find out anything else?"

"Yes. You sitting down? You ready?" She leaned forward. "Matt wasn't the only man. Gao Lan was seeing another foreigner at the same time. The grandparents believe the chances of Shuying being Matt's are only fifty-fifty."

"How could you know that?"

"The grandparents said so."

"I can't believe they'd tell you that."

"They didn't know they were telling us. My friend pretended not to speak Chinese. They provided a translator — and then they spoke with complete freedom in front of us."

"Oh." He smiled at her, admiring. She had guts. "Your friend is Chinese? Or Western?"

"Half," she said.

"Ah. A woman?"

"A man."

"I see." He looked Maggie over again. Maybe this was the reason for the lift of spirit he had noticed when she walked in. Good. He would like to see her get her soul back. Why? he wondered. Maggie was not really his friend. He had liked her when he met her three years before, but that was because she came with Matt, and Matt had become his friend in the course of the all-night rambles that had taken them to the very edges of what the Chinese called the *guiding*, the fixed rules. *Don't worry, I'll keep your secrets,* Carey had said to him. Naturally this meant he might someday have to lie to Matt's wife, but since he didn't know her back then, it was easy to promise. Now Matt was gone, and he was helping the wife — of course. It was his job. *Shi wo yinggai-de,* he thought, one of the first simple Chinese expressions he had learned, It's what I should do.

He opened the file in front of him, slid the permissions into it. In the beginning and the end, he was a lawyer. He was always grateful for the way structure held things together. He drew out a sheet he'd prepared.

"I think you'll feel better once you see this," he said. "Maybe you're right and there's only a half-half chance the girl is his, but let's just say she is. I figured out that your exposure isn't as high as you think. Matt left you the house, right?"

"Yes —"

"I hope you don't mind that I looked all this up. It wasn't hard. The firm handled the will, after all. So — the life insurance was enough to pay off the house. And you did that. Right? That's what it says here. Paid off the house."

"Yes —"

"That means you're in good shape. If you hadn't paid off the house, I'd be worried. Where you're exposed is in what's liquid. See? Your primary residence is off-limits. So if everything he left you is invested there, you don't have to worry, no matter what happens. They can't touch it."

"The house," she said.

"Right."

"I sold the house."

A silence. "But you bought another," he answered. It was one of those hopeful statements that stops just short of being a question.

"No."

"Then where do you live?"

"A little place I rented." *How* little, she knew he couldn't imagine, so she left it at that.

"Where's the money?" he said.

"In cash."

His voice tightened up. "Then you can lose half of everything."

"Clearly," she said. "But first of all, that's only if she's his daughter. And if she's his daughter, why is that losing? She *should* have it."

"Half of everything? In cash?" He withdrew the spreadsheet and put it away, realizing she wasn't even going to look at it. "I can't believe you're saying that."

"Well, I am."

"Am I wrong? Or do you sound like you actually wouldn't mind a match from the lab too much?"

"It's not like that. Some things you don't get to mind or not mind. They just *are*. Maybe that's what's changed — I met Shuying. She's not theoretical anymore. She's a kid. If she's Matt's, I'll take care of her. I can't believe you'd even suggest I do anything else."

He bristled faintly in response. "There *are* degrees, you know. Anyway. Maybe she's his. And maybe she's not. If she's not, that's it. We get rid of the claim and we're done."

"And Shuying?"

"Then Shuying is not our problem. They file against the other guy. At that point it's none of your business."

"What if they need help doing that?"

"Maggie," he reproved her.

"I don't want the kid left out in the cold."

"Stop. Get the test back. Then we'll talk."

"All right," she said, "but only for now. Until I hear." She rummaged in her purse and came up with the newspaper clipping. "I brought this to show you. Did you ever see it? It was in the news after Matt died."

Carey looked at it and felt his heart contract. There was Matt, the man by whose side he had prowled the magical night and returned, again and again, to the rigor of day. There was Matt on the ground, stilled, splayed. Purses and briefcases were scattered around. Carey had imagined Matt's death so many times, seen it, thought of it. Now here it was, the street corner, the crowd. Pain crept up and stung at him. People clustered around Matt in the picture. A woman bent over him, caught by the camera looking up, eyes frightened wide.

The woman. He stopped. His skin felt like it was going to lift right off his body.

"What is it?" Maggie asked.

He pointed to the grainy, shaded picture. "That woman there? See?"

"I see," said Maggie. The woman bending over Matt, yes, she had seen her a thousand times. Studied her face. "Nobody ever got her name. I'd have given anything to talk to her. Maybe he said something, at the end. If he did I'd like to know. But nobody knew who she was."

"I may."

His voice was a thin, hesitant thread, but it made her head snap up.

"It's just possible —"

"What?" Maggie felt all the air go out of her, leaving nothing.

"This is not a good picture. It's not clear. Maybe I shouldn't say anything. But." He brought the tip of his finger to the grainy uplift of the woman's face. "I think you should prepare yourself for the possibility that this could very well be . . ." He swallowed. "It looks like Gao Lan."

Maggie burst out the front door of the building like somebody swimming up from the deep, holding it in, lungs screaming for air, her heart refusing, denying. On the sidewalk she could not get her breath. Everyone passing her was safe in a group, twos and threes and fours. She jostled and bumped among them, the only one alone. She'd had a pattern in her life once, a pattern of two. Her and Matt. No more.

If Gao Lan was with him the day he died, everything shifted. The wheel turned again. That meant they had a relationship. Then there was a much better chance Shuying was his, or at least that he *believed* she was his. If he even knew. Did he know? Maggie followed this scenario several moves down her mental game board. Matt may have known nothing of the other guy. He may have known only that his own timing had been right. That would have been enough. His generous nature, his goodness, would have done the rest. That and how much he was starting to want a child of his own. So maybe he knew, after all. Maybe he lied to Maggie more than she wanted to believe.

She felt she was falling down a dark hole. The man she'd always thought she'd known, who had lived in her memory all this past year, was ebbing. In his place there had materialized another, darker one, a shadow of her husband, a man who kept secrets and was divided. *Ask me,* he seemed to be saying to her. *Ask me what really happened.*

And yet she had known him, had she not? Was he not real then? He had been good. *Remember that too.*

She remembered the day she started bleeding mid-month, two years ago, a year before he died; she knew instantly something was not right. She called the doctor and they said to come in. She called Matt, just to let him know. He insisted that he would take her and she should wait there until he arrived.

He came in thirty minutes, calming her, encircling her, bundling her into the car. In the doctor's office he stood next to her with his large-knuckled hand cupping her shoulder. She had fibroids, the doctor said. Bed rest until the heavy bleeding stopped. No getting up except to go to the bathroom.

"I'll take care of her," said Matt.

"It should stop within twelve hours, or call me. By the way, these don't tend to get better. And they can complicate pregnancy. So if you're going to have kids you might want to do it soon." He glanced at the chart. "You're thirty-eight," he said to Maggie, and to Matt he said, "You're . . . ?"

"Forty-two."

"I see," said the doctor. "Well."

Maggie felt she might cry.

Matt saw. "Thank you," he said, his voice firm. "We appreciate what you said." He talked the doctor out of the room, steered Maggie out the door and to the car, took her home, and put her to bed. For a long time, even though it was the middle of the afternoon, he lay on the bed beside her. "Don't feel bad," he said. "He doesn't know us. Nothing matters but the two of us, what we think."

"Everyone in the world is in league against me. They all think I should have your child."

"None of that," he said. He was serious. No more silly jokes. When they first started to wrestle with this she had often taken refuge behind amusing, deflective ironies — *Children? But I can barely stand to have wineglasses! How could I have children?* — but that time was past. "Listen to me," he said that day on the bed. He laid his hand on her midsection. "You're the one I want. That hasn't changed. Yes, it's true, I want a child too. But not as much as I want you. Even if you say no, never, out of the question — I might not like that too much, but I'm still not going anywhere. You're my wife."

She had cried then, letting out everything she'd held in before, seeing love, feeling it. And now she had Carey telling her Gao Lan might have been with Matt when he died. Maybe.

Anger rose in her, hissing through her brain. She snapped open her phone and dialed Zinnia. "We have to find Gao Lan," she said.

"Something happen?" Zinnia was on the floor of her apartment, playing with her two-year-old son. At the sound of Maggie's voice she sat straighter and pushed her hip black glasses higher up on the small, prim bridge of her nose. She held the boy loosely while she listened. When Maggie had finished she said, "Do you think it can be her?"

"How can I know? He thinks so — maybe — and he's the only person I happen to know who's ever seen her. We have to find someone else who knew her. We have to find *her*."

"You're right," said Zinnia. "I will try even harder. Already I have been to many offices in the Sun Building, where Carey said she used to work." Inside, Zinnia thought of Carey. He was going to have to help now. She had asked him to call one or two of his former female friends. Some were likely to know Gao Lan, and those who didn't knew others, and somewhere on that chain was a Beijinger who knew where Gao Lan was right now. And knew why no one in her old work circle had seen her in the last three years. Logistics, was what Carey had passed on from Maggie. That could mean many things. It was not enough. They needed someone who knew.

Yet when she had pressed Carey about these women, he evaded her. "I've fallen out of touch with her," he said of one, and "It was not good the last time we spoke; I can't call her," of another.

Zinnia was a composed professional who always observed propriety, and there were certain questions she would never ask of a man at work. His private life was not her business. Still, it was obvious something was wrong, for he was well past forty and not yet married. This was an aberration. She didn't know why he remained this way. He was not an invert; he liked women. Maybe too much. Maybe that was the problem.

The direction of life was important. She believed all men and women should marry and make families. That Carey did not do this, that he grew older and continued prowling the world of love, had at first seemed to Zinnia merely American. In time, though, after meeting a number of others from his country, she realized it was not a national trait but individual to him. She watched him with fascination, wondering always which girl would fall for him next. He was appealing, in a rangy yellow-haired kind of way, but he was old. The skin on his face was loosening. Still he drew women, though he always seemed to break with them before they knew him well enough to really see him. Perhaps, Zinnia had concluded, it was that he did not want to be seen.

The door jingled and her husband came in, flush from the climb up three flights, string bags of vegetables and a fish for their dinner bouncing against his legs. He put the food down and beamed as the little boy toddled to him. She watched them with love. "We'll find her," she said to Maggie on the phone, her eyes on her two men. "We'll make sense of everything. There *is* a pattern. Always. We just have to see it."

When Sam had finished reading the long document in his father's jumpy, idiosyncratic English, he went back to the start and began to smooth it out. It went quickly, since this time there was no need to compare the approximated English with an original text in characters. He liked doing it, just as he liked working with his father on the translations; it was the only way they had ever really collaborated. When he was done, he felt close to the old man, sure they'd be able to talk. He called him again.

"Ba," he said when Liang Yeh picked up, "I love what you sent me. Can we make it the epilogue of the book?"

"Maybe."

"Think about it. But Baba. What happened to you is not unique. Everybody had a bad time — but it's the past. I can't say it's not cynical here, and internally bankrupt in a certain way; it is. Maybe that's what's left, now, of everything that's happened: nobody believes anymore. But as far as life goes, and whether it's safe or not — believe me, they have left all that behind."

"Do you think I have no heart?" Liang Yeh shot back. "I do what I can. Do you know how often I call Little Xie now? Every day! That's right! Do you know how much that costs?"

Sam heard fumbling, and then his mother came on the line. "Sammy," she said, "I know it's hard. But let him be."

He hung up, disappointed. He read his father's story through again. It wasn't enough just to read it. He wanted to show it to someone.

Various friends went through his mind. The one he kept coming back to was Maggie. She had been to Hangzhou. She had met the Xie family. She would know.

He rooted in his pocket for her card with her e-mail address. No. He didn't know where he had put it. He took out his phone to call her.

At that time Maggie was scrolling down her computer screen through all the e-mail messages Matt had sent her, everything from the last two years of his life. For the first time she was thinking about blocking them and deleting them, all of them. There was no backup. She could erase him. Push all this out of her life once and for all.

She blocked them. They all turned blue.

Her phone rang.

She didn't want to answer. She was busy. This was important. She was getting rid of Matt. But the small screen said it was Sam Liang.

"Hello," she said, "can you wait a minute?"

"Sure."

Carefully she clicked through the sequence until she had unblocked the messages and exited the program. If she deleted them, she wanted it to be when she was paying full attention. Not now, with someone on the phone. "Okay," she said to Sam, "I'm back." There was a vulnerability in her voice, but she covered it. "How are you?"

"Fine," he said. And then: "What's wrong?"

"Nothing."

"Maggie," he said.

"You have so much to do. You don't want to hear my problems."

"I'm asking," he said.

Still she hesitated. Infidelity and lies had a taint to them; she knew telling him could be a mistake. But he already knew half the story. "There is this picture from the news, of my husband's accident. You can see Matt on the ground, part of Matt, dead, and a woman leaning over him."

"What part of Matt?"

"His feet and legs."

"Okay," said Sam slowly, as if visualizing it.

"This woman. Nobody ever got her name. It was odd because usually people like that come forward. But then today I happened to show the picture to this guy in the law firm here. He thinks he recognizes her. He thinks it's Gao Lan."

"With your husband when he *died?*"

"That's what he says."

"Is he sure?"

"No. The face is not distinct."

He was silent with her for a minute, or at least his voice was silent. She could hear him chopping. She liked that they could be quiet together. It was like being in a room doing things, different things, two people in proximity but separately productive. It had been that way with Matt, even if they needed their time apart to keep it working.

"I feel like I can't think about anything else but finding her. It's like with Shuying, where I had to get the sample, I had to see her face, but even more powerful. I need to see for myself what kind of woman this is."

He was silent for a minute. "I just hope when you do see her, it's going to make you feel better."

"It's always better to know." Maggie needed to place the woman in her ladder of esteem, drink in her aura of looks and personality, judge her. She needed to steady herself that even if this woman had attracted her husband's attention she still was no match for Maggie. That she had never been. It was basic female power restoration.

"I can't believe it when I hear myself," she said to Sam Liang. "I tell you the most personal things."

"I like that," he protested.

"I think I've told you too much."

"Why? I'll tell you one about me. Will that make you feel better?"

"Yes."

"All right. This happened right after we came back from Hangzhou. By the way, it was strange, wasn't it? Coming back from Hangzhou. After being together for two days. Always the two of us, and then boom."

"It was strange," she agreed, glad he had said it.

"So we came back. I called my father. I told him this was it, Uncle Xie was dying, please come. Get over your fears. He needs you. And by way of explaining why he couldn't, he sent me the story of his life, up to the time he escaped from China. As if I was going to read this and say, Oh, Dad, I see now, you're right, this was so bad you should definitely never come back to China. But I didn't feel that way. I called him and said, I understand, but really, you are safe, nothing will happen, and please please come see Xie before he dies. You must. Please. I begged him."

She felt a pang for him. "Did it work?"

"No. He said no."

"I'm sorry."

"Even me, his son, asking like that, it wasn't enough."

"You can't change him. I don't know what his deal is, but most likely it's beyond your reach."

"You're right."

"At least now you have his story."

"It was worth the wait."

"Will you send it to me?" said Maggie.

"Yes! That's why I called you, if you want to know the truth. I want you to read it. But I can't find your e-mail."

"Send it," said Maggie, and dictated her address.

He moved over to his computer and clicked a button. "There. I just e-mailed it. Let me know what you think."

"I will." She felt a little better, talking to him. The way he was, the way he thought, left her feeling lifted. He reminded her of the world beyond herself. What was more, he had the makings of a great cook. She felt he deserved this prize with every inch of his soul. "Do you know what I want more than anything?" she said. "I want you to win. I want you to have this."

She could hear a smile in his voice. "Then for you I will try to get it."

"Not for me! For your family."

"Okay," he said. "For them."

11

The most important thing is to preserve civilization. As men we are the sum of our forebears, the great thinkers, great masters, great chefs. We who know the secrets of food must pass them on, for our attainment in food is no less than our attainment in philosophy, or art; indeed, the three things cannot be separated. These are the things that make us Chinese. In the West, it is different. There, Plato is one of their favorite sages. He teaches them that food is the opposite of art, a routine undertaken to satisfy human need, no more — worse, a form of flattery. We Chinese look instead to the Analects of Confucius, where it is written that there is "no objection to the finest food, nor the finest shredding."

— LIANG WEI, *The Last Chinese Chef*

⁑ ⁑ ⁑ I was born to my father late. He may have been one of the great chefs of his time and written a book that made him gastronome to a generation, yet he did not have a son — not at least until his wife died in 1934 and he at last — for he had long ignored the urgings of his friends — took a second. He could have done it sooner. Many men in those days did. They chose a concubine. Liang Wei could have done it without raising an eyebrow, for his wife had proved barren, but he never did. He wanted to be modern. He was a traditional chef, a product of the Forbidden City, of feudalism, but he would not take a second.

And then she died. He put on a grand funeral, more than he could afford. The sutras were chanted for forty-nine days. When Qingming came in the spring, the day of Pure Brightness on which the dead are honored, he offered his prayers at her grave. Then he sent for the matchmaker.

He wanted someone young, he told the older woman, but not too young. He wanted wide hips for bearing. And he wanted a girl who could cook. Someone had to oversee his kitchen at home while he ran his restaurant. His own hired cook was not enough. For my father, even the food at home had to scale the heights. He was one for whom every mouthful, even the most insignificant snack with tea, was worthy of talent and attention.

Wang Ma the matchmaker brought him my mother, age twenty-four. Her name was Chao Jing, Surpassing Crystal. She didn't look anything like her name. She was a plain jug of a girl with a flat, freckled nose. Yet her eyes sparkled with intelligence and humor. She was strong in the kitchen and superlative at the market, the latter a skill for which my father had not dared to hope. No one could outdo her, not even Ah Heng, the hired cook. It was Ah Heng's right to do the shopping. He gained a critical slice of his income through the small commission he took on each purchase and, like so many cooks in Peking then, he had used that little cash stream to build up a gambling operation that he ran in his family home nearby. Despite all that, he would step aside sometimes and let my mother shop. She cared about food; the vendors knew it and they loved her. They all wanted to please her. She always brought home superior ingredients at a lower price.

And she ran a great kitchen. I think often of the banquets my father served at home almost every night, taking a few hours' leave from the restaurant to come home and dine — great meals that he could never have staged without Ah Heng and above all my mother. Even if the meal was a simple one, even if the guests were few, he always expended as much care and love on each dish as if he were entertaining Yi Yin himself, the greatest chef in history, who like him started as a slave. He would think many days ahead and call together friends whom he loved. He would send out a poem of invitation. All the recipients would fall into a passion of expectation. There would be a thematic reason to gather: the Osmanthus Festival, the anniversary of the birth of a poet, the first crabs of the season. Guests might present a painting or a work of calligraphy to accompany the meal. Remarks on cuisine would lead naturally to remarks on poetry, the two subjects sharing to a surprising degree both vocabulary and a style of critical expression. Eventually poems themselves would be invented, inspired by food, lubricated by wine.

People think of the history of cuisine as being a story that is told in restaurants, but in China it is very much told in the kitchens of the great houses. It was true of my father. His reputation had three legs, like the bronze vessels of yore. There was his famous book, there was the restaurant, and there was the cuisine of his home and family. Sometimes I felt that his home kitchen on Houhai was where he really created his food, with his wife shopping and helping. This was his real child in life, his bequest: Liang Jia Cai. Liang Family Cuisine.

Preparations for the evening meal started early in the day. I learned there was no better place to be than behind my mother on the way to market, weaving under the crystal autumn light through the crowd on Hata Men, soaked in the gay chatter and the golden laughter and the calls and whistles of the sweets vendors with their bright, fluttering flags. The world was a festival to me, one that could not be dampened even by the Japanese occupation with its columns of soldiers and its strange kimonoed women. Once we got to the market we were back in our own world, the Chinese world, and we chose with unfettered joy from the capons and bamboo shoots, water shields and fresh duck eggs, prawns, succulent live river eels, wild herbs from the marshy estuaries of the south, and three colors of amaranth. Walking home we would sing songs.

As I grew, my father and Ah Heng let me watch them cook. They loved having me there, even if they usually grumbled and shouted me out of the way. Then one or the other would hiss me over to his side, pull out a secret ingredient — some crumbled herb or paper-wrapped bit of paste — from his pocket, send out an exaggerated, theatrical pretense of a glance to make sure the other wasn't looking, and then add it to the dish. As if they had anything hidden from each other. But each loved the special surge of face that came from imparting a rare secret, and so they played the game. And I learned.

Some evenings, when the meal was over and the guests had gone home, my father would sit a while in the kitchen. He would smoke a little tobacco in Ah Heng's water pipe and tell stories of the Forbidden City while the kitchen was cleaned.

At those times, depleted from yet another elegantly conceived and crafted meal, he often spoke most yearningly of the rustic. To hear him then, nothing was better than plain, everyday foods. He would insist that true cuisine was the perfect preparation of the simplest food, though we all knew he did not cook that way.

He also told us how the Empress Dowager Ci Xi would make periodic demands for the rustic road food she was forced to eat when they fled from the Boxer Rebellion. This was part of the lore of the palace and taught to Liang Wei in the most meticulous fashion by his own master, the renowned imperial chef and antiquities connoisseur Tan Zhuanqing. Master Tan taught my father to make *xiao wo tou*, the rough little thimble-shaped corn cakes that the Empress remembered her bearers buying from vendors along the road, stopping their bumpy caravan in the flapping wind of a mountain pass to eat them, tiny and hot. Years later she would call for them when she wanted to feel alive again. She had been ordinary for a moment, almost poor, outside in the open air like any lowly person. Strangely, of all her memories, it was one of the most thrilling.

My father used to say he detected a smirk on the face of Tan Zhuanqing when he prepared *xiao wo tou* for the Empress. Like many Chinese dishes, *xiao wo tou* has a second layer of meaning beyond how it looks and smells and tastes. Indeed, in the decades that followed, among food people the dish acquired a certain connotation. To cook *xiao wo tou*, to serve it, even to refer to it, was to speak of China's Marie Antoinette. Ci Xi cared nothing for her people. Her reign brought a system that had endured thousands of years to its end. Father taught us that when we made *xiao wo tou* we were making reference to the worst kind of imperial disregard for the common people, and so we must be extraordinarily careful where and when we served them. Delightful and rustic mouthfuls, they were also powerful political statements and could bring about a chef's downfall. Be careful, he told us.

I never made them outside the house. In fact, after I went to work in the restaurant at sixteen, I never made them again.

When I began in the restaurant in 1951, the government was getting ready to close down the industry. Liang Jia Cai was a favorite of everyone, even party royalty. They loved dining there. They always commanded the best tables. So our place was one of the last to go.

I made the most of my few years at Liang Jia Cai, adding eight dishes that became top sellers. People started to say that the Last Chinese Chef would have a successor after all. I gave an interview in the new state-run pictorial magazine. Father was pleased. He worked with me every day to show me as many of the old dishes as he could remember.

In 1954 our door was closed. They chose a final few restaurants to stay open for officials and guests of state, and shuttered the rest. At first Father was livid that ours was not one of the few left open. Yet we were lucky. A few years later, to run an imperial-style restaurant, even one sanctioned by the Communist state, would become very dangerous. This fate he was spared.

When Liang Jia Cai was closed I was transferred to Gou Bu Li in Tianjin. It was a lucky placement, for Tianjin was not far, only 120 kilometers, and I could visit my parents often in their last years. The restaurant itself was one of the most famous eating places in all of China, but it was a dumpling house. There were few more proletarian foods. Even the name, which grew from the nickname of the original chef and meant A Dog Ignores It, gave the feeling of roughness. I was told they served many types of dumplings before liberation, but when I was there they made only their original steamed stuffed bun, filled with either meat or cabbage. That was all right. A great dish can be made with a cabbage. The best food can rest on the simplest ingredients. And there is nothing higher in its way than a fragrant, light-as-a-cloud meat bun. I made these day after day, week after week, for four years. I lived in the commune attached to the restaurant. We cooks had all been transferred there from other places, without families; we lived in the work unit. We slept in a long, low room with two lines of bunks. It was the best place in the world for me to hide.

My parents died within a year of each other and I had no one in the world except Jiang and Tan and Xie; though sworn brothers we were separated by both time and distance. I lost myself in the great kitchens of Gou Bu Li, which were divided into massive stations for each stage of production. There were the great floury, stone-topped dough surfaces, ringed with workers kneading, mixing, then turning out the perfect circles of half-leavened dough. There were the rows of supersized chopping blocks where the filling was minced and seasoned. There were the wrappers and crimpers with their gigantic shallow bowls of filling and their stacks of wrappers, constantly replenished. There was the cooking: the racks and racks of enormous bamboo steamers, each holding eighty, a hundred, a hundred and fifty *baozi*. I kept my head down. Like so many people at that time, I grasped that the key to survival was invisibility. My only goal was to live. I kept to myself.

Others were not so lucky. First Xie's father went to prison. Then old Ah Heng, my father's home cook, was denounced. I was drawing every breath in fear. I was a Liang, son of the famous Liang who'd written *The Last Chinese Chef*. It was only a matter of time. I trembled every day, waiting.

The first sign was a change in the red-character poster that had long been displayed in the kitchens. The old poster exhorted us to serve the masses with exemplary dumplings. Who would not want to do that? But then this vanished, and a new one appeared, filled with a denser text. I recognized it immediately. It was a passage from the writings of Chairman Mao.

Sumptuous feasts are generally forbidden. In Shaoshan, Xiangdan County, it has been decided that guests are to be served with only three kinds of animal food, namely, chicken, fish, and pork. It is also forbidden to serve bamboo shoots, kelp, and lentil noodles. In Hengshan County it has been resolved that eight dishes and no more may be served at a banquet. Only five dishes are allowed in the East Third District in Liling County, and only three meat and three vegetable dishes in the North Second District, while in the West Third District New Year feasts are forbidden entirely. In Xiangxiang County, there is a ban on all "egg-cake feasts," which are by no means sumptuous . . . In the town of Jiamu, Xiangxiang County, people have refrained from eating expensive foods and use only fruit when offering ancestral sacrifices.

I looked at the bottom — "Mao's Report on an Investigation of the Peasant Movement in Hunan," March 1927. Thirty-one years before. But I knew exactly why it was being posted now. Everyone knew. We were used to messages sent through historical symbolism. It was a signal. There was a shift. Those who had known privilege were in danger.

If you went by what comrades were willing to say, everyone at Gou Bu Li came from a peasant or worker background. We were all completely proletarian. But everyone knew it was not true. Each learned to keep silent about his or her own past while avidly listening for clues or simmering talk about everyone else.

So I waited. I watched. I knew something was going to happen.

When it came, it was in the form of an order for food. I was in the kitchen, in the thrum of almost one hundred cooks, at my station, which was for wrapping. Wrapping was the most difficult, the most pleasing, the most subtle part of making Gou Bu Li's *baozi*. Each glossy-white bun had to be in the shape of a tight-budded chrysanthemum, closed at the top with no less than eighteen pleats. Mine were perfect. I worked with care. I kept my eyes down.

One of the waiters from upstairs approached. "Comrade Liang?"

"I am he." I did not interrupt my pleating rhythm.

"There is a special order from a table upstairs."

I looked up. There were no special orders. Just *baozi,* pork and cabbage. "What is it?"

"They made me repeat it. They said they wanted *xiao wo tou.*"

"*Ei?* Say that again."

"*Xiao wo tou.* They said it was your specialty."

"Nonsense," I said. "Never heard of it. Don't know what it is." Though I did, exactly.

"They said you would know," he said.

He was young, the skin on his face tight as a plum. "Listen," I said, "you go back. Tell them you are sorry, we don't make that at this restaurant. What are you standing there for? Go!" And I watched him scuttle off.

I did not see the boy again that night. When we finished I cleaned my area quickly and returned to the bunk room in time to roll up my few articles of clothing and hide them under my pillow. My *hukou,* my household registration, which gave me the right to exist in China, a home, a place in the pattern — this I left in its sewn-in pouch in my inner pocket. Later I would have to find a way to get rid of it.

I washed thoroughly, scrubbing every patch of myself, thinking it was possible I might never wash again. I crept back into the bunk room after the lights were out, so nobody saw me hoist into my bunk with all my clothes on, even my shoes.

I lay as quiet as a stone while the moon rose over the Tianjin rooftops. The roomful of men, worn-out kitchen men who had cooked by hot steamers and cleaned and gone finally to their beds, quieted to a soft forest of sighs and snores.

I waited hours to get up. To climb down I had to step on the bed of the man below. "I'm sorry, Comrade." And I whispered a local slang word for the bathroom. The man snorted and returned to sleep. I hunched down the center aisle, holding my midsection as if ill, concealing my bundle. I slipped out and passed the rear of the kitchens. The last of the men were inside cleaning, and they had set racks of leftover buns in the doorway, which they would divide up later and take home. I took five dozen, wrapped them in three tight cloths in my bundle, and continued on, holding my middle, into the latrine, then out again through a back door that gave onto a Tianjin alley. We were never prisoners in our workers' collectives, but if a man did leave, there was nowhere else to go.

I set out walking. First I cut across the city, with its silent shadows, and then through the hours of thinning buildings and finally the countryside, due east, by the stars. Later, by the sun. I walked without stopping until I came, finally, to the flats that led to the sea. The air was cold, which was good for the *baozi.* As a cook I was well fed, better than most people, and I had the reserves to walk a night and a day without food. I only drank, stopping when I could at farmers' pumps.

By the time I reached the flat, fine, oily sand it was night again, and I could walk no farther. I stumbled out onto a pier crowded with boats. There were fishing boats, squat, of dark, heavy wood, and lined up in their berths, the larger craft — metal-hulled diesel-engine boats scavenged from the years of war, patched, remade, bumping the wood pilings, lines clinking. I had taken my last steps; if I did not lie down, I would collapse. So I staggered out along a wooden plank beside one of the berths, maneuvered my leg over the rail, and stepped aboard a boat. It was a large one, fourteen meters of hull at least. Three metal doors. I pulled at one; it opened. Down a ladder was a wedge-shaped space, and a bunk. I untied the *baozi* from my waist and collapsed.

When I awoke, a man was bending over me with a long knife, the tip of which he pressed ever so gently against my throat. I felt my eyes popping wide as I shrank away, but he followed me easily with the sharp point.

"Don't move," he said in the Tianjin dialect. With his free hand he checked me for weapons, feeling only my sewn-in *hukou* and a few unpromising coins in my pocket.

"If you want to kill me, it's no problem," I croaked. "I am dead already."

He grazed me again with the knife, as if considering it. He had a wide, squat face, creased and salt-burned with thick caterpillar brows. It was impossible to tell his age. "You look alive to me."

"Not for long."

"Unless?" he prompted.

"Yuan zou gao fei," I whispered, Travel far and fly high. Slip away. Disappear. Start again.

I saw in his face that he understood. "Where?"

"Anywhere," I said. A minute ago I had been a dead man. Now my heart raced with hope.

He looked me up and down. "You don't have anything."

"I have that," I said, and pointed with a look. "Open it."

He finally pulled the knife back a few inches and reached for the bundle, still keeping his eyes on me.

He untied the first knot and I could see the change in his face when he caught a whiff of the aroma, and then he laid back the cloth and saw the *baozi,* cooked, in their neat, slightly compressed rows. He leaned his face close to them and breathed. In those days meat dumplings were festival food, and though a man like him was blessed that he might eat his fill of fish, a meat dumpling was something he tasted only a few times a year. And these were buns from Gou Bu Li.

He glanced back at me. He had decided. "All right," he said. "I'm going south. I have cargo going to a work unit in Fuzhou. I can drop you near there. It'll be eighteen days, maybe twenty. I have four men. We go out on the tide tonight. You stay here until I tell you." He threw me a boiled-wool blanket, left, and locked the door.

It was twenty-one days to Fujian Province, around the Shandong peninsula and down the coast past the great mouth of the Yangtze. When finally we came to the first wet fingers of the Min Jiang estuary, north of Fuzhou, he said I should get off there instead of near the city. Go ashore in some quiet place. Hide for a while.

Hide where? I thought. How? But we came to a small cove and the captain took the dinghy down and put me off in calm, waist-deep water. We parted like brothers, with promises to meet again in this life or the next. I waded ashore in what felt like liquid ice, with my dry clothes over my head. They hauled up the dinghy and waited until they saw me emerge on a beach of pebbles and dry myself before they reversed their engines. Even then I stood waving until the lights of the boat had receded far out onto the water. Then I turned and walked straight inland.

The trouble was, there was no land. Once I stepped off the pebbles I was in knee-deep water. I thought if I kept going I would be out of it, but the opposite happened. I was swallowed by water. Darkness fell. Creatures awoke. I heard the calls and slithers of every kind of inhabitant. I sloshed forward. I didn't know where I was. I was not cold; instead I burned with fever. I had to stop, lie down. I couldn't find a dry spot big enough. The best I could do was to sit in a wet lap of roots, half in the water, half out, my head against the tree, until I lost consciousness.

When I awoke I was lying in a flat-bottomed boat, warm, heavenly, covered with a blanket, looking up into the freckled face of my mother. She was poling the boat. Surpassing Crystal, with her kind face and her strong hands; what was she doing here? Sitting behind my head with his hand on my shoulders was a young boy. It was myself. It was a dream. No. It was death. I had died. That was it.

I was not dead, I was ill, and I was taken through the sweet milk of human goodness to a rough house on stilts, where I burned and sweated with fever. The woman cared for me. Hers was the face of God to me. She rarely left me when it was at its worst. She cooled me with wet cloths. The boy, called Longshan, came and went, helping her.

I grew better. They lived in the swamp, far from their nearest neighbors in the rural commune. I sat on the porch, weakened, watching the light change over the waterweeds, which teemed, full of life, even in the approaching winter. Liuli — that was the woman's name — was a deft hunter and trapper. Her job in the commune was trapping eels for the workers' kitchens. This was the year when Chinese had to cease cooking at home and eat their meals in mess halls run by their work units. Luckily Liuli lived far from the village, and so from this particular social experiment she was excused. She delivered live eels twice a week and in return she received a modest quantity of rice, flour, oil, matches, and other staples.

Naturally she was able to supplement this with the skimmings from her catch, but eel was only the beginning of what Liuli managed to bring to the table. She and Longshan went out and came back with snakes, waterfowl, frogs, and all manner of waterweeds and lily bulbs and lotus roots and aromatic marsh plants. I watched them with awe and ate their good, simple food. I grew strong again.

They understood that no one should know I was there. Liuli said nothing on her trips to deliver the eels, and outside of that they saw almost no one anyway. The boy did not go to school. He had no father. What became of the man who begat him I never knew. He was a lonely child, half-wild; he attached himself to me as quickly as a water vine.

I could have stayed there forever. Liuli was a simple woman, almost too shy to look me in the face, though she had nursed me away from death and washed every part of my body when I was sick. I respected her and would never have so much as looked at her in the man-woman way without her invitation. But I loved her. I don't know if I loved her as a woman or a sister or an angel, or in a part of the heart where those things don't matter. Yet with her and the boy Longshan I was, in those weeks, as happy as I have ever been. Barely able to communicate — for she spoke only a local Fujian dialect I could not understand — we had come to know each other's human spirits through the unfolding days, first of sickness, later of laughter and shared chores.

One night, before I left, I cooked for them. I waited until they were out trapping eels. They knew nothing of who I was or what I could do, so when they returned and found my meal upon the table their chins all but brushed the floor. Such heights of pleasure I felt then.

I had prepared eel, of course, but not the stewed eel she made almost every night. Instead I made salt-and-pepper eel, thin little crisp-fried slices of fillet with a pungent wild pepper dip. I roasted a duck in the manner of Tan Zhuanqing, using the method passed down by my father, and then I made a second duck entirely of soy and gluten, and stuffed it with lotus root and lily bulbs and dried tofu and wild garlic, all bound by a mince of the dark green waterweeds that grow among the grasses. I roasted it until its skin was as crisp and shiny as that of the real duck.

The food was too much for them. The way it looked and smelled and tasted overwhelmed them. They had never had such dishes, even though each was prepared from the same foods they ate every day. Their faces lit up when they tasted it, and yet it made them almost frightened of me, of the fact that I could turn their food into a meal such as this. Liuli carried the things to the sink afterward and refused for the first time to let me help her clean. She deferred to me. She avoided my eyes.

That night, I mentioned going. She was neither sorry nor glad. Of course I had to go. I did not belong there. I was not of their home or their lives. By cooking for them I had broken the bubble. Our separateness, the vast differences between us, now defined us. Liuli was self-conscious in front of me. She held herself away. I wanted to reach for her more than ever, but I did not. She was a good woman, a good mother; she and the boy had saved my life. Above all I had to show respect. I spent my last days on the water, playing with Longshan, unable to stop myself from casting long, speculative glances back up at the house where I knew she sat, divided, thinking of me.

In the end she gave me some money she had saved, and that decided it. She pressed it on me; she insisted. I think we both knew if she hadn't done this I might never have left, and she didn't want that. She knew I would never have been able to look at her straight across, as an equal, which is the least any woman deserves.

So she gave the money and I took it. Living as she did, on the water, she knew people who plied the sea for their living and could not be contained by governments or laws. Such people would take a man to Hong Kong and drop him on an outlying beach amid incurious fisherfolk — all it took was money. In China there has always been the *hou men,* the back door, which can be opened by money or relationships and through which many things can be negotiated. Thanks to her that door opened for me. When I went through it I was to keep going until I reached America, but I didn't know that then. I only knew it was the last time I would see her. I climbed into a boat at the edge of the swamp. She poled away backward, her eyes on mine, her face still, remarkably, like the face of my mother. ❦ ❦ ❦

12

In the Peking dialect of my youth, food was always used to describe the basic things. To have work was *jiao gu,* to have grains to chew. To have lost one's job was *da po le fan wan,* to have broken the rice bowl. These words made the difference between life and death for people who were poor. So these words contained a world.

— LIANG WEI, *The Last Chinese Chef*

On Thursday evening, after several days of cooking and sleeping and more cooking, Sam found his eyes straying to the clock. Tonight was Yao Weiguo's banquet for the committee — Yao, his main rival. Tonight was Yao, tomorrow Wang Zijian, and then, Saturday night, the last and tenth night of the competition, Sam. Although radio call-in shows had been burning with exchanges over the merits of the ten chefs, and wagers had been laid, the panel itself had kept completely quiet. None of them had leaked anything about the banquets thus far. Everything in the media was speculation. Sam had not heard a thing.

He felt blessed to have the last slot. His flavors would be the final ones to linger in the judges' minds. On the other hand, they might be exhausted. He would take care not to overwhelm them. Better to reach for greatness in simplicity. This was what he had in mind anyway.

196

He had forty-eight hours left. What remained was the last rehearsal of each dish, especially the ones that were new to him — these had to be done over and over. He was also still assembling bowls, plates, platters, paintings, and calligraphy in tune with the arc of the meal. Once any facet of the meal had struck a resonance in the diner, he wanted everything else in the room and on the table to multiply the effect. The effect could not be overt. It had to build quietly.

He looked again at the clock. There was so much to do. He should work. But he felt a nervous and unceasing tug to go out, too, to go to Yao's side of town, to walk down the *hutong* that ran behind Yao's restaurant, the Red Door, to get close to his banquet, see what he could feel, what he could hear, what he could smell. He closed his eyes. *Don't do it.* But he knew he would.

Night was dropping as he locked his gate, shadows growing, and he felt a familiar wave of love for the area he lived in. His neighbors felt the same. He could see it in the way the grandmas walked the small children, the old men shouted over their card games and in hot weather pushed their undershirts up to their armpits. It was in the way packs of young girls walked the lake, showing off their gazelle bodies in the latest formfitting clothes. He loved it for all these reasons, and then doubly, because in addition to everything else he was living in the house in which his family had lived, on and off, for more than eighty years.

The amount of effort and money Sam had poured into restoring all but the small north-facing room was another sore spot in Liang Yeh's refusal to come back. Sam wanted to bring him here. Show him. *Here, Ba. Look.*

He had told him as much when he called him again, this morning. "The main thing is, Xie needs you. He's hanging on to see you. And you should come. Your house is waiting, your father's house. It's safe."

In response to this, at least, Liang Yeh had been merely silent. This was an improvement.

Sam walked to the subway, went south and changed lines. A few stops to the west brought him to the neighborhood of Yao's restaurant. He walked for a while, distracting himself as if on an aimless stroll. In time he gave in and drifted into the *hutong* that ran behind Yao's place. No one would see him walking. It was dark.

The high rear windows of the place were flung open. As he crept closer he heard laughter from inside and the clink of dishes, then a rising cheer. *"Hao! Hao!"* came the voices, Good! Good! Sam felt the reflexive curl of tension. He shouldn't have come.

He heard a sound to his right and turned to see a figure step out of the shadows — no, not one figure, two. Who?

Sam made a silent mental shriek. It was Jiang. And Tan. Their mouths dropped in recognition too.

The long stare devolved into suppressed laughter, and in a second all three of them were heaving and holding their sides. They hushed one another, which only made it worse.

"Shh!" Sam sent a look to the back windows of Yao's restaurant, which were open.

"Come!" Jiang croaked, wiping his eyes. "Why should we stand here? Let us walk over to the Uighur night market. It's just a few blocks. Have you eaten? I have not. I may faint from starvation! I may die! Come." And the three made their way down the *hutong*.

In the market, cheap lights were strung across the alley and vendors shouted behind great wok rings with lids that lifted off to stately puffs of steam. Row after row of Uighur men with dark Eurasian faces ran charcoal grills, where they produced lamb in every form, from skewers to the tender minced meat that was marinated, griddle-fried, and stuffed in split sesame flat cakes.

No doubt Yao's meal had been brilliant, Sam thought as they walked through the people and the tables and the hot smoky aromas. But what was that to him? His meal would be brilliant too. He felt confident when his uncles were beside him.

After much surveying, they settled on thick hand-cut noodles with green vegetables in broth and a huge platter of dense, chewy, cumin-encrusted lamb ribs. They ate in the companionable silence of relatives assigned to one another long before any of them were even born.

As Sam ate, his eyes roved the crowd. After a minute he saw a distinctive curtain of black hair coming toward him — Xiao Yu, the girl he had seen David Renfrew approach that day in a restaurant. "Hi," he called out when she came close.

She looked over, surprised. "Oh, Liang Cheng," she said, using his Chinese name. "I read the article in the paper about the competition. I hoped for the best. How was your banquet? Was it successful?"

"I haven't gone yet," he said. "Saturday night."

"Wish you success."

"Thank you. And you? How are you?"

"Very well. *Hao jiu bu jian.*" I haven't seen you in a long time.

"Actually," Sam said, "I saw *you* a week ago, but I don't think you knew. It was in a restaurant. I was on the other side. I saw David Renfrew go over and talk with you." They were speaking Chinese, but to say David's name he dropped back into English. The sound of it made her mouth tense. "Sorry," said Sam, seeing it.

"Don't be sorry." But abruptly she looked at her watch. He had touched a sore spot. Something had happened. Sam remembered the odd trepidation he had felt when he saw Xiao Yu and David together. He felt it the minute David asked him for her name. He couldn't have said why. Sometimes it was not necessary to know, only to feel.

"I should go," she said.

Looking at her, he saw he had not imagined it. She wore the proud, taut chin of a woman slighted. "Please take care of yourself."

"You too," she said. "Success to you."

"Man man zou," he said, Walk slow, as he watched her wave and turn and disappear in the close-pressed night crowd. People moved by, under the lights, jostling, their talk and their laughter borne along with them. She was gone.

Jiang and Tan were speaking, and he turned back to them, away from the crowd. He belonged with them. He ate the choice lamb ribs they deposited with love on his plate, and he picked out succulent pieces to place on theirs.

*   *   *

Before leaving work for the day, Zinnia stopped off in Carey's office. "Have you made any calls yet?"

"No." He felt irritated. "I'll get to it."

She sent him her look of prim displeasure, which he knew to be one of her most insufferable and therefore effective weapons. "But you must do it soon. Quickly."

"Why?"

"It's Thursday. Tomorrow people will leave for the weekend."

Carey pursed his lips. "I hate mixing business and pleasure."

"Really! Is that what you believe?"

"Yes."

"It's your philosophy?"

"Yes."

"Who took Matt out, those nights, when he met Gao Lan?"

Carey sighed. "I did."

"Look what happened then."

"All right, Zinnia, Jesus. Okay. I'll do it." Defeated once again by a Chinese woman. He was no match for them. Waving her off with one hand, he reached for the phone with the other. "I'll call."

Carey got lucky with the fourth call, and within an hour was on his way to a restaurant to meet a woman he had dated a few years before. Still unattached, was what he'd heard. As soon as he called and she answered the phone he knew it was true, for she jumped. Yes, of course she would meet him. Tonight? Certainly. She would be disappointed when she realized Carey had not called her for any personal reason. So be it. Zinnia was right, he needed to help. So he made the call.

The restaurant was on the capital's northeast end, in a quarter that had once been home to diplomatic offices and hotels but had now been swallowed by the relentless swell of commercial buildings. Inside, the place preserved some semblance of the old décor, with stone stools and wood-scrolled tables. He arrived first and sat drinking tea, watching the door for her to come in.

It was romantic, living in China. There was beauty in it. He heard parrots screeching in cages on the other side of the dining hall, caught the happy tide of dinnertime Chinese as it rose and fell. Always there was something to please him. Wonderful food. Gorgeous women. They never stopped attracting him, even if he had yet to meet one he wanted to stay with.

He knew that staying here was a sort of delaying tactic, a way of stretching out his youth. It was at home he'd be much more likely to find a woman. *Laowai* men, even the ones most flat-out crazy about Chinese girls, generally went home to marry. They chose one of their own. Girls they knew from high school. Girls from their hometowns. Girls who looked like their mothers, like the men themselves. But not Carey. He reached for his small, thick cup of aromatic tea and sipped it, listening to the ambient well of Mandarin conversation. He would not go home that way.

It was probably moot — the time to go home had come and gone. He had passed the golden point sometime in his late thirties. Now he was forty-five. If he went back he'd step down — on the job, in society, among friends, and with everything having to do with women. Here he was like royalty. Just being a foreigner gave him unassailable value, but it was value he couldn't take with him. Either go home and retire that part of himself forever which had grown to love his position, or stay here in China. Grow old here. Choose a woman. Just choose one. Die here. He stared gloomily out the window at the blue-bowl October sky.

The door opened and Yuan Li came in, ultra-chic in leopard heels and a fashionable fringe of black hair. She was glorious, in her thirties now, confident. Perhaps he should look at her again. Carey toyed with the idea. She was kind, supportive, lovely. She had bored him, though, as he recalled, and he had ended it. No doubt he would end it again, in time, if they were to restart, which was why he would not. It was clear that she was willing. He could tell by the way she looked at him. No, he told himself, don't act interested, not that way. Be friendly.

For the first hour of their meeting he engaged her in a sweet, solicitous conversation that traded all kinds of news: about jobs, relatives, travels, hobbies, vacations. He had been in China long enough to know how a meal should be done, with a long exchange of pleasantries and moods preceding any hint of a disclosure or request.

Finally, after they had talked long and the food he'd ordered had arrived and been eaten, he spoke casually. "It happens I am looking for someone. Gao Lan. Am I correct in recalling that you knew her?"

As he spoke he watched her face. First he saw the trace of insult. She understood now why he had called her. Then in her eyes he saw caution and calculation. Good. That meant she knew her.

Still, she took her time before she answered. "I have not seen her in quite a while. Maybe a year or two. I don't know where she is right now."

The waiter came with the check, which Carey took.

"So I'm not too clear," Yuan Li continued.

"I'd appreciate your telling me if you do hear."

"I can ask."

"Thank you," he said, and then returned smoothly to their previous topic, which was the leasing of a building on which she had been a project manager. Altogether he sat with her for more than two hours that night. They consumed three appetizer cold plates and three entrée dishes, plus a small forest of beers, most of which, admittedly, were drunk by him. They observed every nicety and parted as friends, even trading warm and potentially meaningful embraces. And all of it was for those few sentences uttered in the middle, cast lightly on the table — Do you know where she is? No. Will you find out? I'll try. Thank you.

Carey steered Yuan Li out to the sidewalk and saw her into a taxi, waved warmly from the sidewalk as she pulled into the street. Ah, it was a nice life here, in its way; the gravity of history, the traces of gentility, and the pleasure of now. He liked the freedom and the forthrightness, which had their own way of coexisting with the oppressions of the government. It wasn't so much that people liked the government or approved of it, such questions being irrelevant anyway; it was that they were good at living with it. Against all odds, despite its severe gray undertone, Carey found China a joyous place.

He sighed. Had he stayed too long, had he let things go sour, was he trapped? Maybe he should have been more like the other lawyers in the firm, like Matt; he should have based himself in Los Angeles and just made sojourns here. But he had been seduced by China. It felt so exquisitely good here. Once he arrived, he had really never wanted to leave.

He held up his hand for a taxi. It was not his world, though, and no matter how long he stayed here, it never would be. He would always be an outsider, and despite a marvelously warm mix of etiquette, kindness, and convention the Chinese did not truly welcome outsiders.

So if he went home — but who was he kidding? It was too late to go home. He was too old. And he climbed into a car and drove off into the Beijing night, thinking instead about where he would go to drink, to hear music, to run into old friends and maybe, with any luck, meet new ones. He named a club to the driver, an address in a *hutong* off Sanlitun, and lay back to watch his adopted city pass him in a pleasant procession of lights, skyscrapers mixed with the old-fashioned red lanterns that still hung outside restaurants as they had for centuries, wherever people gathered to eat and cement their relationships.

Maybe he would have to stay.

The next morning was Friday. Maggie went by Sam's house to drop off a good-luck gift. The taxi waited with its engine idling while she knocked on the gate. It was a polite, preemptive knock; she didn't expect him to be there, intending, if he was not, to leave her gift outside. Where it belonged.

But his footsteps came across the court, a little impatient. He was working. Then he unlatched the gate and saw her, and his face changed. "Hi," he said.

"Hi." She smiled a little. He was glad to see her. "I brought you something. I can't come inside or anything, I know you have to work, I just want you to have this. For luck."

"You're so kind," he said.

"You'll have to give me a hand." She stepped back toward the taxi and he followed her out over the sill. As they approached the trunk the driver released the catch and she showed Sam what was inside, a potted evergreen tree that filled the entire space.

He stared. It was the last thing he had expected.

"I brought it for your court," she said. "It will get tall." They hauled it out together, and he set it by the gate. It had a shape like a spiral column.

"Of course, if you don't like it, hey," she said. "If I ever come back to Beijing and dine in your restaurant and it's not in evidence, I won't be hurt. I promise."

"It'll be here," he said, and she could tell by the way he was smiling that it was true. "Thanks."

"No problem," she said. It had been easy, with Zinnia powering her through the city flower market and subjecting vendors to penetrating inquisitions on the suitability of various potted shrubs and trees to a Beijing courtyard, to choose one. The whole idea, Zinnia confided to Maggie on the side, was almost quaint now, for no one had courtyards. It was a way of life which had vanished. Nevertheless they settled on the spiral tree, and Zinnia had the young vendor's assistant carry it outside. When it was in the taxi Zinnia said suddenly that she would take the next one; her lunch hour was over. Maggie could see her busy eyes already thinking ahead to the work that waited on her desk. Maggie hugged her. "Thanks," she said.

And now the tree was on the ground, outside Sam's gate, with him looking at it. He did like it. "I loved your father's memoir, by the way. It was beautiful," said Maggie. The taxi was still there, engine running.

He looked up slowly. "He came. He's here."

"Your *father*?"

"He got a visa, bought a ticket. He did it. He's here."

"You said he'd never come."

"I said wrong," said Sam. "It was Xie that got him here. I don't think anything else could have."

"That's where he is?"

"In Hangzhou."

The news, and the look on his face, gave her a flush of happiness. "That's wonderful. Good for you. Good." She looked at the taxi. "I've got to go."

He nodded. "Thanks for the tree."

"That's for luck," she said.

And he said, "I'll take it."

That afternoon Maggie worked on her story. She didn't yet know the ending, but there was no reason not to go all the way up to that point.

As she often did when she started a piece, she began by just writing, following her spine, which in this case was connectedness. She spent some hours re-creating scenes, conversations, and explanations, weaving them in and around her notion, which was her sense of what he had shown her.

Then there was the question of the piece's forward propulsion. She took a fresh sheet of paper and wrote six words in block letters on three lines:

TEN CANDIDATES.
TEN BANQUETS.
TWO SLOTS.

This was the logical forward movement — the announcement, the whirlwind preparation, the banquet itself. She would write to this. She taped the page up on the wall in front of her. Now she could go back to the beginning. She turned back to her computer and opened a new file. Like any blank page it was filled with possibility. She typed the words *Sam Liang* and then jumped so hard she almost broke her chair. Someone was knocking at the door.

She pressed her eye to the peephole. It was Zinnia, leaning toward the tiny glass circle with that hurried look in her eye. Maggie pulled back the door. "Hi."

Zinnia pumped past her, glasses flashing in triumph. "Sorry! So sorry to come without calling, but I just found out, and I was near here."

"You can come without calling anytime. Found out what?"

"I know where Gao Lan is."

"Sit." Maggie steered her to the couch. "Where?"

"Here. Not far. She lives at the Dongfang Yinzuo. The Oriental Kenzo. It's a big residential and commercial development downtown."

"How'd you find out?"

"Carey found out."

"That's where she lives, or where she works?"

"Where she lives. I don't know where she works yet. But I called her already. She is home today. She says we can meet her there in an hour. You want to?"

"Yes!" said Maggie.

"*Zou-ba,*" said Zinnia, happy, Let's go. She never even sat down. She turned for the door and Maggie followed.

In the back of a taxi, stuttering through choked side streets toward the Dongfang Yinzuo, Gao Lan closed her eyes and cradled her small packages. In her lap she held a packet of tea, an exceptional orchid oolong, and snacks — melon seeds and biscuits — the things that must be offered to guests, and which she did not keep.

Her man was not in town. He was in Taipei with his wife and children, which was why she could receive these people. She wouldn't want the man anywhere near an encounter like this. He did not know she had a child. If he did, he would end her employment. That was unthinkable. Shuying and her parents lived on the money she sent home every month, though they had no idea what she actually did. She sent home almost everything she earned. She did nothing except work out in the gym, which he paid for. She ate in the apartment, taking as little as possible. Sometimes she walked. She never bought anything, she just walked. When he came she bought the foods he liked just before he arrived. While he was there her only thought was to please him.

Before Shuying was born, life had been different. She let out an ironic laugh. She certainly was not living the life her parents had once had in mind for her. Far from it.

They were old-fashioned, the first people she knew to express nostalgia for the Cultural Revolution. They continued to see it as an experiment of tragic but also noble dimensions. Having been a child in the optimistic eighties, when state-owned enterprises were closing everywhere, Gao Lan remembered being embarrassed by her parents' pronouncements. Standards of living were improving vastly. Everyone else welcomed the change. It seemed to her back then that her mother and father were the only ones who looked back with longing.

They thought she should seek a simple life close to home, but she had other ideas. She went to school, did well in English, and moved to Beijing to work. There was work in the international sector. The pay was modest but sufficient. It was never stable, for businesses came and went, but there was usually something.

And it was wonderful to be young and unattached in the city at that time, with things opening up so fast. She went with her friends to clubs, to parties, to receptions. She learned about life, and being on her own, and falling in love.

She saw girls around her during those years who went out at night as she did, forming liaisons as she did, yet who turned out later to be married. The husband lived in some other city. Sometimes there was a child, and in that case the child was usually with the grandparents. The women lived as if single. They were not libertines, but if they fell for someone, they had an affair. Gao Lan remembered how shocked she was the first time one of them admitted to her that she was married, that she had a little girl. "I have two minds," the woman had said. "Two hearts. One loves my daughter and misses her. The other one is here."

In time Gao Lan had come to understand that many of these girls, when young, had married men toward whom their parents had steered them. At that age obedience was all they understood. Now, though, the deed done, they found it easier to live apart from those husbands and maintain lives of their own.

Gao Lan had been proud then, when she was young, that her life path was hers to choose. Now of course she was alone forever, most likely — especially considering what she had been doing the last few years. Back then, though, she had only been full of joy and freedom.

Her fourth year in Beijing she started a relationship with a foreigner. He was marvelously exciting to her at first — perhaps simply because he was foreign, and so different. He was strong, for one thing. He handled her with confidence. She loved it, but in time she came to see the dark side of the relationship: always, he had to control. He would make a date with her and be effusive in his anticipation, then call her an hour before to break it off. He became cold if she showed too much feeling for him.

Get rid of him, her friends told her. But she felt empty when she tried to do so. Unwise as it was, she cared for him. She kept going back to him, even when he infuriated her. It had become like a game between them, to be cared for, be accepted.

During this time she met Matt. She was in a club with some friends. The other man had angered her and she hadn't spoken to him in a week. She was bored, tired; even though it was still early she was ready to leave. Then she saw Matt across the room at the same moment he saw her. It was impossible to say who approached whom first; they walked toward each other, smiling. They talked. He was courtly and charming. She wanted to know everything about him. His English was clear, easy for her to understand. She told him about her life, her childhood in Shaoxing, her parents. He seemed to take an interest in everything she said.

After a time his friend, another American from his company, thinner, older, more sinuous, wanted to leave. Matt refused to hear of it. He wanted to stay with her. The other man grew annoyed. Finally Matt said they could go if she could come with him. The other man resisted. They argued, in English too fast and slurred for her to understand; then suddenly it was all right and she was leaving with them. They went to another bar. She and Matt sat close, talking. They went from place to place. She sensed the other man's displeasure, but neither she nor Matt was willing to leave the other's company.

Finally at four A.M. the three of them left the last bar. She and Matt left first. They climbed into the back of a car, close.

"Do you want to go someplace else and keep talking?"

"Yes," she said. She wanted never to leave his side.

His face was a few inches away in the night-dark. "Or do you want to come home with me?"

"Yes," she said. "That."

He leaned forward and gave his address in memorized, approximated Chinese, and as soon as he was relaxed in his seat again he slipped his hand under her skirt. He amazed her. She had never known anyone so free. It was as if her saying yes had burst the tension of not knowing that had held them apart all these hours, and now he couldn't wait another second. Her excitement rose with his, and by the time they got out at his building they could barely make it inside and up the elevator.

He was pure and joyous with her; she felt she had never known a man so openhearted. She was breaking all her own rules by being with him — *If a foreigner, it must be someone who lives here, never a tourist or a visitor, never, for such a man will soon leave* — but she also felt unaccountably happy. He was present. With him she felt *seen.*

Afterward he didn't drop immediately into sleep as she expected. He was awake again, talking. He told her about his life, his travels. He talked about his wife. She lay on top of him like a child, listening, following, realizing things were not simple. It was good with his wife, but not perfect. He loved her, yet he wanted a baby and she did not. How strange, Gao Lan thought, her hand idle on his chest, that she would say no to him.

He had already told her he was coming back to China in several weeks' time. He promised to call her. Then he left. As the days went by after that, as she relented at last and took her other boyfriend's calls, she understood a little better that she in her own way had been using Matt. She felt better after their night together, more confident.

She started up again with the other man. Almost at once it turned difficult. She began to think of Matt. By the time he returned she was aflame with anticipation. The day he had mentioned came and went. She watched her caller ID screen constantly.

If he was in Beijing, why had she not heard from him? She held out another half-day, then called the cell phone number he had given her.

"Hello, Gao Lan." His voice had a heavy quality. He didn't want to hear from her. She dropped as fast and deep as a stone anchor.

Still she was warm and cheerful and said they should get together. "I don't know," he said, politely perplexed, as if they were on a business call. "Appointments all day . . . I have something on tonight . . ." She heard him turning pages. "Gao Lan, I'm sorry. This doesn't look good."

She was shocked by his rudeness. Her opinion of him plummeted.

"Hey," he was saying, "I'm only here for a couple of days."

A torrent of curses burned in her throat, but she limited herself to a few cool sentences. "My opinion is like this. We did too much already for you to leave it that way. Whatever you have to say to me, you may say to me directly."

There was a silence. She heard a long, heavy breath.

"Meet me at four o'clock at Anthony's on Wangfujing," she went on, stronger. "It's right behind the Pacific Hotel."

A long silence, and then he said, "All right."

She was waiting there when he arrived. He came in ready, as if he'd rehearsed, which he no doubt had. He moved his big, square body with ease into the seat opposite her. "Before I say anything else," he began, "I want you to know our night together was special to me. Exceedingly special."

She was not moved. He seemed so shallow now. "But?" she said.

"But that's it. I can't do it again. I'm sorry."

"No problem," she said. "All right. But you can *tell* me. To my face. That's all." It almost didn't matter what she said. The toxic jolt she had felt when he dismissed her on the phone needed to be aired in order to be erased.

"Okay," he said, chastened. Suddenly he looked helpless. "It's my wife," he said, as if bewildered by the force of his own emotions. "I belong with her. I love her so much, I can't lie to her. She would never know, she would probably never find out, but I still can't do it."

"The night we were together you didn't think this way."

"I didn't think about anything else but you! I'm sorry. I take responsibility. But I can't do it again. Can't turn off reality twice. I'm sorry."

"*Bu yong*," she said, Don't be sorry. "I don't care," she added, which was not entirely true, and then, "But I wanted you to say it," which was.

A short time after that she found out she was pregnant. Late the following summer Shuying was born. To Gao Lan, she was always the child of the other man, for he was the one who had vexed her and hurt her and also carried her to the heights. He was the one who against her creeping knowledge of what was right and wrong had become part of the pattern of her life. There had been only the one time with Matt. One time, and then the insult of his dismissal. What were the chances? None. Next to none. No more.

Gao Lan stayed away from Beijing for almost a year. She returned with a story about having gone home to help with a family illness, but work was spotty. The world had moved on. She was not in demand as she had been before. It was difficult to make money enough for herself, much less enough to send home so her parents could care for the baby.

She was also tormented over her inability to identify Shuying's father. Because of that one night with Matt she could not be sure. It was as if she were being punished over and over for that night. This doubt had kept her from telling either man there was a baby. She knew this was a mistake. At first, though, she had felt that the best thing was simply to wait a little, until Shuying grew into herself and began to look more clearly like one or the other. Then she would approach the man. Meanwhile she kept working.

She lost her job. She didn't get another one. She refused to give up. She went out every day on interviews until she lost her apartment, too, and then she moved in with women friends, first one, then another. Her parents were calling. They needed money.

Shuying, her little *yang wan wan,* her sweet foreign-doll baby —
she was the sun and the stars, but she needed so many things. Then
her girlfriend told her she would have to find another refuge, for
she was giving up the apartment and moving to Shanghai. And that
was Gao Lan's last stop.

She remembered meeting a woman — not someone she knew
well, a friend of a friend — who told her she could do well working
for a man, as a woman who was kept. The woman meant this partly
as a compliment to Gao Lan's beauty; not all women were qualified
for this work, only women for whom certain men would pay. At
the time Gao Lan had laughed, embarrassed. She had waited until
another time and place entirely to ask someone what such a man
took, and what he gave; and how working as an *ernai* might be arranged.

She still saw clearly the first man who took her, Chen Xian from
Hong Kong. Fifty-six, hair dyed black, rich, careful about how
much he spent on everything, including her, yet fair. He used her
for his pleasure, used her hard sometimes, but that was his right.
That was what he paid for. He was always kind to her. Him she remembered with affection.

He had met her for the first interview in a bar off Sanlitun. It was
a dim place, and they lounged on a couch together while they
talked. She could feel him looking at her. Finally he asked her if she
would like to dance. She said yes and they went out on the floor. At
first they danced apart, but then he pulled her to him and she felt
him feeling her body. She could tell that he liked her. She liked him
too, well enough. It would be all right.

They went out together a few more times, and on their fourth
meeting he made an offer.

"Here's how it works." They were in a bar. He signaled for another round of scotch. His was empty, though she had barely
touched her own. "I pay you three thousand *ren min bi* a month,
plus an apartment. You'll have a membership at the gym downstairs. I'm in Beijing only a week and a half a month, maybe two.
The rest of the time I expect you to keep my face."

She swallowed. The pay was far more than she could make at a job, especially considering that she'd have no living expenses. He was old. About that she didn't care. She saw his hand come up from his lap, brown, assured, perfectly manicured. For a second she thought he was going to reach for her, but instead he counted out money, three thousand, the first month. She couldn't take her eyes away from it. "What do you say?" he said.

She said yes. They were together eight months and then he left her, but only because his wife insisted on it. He let her stay two more months in the apartment. That was the sort of person Chen Xian was, kind.

Since then she'd had her education. Some of it had been cruel, and some of it had been satisfying — like the money she'd been able to send home. *That* was satisfying. It was good to know Shuying was taken care of.

As the little girl grew, she looked frustratingly like herself, and not really like either man, but Gao Lan still felt pretty certain she was not Matt's. She was not developing Matt's type of body, for one thing. Gao Lan had to approach the other man, and she knew it. She kept planning it, and putting it off. She could not stand to see him now, given what she was selling to survive. It would cost her more than she was prepared to pay. She could not bear to tell her parents, who loved her; how could she tell him, who had toyed with her for months and then dropped her so cruelly? When he ended their affair with a terse, abrupt phone call, she demanded he meet her to talk in person. It had worked with Matt, and even though their liaison was over, the fact that they spoke face to face made her feel better. She at least received a minimal level of human respect from Matt. The other man gave her no such thing. When she asked, he hung up on her. She could not tell him about the child.

At first she reasoned that she'd get a real job soon, and after that she'd approach him. But it did not happen. Three months, she vowed. Six. Then it became a year, then two.

She had finally gone to see him a little more than a year before. She had given up on waiting. She carried a picture of Shuying. His response was to curse her out of his office for suggesting any child of hers could be his. He hadn't seen her in years. It was outrageous. If she ever tried to do it again he would ruin her.

Gao Lan knew he was well connected. He could make it harder than ever for her to return to work if he wanted to. And she had to return to real work eventually or she was finished. She'd take a cut in pay when she did, and she didn't yet know how she would manage, but she also knew she had no choice. In just a few more years she'd run out of time.

It was soon after that she heard that Matt had been killed. She still remembered her physical reaction, a jolt in her midsection. She knew then she had cared for him, despite the brevity of their encounter, for she'd found her body, in its visceral reactions, to be incapable of a lie. Yet she still didn't believe Matt was Shuying's father.

After the Treaty was passed, her parents pressed her to file a claim and she said all right, but not against the other man; against Matt. He was gone. He could not take revenge on her, at least not on this side of the veil.

Not that his wife would be pleased. Gao Lan shivered. That was the woman coming to meet her now. So be it. Just as they said all men were brothers, all women were sisters, and Gao Lan vowed to tell her the truth. She would regard her with respect. The two women already had a connectedness between them, because of Matt.

In the apartment, after she had prepared tea and set flowers in a plain jug, the doorbell rang. She pulled it open to two women. One was American, the widow — older, attractive in the sharp, speckled, brown-eyed way some Westerners had. Almost friendly. "Welcome, welcome," Gao Lan said, drawing them in. She was relieved she would not have to use English. This big-glasses girl, Chu Zuomin, was obviously here to translate.

In the living room she poured tea, which sat untouched. She and the Chinese girl made small talk about the apartment, and Gao Lan waited for Matt's widow to begin.

Yet the woman was not in a hurry. She followed right along behind the translator, observing manners, talking, laying small increments of relationship. She complimented the big, modern complex, the neighborhood. She asked about nearby restaurants, and Gao Lan told her of Ghost Street, a nearby stretch jammed with eateries, which was one reason so many men kept mistresses in the Dongfang Yinzuo, few things in life mattering more than proximity to a good meal. The widow even praised little Shuying for being bright and pretty. She seemed to be thinking of ways to advance the conversation, even as she studied Gao Lan centimeter by centimeter. Finally she said that she understood Gao Lan was working hard at the logistics company.

Gao Lan stared. "Logistics?"

"I thought you worked at a logistics company."

"Oh. My parents must have told you that."

"Yes."

"Well, that's what they think. Would you blame me? Of course I tell them that. It's not true. I haven't been able to get that kind of job. I work for the man who rents this apartment. Naturally I would not want them to know this." Gao Lan saw that the translator colored a slow pink as she put this into English.

"I thought this was your apartment," said the widow.

"Not at all. Living here is part of my pay."

"And what is it you do?" said the widow.

"Whatever he wants," said Gao Lan. "Do you understand my meaning or not? He has a wife and children in Taiwan. He is only here sometimes."

"Oh," said the widow suddenly, when she heard the translation. "I didn't know."

"My parents also do not know," Gao Lan reminded her.

"They won't learn it from me," the American said. "Don't worry."

"*Bie zhaoji,*" Chu Zuomin translated.

Gao Lan filled the ensuing silence by insisting they have melon seeds and small candies. They thanked her without actually eating any, again showing manners.

Then the wife of Matt sat up straight. "May I ask you a question?" she said.

"Please."

"I *do* understand why you would seek support from the father of your child. Why you *should*. What I want to know is, why did you file against my husband? Why not the other man?"

A charged silence hung, like the kind before a storm's first crack of thunder. How had the widow known? Finally Gao Lan broke it with a short, formal laugh. "You've made a wide cast of your net."

"If it were your husband, would you do any less?"

"I suppose not."

The woman went on. "Look. I know there is a chance Shuying is Matt's, and a chance she's this other guy's. You're the mother. You're the only one who can say which is more likely. So all I'm really asking is, why Matt? Is it because you think she looks like him? Because I'll tell you, I went there and met her with an open mind, and I'm going to be honest: I don't see it."

Gao Lan nodded. It was true; Shuying did not look much like Matt. She had been aware of it since the girl grew out of her split pants and left babyhood behind. "I did go to the other man first."

The American woman sat higher in her chair. "And?"

Gao Lan was a woman who hated to show she was afraid, but this man she feared. She had done many things in her life which showed her bravery — she had struck out on her own; she had refused her parents' suggestions for husbands and come to Beijing to make her way instead. This man was different. She didn't say his name anymore. She didn't even like to think it. "He threatened me," she said.

"What?" The American widow almost rose from her chair, a fierce, instinctive movement.

"He said if I ever said such a thing again, implied Shuying was his daughter, or did anything about it, he would make sure I did not work in Beijing again."

"He can't do that."

"But he can. He can spread talk about me easily, if he wants."

"Does he know this work you do?"

"Not now," said Gao Lan. "At least I don't think so. But secrets are hard to keep. And if he found out, and passed this around" — she trailed her eyes over the apartment, the sparkling plaza down below outside the windows — "the door for me would close."

"But if he's the father, he's responsible for Shuying under the Treaty. He must take care of her."

"Asking him to do that is like asking a tiger for its hide."

The American's eyes softened in understanding. "I see why you'd feel that way. But he *still* can't intimidate you. I don't know about the laws here, but he couldn't do it in the States. Impossible."

Gao Lan felt a frisson of surprise. Something in the American woman had changed. It seemed as if she didn't like hearing that this other man had threatened her. "Unfortunately, though, I don't know of anything that could stop him here in China," she said.

"I do," said the widow. "Carey could stop him. He could straighten him out. Carey James? Remember? You met him."

The name did not click at once in Gao Lan's mind. She shook her head.

The foreign woman closed her eyes. "The night you met my husband. The night the two of you were together. The first time."

"The only time," said Gao Lan. "I remember. Your husband's friend." Now she could see Carey: tall, blond, remote. He was the one who had been with Matt, who had urged Matt over and over to say goodbye to her and go someplace else.

"He will help you," the widow said. "I'll make sure of it. That's if the child is this other man's and not Matt's — and we'll know the answer to that in a few more days."

Gao Lan decided to give voice to what she noticed a minute before. "Why would you help me? If Shuying is not Matt's."

"I'll tell you why. Women don't stand by and watch another woman being bullied. That's a law of nature, as I see it." The Chinese woman translated this, even though Gao Lan found she could more or less follow Matt's wife's English.

Now Gao Lan felt her own guard dropping and tears, for the first time, gathering in her eyes. "You know what? I am sorry. Sorry two ways. First and forever, I'm sorry he took leave of this world. I felt so sad when I heard."

This made the widow's tears start up.

"I'm sorry for what we did together, too. It was only once. I thought it would be a secret, safe, separate from you and your life.

Well water not intruding with river water — that's what I thought. I was wrong. *Duibuqi.*"

"That means I'm sorry," said Miss Chu.

The American nodded, now with shiny tracks down her face.

Gao Lan pushed on. "But I want to tell you this. Matt was the one who stopped it with us. Not me. I wanted to go on. I'm sorry, but it's true; I did. He said no, he wouldn't, because he loved you. He said he had done it once and he would have to live with that, but he would never do it again. He told me, 'I love her so much.' That's what he said."

Gao Lan had to stop, and she sat in a tremble while the Chinese woman put this in English. The American listened, then reached out and brushed her dry fingers across the back of Gao Lan's hand. "Thank you," she said.

"Drink some tea," Gao Lan said, with a gesture to the table. The other two women murmured agreement, though they still did not touch their cups.

"There is one more thing," said the American.

"Hai you yijian shi," translated Miss Chu.

The widow wiped her face with the back of her hand in a movement she had obviously made many times before. Gao Lan felt for her.

Then she opened the bag she had brought with her and withdrew an envelope, and from this she took a picture. She handed it across. "Have you ever seen this?" she said, and Miss Chu translated.

Gao Lan leaned to the left to hold it under the light. She saw a street corner, people on the ground, a car on the sidewalk. She swallowed.

"It's the accident." The widow's voice was thick.

Gao Lan looked at it again. Her heart rushed up into her mouth. That was Matt. On the ground with the woman kneeling over him.

When Gao Lan looked up her eyes were wet again. She handed it back. She didn't want to look at it anymore.

But the widow stopped her. "Wait." She pointed to the picture. "See that woman?"

"Yes."

"Carey says that looks like you."

"Like me? But how?" Gao Lan looked closer. "Maybe. In a way."

"So you're saying it's not you."

"How could it be me?"

"You were not there?"

Gao Lan stared as she listened to Miss Chu's Chinese. Her, in San Francisco? Kneeling over Matt at the moment of his death? "No. I haven't even been to Hong Kong. The farthest I've been from home is here, Beijing."

The American looked at her again, then at the picture. A tightness faded from her face. "You're right," she said slowly. "I see. It's not you." She looked at Gao Lan for a long moment, then replaced the clipping in her purse. "Shall I call you when I hear from the lab?"

"Please." Gao Lan gave her a card, no title, no company. Just her name in two Chinese characters and a cell number. "Get in touch anytime. Dark or light."

"I will," said Matt's wife, and handed over her own card. Maggie McElroy. Writer, *Table* magazine. "Look, I didn't say and you didn't ask, but I want you to know something too. If Shuying is Matt's, you won't have any trouble from me. I'll take care of things."

"Thank you," said Gao Lan.

She stood up with them and walked them to the door, where she and the widow clasped hands for a second. "Three days, maybe four," Matt's wife said. "I'll call you."

The next day, Saturday, Uncle Xie died. Sam called her about it in the morning. She consoled him, sharing the weight of it, as friends had done for her during her year. She also told him how sorry she was about the timing. It could hardly have been worse. Tonight was his banquet.

"It's true," he said, "everything's crazy. So much so that I don't even have time to call more than one person with this. Just you. And isn't it funny that I'd call you? Someone I've known for only a week."

"How can you say that? We've been to Hangzhou together. I've met your uncle."

"He liked you. They all liked you."

"That's why you called me," she said, "because I was there. I saw how much he loved you. And he believed in you, too. I'm sorry, Sam. I know it's a blow."

"It is," he admitted.

"And don't think of me as an interviewer. Not anymore. We've done that. I've written almost all of the article, leaving only one part blank, the ending. What I mean," she said delicately, "is that when we talk now we talk as friends. I don't write it down anymore. I don't use it. You can say what you want without worrying."

"I wasn't worried," he said.

"Just so you know."

"Well, you might want to write this down," he said. "Something strange is happening in Hangzhou. It's beyond Uncle Xie. It's the whole city. It's very rare. The bamboo is flowering."

"All over the city?"

"It will be all over the province before it's done."

"What does it mean?"

"The end of an era."

She thought about this for a second. "If there's a new era, Sam, I think it will be yours. I wish you luck tonight. I'm sorry about your uncle, but I also think if he's anywhere, watching, then this is what he wishes too. For a great meal. So good luck."

"Thank you," he said. There was a silence and then, almost to his own surprise, he said, "I would like you to come."

"This is your night. You don't have to ask me there."

"I know. I ask because I want to."

"What if I were in your way? It's too important."

"That's exactly why I want you there, because it's important. I feel better when you're around."

She was silent. Then: "Are you sure?"

"Yes. Please come, well before the panel. Come at six. My grandfather's house behind the red gate, soon to be my restaurant. You know. Liang Jia Cai."

13

When does the bamboo flower? A man may wait his lifetime for the answer and still not see it. The bamboo might flower only once in a hundred years. Once it begins, all the bamboo around it will flower too, for hundreds of miles, all over the region. All the bamboo will flower and bear seeds and then die. So it would seem that the bamboo flowering portends disaster. But many are the tales of famine, of men driven mad by starvation, and then suddenly at that moment the bamboo flowers. Bamboo rats gorge on the seeds and overpopulate; the starving people eat them and their lives are saved. Enough seeds work their way into the soil to begin the new plants, and the cycle of man and his food starts again. Thus the time of the bamboo flowering means both the end and the beginning.

— LIANG WEI, *The Last Chinese Chef*

Later that morning Maggie went into the office to tell Carey she had decided what she wanted to do.

"I ought to have the results in two days, three at most," she said. "If she's Matt's, cooperate fully."

"There's nothing else we can do," said Carey, and Zinnia nodded.

"But if she's not, if she's the other guy's daughter, I want you to help Gao Lan. Zinnia told you, right? About him threatening her?"

"She did," said Carey. "I still say that has nothing to do with you."

"She's afraid of him," Maggie countered. "More than she should be, I think, but she is. She's taken that fear in. She's holding it dear." *Like I did, with my grief, all last year.* "She can't approach him. Somebody needs to intervene."

"What did you have in mind?"

"You telling him what's up with his responsibilities, that's what. Only a man can do it. And a lawyer. In twenty minutes you could talk some sense into his head."

"I'm still not sure it's our province."

"If I pay you by the hour and ask you to do it, will it be our province?"

He raised his hands. "Okay. I get it. Okay."

She and Zinnia traded glances of satisfaction.

"But get the test back. Okay? Call me. Call anytime." Then he gave his wicked smile. "Because as you know I'm up until all hours."

At lunchtime Maggie stopped at a Chongqing-style Sichuan restaurant, and ordered savory, chewy strips of eel fillet cooked with pungent shreds of pepper and soft whole braised garlic cloves. As soon as she tasted it she knew she would not be able to stop eating it, and so she continued to pluck up the succulent bits until she had eaten most of what was on the plate. While she ate, she let her mind go. She thought about what had been wrong in her life, what had been right. Matt had been right. She still felt that way, even now, after Gao Lan. So he had slipped. She also knew he must have suffered for it. Nothing burdened Matt more than a confession unmade. Poor soul. She suddenly wished that he had told her while he was alive so she could have forgiven him. She would have forgiven him, just as she forgave him now. Their love had been greater than one mistake.

She remembered the day a month or two before he died when they were both getting ready to leave again on their trips. Usually they looked forward to their travel. On this day, though, she woke up knowing that she did not want to be away from him. She did not feel the customary pull to her freedom, to their separation, to a quiet, private house or a hotel room. She wished they could both stay home.

There were no presentiments. She had not the remotest inkling of the fate that would take him a few weeks later. She only knew at that moment that she loved him differently, that she did not want him to leave. She thought about this as she ate the bag of candy corn he'd left for her on the bureau.

That night she knocked on Sam's red gate precisely at six and over the wall heard the now-familiar *phit-phit* of his cloth shoes as he crossed the court to open it. She saw the anxious sheen of sweat on his cheekbones.

"Big night," she said softly. His apron was already marked, and sweat was gathering on his T-shirt underneath. She wanted to hug him, just a quick squeeze of sustenance, but she stood her ground and let her support show in her eyes. It would not be right to step across that line and put her arms around him. Nothing should upset his equilibrium tonight. Besides, she was doing a story on him. And she still had that last, all-important paragraph left to write, the one about tonight.

"We're on schedule, at least."

"I'm glad." They walked around the screen and she noticed her spiral evergreen, appealingly placed near a small stone table with four stone stools. She felt a surge of warmth. "I know it's going to be great. I can feel it."

"Your lips to my kitchen gods." They walked up the porch steps to the dining room, and he pulled back the door for her.

"I keep thinking about your father," she said, "that he came. Is he going to come up to Beijing now?"

"He says he will. He may get here tonight. We're not sure. Everybody's so sick with sadness about Xie."

"I hope you can set it aside."

"We're trying."

"Does he like being back, your father?"

"He loves it! You should have heard him go on. How the Zhe-jiang Food and Restaurant Association met him with flowers — just because he was a Liang. I told him he deserved it. Look what I did in here."

She followed him across the dining room, lit with silk lotus-shaped lamps, set with one exquisite table for the panel. "Beautiful," she said. The room was not bare, as it had been before, but warm with purpose. There were enormous candles in tall stands, which she knew he would light later. Divans were built into the walls. Doors closed off small private rooms. The outside world had fallen away. She had the strange sense that they could be standing here at almost any time in history.

The kitchen was different from the serene dining room, shouting, chaotic. On every surface were bowls and baskets and plates of fresh ingredients, every sort of vegetable and herb and paste, chopped and minced and mixed. There were freshly killed chickens and ducks. One of Sam's old uncles — these were the other two, the ones she had not met — groomed one of the birds, turning the warm, fresh carcass around in his lap.

"Do you know my Second Uncle Tan?" Sam said.

"Ni hao." Tan dipped his head.

"And this is Jiang, First Uncle," said Sam.

"Hello."

"The writer!" said Jiang in English. "Very good. Come in!"

"I'm only going to watch," she said. "And please know I'm sorry for your loss." Sam translated this, and both uncles thanked her. "They're your assistants?" she said to Sam.

"Each chef is actually allowed three assistants. I'm using only two. As you know, my Third Uncle couldn't travel. These two have been terrific."

"I'm sure," she said, and surveyed the room, the brilliant sheaves of chives and greens and shoots, pale mounds of cabbage, glistening white bricks of tofu. A blue-and-white bowl held raw fish heads, pink flesh, silver skin, brilliant shiny eyes. Oh, the soup, she thought, excitement picking up. From Hangzhou.

Sam was packing a round mold in front of her. In the bottom went a geometric slab of dark-brown braised pork, upside down on its fat and skin. Around the pork he pressed rice mixed with ginkgo nuts, dates, lotus buds, silver fungus, pine nuts.

"Eight-treasure *dongpo* pork," he said. "My version of a classic." He pressed foil around it, whip-tight. "I'm going to steam it two hours. The brown sauce suffuses everything. I *am* going to drain off some of the fat before I serve it, though — and you wait. You'll see. We'll have an argument over it."

Across the room Tan had finished with the chicken and was now preparing to carve vegetables, turnips and large, pale daikon radishes. "He's great with a knife," Sam said, looking at his uncle. "He taught me. Now watch this."

Sam picked up Tan's warm, fresh chicken and positioned it on his chopping block. He applied a small, sharp knife to the rim of the chicken's body cavity, working his way in. He separated the skin from the carcass with love, one millimeter at a time, teasing the two apart without creating the slightest nick or tear. She barely breathed. In a minute he had the entire skin off the chicken, in one piece, and he held it up, grinning.

"Oh, bravo," she said.

"How about it?" He was proud of himself.

"You should have been a surgeon."

"No! I should have been this, just what I am. Okay. We call this the chicken's pajamas." He laid it aside. "You watch. You're going to see it later."

"Can they take the skin off like that?" She looked at the uncles.

"No," Sam said. "They can't do it. Neither of them. Not many chefs can. You have to be able to feel it." He switched to Chinese and shouted something to Uncle Jiang, who was at the next station mincing ingredients Sam would combine to stuff into the chicken skin: cabbage, exotic dried mushrooms, tofu skins, chives, and minced salt-cured ham from Yunnan.

"You should add rice to the stuffing," Jiang said in Chinese.

"No," Sam insisted. "No rice until the end." Because then there would be the glutinous rice in the pork mold, profound with the rich mahogany sauce and its eight treasures, and the *dongpo* pork itself. That was rice enough.

Maggie could not understand these bursts of Chinese, but she could see Sam's Second Uncle Tan get up on the other side of the kitchen and move to lift the cover off a large stoneware crock. He hefted this and tipped it to fill a cup, which he then drained, quickly.

"*Xiao Tan,*" Jiang reproved him.

Tan raised his hand. He didn't want to hear it. "My old heart," he protested.

"Mine too! How do you think I feel, with Little Xie gone from this world! The same as you. I burn inside. But right now we need our wits. We must help Nephew."

"I have my wits," Tan grumbled, but he capped off the jug and returned to his vegetables. He was ruddy, glowing, visibly happier for his drink. Maggie watched it all.

Sam watched it too. "Tan's been up half the night," he explained. "My father called him and woke him up the second it happened."

"So hard for them. And you."

"Yes. Thanks."

But she could still feel unease in the air. Sam and Jiang didn't like Tan's drinking. It would be better for her to get out of the kitchen and take a walk before the panel came. "Do you mind if I look around?"

"Go," said Sam. "Go anywhere."

So she slid off her chair. Sam was bent over his cooking. She traded nods and smiles with the uncles and pushed open the heavy door. She liked how hard it was to push. She liked some things heavy, a fire poker, bedcovers, keys on a piano. Matt had been heavy, much larger than she. A protective weight on top of her.

In the dining room, the standing wood lamps made pools of light against the pitch of the fitted rafters and the black tile floors. Tall windows were cranked open to the courtyard, where garden lights glowed among the potted flowers and wood filigree.

She peeked into the small private rooms. Two had round tables and chairs. One had a piano. A piano! The sight of one always brought back the warm feeling of her mother's apartment. She wondered if it was in tune.

She walked across the courtyard. The light was starting to fail. The second dining room was here. This one was done differently, with white walls and contemporary art, and also doors to private rooms.

She looked into the smallest, north-facing room. It had not been restored. This was where he had lived while the place was being done. The high wooden ceiling was weathered, its paint half flaked off. The walls were seamed with cracks. Black-and-white subway tile, pieces of which were missing, covered the floor.

She turned out the light and crossed to the last, south-facing room. This was where he lived now. It was a warm room; it contained a life. The bed was rumpled. A laptop blinked on the table. Clothing lay in folded stacks beneath the window.

He had said to go anywhere, but here she was intruding. This was his private place. She did not enter, just stood in the doorway and looked.

Like the other rooms, this one had high rear windows. They were screened and hung open on chains. Through them she could see patches of rooftops and sky.

She leaned on the door frame. It was comfortable. There was a stillness to China in unexpected places, and once again she had the curious sensation of being anywhere in time. She felt relieved of her life, of the world she knew, stripped away from herself. It was a strange place, far from her home. She really didn't belong. So why did the surprise thought keep rising like a bubble inside her that it might be nice to stay?

She backed out of Sam Liang's room. As she crossed on the path she could hear the Chinese voices from the kitchen. The interplay of sounds was like abstract music to her. When she pushed open the door to the kitchen she saw that Jiang was disagreeing with Sam about something. Tan was off by himself carving furiously. He already had made birds and animals. He looked slightly melted.

"Perfect timing," Sam said to her. "They'll be here soon."

"Were you arguing with him?" she said when Jiang turned back to his task.

"He thought I was using too many crabs."

"Is there such a thing? Ever?"

He laughed.

"I didn't think so," she said, triumphant. "What's the dish?"

"Spongy tofu. It's a simple, plain dish — but the sky-high imperial version. The thing about tofu is, if you boil it rapidly for thirty minutes it will fill with holes. It becomes a sponge, ready to squirt its sauce when you bite into it. Now the average kitchen might dress it with green onion and oyster sauce. You know, whatever. Not me. I am making a reduction sauce from thirty crabs."

"But that sounds great!"

"And not even their meat. Their shells, their fat, and their roe. Reduced and thickened until it's just thick enough to soak into the tofu and stay there. Until you bite into it. This is a dish of artifice. See? It comes to the table looking like one thing. Like the plainest of food. Tofu. But you taste it and it's something different."

"Don't listen to them. Do it."

Sam stopped and turned his head to a sound, the gate. A knock. It was the smallest of sounds by the time it got all the way back to the kitchen, but this was his home and he knew that small sound by heart. "First Uncle! They're here."

"Oh!" Jiang yanked off his apron and brushed his pants, anxious suddenly, fussy.

"You're fine," said Sam. "Go."

Maggie held the heavy door and watched him pause to light the candles and switch on more lamps to illuminate the couplets of calligraphy around the walls. Then he hurried out to the gate.

"How many judges are there?" she asked Sam.

"Six. All food people, from the Ministry of Culture and the Beijing Restaurant Association."

"Here they come." She peeked through the door.

Sam put his knife down and came over to stand next to her and look through the crack. The panel filed in, all men, with one senior member, all in dark suits, smiling, First Uncle welcoming them. It was right for him to be the one to do it; he was the eldest. Once he had them settled in their seats around tiny dishes of pickles and salt-roasted fava beans, he poured a rare aromatic oolong while he delivered a sparkling little introduction to Liang family cuisine.

"Now!" he hissed as he swept back into the kitchen. "Are you ready?" But Sam already had the first appetizers laid out. After an interval for the diners to relax, Jiang carried out a mince of wild herbs and dried tofu, sweet-savory puffs of gluten, and pureed scented hyacinth beans. He came back for the fragrant vinegar duck, spattered with brown Shanxi vinegar. The last appetizer was fresh clams, marinated in a dense bath of soy, vinegar, and aromatics. "That's *nong*," he said, bringing the sauce close to her to smell. "The dark, concentrated flavor."

A shimmering interval of eating and happy laughter floated by in the dining room. Appetizers were consumed, along with tea and the first toasts of wine.

Sam himself carried in the first main courses. According to the classical pattern he started with a few lacy-crisp deep-fried dishes: pepper-salt eel fillets like translucent little tiles, similar to those his father had described making for the mother and son in the swamp; and an aromatic stir-fry of yellow chives studded with tiny, delicate fried oysters.

Back in the kitchen, he stir-fried tender mustard greens with wide, flat tofu-skin noodles and plump, fresh, braised young soybeans. These glistened on the platter in a light crystal sauce. After that there were lamb skewers, delectably grilled and crusted with sesame.

On the other side of the kitchen Sam noticed Second Uncle looking distinctly glossy as he bent over his knife. Too much to drink. It was bad enough that he was using a knife to carve vegetables; he had to be kept away from food. Sam and Jiang would need to do everything by themselves. Could they?

"When is Baba getting to Beijing?" Sam asked in Chinese, loud enough for only Jiang to hear.

Jiang understood; he sent the smallest look in Tan's direction. "Actually, he is here."

Sam jerked around. "Already here?"

"He came a few hours ago."

"Why didn't he call?"

His eldest uncle regarded him patiently. "This is your night."

Sam understood, but still — to stay away from his childhood home? "Where is he?"

"At Yang's house. Not far from here."

"We may need him," said Sam.

"We may," Jiang agreed. "But let us wait. Do you know, it was always difficult for your father to be his father's son. He was never the original one or the real one, only the son. He knows well that you have been here alone for four years, with us. He wants you to win tonight the same way." Jiang raised a white eyebrow. "I agree with him."

"Unless we need him," Sam qualified.

By now there was a palpable surge of success from the dining room, the sound of pleased conversation, laughter, delight, comprehensible in any language. Everyone in the kitchen was smiling, Jiang, Sam, even Tan, still on the side carving daikons.

Sam signaled Jiang that there would now be a pause. Shaoxing wine was to be served, thick, aromatic, in tiny stoneware cups. Uncle Jiang poured it from the large crock into the smaller, more precious one that would be borne to the table; it was inscribed with the words of the ninth-century poet Po Chu-I, *What could I do to ease a rustic heart?* Sam had planned every small thing this way, to support the theme of the meal. He positioned the jug with its words on the tray. He hoped the diners would have their own rustic thoughts. Perhaps they would be reminded of the words of Confucius — *With coarse grain to eat, with water to drink, and my bended arm for a pillow: I still have joy in the midst of these things.*

When the tray was ready Jiang closed the wine crock and stowed it high in the cupboard, out of reach. "I saw that!" said Tan.

"I hope so!" Jiang shot back.

While they were drinking and toasting the dishes at the table Sam took the next course from the oven, a perfect plump chicken, roasted to a crisp honey brown. No, she thought, not a chicken — this was the chicken *skin*. "Is there any chicken inside?"

"None," he said. "Minced vegetables and ham. You cut it like a pie. Here we enter the part of the menu which toys with the mind. You see one thing, you taste something else. This is supposed to wake you up, make you realize you've been daydreaming. You know what I mean?"

"I feel that way all the time here," she said. "Seems like my whole life before I came to China was a daydream."

"Wo yiyang," Sam said, Me too. He turned to Jiang and Tan, who had magically risen from his corner and joined them at the center island. The three of them quickly created a monumental platter by settling the whole crisp chicken on a papery bed of fried spinach next to a pearly white woman in flowing robes carved from daikon, her lips and eyes brightened with food coloring, her hands spread in universal kindness. This provocative creation was borne out, thwacked open, and shouted over by the diners. In the kitchen, Sam lifted the steamer to check the ribs in lotus leaves. Almost time.

Behind them they heard a cry. Maggie turned and saw Tan's hand raised, the clutch of his other fist not quite hiding a little up-rush of blood. He had cut himself. She grabbed a clean towel and leapt to him, applying pressure.

"Thanks, Maggie," Sam said, and then to Jiang, in Chinese, "Let's go to the soup."

This he assembled in an enormous blue-and-white tureen — the intense, delectable fish broth, the fish balls like fresh clouds, the silky tofu, the mustard greens. The great bowl was too heavy for Jiang.

"I'll take this one," said Sam, hoisting it.

When he walked into the dining room with the soup there rose a general murmur of approval which escalated to a cheer. He told them the soup was a tribute to Hangzhou.

Then they were ready for the tofu with crab sauce. Tan's finger had stopped bleeding and been bandaged, so Maggie came over to watch. Sam reduced the sauce and then thickened it with emulsified crab fat and crab roe. Just enough, he said to her, so it would penetrate the tofu and stay there.

When it was right he dropped in the slices of spongy tofu, immersing them. "This cooks on low. The tofu will drink up all the sauce. It looks like tofu — a peasant dish — when it comes to the table. Then the crab squirts out when you bite into it. So good. Here — try. This is what they will taste." He took a spoonful and dropped it in a small clean dish, which he held up and tipped to her lips. "Go on."

She opened and let him pour it into her mouth. It was crab flavor multiplied further than she had ever thought possible. "What *is* that? I never tasted crab flavor so intense."

"The shells are the secret," he said. "The part most people throw away. It's almost ready." He stood over the tofu, monitoring it. "Now! Let's go."

He took the rustic-looking platter he had selected and piled it on. Yuan Mei said nothing was more sophisticated than the simplest bowls and plates. This platter said "plain food." It completed the illusion — all of which would be shattered when the diner bit into the crab sauce. This, he thought, might be his best dish.

"Ready?" said Jiang, and he took the platter and bore it toward the door. Just at that moment Tan rose from his chair, lost his footing, and stumbled backward into Jiang.

The platter flew from First Uncle's hands. They all saw. But nothing could stop it from arcing through the air and shattering on the floor. Big, powdery shards of smashed porcelain came to rest in the tofu and crab sauce.

They all stood staring in a circle around it.

Sam was heaving. The thirty crabs. The glory of the taste.

"Who moved this chair?" Uncle Tan glared. "Nephew? Was it you? It wasn't there before."

Sam ignored him, turned to Jiang. He was drained of color. "Now we're short one," he said.

Jiang nodded. "I'll call your father."

"I'll do it," said Sam.

"Nephew," Tan persisted drunkenly, "did you move it?"

Sam just looked at him. He knew when to raise the barriers so he could keep going, and this was one of those times. He turned away. As he thumbed Liang Yeh's number into his phone, from the corner of his eye he saw Maggie step over to Uncle Tan and put her hands on his shoulders. On the other end of the line the phone was ringing.

"You should sit down and take a rest and let us clean this up," he heard her say. "And don't say another word to Sam right now." She gently pushed him down into a chair.

In his half-lubricated state a foreign woman coming at him and then actually touching him was too much; he did exactly what she said and sank into the chair, mute. *"Wei?"* Sam heard Liang Yeh say on the other end.

"Wei," said Sam. "Dad. I need you. Please come right now."

"My son, this is —"

"Now," Sam cut in. "I mean it. Please."

"Wh —"

"We've had an accident."

Quiet. He heard small faraway sounds. "Right away I will come," Liang Yeh said.

It was only a few minutes until he arrived, a small older man, stepping quietly in through the back kitchen door.

Tan looked up at him dumbly. "How did you get in?"

"No matter how far a man may travel, he still knows how to return to his native place," joked Liang Yeh.

"Baba," Sam said, and the two walked to each other. Sam held his father for a long time. He could feel Maggie watching, unable to take her eyes away. *This is me. Take a look. He comes with me.* They stepped apart and he introduced her.

"Hi," she said, smiling up at him. She was on the floor, wiping up the last of the crab.

She had insisted on doing it while she kept an eye on Tan. Sam was grateful.

He led his father to the cooking area, explaining, and gave him a taste of the crab sauce that had just been lost. "Wonderful," Liang Yeh whispered, his eyes wide, his face split in awe. It was a look Sam didn't think he'd ever seen on his father's face before. "How many crabs?"

"Thirty."

"Thirty!" Liang Yeh's gray eyebrows shot up. "Magnificent! I love crabs."

"'As far as crabs are concerned,'" Tan intoned, "'my mind is addicted to them, my mouth enjoys the taste of them, and never for a single day in my life have I forgotten about them.'"

"You're drunk," Liang Yeh said.

"But accurate," Jiang said. "That's Li Yu, 1650. Word for word."

"Still drunk. Old friend." And Liang Yeh embraced Tan, who cried a little on his shoulder, and then Jiang, who squeezed him in a tall, quiet way. They had greeted each other a few hours before, but still seemed overcome by being together — old now, but together.

"Gentlemen," said Sam, "I need another dish. Fast."

But Liang Yeh was on his own time, as always. Now he was looking at the white woman over there with her rump up in the air, cleaning the floor. "Is she —," he said.

"No, Baba. Just a friend. Actually she's interviewing me for a magazine. So only sort of a friend. A colleague."

"Sort of," repeated Liang Yeh. "She doesn't talk?"

"No. But you speak English, last time I checked. Now come on. A dish."

"All right." Reluctantly he tore himself away from the natural speculations arising from the sight of Maggie on Sam's floor. "Where are you?"

"Here. See the menu?" Sam pointed to a spot on the page.

234

"The spongy tofu," said his father. "What else can you tell me about the room, the poems, the serving pieces?"

"There is the couplet on the wall," said Sam. "It's something we chose from Su Dongpo, a poem about taking a boat down the Grand Canal. Uncle Jiang did the calligraphy. It says:

> "The sound of chopping fish comes from the bow
> And the fragrance of cooking rice from the stern."

"Good," said Liang Yeh. "Let me see through into the dining room." He moved to the door and peered through the crack. "Ah! You have made it beautiful."

"I'm sure I could have done a better job," said Sam, knowing that he couldn't have, but using the automatic modesty that came with Chinese.

Sam was startled when he realized they were speaking Chinese. His father had not spoken it much during Sam's childhood, sticking stubbornly with his simplified English and thus allowing himself to be simplified before the world. *No wonder you retreated.* Now the deep-throated, *rrr*-inflected Mandarin of Beijing had settled back over his father. "You can talk, too," he said to Sam approvingly.

"Still learning. I'll show you the house later. I did over everything except the little north-facing room. That's where I lived while they were doing it. But it's not what you remember, Baba. It's just one court."

"This was my mother's court," said Liang Yeh softly, "Chao Jing." And Sam saw the rain gathering in his eyes. "This was her main living area. She had her bed over there." And he pointed to the private rooms. "All right." He stepped away from the door. "Go on. Other serving pieces?"

"We brought out the Shaoxing wine in the 'rustic heart' jug — you know the one?" said Sam.

"So well! It was my father's." Liang Yeh followed him back to the cooking area, picked up the menu, and studied it. "The spongy tofu was your second artifice dish."

"Yes. The first was the whole crisp chicken skin, stuffed with other things."

"Then you lost one artifice dish. We need something intellectual," said Liang.

"Or historical," said Sam. He switched into English. Chinese was for allusion, English for precision. He was in another realm with his father now that he could speak both. It shifted everything between them. "See, nostalgia is powerful here right now because of how fast things have changed. Anything that really nails the recherché is automatically provocative; it unleashes a whole torrent of ideas in people's minds."

"All right." His father paced the counters, scanned the ingredients. "Can you buy me a little time?" They were still in English. "Serve something else?"

"The lotus-leaf pork ribs," said Sam. "Uncle Xie's recipe. They're ready."

His father turned. "He taught you? Go ahead, then."

By the time Sam had served the ribs and chatted with the diners and come back, Liang Yeh had something under way. Sam watched him working with chestnut flour and cornmeal, mincing pork. He did it so easily. *Why did you hold back all those years? Why wouldn't you cook? Was the fear worth it?*

"You don't need this pork, do you?"

"No," Sam said. "It's from the top of the ribs."

"Never waste food," said Liang Yeh.

Jiang gave a chirp of laughter from where he stood, cutting, but Sam did not laugh. He took a deep breath in, loving it. It was home, being in the kitchen beside his father. It was the root of his chord, even though he had never heard it played before. "Yes, Baba," he said, obedient. Don't waste food.

His father made three cold vegetable dishes, one of macerated bite-sized cucumber spears shot through with sauce, and another of air-thin slices of pink watermelon radish in a light dressing. Braised soybeans — those left over from yesterday's prep — had been dressed with the torn leaves of the Chinese toon tree.

Then the meat and the cakes. First he marinated the minced

pork. While it soaked he worked with the wheat flour and a little fat until he had just the weight he wanted, then formed the dough into balls that he rolled in sesame. The next step was to add minced water chestnuts to the pork and fry it quickly on a griddle with garlic and ginger and green onion and soy until it was deep brown and chewy-soft. Then he held another wok upside down, dry, over a high fire until it was very hot, after which he pressed the dough balls into little disks all over the inside and flattened them slightly with his fingers. "This is another dish of the Empress Dowager's," he told his son. "This one came to her in a dream. Did you know that? The Old Buddha dreamed, and then she ordered her chefs to make it." He smiled. "Actually it's not bad," he said.

The wok with the dough disks inside it went back over the fire, upside down and angled, constantly turned, carefully watched, until all the flat cakes were golden brown and ready to be popped off.

"Split them," Liang Yeh said, handing the steaming plate to Sam. "Stuff them with the meat." Sam started this, fingers flying. Each one emitted a fragrant puff of steam when he opened it to push in the meat. Meanwhile his father turned to his other bowl of dough, this one of corn and chestnut flour, and worked it until it was ready. From this he shaped a swift panful of tiny thimble-shaped cones.

"After all these years?" Sam said, because he recognized what his father was making — *xiao wo tou*. This was the dish that had caused him to flee Gou Bu Li that night. This was the rustic favorite of the Empress, which Liang Wei had warned his son never to make. "Why now?"

"Better than being haunted by ghosts, isn't it? Besides, it's another resonance on your rustic theme. For those who know their history, the connection will satisfy." Watching the speed at which he moved, it was impossible for Sam to believe that those fingers had been resting for forty years.

The corn cones went in the oven only briefly — fuel had been scarce on the road when the Empress fled — and then came out. He arranged them on a plain platter with the tiny meat-stuffed cakes. "Think of it as a pause by the side of the road," he told his son as he packed everything on a tray around a turnip that Tan had turned into a fragile pink peony.

"Should I tell the panel the background story?" said Sam, before he carried it out. "Because I don't think they will know."

"Surely they will know," said Liang Yeh. "It's the Empress Dowager."

"Brother," chided Jiang, "they won't know. They have forgotten."

Liang Yeh shrugged. "Then let it be."

Sam took the platter from his father. He saw that his father was different here, light, almost at ease, in the way he must have been when he was young. Gone was the ill-fitting cloak of exile he had worn for so many years, the hunched and anxious shoulders. Sam wished his mother could be here, seeing it. She loved Liang Yeh, loved his kindness and his mordant humor; she would be uplifted to see him so happy. Sam felt a pang of longing for them to be together, the three of them, with his father like this, here in China.

Back in the kitchen Sam noticed Maggie sitting now, watching. She was so attentive. Her presence reminded him that most people did not watch things very closely. Well, it was her job. She was a writer. He liked knowing she was there. She saw everything. He almost seemed to see his own life more clearly when she was here to witness it. Soon, though, she would be gone. "How much longer are you going to be in China?" he said.

"I try not to think about that."

"Why?"

"I guess I don't want to leave. I would never have thought I would like it here, this much. But I do. It feels good."

"So stay," he said.

"I can't. I have to work. By the way," she said quickly, changing the subject, "he's amazing, your father. He really kept his skills up. I thought you said he never cooked!"

"He hasn't, for many years," said Sam. "He's just naturally great. He's the last Chinese chef."

"No, Sam," she said. "You are."

He smiled. "That's why I wish you didn't have to leave."

"I feel the same."

"So maybe you'll come back."

She said nothing. He held the first of the three molds over the sink and, supporting it with a sieve, dislodged it in one piece. He opened the crevice just a bit, and sizzling pork fat ran off and hissed into the sink.

"Nephew! Your sense has vanished and left you!" Jiang flew across the room at him.

"Remember?" Sam said to Maggie in English. "I told you this would cause a fight." Then he went back to Chinese. "Uncle, we don't need *all* the fat."

"But this dish is *you er bu ni*," To taste of fat without being oily. "That is its point!"

"This is enough fat."

"Leave him!" cried Liang Yeh. "Do you not think he knows the right amount? To the droplet? To the touch?"

A change came over the room. Even Maggie felt the fine hairs on her arms stand up.

"Perhaps you are right," said Jiang in Chinese.

"Thanks, Dad," said Sam, using English. Then, in Chinese: "It's so rich already. And this is the first rice we've had. I assure you, for the *meishijia*, the fat is waiting, delicate and aromatic as a soufflé, right under the skin." He turned to his father. "You serve it. Please. I served your corn cakes and your sloppy joes."

"*Xiao wo tou* and *shao bing jia rou mo*," his father said. "Learn the Chinese names."

"I will," Sam said. And Liang Yeh carried the tray in high, with a flourish. They heard his smart steps across the floor, the click of the plates on the table, and then, from the panel, low shrieks of disbelief, submission, almost weeping.

"They're going to eat the fat," Tan predicted.

"Five to two says no," Sam said. "A hundred *kuai*."

"Done," Tan said, satisfied. He had cooked for the *meishijia* all his life. He knew they would eat the fat.

Jiang stood back to let Liang Yeh back in and peered out through the crack in the door. "You win," he said to Tan. "They're eating it. Any more dishes?"

"One," said Sam. "The last metaphor. It's easy now. I made the broth yesterday." From the refrigerator he took a bowl with about six cups of rich-looking jellied broth. "Lamb broth. I boiled it for three hours — lamb meat and bones, and wine, and all kinds of aromatics. Then I cooled it, took out all the fat." He dumped the jellied broth into a pot. "Every great banquet ends with a fish," he told Maggie in English. "This is going to be carp in lamb broth."

"I don't think I've ever heard of that combination," said Maggie.

"It's a literary finish. This last dish creates a word, perhaps the single most important word in the Chinese culinary language — *xian*, the fresh, clean taste. The character for *xian* is made up of two characters — the character for fish combined with the character for lamb. In this dish the two are joined. They mesh. They symbolize *xian*. They are *xian*."

"Is it hard to make them work together, carp and lamb?"

"Harder than you think. It's about the balance of flavors. Lamb cooked in wine is sweet and strong. Carp is meaty and also strong. If you can find just the right meeting point, they're perfect." The broth was heating up.

"It smells wonderful."

"Watch," he said. "As full as the people out there are, they'll eat the soup, all of it." He added the fish, brought the broth and the fish back to a boil, and immediately turned it out into a famille-rose tureen. The smell was the two natural musks, of lamb and of carp, made one.

"Mm." She drew it in. "In the beginning was the Word."

He laughed at her, delighted, and took off his apron. "That's it!" He lifted the bowl. It was done.

Dessert was a platter of rare fruits, trimmed and carved into bite-sized flowers and other small pleasing geometries, then assembled like a mosaic into the shape of a flying yellow dragon — imperial style, with five claws instead of four. This was another of Uncle Tan's creations.

Crafting thematic images with fruits and vegetables was a common Chinese culinary trick, practiced at all the better restaurants, so when Sam first brought the fruit mosaic to the table the only comment it excited was on the perfection of the dragon and the pleasing way in which the finale reinforced the Liang family's roots in imperial cuisine. It was only after the panel began to nibble at the fruits that the cries of happy surprise once again rose from the table. None of the fruits were what they expected. They were from every corner of China and her territories, like the delicacies that had always been brought to the Emperor. There were mangosteens and soursops and cold litchi jelly from the south, deep-orange Hami melon from Xinjiang, jujubes and crab apples and haws from China's northeast.

If the members of the panel ate enough of the fruit to see the line of calligraphy alongside the painting of peaches on the plate, they would also find an excerpt from Yi Yin's famous description of the tribute fruits brought to court, written in the eighteenth century B.C.: *North of the Chao Range there are all kinds of fruit eaten by the Gods. The fastest horses are required to fetch them.* If they ate far enough, they would read these lines and the connection would be complete.

Sam didn't know if they would reach the quotation or not, but by now he saw that it didn't matter. The act was enough. There was totality in the act.

Now, from the dining room, they were cheering and calling out. Maggie touched his arm. "I think they want you."

So he walked in. They rose to their feet, crying out their happiness, applauding. "Marvelous!" "Unforgettable!" "The Liangs have returned."

"Thank you," he said back to them, "thank you." He felt himself practically vibrating with happiness. He introduced his assistants, his father and his uncles, one by one. He bowed. He thanked them again.

After hearing the names, one of the panelists addressed Sam's father. "You are Liang Yeh? The son of Liang Wei?"

"I am he," the old man said.

"So interesting. There is another face to the family name!"

"Yes," Liang Yeh said simply, smiling at the panelist, saying no more.

Sam watched. He remembered what First Uncle had told him about Liang Yeh laboring under his own father's fame, and once again he saw his father differently, not as his father but as a man with his own private mountains in front of him.

Sam continued thanking the panel for their compliments, aware that very soon now they would leave. Chinese diners never lingered around a table as did Westerners. After completing a meal and taking the appropriate time to exchange moods of surfeit, gratitude, and admiration, they would rise as one and politely depart as a group. It was the custom.

Sam saw his problem. Someone had to go out, quickly, to unlock the front gate. Originally this had been Tan's job, but Tan was out of commission. And he could not go himself. As the chef he had to see the panelists out.

Head averted, just enough, he managed to catch Jiang's eye and signal toward the front. Jiang understood. He made a small confirming nod and stepped back from the group, quietly, to turn for the door.

When Jiang Wanli caught Nephew's signal, he remembered that Xiao Tan was in no condition to run out and open the gate. Nephew was right. Someone had to go. He excused himself from the dining room, slipped back into the kitchen, and quickly crossed it to walk out through the back door. He hurried past the slab of stone where Nephew did the butchering, through the small arch, and into the courtyard, his old wisp of a frame quiet. The sky was clear now above the gathering trees, the small spotlights shining along the path. He kept to the quiet shadows along the side, by the south verandah, in front of the one room Nephew had not refinished. He pulled his old cardigan close around him.

Just as he rounded the spirit screen he heard the door from the main dining room clatter back. Nephew was leading them out. He stretched his arm out, shaking a little, and turned the lock to release the gate. There. Now what? They were halfway across the court. Where could he go? There was the door into the little guardhouse. He didn't know if it was locked. He tried the handle. It turned. He heard Nephew's voice saying goodbye, moving toward the ceramic-faced wall. He opened the door and stepped trembling inside.

It was a cramped cubicle, full of dust. They came flowing around the screen and their voices drifted right through the grillwork window to him. "Work of art . . . *Meizhile* . . . Beautiful . . . Above everyone except possibly Yao . . . Yes . . . Too bad, isn't it? . . . About the minister's son! . . . Oh, yes . . . Too bad . . ." Jiang stood in the darkness, listening. He held his breath so as not to sneeze. "Too bad . . ." Their voices faded as they passed into the street.

Old fool, Jiang told himself, *you knew this. You heard it from the Master of the Nets the day you took Nephew to meet him.* Still, it hurt. Because from the meal tonight there had risen the fragrance of genius.

When First Uncle had locked the gate again and made his way back to the kitchen, he found the family embracing one another, pouring wine. Even Tan was allowed to drink again. Young Liang and Old Liang had their arms linked, Nephew and his father, a sight Jiang had lived long to see. Everyone was happy, even the foreign woman, who, he noticed, did not like to take her eyes off Young Liang. If Nephew didn't see why she was here, he was blind. Jiang might take him aside and tell him.

"Uncle!" Sam cried. "What do you think? They loved it!"

"They did," said Jiang, his heart swelling for the boy who had cooked so well. No, he decided; he would not tell him what he'd just heard at the gate. Let him enjoy his success. In any case, speaking technically, it was nothing Nephew did not already know. He had been in the fish purveyor's office that day too. He knew.

"Listen!" cried Liang Yeh. "I vow that by this time tomorrow it will be *kuai zhi ren kou,* On everyone's lips. You will succeed! I am sure!"

"I agree," said Jiang.

Tan drained off another cup of wine. "Now let's go eat!" he said. "Before I die from hunger."

"Do we have to go out?" Jiang complained.

All five of them looked at what had been the kitchen. It was a wreck.

"There's nothing to eat here," Sam said dismissively.

They accepted this instantly. The talk bounced ahead to an animated discussion of possible restaurants. Eventually it was decided that the three elders must have *jing jiang rou si,* a celestially delicious local dish of shredded pork in piquant sauce rolled up with spring onion in a tofu wrapper. This specialty was available at many places around Beijing, but they had to have the choicest and most succulent, and for that they had to trek to a certain restaurant on the northeast side of town.

"Not me," said Nephew. "I can't eat right now. You go." And they all walked out to the lakefront together so he could get a car for them, get them comfortable inside, and chat with the driver for a minute about finding the restaurant, which was down a side street and easily missed the first time one looked for it.

Jiang clasped Nephew's hand one last time. He understood some English, just a little, and before they drove away he heard Young Liang say to the American girl, "Come on. I'll lock the gate and take you home."

14

Yuan Mei wrote that cooking was similar to matrimony. He said, "Two things served together should match. Clear should go with clear, thick with thick, hard with hard, soft with soft." It is the correct pairing on which things depend.

— LIANG WEI, *The Last Chinese Chef*

On Sunday morning, Maggie woke up to an e-mail message from the DNA lab: the results would be posted on the Internet at nine A.M. Monday, beneath her password — midnight Monday for her, here. She turned back to drafting her article. She felt the old thrill of insight as her fingers flew over the keys. How long since she'd written with such excitement? It really was more than food, this cuisine; it was *guanxi*, relationships, caring. She saw Uncle Xie and his family along with Sam as she wrote, the warmth and love and grief of the house in Hangzhou.

There was another level too, one she understood only after watching Sam stage the banquet. In addition to connecting people to one another, food was the mediator between the Chinese and their culture. By its references to art and the achievements of civilization, it bound the diner to his or her own soul. Okay, she admitted, it was clubby, and maybe possible only in a closed society of long history, but she had never been in a place where the web was so rich.

The next night, Monday, after walking outside all day, she decided to start the last part. The press conference was scheduled for Tuesday evening. She would watch it on the news, praying, repeating mantras all the while. For now she could write about the banquet itself, about his triumph, even after the loss of spongy tofu with a sauce of thirty crabs. What a sauce. Genius.

She came as close as she could to the end of the piece before she had to stop. She could not finish until the winners were announced. And even though she had been careful to sound appropriately dispassionate on the page, she knew she badly wanted one of them to be Sam.

She thought about this as she closed the file and switched off the computer. She liked him. She surprised herself. She didn't make real friends, as a rule, when she traveled. Not that she was unfriendly; the opposite. She had been doing her column for years. She thought of herself as an expert on the transient relationship. She had learned to create a friendship in a short time, have it lend mutual enjoyment and human glow to the work, and then let it go. Sometimes there were a few calls and e-mail messages after, but most of these column connections, even those that seemed full of possibility, would in time fall away from her. She never felt the way she felt now, that she actually wanted to put off leaving a place because she enjoyed being around someone so much.

Was it him, or was it his family? It was both of them, and his whole world. Maybe she would break her mold on this story and they would actually become friends. No more than friends, she was sure, for she had never felt him look at her in the other way, but friends. She would like to know him, she realized. She would like to stay here, and stay connected, a little longer.

There was time, at least as far as *Table* was concerned. She didn't even have to turn in her copy for another eight days. That was far more time than she needed to get the lab results, act on them, learn the outcome of the contest, and write the last sentences of her story.

She could just be here, a place she was realizing she liked. Be here, enjoy it, and finish with the past. That was another thing that was in pure, sharp focus here — all of her memories. She moved to the couch in front of the windows and watched the lit-up buildings. Never had the memories been so clear. She could see everything: the dark side of Matt, the light. The odd times and places she had really felt at home. The truth of certain moments.

The last morning of his life floated before her. He was dressing and getting ready to fly to San Francisco. First she had made him coffee.

She remembered it was French roast she had brought back from Louisiana, which released a wonderful burnt-caramel smell. He had declared that on the basis of that coffee alone it was difficult to leave her for so much as a single night, a day. He flattered her. Coffee was the only thing she ever made. She remembered how this made her laugh as she brought the coffee back to the bedroom with the first lightenings of the sun beyond the window. She remembered their feeling of calm together. She remembered the good feeling once again of not wanting him to leave, and the simultaneous sensation of having plenty of time, having years. She was thirty-nine then.

She lay in bed and watched him get up and get dressed. She was still feeling as if they should change their schedules, do something about the traveling. Move closer to the kind of life he wanted. This might be the moment.

"I've been thinking," she said from the bed. "I've been starting to wish we didn't have to be apart."

He looked at her in surprise. "And not travel?"

"Just a thought."

He zipped up and buckled his belt. "Let's talk about it when I get back."

"Okay." She was a little surprised by his reaction. For her to even say this was a big step. She had half expected him to leap on it. But he was preoccupied with his trip to San Francisco. He was late.

He came over to the bed and kissed her, but it was short, chaste, the kiss of a man whose mind has moved through the door to where he has to be. No candy corn. "See you tonight," he said, and walked out the door. She never saw him again.

She could still envision the door, smooth, light, empty, which he closed behind him softly. This was the door between her old life and the year that came after. The world of now. She could still hear his footsteps tapping down the hall, soft, precise for a man of his size. She could hear the sputter of his motor, the whine of it reversing out the driveway, the fade as he drove away. A few days later she went to the airport to retrieve that car, numb, trembling, eyes puffed nearly shut from crying. She signed forms, filling in a blank line with the word *Deceased,* drove the car home, got out, and never climbed inside it again. She sold it. Then she stored her possessions. She sold the house. All those things made her feel bad, was how she explained it to people when they asked. So she got rid of them. She couldn't let herself have a life when he did not. Especially when he was so undeserving of his fate, so damned *good.*

Good? she thought now. Maybe not really.

The clock showed almost midnight. It was time to see if Shuying was Matt's child.

She flipped on the machine, went online, and put in her password. Then for security she entered it again. Then the last four digits of her credit card, and her mother's maiden name.

She watched the screen, waiting. *We're even now. I'll never again feel guilt for not giving you a child.* Strangely, she felt serene.

Then it came up. Right in front of her.

Matthew Mason and Gao Shuying.

Match: negative.

She read it again. Again. She didn't believe it. So she exited the site, went offline, reconnected, and started over. Same sequence. She clicked for the second time on "Get Results." There it was.

Matthew Mason and Gao Shuying. Match: negative.

Maggie stared at the words. She felt like a car with its motor cut, rolling to a silent stop.

She read farther down. Written lab results were being expressed to her with a duplicate set on their way to Calder Hayes in Beijing.

Arrival in thirty-six hours. That was still two business days before the ruling. Not much time. But enough.

Gao Lan had said to call anytime — what had she said? *Dark or light* — but it was past midnight, so Maggie would wait. There was always the possibility that her employer was in town.

Carey was a different matter. Maggie *knew* he was up. It was possible he was with a woman, she supposed, but she doubted that would stop him from answering his phone.

Her intuition was correct. He picked right up.

"You told me to call anytime," she reminded him.

"Of course."

"Well, here it is. Shuying is not Matt's."

No sound. Just his breathing. "That's a relief," he said at last.

Maggie heard the complex tangle behind his words. He was glad. But now he was thinking that he'd told her, put her through all this, for nothing. No, she thought, for everything. She grew taller in her chair. "You'll get your set of documents Wednesday morning. But you don't have to wait until then, right? You can call the ministry?"

"Oh, yes. First thing tomorrow. And someone else at the top of my list is Andrew Souther. That's the guy, that's his name. I pried it out of Gao Lan."

"How'd you do that?"

"There's this restaurant out toward the Beijing Zoo, a Uighur place — you should try it."

"Ah," said Maggie.

"I'll set up a meeting with him here in the office. I'm going to pack it with a few other lawyers, just to drive my point home."

"Which is?" said Maggie.

"To make the law very clear to him."

"Thank you. That's what I was hoping for."

"At first I was surprised you wanted to help her," he said.

Maggie spoke slowly. She had given this a lot of thought. "We are connected, she and I, by something that happened in our lives. After I met her I felt that, and then the rivalry part didn't matter anymore. Also, I'm human — and I met the child."

"There, you were right. Someone may have to intervene. Zinnia explained a little more to me after you left about Gao Lan — let's face it, she has only six or seven years left doing that kind of work. And none of this is the kid's fault."

"Now, should I pay you for this?" said Maggie. "Because I will."

"No! No problem. Everything has to be done soon, though, because I'm going home next week. My mother's sick."

"I'm sorry," said Maggie. "I didn't know that."

"She's dying."

"That must be difficult."

"It's not sudden. She's been sick for a while. Got to go, though, you know? It's important."

"I know."

"Family."

"Right. *Guanxi.*"

A smile came into his voice. "Listen to you! You like China."

"Funny you say that. I've been sitting here all night, waiting for these results to be posted, staring out the window at Beijing. It's very mind-altering. I've decided China makes me high."

He laughed. "I know what you mean. This is the only place I've lived where I don't really need any substances. Just being here is enough. It's like a drug. And if it turns out to be *your* drug, you never want to leave."

"I've thought about that," she said, "staying. Believe it or not. Which is crazy."

"Not necessarily," he said. "People come here, they do strange things. Wait and see."

Sam spent the first day after the banquet cleaning, refusing his father's help, grateful for the hours of dishwashing and pot-scrubbing and finally floor-mopping, begun when he was already so tired he could barely stand. He finished everything in the early evening when the clear lake light was just starting to wane, and even though it was not late he fell on his bed and was blessedly, instantly asleep. He slept deeply, straight through, without dreams, oblivious to the night noises of the neighborhood outside. When he awoke in the morning he felt cleansed. It had been years since he'd slept so long, more than he could remember, maybe since he was a child. He rose with an easy stretch he seemed to have known once and then forgotten. The job was done. It was past. Now he would wait, and proceed as the way opened.

He spent that day with his father, taking him around to see how the city had changed. They did not visit famous places such as palaces and temples, but the places his father remembered from being a boy: the site of his elementary school, once tucked in a leafy *hutong*, now obliterated by a massive concrete-faced apartment building. They took a taxi down Chongwenmennei Boulevard, now wide, soulless, streaming traffic past intersections that led off to gritty, almost sad-looking streets and alleys. This had been Hata Men, and it was the only thing that brought tears to his father's eyes. "It was so crowded," he said, "so gay! The crowds, the vendors — we always walked through here when we shopped for food." He stared out at the wide modern artery in front of him as if he were not seeing it at all but an entirely different world. "My mother and I."

"I know," said Sam. "Surpassing Crystal." And he and his father touched hands.

That night they joined Jiang and Tan to dine at Fang Shan in Beihai Park, another imperial-style restaurant that had been established the year *The Last Chinese Chef* was published, and with which the three older men had lifelong ties. Located in buildings that had once been part of the imperial pleasure grounds, the place had been started by chefs from the closed-down palace kitchens at the same time Liang Yeh's father opened Liang Jia Cai. Fang Shan was one of the few restaurants left open by the government in the 1950s. For long stretches it had been only for guests of state, and it was closed entirely during the decade of the Cultural Revolution. Now, though, like the rest of China, it was back to a booming business. They welcomed Liang Yeh like a returning prince, and pressed on the four of them a long and extravagant meal of the chef's devising. Sam secretly found the food tired, but the tea snacks, the tiny pastries meant to clear the palate between courses — these were exceptional. They even had *xiao wo tou* and *shao bing jia rou mo.* "Yours last night were better," Sam whispered to his father.

The next day Sam's father, Jiang, and Tan left on an excursion to a temple outside the city, leaving Sam alone in the courtyard rooms, clean now, and ordered. The dining room was still hung with the calligraphy from the banquet, and each time Sam passed through on his way to the kitchen he remembered the meal, the way it had soared even after the loss of the thirty-crab sauce, the up-rush of triumph he had felt when the diners applauded him at the end. Tonight he would hear. The press conference was at eight, and the two winners, the ones who would be given the coveted north-ern spots on the Chinese team, would be announced. He knew he had a chance. He had surpassed himself. Every time he thought of it he felt a churn of excitement. By the time late afternoon came and the sun was low, he could stay inside no longer. On top of eve-rything else, the place felt empty to him without his father, which was strange because Liang Yeh had been there only a short time. Sam went out, locked the gate, and started to walk around the lake.

It was the perfect time of day. Twilight would fall soon; right now the long light was glorious. The streets gained a second life af-ter dark, especially in the warm summer months and the golden weeks of autumn. Out walking then, Sam felt that the city, its sub-tleties enhanced by shadow, was all his. That was a good way to feel tonight. He wanted to win.

He walked the rim of the lake, its lively line of restaurants, shops, and teahouses, its foot-pedaled boats now tied up at their little docks. His chances were strong. It all depended on how good Yao Weiguo's banquet was — it was between him and Yao. That was if one of the two spots went to Pan Jun, which it would. Sam felt the frustrated contraction inside him. *It's life,* he thought, *live with it.* It was the dark side of *guanxi,* another truth of being here. *Still, I can win. It's either me or Yao Weiguo.* As he walked, only the balls of his feet touched the ground, as if he were lifting right into the air. With every breath he felt himself praying to fate.

By the time it grew close to eight he had made his way to the club end of the lake and taken up a resting post by an old marble column left from before, when the lake was a quiet place. Sam had never seen it like this, but his uncles had told him. Most of what he saw around him now had been built in the last decade.

Five minutes, he thought. There were bars behind him with TV screens; he had been in them before. He knew this was a place he could see the news. His feet had known where to bring him.

He walked into a bar full of people. He heard a wall of voices and the crack of billiards from a spotlit table in the corner. There was a TV flashing images from the wall with its sound turned down; good. He could sidle over and turn it up when the time came.

He ordered cognac, not currently a hip drink. It was what his uncles ordered when he was out with them. That was why he liked it, and why he ordered it now, to feel connected to them — that, and the golden, half-punishing flavor, which he loved.

He drank it slowly, in tiny tastes, holding down his excitement. A glance at the screen, no, not yet, a commercial. Then the news would start. They would either go live to the press conference or do a story on it right after. He took another sip. He knew no one in this bar. He was also the only foreigner. He could have chosen to be with friends tonight, to have gathered a congenial group around him. He knew enough people in Beijing to have done it. But he didn't. He put it off, waiting. Then his uncles and his father went away for the night, and he realized he wanted to hear the news alone. So he was here. Because often, in China, being in a crowd was being alone.

It was time. He saw the story's introduction. First there was a slick preamble about the Cultural Games, with a montage of traditional performers and martial artists and chefs, and then there was a similar profile of the contemporary arts festival that was scheduled to take place at the same time. Finally they cut to the press conference. There was the committee. He recognized them.

Sam rose from his stool. He was about to move over and raise the volume when something semi-miraculous happened — a young man seated closer got up and did it first. As the sound went up, the announcer was reading names, and photos of the ten contestants were spilling across the bottom of the screen. There was Sam. He sat back on his stool, taut and quiet, waiting, his mind saying, *Yes. Yes.*

The panel's senior member, a quiet, block-faced man, gave a carefully written, flowery little speech that culminated in his raising his voice to an abrupt and unaccustomed shout as he called out the name of the first winner.

Pan Jun. His face, enlarged, detached from the other nine, floated to the top.

Well, Sam thought, still strong inside, he knew this. Ever since the day he and Uncle Jiang went to visit the Master of the Nets, when he saw Pan Jun and found out he was the son of the minister; ever since then it had been clear. He wet his lips. They were like paper.

Another flowery buildup, and then a second shout — Yao Weiguo. Yao's face detached and rose to the top, taking its place beside Pan Jun's.

Sam felt he was in a bubble of agonized silence. *But I cooked a great meal.* He stared at the screen. *How could I lose? You loved it. All six of you.* But then they cut away from the panel and went on with the news. Obviously, Yao's meal had been better. That was it. Simple.

He turned away on his stool. The sound was lowered again. He took his glass and drained off what was left, grateful he was alone, grateful no one knew him. He paid the bartender. Now he just wanted to leave. He should go home.

Outside, the air cleared him somewhat. He stood staring over the dark water, hands in his pockets. He remembered the story he'd been told, how in past centuries young scholars who had failed the imperial examinations drowned themselves in this lake. Some people claimed to see their ghosts. Was it just his defeat and his dark imaginings, or could he feel them tonight? He stood quiet, watching, turned away from the voices and the sounds of laughter drifting from the string of lights and restaurants behind him, focusing on the water, which he imagined to be filled with souls. Was it real or only a feeling? He didn't know, but he liked the fact that he felt these things here. Back home he had never had this sense of the past. Maybe it was natural. This was where half of him originated.

He felt a pang for his father and his uncles. He was in the river of life with them. It was time to talk. They were probably waiting for him to make the call. He took out his phone, dialing Uncle Jiang's number. "First Uncle," he said, when he heard Jiang's voice.

"I know, my son, I heard," said Jiang softly. "My heart is too bitter to bear words."

"I thought I had a chance, truly."

"You did!" said Jiang. "Come now. Here. Your Baba." Sam waited while the phone was passed to Liang Yeh.

"I'm sorry," his father said.

"Wo yiyang," said Sam, Me too.

"I told your mother. She cried."

This made Sam feel blanketed in sadness. "I wish you didn't have to tell her," he said, and even as the words slipped out he knew they were not really what he meant; he meant he wished he had not failed, that his father had had good news to give her.

"I tell her everything," Liang Yeh said, surprised.

"I know, Baba. It's okay." It was not his father's fault. He had lost, that was all. It had been between him and Yao, and Yao had won. Sam felt his head throbbing. Yao was a great cook. That was all there was to it.

"Ba," he said, "listen, I want you and First and Second Uncle to put this from your mind. Enjoy the temple. You know how famous the food is, and you know you cannot enjoy it when you are tasting bitterness."

"Yes, but," said his father, "how can we put it from our minds when we know you will not?"

"I will, though," Sam promised him. And then Jiang and Tan each got on the phone, and he assured them of the same thing, and told them to eat well. When he hung up he was glad they were away. It would be a relief to be by himself now.

Should he go home, then? The moon was narrow, waning, and later it would rise. One of the charms of his courtyard was that no one could see into it from anywhere outside. Would that be enough for him tonight? To lie outside on a wicker chaise, in drawstring pa-jamas, and listen to the leaves? That was what he had missed, not growing up in China. If he had been a child here he would have heard poetry recited on a night like this. No. If he had been a child here he would have suffered.

His head hurt.

I should go home, he thought. Yet he recognized inside him a concomitant need for the laughter and reassurance of a friend. Who? Because this was a naked moment.

He opened his phone and scanned the screen. Restaurant friends, drinking friends, friends who knew women. He had connected with a lot of people. A stranger in a faraway place had to know a lot of people. That was the cushion beneath him. But how well did he know them? There were few he felt like being with right now.

He came back to Maggie's name, paused on it, cycled on. He had gotten to know her so quickly, it was hard to believe she had been here less than two weeks. Soon she would leave. Best to pull back now. He went farther down the list.

But she had been there. She had been at the banquet.

And anyway he had promised to tell her.

He went back to her name. *She's the one you want to talk to.* He pressed the button and listened to it dial.

"Hello?"

"Maggie?"

"Sam?"

"It's me," he said. His gray tone was probably enough, but in case it wasn't, he said the words. "I didn't get it."

"You *didn't?*" she said.

"I didn't."

He heard her long, shocked breath. "How can that be?"

He almost laughed. *That's why you called her.* "Well, one spot went to Pan Jun, the son of the culture minister. Remember, I told you?"

"Oh, yes," she said. "The back door."

"Very important concept; one of the keys to life here. So that left one spot, and we all more or less thought that one would come down to me and Yao Weiguo. Well, he got it."

"I'm sorry."

"Don't be. He's an incredibly good cook. Sometimes he's inspired."

"I'm still sorry."

He almost smiled. It was the sound of her voice. "Where are you?"

"In a restaurant. I just ordered."

"What restaurant?"

She read him the name off the menu.

"I know the place." He felt a click of decision inside him. "Wait for me. I'll come over."

"Really? You will?"

"Yes. Can you wait?"

"I'll be here," she said.

Maggie sat at her table in the bright-lit restaurant, wondering what kind of state he would be in when he got here. She so felt for him. He should have won. She had been there that night.

As she waited she decided she would think of things to say that would comfort him. She could begin now being his friend. The interview chapter was closed. The story had ended. She might not have technically finished the last paragraph, but she had written it in her mind. From the moment they hung up the phone, as she sat at this table waiting for him, she had composed the last sentence over and over.

When he came in she saw him first, and watched him loop his body through the tables, anxious, scanning for her. She lifted a hand and his eyes came to her, relaxing a notch. Then he stepped close to the table and saw her food still undisturbed. "Why didn't you eat?"

"I was waiting," she said.

He eased into a chair. She saw him favoring his body. He was holding himself oddly. "Never waste food."

"It's not wasted. I thought you might like some."

He spoke slowly. "I don't think I can eat right now."

"You must feel so angry," she said.

He made a weak shrug. "It's my fate," he said.

"I found out some fate too," she said, "since I saw you. I got the lab results."

He looked up.

"Shuying is not Matt's child."

Implications tumbled across his face. "That's good for you," he said.

"Yes. Strange, but good."

"Strange how?"

"It's the end of Matt. Truly the end."

"That happened a while ago," he said.

"I know." She looked at him. His dark eyes were closed, and he was pressing his fingers to the side of his head. "Are you okay?"

"I'm fighting a headache. Please," he said, "eat."

She took small bites from the plates and nibbled at them, but he, with every passing moment, looked worse. His eyes took on the unmistakable crinkle of nausea. Then of course she could not eat either. The appeal of the food drained away. She put down her chopsticks. "Sam," she said. He winced at her voice. "What is it?"

"A migraine, I think. I haven't had one in so long, since I was a kid. I didn't think I'd ever have one again." It seemed to hurt him to speak.

"Look what happened tonight," she pointed out.

He made the smallest movement of assent with his head.

"What helps?" she said, her voice soft.

"Lie down," he said, with effort. "In a dark room, quiet — if I can fall asleep, even for a little while, it'll be over."

"Let's go," she said, and signaled the waiter for a check. She paid and then stood up and walked behind him and slid her hands underneath his armpits. He shivered when she touched him. "Stand up," she said gently. "I'll help you get home."

This promise seemed to go through to the part of him which could still respond, and he rose with her, walking steadily out even as he kept one hand over his eyes. "It's not dangerous, is it?" she asked, and he managed to shake his head. Relieved, she raised her hand for a taxi.

One pulled over and she got him into the back seat, then gave the driver her approximate pronunciation of the intersection next to Sam's house. She said it wrong, no doubt, but it always got her there. Now when Sam heard it he made a twitch of a smile through his pain. He uttered a few words of the guttural Beijing burr and the driver nodded. Then he sat, still as a stone, eyes closed, every sound they heard as they drove through the streets seeming to magnify his pain. Maggie could almost see his head throbbing. First losing; now this. She would help him get home, to quiet and darkness. That was all she could do.

At his gate he fumbled in his pocket and brought forth the key. She unlocked the gate and then relatched it behind them. She slipped the key back in his pocket. She felt the knob of his hipbone. With her other hand she held his elbow, guiding him. He could barely walk. *I know. Just a little farther.*

To get to his room she counted off the three steps up to the verandah. Inside the half-glass door she steered him across the floor and to his bed. He lay down slowly, gingerly, not wanting her to touch him, cringing even when she unlaced his shoes. She turned off all the lights, which made him exhale in relief.

She wanted a wet towel. The closest bathroom that she knew of was across the court in the restaurant's main dining room. Just inside the door, she found a switch that made the white, lotus-shaped lampshades in the room spring to light. She walked across the dark, liquid-looking tiles to the small restroom, soaked a towel in cold water, wrung it, and walked back.

When she reentered his room he was lying still. She stepped quietly. All his attention was turned inward. She came quietly to the bed and, not wanting to startle him, touched him softly with her fingers first, above the brow. His head made a tick in response. She laid the cloth on him, first one end, so he could feel the cold wetness, then all the way across. He looked grateful. He reached up and pressed it to his temples. Then one of his hands came out and found one of hers, and quickly, naturally, their fingers laced together. He gave her a squeeze of thanks. Then he withdrew and folded his hands on top of his chest, motionless, the way he had been holding them.

She eased back. Quiet. Silence. She wanted him to fall asleep. Three steps from the bed was a frayed leather armchair. She lowered herself into it without a sound, an inch at a time, and sat quietly.

The room was dark, the only illumination the two silver squares of streetlight from the *hutong* behind, bent in half at the seam of wall and ceiling. Occasionally she heard sounds from outside, people passing, a few cars, but mostly the room was silent.

She could leave, she thought. He was settled. He would surely fall asleep now, and when he woke up he would be better.

She would leave, but not yet. Right now she wanted to watch him. Time went away. She saw his breathing turn deep and regular. When a noise intruded from outside he no longer winced. She thought he might be asleep. Good. Sleep. She liked the forever feeling of the room, the old wooden furniture, the sight of him so undefended. It had been a year since she was alone with a man in a room while he slept, and a decade since it had happened with anyone but Matt. No, that was not true. She and Sam had slept for a few hours in the little upstairs room at his Uncle Xie's house. That had been different. Now she was on watch. She was the guardian, the one caring. She kept her eyes on him until slowly she felt them starting to close. She was drifting into sleep. It was comfortable in the chair. That was the last thing she remembered thinking.

When she awoke she moved with a jolt. He was awake. He was sitting up on the edge of the bed. He looked dazed, and shiny with relief-sweat, but once again like himself.

She stirred. "Are you okay?"

"I am. It's over. I fell asleep."

"Good."

"Thank you."

"I didn't do anything."

"You brought me here."

She shrugged. "You feel all right?"

"Fine." He appeared to be at an odd midpoint between exhausted and exhilarated. He massaged a ring around his scalp.

"Here. Let me." She went to stand behind him, but the angle was wrong, even though he turned his body to help her. Then her fingers caught in his tied-back hair.

"Sit down," he said, and touched the bed behind him. She climbed up, settled a few inches from the back of him, and touched the coated elastic band that bound his hair. He brought up a practiced finger to hook through it and pull it off. His hair fell straight and heavy. She had never seen it loose. He looked different. She slipped her fingers underneath it to massage up, from the base of his scalp, following the arc his fingers had marked earlier.

She saw him relaxing. The jumpy little trigger points around his head seemed to disperse. His spine straightened. It took her a while to work her way to the top of his head, to the midpoint above his forehead, where she finished.

He caught her hand as it fell away, carried it around to his face, and pressed it to his cheek. Then he moved until his lips were in the center of her palm. She knew he was going to kiss her there and he did, but instead of the single lip-press she expected, he did it slowly, for a long time, and with all the care and attention he might have lavished were he kissing her on the mouth. There was no mistaking what he was saying. A torrent of pain and hope poured through her brain, threatening to short-circuit everything, but her hand moved against his face by itself, responding.

What to do now? Cross this line unthinking? Neither was young. They were fossils. He was older than she, which was saying something. She knew little about his past, but for the first time in her life it didn't seem to matter. Of course he had pain and remorse in his suitcase. So did she. Hers was different, though; it was total. Being widowed wiped a person clean. There was nothing unfinished; everything was finished. She was empty. She carried nothing. She never expected to love again. Don't think of love, she reproved herself. Don't even allow the word to form. This could be only a moment. No pretending. She held herself still, moving only her hand against his mouth.

In the end her body decided for her. He brought his mouth to the cleft between her fingers with so much love that she found herself inching up, just a little, until she was against him from behind. She slid her left hand around his waist, he caught it with his, and again their fingers interlaced. In this way they held each other and exchanged promises and trepidations, all without speaking, all without hurry, for each wanted to be sure. This was the long moment that was like a question. She let the question play, loving the strong, wiry feeling of his body from behind. Her hand played with his stomach and he tilted himself up to her. She put her lips on the back of his neck. That was it. She had answered. His hands loosened, his body turned, and in a long second she saw the prismatic potential of their lives unfolding. *Don't think about that.* Then he was facing her, undoing her clothing, cupping a gentle hand behind her head to bring her mouth to his, and she felt the future and the past fall away from her.

When they awakened it was deep night, and cold. They were naked. Her legs were wrapped around him. She saw the blankets on the floor and remembered the moment they were pushed off the bed. His eyes followed, and they both started to laugh.

"Look at us," she said, touching his chest. "Like a couple of teenagers." Then she said what she was scared to say. "Sam, that was so good."

"I know." He caught her under the rib cage and stretched, first back, then forward, taking her with him. She felt a gentle pull up and down her spine.

He let her go. There was a shine to his face. "You want to get up and sit in the courtyard? The moon's up. The city's sleeping. I like this time," he added, but with a different tone, as if now he would start to tell her about himself; as if there were many things she would need to know.

"I like it too," said Maggie.

He rose and drew some folded things from a pile, pajamas — his, but they fit her. Not like the capacious things she used to borrow from Matt. Matt. She swallowed at the new strangeness of the thought of her husband. The dial had moved. She had made love to someone. Sam had put on pajamas and was tying the string at his waist, free in front of her, his hair still loose. She reached out and gathered it and let it drop. The touch made him raise his face, happy. She felt it too. This was the night Matt would start to become a memory.

Sam set out two rattan recliners in the court and lit a sheltered candle between them. They lay side by side and watched the leaves above their heads. The waning moon made a lazy letter *C* atop the rim of the wall.

"It's so quiet," she said. "I thought your father would be staying here."

"He is, in that room." Sam pointed to the north-facing room across from his own. "But he went with Jiang and Tan on an overnight pilgrimage to a temple."

"Are they religious?"

"Only about food. This place has the best vegetarian cuisine in north China. They pray with the monks, sleep at the temple, and eat like kings. They come back tomorrow."

"So they were already gone when you got the news."

"Yes."

She looked at him across the candle. They had been so close to each other a few hours ago, inside each other. She had seen so much about him. She felt a surge. She was aware of how much she wanted him to be happy. "Don't worry, Sam. This thing means nothing. Your career's going to take off. Nothing can stop it."

"You sound like my uncles."

That's because I love you as they do, was the thought that blurted up from her subconscious — but which she could not say out loud. "They know. So do I." Then she kept talking, so the words could more easily pass by. "And in time the world will know, too. My article will help. You will be really happy with its portrait of what you do. And I wrote it before this happened" — she touched his leg — "so don't worry." She paused. "I didn't expect this, Sam."

"Neither did I."

A smile crept over her. "Any more than I expected the food to be so great. Maybe that's what makes the article about you glow the way it does. Do you know what they say? That writers do their very best stories on a foreign place the first time they see it — and then again the last time, when they are saying goodbye, just before leaving. That last one they call the swan song. So maybe my piece on you is just my first piece on this place and this food, and everything seems so marvelous — *is* so marvelous — that it comes out on the page."

"I love that you got it about the food," he said, "that you understood it, that maybe — I hope I'm not projecting — you might even be on your way to loving it."

"I could get there," she said, seriously. "Given time, and exposure."

"That would best be done here," he pointed out.

She didn't say anything. She thought she understood what he was really saying, and she couldn't promise to stay here any more than he could say he'd come back home. She stood up, redirected the moment by stretching a bit, then excused herself and started to walk away on the path toward the main dining room.

"Bathroom?" he said. "Restaurant's closed. Use mine." He pointed to a door in the corner between the room where he lived and the second dining room. She had not seen it before.

She would ask nothing, she decided, as she walked across the court. Expect nothing. A world separated them. There was no way anything between them could take hold and keep going. She knew that already now, at the beginning, and once she adjusted to the idea it gave her a certain peace. Just as being widowed had given her peace, though of a different and far more bitter kind. Being widowed had made her feel that nothing else she could ever lose, ever again, could really hurt her. But that was wrong, because this would hurt her, losing Sam. Already she knew it would hurt.

The bathroom was small and homey, with a stall shower. She felt comfortable in here. She brought his towel to her face and closed her eyes and sank into it. It was full of him, his smell. She loved it; she could stand here breathing it forever.

It was amazing how a feeling could be so powerful and still impossible. As if she could stay. She put the towel back on the rack. The city was so quiet. Was it four in the morning? Five? She walked back out under the rustling leaves. She was aware of the freedom of her body, the ease of no underwear. She had a strange, dreamlike sense that she had always lived here and had merely forgotten it, that every day of her life she had seen Sam reclining in just this way, his chest bare, his drawstring pajamas. She felt a cramp inside her.

He moved to one side of his chaise. "Come here with me. There's room." And she lay down next to him, nestled under his arm. As soon as he was holding her again and they were breathing together, she felt herself relax. Her thoughts and questions ebbed. "I do wish I could stay here," she said truthfully.

"I was going to propose that," he answered. She laughed. She did not stop to wonder if he spoke lightly or seriously. Somehow she knew at that moment, in the circle of his arm, that the few words they had just spoken were the simple and sufficient truth.

15

In this humble book I have tried to give the facts about the cuisine of the Chinese imperial palace. It was a place of tragic beauty. Of everything I learned there, one thing stands out. Food was always to be shared. When my master sent out his untouched dishes from the huge imperial repasts to the families of the princes and the chief bureaucrats, he would send them only as complete meals for eight people in stacked lacquerware. Never any other way. Always for eight. The high point of every meal was never the food itself, he taught us, but always the act of sharing it.

— LIANG WEI, *The Last Chinese Chef*

They awakened to a sound, too early. They were naked under the blankets, their arms and legs twined like one being. With Matt, when she woke up, she had always been off by herself in the bed. This was different. She moved closer to Sam's smell, his black hair, his body the same size as hers. Then the sound crashed through again, and right behind it she heard another sound, one she recognized — the creak of the red gate pushing open. "Sam." She nudged him, whispered in his ear.

He stirred. Then they heard Jiang's quavery voice calling. *"Zizi!"* Nephew!

"They're here," said Sam. He jumped out of the bed, his dark-ivory skin flashing in the daylight before her eyes, his hands quick on his pants. "Here." He threw her clothes. "Sorry. Damn. No privacy in this family."

"But what do I do?"

"Nothing. Just be normal."

"It's not," she said. "It's not normal."

"I know that. But it's the best kind of not normal."

"Zizi!" Jiang called again from the courtyard.

"Wo lai!" Sam called back, Coming!

"Should we say anything?" she asked.

"Why?" he said. "They'll know everything the instant they see you. You're here, in my room, it's not even seven o'clock, and look at you. Anybody can see it. You're brimming with it. You're a walking light source."

"So are you," she said. He was smiling nonstop.

He zipped his pants. "Just come out." And he turned and slipped out into the courtyard.

She followed a minute later, stopped in the bathroom, then came out and there they were, a fussing, loving clot of old men. "Miss Maggie!" Tan called, waving her over with a smile. They were all beaming welcome. They all knew. She felt naked as she walked over and said good morning to them. She felt as if they had seen everything she and Sam had done. Yet they were happy. She was happy too, she realized. She relaxed.

Sam had gone ahead to the kitchen and now called out that he was starting breakfast — in English, which was for her.

"How was the temple?" she said to Sam's father.

"Ah! So delicious! You have never eaten a vegetarian meal like this one. The gluten duck, the crispy pepper-salt oysters made from rice puffs — you must go."

"Would I have to get up and pray?"

"Naturally! Four-thirty in the morning! Why do you think we are home so early?"

"I'll go if he goes," she joked, shooting a look toward the kitchen, where Sam was clanging pots.

"We will all go," Liang Yeh said.

Jiang and Tan were preparing the single table in the dining room, having pulled it over by the windows to drink in the morning light. They set five places and were steeping tea of various kinds. She tried to help them, but they batted her away and sent her on to the kitchen.

Sam was at the stove. She slid onto her stool in her now-accustomed spot. The stool was hers now; it fit her body.

"I feel so humbled by what happened," he said.

"I do too. Humbled. Awed."

She watched him while the rice cooked, happy even though nothing was certain. "What are you making?"

"Congee. It's the simplest food, the most basic. But it takes care. It's like love." He looked straight at her; she could feel him looking right through her clothes to her body, to her heart. He gave the pot a stir. "First it must have that fragrance of fresh-steamed rice. Then the toppings." He gestured at the side counter, which was crowded with little bowls he had been preparing while the aromatic rice was cooking. There were tiny squares of crunchy pickle, slivers of greens, velvety cubes of tofu, tiny smoke-dried Hunan fish mounded up in a crispy, silvery tangle. There were peanuts, shreds of river moss, crunchy soaked fungus, and matchsticks of salty Yunnan ham. "You can take those in," he said.

"Okay." It felt good bearing dishes for him, having a place in the pattern. She put all the side dishes around the rim of the inner wheel. She had seen the enormous tureen for the congee; Sam was warming it now, by the sink, with boiling water. She left room for it in the center of the wheel.

He brought the tureen in. All the dishes around it made a pleasing circle. They sat down together. *"Lai, lai,"* said Sam, Come, and they all passed their clean bowls to him. The first one he filled, he handed to his father. Then he served Jiang, the eldest, and then Tan. And then her. When he handed her the bowl and their fingers touched he looked into her with a gladness that was unmistakable. She knew they all saw it. That kind of feeling could not be hidden.

She surveyed the condiments. She selected greens, pickle pieces, and the tiny fish. Following one more suggestion from Sam's eyes she took slippery cubes of fresh tofu too. There. He looked satisfied. She felt another satisfaction bloom. He cared what she ate. That was not something she had known before either. She and Matt had been servants of convenience. There could never in their house have been a meal like this.

Chopsticks flew as they piled ingredients on top of their congee, and the Chinese conversation burst forth like birds from a box. She loved the sound of it. If she learned the language, if she understood it, would it still be so? Would she feel loosed from her old fetters whenever she heard it, freshly born? Maybe. Maybe more so.

She mixed her congee with her spoon and tasted it. Oh, so good. She shivered. The salty and piquant flavors against the delicate fragrance of rice, the crispy fish against the tofu and the soft gruel. Sheer goodness. She caught Sam's eye and said one word, "Wonderful."

The uncles agreed. "I would come back from the dead for this," said Jiang. "What is that poem? The one that calls back the soul to the table?"

"Oh! From the Zhou Dynasty," said Tan.

To their surprise, it was Liang Yeh who started to intone, in English.

> "O Soul, come back! Why should you go far away?
> All kinds of good foods are ready:
> rice, broom-corn, early wheat, mixed with yellow millet —"

He could not remember the next line. Jiang murmured to him in Chinese, and he continued:

> "Ribs of the fatted ox, tender and succulent;
> Sour and bitter blended in the soup of Wu.
>
> O Soul, come back and do not be afraid."

"Ah, the soup of Wu," said Tan as he ate his congee. Wu was the archaic word for the region around Hangzhou, which made the connection to their friend's death complete.

"To Uncle Xie," Sam said, raising his teacup. They drank.

After this Sam refilled their bowls from the tureen and the condiments went around again.

"You are a great chef," Liang Yeh said to his son.

"Thanks," Sam said, reddening. He caught Maggie's eye. This was the moment for him, she understood. More than the prize. More than the restaurant.

"You are! I saw three nights ago. We all saw."

"Yes," said Jiang and Tan, on top of each other. "We did."

Under the table she touched his knee. He caught her hand and held it.

Liang Yeh could feel the current between them. "Now, we must take your lady friend to the temple. What do you say? I am happy to go again this very week."

"She's leaving in a few days," said Sam.

"Leaving? No! She just arrived! Isn't that true?" He addressed himself to Maggie. "Didn't you just arrive?"

"More or less," she said. "But I have to go back. I have a job."

His face fell.

Sam said, "Dad, it's okay."

"I know." Liang Yeh raised a hand. "Because you will return." He touched Maggie's arm lightly. "Isn't it so? Won't you be back? Very soon?"

All of them were watching her.

She sneaked a look at Sam. His face was full and unafraid. *Go ahead,* he seemed to be telling her, *say it. Tell them.*

"I think so," she said. "Yes."

"Good. You see?" said Liang Yeh. His eyes crinkled with gladness as he took slivers of ham and greens and added them to Sam's bowl, and put another scoop of the crisp silver fish in hers. "Now eat, children. Another day lies ahead."

The Last Chinese Chef is a work of fiction, yet the Chinese culinary world that comes to life in its pages is real. I could never have captured it without the help of many Chinese who shared their knowledge, analyses, reminiscences, and recipes, nor could I have written it without the published works of literary gourmets, culinary thinkers, and food-obsessed poets dating back through the centuries.

In a deeper sense my research began thirty years ago when I started doing business in China. Arriving there to buy woolen textiles in 1977, just six weeks after the Cultural Revolution had formally ended, I sat down to my first government-arranged banquet and found my mind and senses exploded by a cuisine more exciting, diverse, and subtle than any Chinese food I had encountered in America. Real cuisine was available to only a handful of people in China then, for the country's population was not only poor but traumatized by a long era of successive terrors that had turned many of life's pleasures, including food, into ideological evils. At a time when most people around me had limited choices and rationed food, I, as the guest of one of China's large state-owned enterprises, was given many opportunities in those first few years to experience a cuisine that was as fantastic as it was — to me, an inexperienced young woman trying desperately to figure out how to do business in a socialist country — incomprehensible.

Over the next eighteen years, as I ran my textile business in China, I came to know this remarkable cuisine better. Working with provincial state-owned textile mills in different parts of the country and returning to school at night to learn Chinese, I slowly saw how *guanxi* — the net of relationship and mutual responsibility — grew from a succession of special meals. Each meal celebrated our *guanxi* and improved it. These meals, over almost two decades, formed my first education into the hidden language of Chinese cuisine — the codes of seating and serving, the messages conveyed by a menu, and the social signals that substitute for the concrete business conversations we Westerners are used to having at table.

In 1999, a few years after I closed my textile business and saw the publication of my first novel, I began writing about Chinese food for *Gourmet* magazine. Here was the start of my second education in Chinese cuisine. Covering the food scene in major Chinese cities gave me the chance to interview chefs, restaurant owners, restaurant managers, sociologists, home cooks, and diners.

Still, to write *The Last Chinese Chef,* I needed to know a lot more. Almost all of the characters in the book are food experts, and the eponymous book-within-a-book is a faux food classic. To create this world of erudite cooks and diners, and to create an excerpted food classic they would all admire, I had to learn what they knew. Fortunately, much has been written over the centuries on Chinese gastronomy. I digested a good deal of it in translation (my Chinese literacy is nonexistent) and also returned to China to interview more chefs and restaurateurs.

While I could never list every person in China who has taught me something about cuisine over the last thirty years, certain people gave so generously of their time as to deserve special note. Vivian Bao shared her knowledge of Shanghainese cuisine, helped me connect with chefs in various places, and related her personal memories of China in 1958, the year Liang Yeh made his way from Gou Bu Li in Tianjin to the coast of Fujian Province. Yu Changjiang, a sociology professor at Beijing University with a special interest in restaurant and food culture, opened my eyes to the deeper meaning of food in China, helping me connect cuisine to patterns of ideology, history, and the contemporary Chinese economy. Anthony Kuhn, then of the *Los Angeles Times,* took me to meet Yu Changjiang and translated some of his academic papers so I could study them.

Many restaurant owners and managers took time from their busy lives to help me understand their world. In Beijing, Yu Jingmin (of Fang Shan), Li Shanlin (of Li Jia Cai), Li Jun (of Mao Jia Cai), and David Tang (of the China Club) each gave me an education. In Shanghai, Walter Wang, manager of Xian Yue Hien, and Dr. Wang, a home cook who demonstrated Chinese concepts of healing through food, were both helpful, and I thank Willie Brent and Jocelyn Norskog Brent for taking me to meet them.

In the San Gabriel Valley east of Los Angeles, Henry Chang (formerly of Dong Lai Shun and Juon Yuan, San Gabriel; now owner and chef of Chang's Garden, Arcadia) worked hard to give me a complete view of his career and has always been generous with recipes. The pork ribs steamed in lotus leaves — the ones Sam's Uncle Xie has him make over and over until they are right — are his creation. Wang Haibo, from Shanghai (chef and owner of Green Village, San Gabriel), and Chen Qingping, from Chongqing (chef of Chung King, Monterey Park), taught me much. Linda Huang (owner of Chung King) joined Henry Chang and Wang Haibo in helping me understand the difference between Chinese cuisine and Chinese-American cuisine, and between the Chinese and the American diner.

My research trip to Hangzhou, home of China's literature-based cuisine, would never have succeeded without the help of Dai Xiongping, who introduced me to chefs and restaurant owners. Restaurant tycoon Wang Zhiyuan explained his formula for success in the new China and led a tour through the cavernous kitchens of Xin Kai Yuan. Wu Xunqu, a chef at Lou Wai Lou for forty-six years, explained the history of the city's literary cuisine and then parted with his famed recipe for beggar's chicken — though not, he cautioned, the complete recipe, for certain secret ingredients had to stay secret. Retired chef Xu Zichuan opened the door to his home and his memories. His daughter Xu Lihua, manager of Shan Wai Shan, introduced me to her restaurant's famous fish-head soup, which is prepared and served by Sam in the pages of this novel.

Outside the realm of food, I owe special thanks to two friends. Zhan Zhao candidly shared his knowledge of the subworld of modern China in which love in many forms, and at many levels, is for sale, even helping me pinpoint where Gao Lan would live. Tom Garnier's knowledge of seamanship made it possible for me to frame Liang Yeh's coastal voyage from Tianjin to Fujian Province more accurately.

Published works were critical to me, especially in understanding Chinese cuisine over time. Among classical written sources, I relied most heavily on the works of Yuan Mei (1715–1797), often considered the greatest of all Chinese food writers; Li Liweng or Li Yu (1610–1680), an erotic novelist, opera producer, and epicure who explored the value of the rustic in haute cuisine; and Yi Yin (at the dawn of the Shang dynasty, dated at 1766 B.C. by a Han chronology but now thought by many to have been about 1554 B.C.), the first great Chinese gastronome. Reading excerpts from *The Yellow Emperor's Classic of Internal Medicine* (third century B.C.) helped me see the philosophical framework behind early theories of curative foods. The lines recited in the novel's last scene are taken from two poems of the Zhou Dynasty period (twelfth century B.C.–221 B.C.), "The Summons of the Soul" and "The Great Summons," translated by David Hawkes. Food passages from the novel *The Scholars* by Wu Ching-Tzu (1701–1754) gave me insight. Even Confucius wrote about food, and some material from the Analects was helpful to me. I also learned much from the poet Po Chu-I (772–846) and from the poet, calligrapher, and rhymed-prose food essayist Su Dongpo or Su Shi (1037–1101), who connected cuisine to the aesthetics of classical literature and was an important influence in the growth of Hangzhou's literary cuisine. The famous pork dish *dongpo rou,* named for him and based on his recipe, appears on Chinese menus all over the world.

Modern sources on Chinese cuisine were also important. Chief among these was the remarkable *Chinese Gastronomy* by Hsiangju Lin and Tsuifeng Lin. This exceptional book helped me grasp the formal goals of taste and texture as well as principles of menu development. I am indebted as well to the scholarly essays on cuisine through Chinese history by K. C. Chang, Michael Freeman, Frederick W. Mote, and Jonathan Spence, collected in *Food and Chinese Culture*, edited by K. C. Chang. An academic paper titled "Tasting the Good and the Beautiful: The Aestheticization of Eating and Drinking in Traditional Chinese Culture" by Da'an Pan was also helpful, as was the book *Chinese System of Food Cures* by Henry C. Lu.

Though this is a novel, and almost all of the characters are imagined, some actual historical events and personages make appearances within its pages. Tan Zhuanqing, Liang Wei's master in the Forbidden City, was a very famous chef in his time as well as an admired scholar; his name is still frequently invoked in Chinese cooking circles. Peng Changhai, Liang Wei's youthful compadre in the palace along with Xie Huangshi, was a real-life apprentice in the palace; the restaurant he went on to found, based on the cuisine teachings of Tan Zhuanqing, was considered one of Beijing's greatest restaurants in the 1950s. The Empress Dowager really did have a late-life lust for the little broom-corn cakes (*xiao wo tou*) she ate on the road during the royal family's flight from the Boxer Rebellion. She also, according to culinary legend, did commission her chefs to create the flat sesame cakes stuffed with minced meat (*shao bing jia rou mo*) after she saw them in a dream. I am grateful to the kitchen staff at Fang Shan, the imperial-style restaurant in Beihai Park in Beijing, for showing me how to make them.

The eponymous book excerpted throughout this novel — the 1925 food classic written by Sam's grandfather — is a fiction: it does not exist. The ideas it expresses are based on the classical sources noted above. The Children's Rights Treaty is also an invention; there is no such treaty. Several restaurants mentioned in the book are real, though: Fang Shan, Gou Bu Li, Lou Wai Lou, and Shan Wai Shan.

Readers who would like to taste the food in this book (almost every dish described is in the repertoire of a contemporary Chinese chef), who wish to cook the food themselves (some of these chefs gave their recipes), or who simply want to know where to find great food as they travel to China, are invited to visit my Web site, www.nicolemones.com.

ACKNOWLEDGMENTS

This book would never have come to fruition without my exceptional editor, Jane Rosenman. Her patience, knowledge, and good nature were topped only by her unerring, almost uncanny ability to see the book's strengths and help me maximize them. My agent, Bonnie Nadell, saw the potential in this book from my very first enunciation of its concept and supported it all the way, from the first stages of research to the last page. Katya Rice's thoughtful manuscript editing improved the book greatly. The Houghton Mifflin team is the stuff authors' dreams are made of, especially Taryn Roeder and Sanj Kharbanda.

I will always be indebted to Ruth Reichl for encouraging me to write about Chinese cuisine for *Gourmet* and for her willingness to publish articles that place Chinese cuisine in the wider context of culture, history, mindset, and patterns of emigration. My editors at the magazine, Jocelyn Zuckerman and Amanda Agee, helped me learn to do better work. In large part it was through the research and writing I undertook for them that I gained the knowledge and confidence to write this novel.

Many friends have been supportive, but Barbara Peters of the Poisoned Pen in Phoenix, Arizona, deserves a special thanks. She has always encouraged me, even writing to me between books to urge me to keep going. Every writer knows the moments of self-doubt. She helped me move past those, and I often found myself writing with her in mind.

My great friend Evelyn Madsen accompanied me on a research trip to Shaoxing and Hangzhou, bringing her good humor and excellent palate to a whirlwind schedule of restaurant visits, chef interviews, and scouting jaunts for scenes. It is my policy to go everywhere my characters go, and she made it more fun.

I'm grateful to my friends Tom Saunders and Nancy Beers, each of whom gave me a private place to work when I needed to block out this world in order to conjure up another one. Thanks too to my foodie friends Anne Sprecher, Linda Burum, John Wong, and Ruth Parvin, for sharing tips and rumors on good restaurants and for our fun and informative outings.

My terrific husband, Paul Mones, has gone far beyond supporting my writing to being an invaluable resource on Chinese cuisine. A talented fusion cook who as a teenager washed dishes in a Chinese restaurant to learn technique and went on to win the North Carolina state pork championship, he chose a Chinese restaurant for our first date, where it was instantly apparent that we were well matched. In my thirty years of travel to China, he is the only person I have ever seen climb up on restaurant chairs to photograph everything that comes to the table.

My last and deepest thanks are for my wonderful sons, Ben and Luke. Not only do they appreciate Chinese food, they have always offered love, support, and a generous understanding of all it takes to write a book. I'm not sure that without them I could ever have produced this one.

The Last Chinese Chef

by

NICOLE MONES

READER'S
GUIDE

For Discussion

1. In the beginning of the book, Maggie has tried to deal with her husband's death by shrinking "her life to a pinpoint." She disconnects from people and seems to be trying to make her world and herself smaller and smaller. When you suffered a loss in your life, did you also feel like withdrawing from the world? If you didn't, how did you feel? And if you did, how did you find your way back?

2. Maggie's trip to China is weighted with deep emotions — confusion over her late husband's possible betrayal of her, nostalgia for the time they spent in Beijing, shock, grief. What does she ultimately find therapeutic about her time there? Do you think people are generally more open to enlightening experiences when they travel? If so, how or why?

3. Maggie approaches China, especially Chinese cuisine, with an initial reluctance. What is it about the culture and the food in Beijing that helps to win her over? What connections does Maggie find between this new world of cuisine and her writing specialty, American regional cuisine?

4. *The Last Chinese Chef* could be described as a novel about human healing through the lessons and joys of cuisine and the bonds between people. Several readers have written to say they felt a healing echo in themselves from reading the novel. Did you sense any of this yourself? How did the book affect you?

5. As the book illuminates China's gastronomical philosophy, we learn that Chinese cuisine is not only about fine ingredients and unique skills; it is also about *guanxi*, or relationship. Is *guanxi* a concept that is solely Chinese, or do other cultures honor connections and relationships in the same way — through food? What does Chinese food teach Maggie about *guanxi*? What did you learn that might change the way you dine and eat?

6. Of all the chefs vying for a spot in the Chinese Cultural Olympics, it could be said that Sam — raised in America, the son of an American Jewish mother and an expatriate Chinese father — is the least "Chinese." Yet his food is described as the most traditional. Why is it important to Sam to honor the traditions of his father and grandfather before him? What do his culinary interests reveal about him and his mixed heritage?

7. Sam hones his culinary skills under the tutelage of his three "uncles." How do these men influence Sam's cooking, and in what way does he work their instructions into his own culinary vision? In your own life, who has most influenced or encouraged your interest in food and/or traditions?

8. Sam's relationship with his father is complex and strained at times. Why has the elder Liang made the choices he has, and how

have his choices contributed to the relationship with his son? Do you empathize with his decisions?

9. What is the significance of the book-within-the-novel, Sam's grandfather's work, *The Last Chinese Chef*? What deeper cultural understanding do the translated excerpts offer to Maggie, and to you as a reader?

10. Her interview assignment starts as a side note to her main reason for coming to China: investigation into the claim against her husband's estate. How does her unexpected assignment end up changing how she feels about her husband's death? How does her meeting with the claimants serve as a breakthrough for her? How did you feel about her ultimate handling of the claim? What does the experience teach her about herself?

11. When Maggie first learns about Gao Lan she is not disposed to feel friendly, yet as she gets to know the full story — slowly — her perspective on Gao Lan changes. Do you sympathize with the shift in Maggie's attitude toward this woman? Has this ever happened to you? Have you ever started out against someone and then, as you got to know more about them, slowly changed your view?

12. Readers have written to Nicole Mones to note that there are no villains in the book. The people who seem to have done wrong to Maggie in the beginning (like Matt and Gao Lan) become just human people who have made mistakes by the end. One reader wrote that she felt there were only two "villains" in the book: the system and the obstacles we place in front of ourselves. In your personal life story, what are your "villains," in other words, what forces

or systems feel to you like they are most against you? What do you do about them?

13. Reviewers have described this book as "tantalizing," "mouthwatering," "delicious." What about Mones's descriptions make them so tempting? Was there a particular food scene that you found especially memorable or mouthwatering?

14. How has Maggie's experience in Beijing altered her by the book's end? What kind of future do you imagine for her, for Sam?

15. Maggie finds her way back through grief by way of a cuisine that insists people be bonded together, over and over, at every meal. How does food and all that it represents — community, nourishment, connection with the past — serve as a balm in both Maggie's life and Sam's life? When have you been similarly affected by the way you eat? When you finished the book, did you feel at all differently about how you cook and eat with others in your own life? If you felt you would like to change one thing about this aspect of your life, what would it be? Could you do it? Why or why not?

A Conversation with Nicole Mones

Your novel comes to life against the unusual background of serious Chinese cuisine. Why did you choose this setting?

Because there is a magnificent world of Chinese food that remains invisible to most Americans. What we call Chinese food in this country is a hybrid cuisine, different and limited, so most Americans have never experienced true Chinese food — even though it is beginning to be available in this country and can usually be found in U.S. cities with strong Chinese communities.

When did you become interested in Chinese food?

From the moment I arrived there in 1977, to do business in textiles. You can imagine what a shock it was to sit down to my first banquet in the People's Republic. I had never dreamed such dishes existed. In the eighteen years I did business in China, I came to see that the cuisine itself constituted a kind of language. Formal meals sent signals without words. Often in those years I would hear foreign businessmen complain that they had sat through a three-hour banquet only to have every attempt to discuss business rebuffed. They did not understand that the banquet itself was the conversation.

Was there much of a restaurant scene then?

No. In the early fifties, the government allowed only a few restaurants to stay open; they shuttered the rest. By the nineties, that had changed. Privatization arrived and the restaurant industry was one of the first to bloom. You might say that food, formerly reviled as decadent, was one of the first of life's pleasures to be rehabilitated in the new free-market China. Now it's really big. There's keen competition to create great cuisine. It's a boom time for the art form.

What was it like when you first got there?

The Cultural Revolution had just been formally ended by the National People's Congress six weeks before. We had no diplomatic relations. To enter China, you had to go to a rural border village north of Hong Kong and cross on foot. British authorities would exit-stamp you to walk across a covered wooden bridge with your suitcase. I remember being surprised that I made it across without fainting. It was very surreal. At that time China was premodern; to enter it was to fall back in time to the 1940s. And people were completely traumatized by the Cultural Revolution and the famine that had preceded it.

A few years later, just as I was gaining the ability to converse in Chinese, the curtain of silence was starting to lift on recent traumas such as the Cultural Revolution. I found Chinese people everywhere filled with the need to tell their stories. In those years I absorbed countless tales of people's lives. This prepared me to write novels with Chinese characters.

What were the three most fascinating things you learned about Chinese cuisine?

First, to a much greater degree than other cuisines, Chinese food consciously seeks to reflect and comment on its culture through a web of references and allusions. It encompasses a world, and maybe that's why it's seen there as a fine art form. Second, Chinese food aims to engage the mind, not just the palate. There is a whole tradition of artifice — dishes come to the table looking like one thing but turn out to be something else. Other dishes call up events in history or great works of art. Still others aim to spur the creation of poetry at the table. Third, the highest lesson of Chinese food, its single most important aspect, is the focus on community. All food in China is shared. Nothing is ever plated for the individual — the opposite of cuisine in the West. Through the ritual of eating together every day, the human bonds that hold the world together are forged and reinforced. That's the journey at the heart of *The Last Chinese Chef.*

Recommended Recipes

MANY READERS of *The Last Chinese Chef* have been inspired to explore Chinese cuisine further. Nicole Mones has gathered the following recipes and offers them as a starting point for your own culinary adventures.

Readers can also taste these dishes at the source by visiting their home restaurants. For current addresses and additional recommendations, visit www.nicolemones.com and click on "Food Lovers."

STEAMED CLAMS AND EGGS

12 Manila clams, scrubbed
4 eggs
⅔ cup lukewarm unsalted chicken broth (lukewarm water and
    powdered chicken bouillon may be substituted)
Salt
Freshly ground white pepper
Sesame oil
Light soy sauce
1 tablespoon minced scallion

In a large pot fitted with a steamer rack large enough to hold 4
(8-ounce) ramekins, bring a quart of water to a boil. Divide
clams among ramekins.

In a small bowl whisk 1 egg until frothy. Whisk in an equivalent
amount of chicken broth and a dash of salt and white pepper.
Pour the egg mixture over the clams in one of the ramekins. Repeat with the remaining eggs. Place ramekins on the steamer rack
in the pot.

Cover the pot and simmer for 12 minutes. Remove ramekins. Gar-
nish each with a small drop of sesame oil, a few drops of soy
sauce, and a sprinkle of scallions. Serves 4 as an appetizer.

COURTESY OF *Wang Haibo, Green Village, San Gabriel, California.*

BEGGAR'S CHICKEN

ONE OF THE MOST FAMOUS Chinese dishes in the world, this is also one of the more elusive. Perhaps the traditional method of first marinating the bird, then wrapping it in lotus leaves, then sealing it in mud before long baking seems too daunting — for not many restaurants actually offer it, at least without ordering ahead. One exception is Lou Wai Lou, which is one of several places where beggar's chicken may have originated. Because they produce so many orders each day, they have abandoned the mud-seal technique in favor of successive layers of lotus leaves and modern baking bags.

When Wu Xunqu, chief chef at Lou Wai Lou, divulged this recipe, he cautioned that it was most but not all of the recipe, since he had a few secret ingredients he wanted to keep to himself. He also insisted on starting with the life of the chicken. This is one of the poultry-cooking secrets of Chinese haute cuisine: the last two weeks of a chicken's life must be spent outdoors, running free.

At home, however, you may start with a whole chicken, cleaned, and
    4–6 whole lotus leaves, soaked 20 minutes in warm water.
With one hand in the cavity of the bird and the other hand on the
    outside, snap as many bones as you can, leaving the whole
    chicken intact.

Create 3–4 cups of concentrated soup broth from pork bone, beef bone, ham, and chicken feet (good quality canned broth may be substituted), onion, ginger, and meiling soy sauce (it's a tiny bit sour).

When cool, combine with rice wine, starch powder, white pepper, salt, and a little soy. Marinate chicken 30 minutes.

Remove the chicken to wrap in soaked lotus leaves, first pouring over and inside 1 cup of the marinade (fortified with about 1 cup of extra slivered ham, other cooked meats left from the soup, and/or soaked, slivered mushrooms).

Follow a layer of lotus with a layer of parchment and then another layer of lotus. Use plastic-style baking bags and a foil wrap to create a tight seal.

Roast at 400 degrees for ½ hour, then at 350 degrees for up to 3½ hours, depending on the bird's size and age.

COURTESY OF *Wu Xunqu, Lou Wai Lou, Hangzhou, China.*

PORK SPARE RIBS IN LOTUS LEAF

THESE TENDER STEAMED RIBS, which Uncle Xie teaches Sam to make in Hangzhou, are infused with the delicate herbal musk of the lotus leaf. They are the creation of Henry Chang, owner and chef of Chang's Garden in Arcadia, California. Chang was trained from childhood in an old-school apprenticeship in Taiwan, a place where all China's cuisines are represented. As a result, he is adept in the cooking of every Chinese province. Lately the cuisine of Hangzhou has captured his creative attention, and he has opened this restaurant to showcase the subtle dishes of that city.

> 1 lb pork spare ribs
> 2 dried lotus leaves
> Crumbled glutinous rice scented with 5-spice
>
> SEASONINGS:
> > 2 T chopped scallion
> > 1 T chopped ginger
> > 1 T each soy sauce, oil, sugar, soybean paste
> > ½ T sesame oil

Trim all possible fat from spare ribs. Cut ribs into pieces 1 inch wide, 2 inches long, then marinate in seasonings ½ hour. Cut lotus leaves into eight pieces and soak in hot water 20 minutes. Remove marinated ribs and discard scallion and ginger. Add crumbled rice and thoroughly mix with rib pieces. Divide ribs into eight small portions. Place each on a soaked lotus leaf, fold, and roll to make a package. Place with the smooth side down in a bowl or deep plate. Steam over high heat for 2 hours until tender. Put a serving plate face-down over the bowl and turn over. Serves 4.

COURTESY OF *Henry Chang, Chang's Garden, Arcadia, California.*

Look for the Reader's Guides available at
www.marinerreadersguides.com.